UNDER GORNSTOCK

Clive Mullis

ISBN:
ISBN-13: 9781671000292

DEDICATION

To Glenn Young
Husband to Carol
Father to Ian and Emma
Grandfather
An extraordinary man and artist — also my friend.
Taken too soon.

ACKNOWLEDGEMENTS

My thanks go to all those who helped me and put up with me not doing what I should have been doing when I was doing this.

Also thanks go to those that read the early drafts and gave me advice, suggestions and encouragement, namely Rémy, Lesley, Katy, Dave, Suzi, Sarah, Nigel, John, Ian and Janet.

Also thanks to my advance reader group in the Black Stoat VIP Club.

Not forgetting my long suffering wife and my son, who've had to put up with me.

ABOUT GORNSTOCK

Gornstock sits on the bank of the Sterkle, a wide flowing river which feeds into the Blue Sea on the island of Inglion. Founded by Morris Dancers, the city is still subject to its rules and regulations and the rancour hasn't gone away.

There is a rent in the fabric of time and space that allows Gornstock's universe to peek into other universes: the little blue planet of Twearth being just one little blue planet among countless other little blue planets — all of them just a shadow away.

CHAPTER 1

Gleb Ironcrust didn't so much hear the snore as feel it, the vibrations enough to stir him from his repose. One bloodshot eye opened and peered into the gloom. The uncomfortable pillow might be on the soft side, but the mattress made up for it, being nice and firm; however, the blankets, smelling of wee, were not of the highest quality.

The one eye struggled to focus: blinking madly, it stared into what seemed to be a cracked mirror, with two evil eyes staring back, but those eyes had a little black point between them, sprinkled with straight looking wires, and behind them, a grey blob with a bit of string stuck on the end. The black bit twitched and the wires danced. Gleb reached out his hand and the rat showed its teeth, then it scarpered, scuttling off down the alley after a less lively adversary.

He yawned and felt his pillow, a crumbling doorstep with lots of flaky bits, which had caught up in his beard. The blankets turned out to be some urine-ridden flattened cardboard boxes which he had pulled over the top of him to keep out just a little bit of the chill, the mattress being the alley itself — he'd slept in worse places.

He rolled over, probably not his greatest idea, especially when lying in an alley, in The Warren, in the city of Gornstock. He received a wash that he hadn't envisaged as he tipped into the gulley, luckily it had been raining and the rain had washed all the little turds down towards the river, the early morning giving the clue that the open runnel had yet to be filled by the neighbourhoods' emptying of their night-time productions.

Groaning and swearing, Gleb climbed to his feet and wrung out his beard. He stamped a bit, hoping to get a little circulation moving and took stock of his surroundings, trying to remember how he'd got there. He used the facilities, giving the runnel its first proper use of the day and then stomped up the alley with his hands thrust deep into his pockets.

The gloomy alley gave out into a narrow cobbled street between two red-brick houses that had seen better days, which matched the rest of the street, teetering on the edge of decrepitude. He scratched his head as the vague memory began to fire up a few more neurones and before long he had a bit of a picture. He stood in the Warren, the second-worst slum in Gornstock, only supplanted by The Brews, which actually aspired to be a slum.

Alcohol had played a significant part of how he arrived here, wherever here actually was; the Warren definitely, but which part? He hoped to find a dwarf entrance, but his brain failed to instruct him: he didn't recognise this bit at all.

As he stomped off down the street, the memories flooded back. He started off in The Black Nag and then The Foundry, and then The Spanner and Nut before moving on to The Wardens Arms for a game of dice. He thought hard, sure that he had forgotten one, so he began to count them on his fingers until he remembered the missing one: The Ring, where he had taken part in the throwing contest, the dwarf throwing contest, the dwarf in question being himself. He made a few dollars out of that, he recalled, and he nearly always had a soft landing in the compost. He then got lost as he tried to get home, eventually giving up when he found himself in a little alley with a welcoming doorstep. It had been a good night.

It started raining again, the droplets pinging down like shards of ice. A crack of thunder boomed overhead and the patter of rain became a sudden deluge — like walking in a waterfall. As Gleb got to the end of the street, he vaguely recognised the avenue that adjoined it. The press congregated here: Pleet Street pumped out newspapers like there was no tomorrow, the high grey stone buildings hiding the printing presses and journalists offices behind a façade of gentility. He stood at the corner and watched as carts screamed down the street, desperate to get their bales of trash journalism into the hands of a gullible populace: a race with no quarter given as the drivers cracked their whips and grimaced with determination. Getting the first edition of the papers delivered quickly meant bonuses, so pedestrians had to be vigilant, and preferably not hungover.

Gleb stepped out onto Pleet Street and immediately wished he hadn't. A puddle pooled in the road just where he stood on the pavement. The tidal wave of water hit him full in the face.

'Bastard,' he yelled, shaking a fist at the back-end of the cart, receiving a one-fingered salute in reply.

The rain suddenly eased off as if making a mockery of it all. He stood dripping water and then turned to walk on just as another cart hammered by — hitting the same puddle with the same result.

Gleb seethed in indignation as the puddle of water transformed into a shower. He spat out the brown sludgy liquid and wiped his mouth with his sleeve, leaving a wet greasy smear on his coat. He sniffed and then began to walk again.

Umbrellas were everywhere and the early risers either used a brolly or wore a wide-brimmed hat, all that is, except a certain dwarf whose leather hat had somehow disappeared during the night. His clothes were so wet that the chafing, especially around the groinal area, were making things raw. Gleb dreaded to think what he would find when he got them out to dry.

Another cart and then a cab continued his drenching but then he grinned to himself as a coach with wide wheels hit a puddle just ahead, sending the said puddle straight towards the two men walking ahead, the inside of the umbrellas acting as a breakwater hurling the water in a graceful cascading arc, hitting them on the back of their heads.

Pleet Street didn't have an entrance to the dwarf mines, but Shafting Avenue, which lay ahead, did; to get there Gleb had to cross the street, a risky business even at the best of times. He stopped and turned his head to gauge the traffic just as a cart slewed across the road towards him.

'Getouthebloodyway,' shouted the driver as Gleb felt the wind from the lantern as it just missed his head.

'Bastard,' replied Gleb, not for the first time that morning.

Then there came a lull in the traffic, so Gleb took hold of his life and limbs and took a chance, sploshing across as fast as his little legs could go. Still safe at the halfway point with just another few steps to go, a coach and four approached fast, but there seemed to be enough of a gap, so he took another look, jumped over the sewer gulley and trod on something soft, squelchy and very very slippery: the gulley had overflowed and the contents had escaped its confinement. He went down, arms flailing, legs akimbo and landed flat on his back. A wave washed over him as the oncoming coach went past, oblivious to his predicament.

The rain may have been a bloody nuisance but the people thought the distraction of watching a struggling dwarf trying to cross the road made it worth their while to stop, to see what would happen next. Gornstock folk were not generally unsympathetic to someone else's plight but it did make for great entertainment.

Gleb rolled over and scrambled to his feet, just as a cart passed by with a grinning driver. As the cart went by, Gleb ran the last couple of yards to the safety of the pavement. A damp round of applause broke out as he hugged the wall of The Herald in relief. Above him, the gutter gave out and a stream of water hit him straight on the head, engulfing him with the addition of moss and leaves and copious quantities of bird shit.

Gleb could have had a better start to the day.

Finally, the sodden dwarf made it to Shafting Avenue, squelching towards the entrance. Dispirited, hungover and just a tad damp, he practically fell down the few steps to the iron-mesh gate which he rattled maniacally until a dwarf appeared on the other side.

'Who's that making all that din?'

'It's me, Gleb Ironcrust,' growled Gleb.

'What you doing out in this weather? You bin swimming?'

'Ha, ha, bloody ha.'

'You look like a drowned rat.'

'Thanks, but I have in fact been walking. There is a lot of weather out there and most of it is on me.'

The dwarf guarding the entrance grinned as he picked out his keys, clicked one into the slot and cranked open the gate. A relieved Gleb fell in, finally managing to gain the security of the dry dwarf tunnels.

'Bastard bloody rain,' he said, dripping wet onto the floor.

As Gleb headed off into the dark, he heard chuckling behind him; he stopped briefly, turned and shook himself, giving the evil eye. Turning around again, he stormed off, swearing and muttering, mostly incoherently.

With the all-embracing cocoon of the tunnels, meaning rock and lots of it, he began to relax. Steam rose as the warmth began to ease into his bones and clothes, magnifying the whiff of wet dog, which, for some reason, seemed to come from him. He shrugged, reasoning that soon he would dry out and the smell should disappear.

A rumble in the distance alerted Gleb to the imminent arrival of the pump-trolley.

The trolley hurtled around the corner with two young dwarfs propelling the thing, each one pumping a handle up and down which turned the wheels by use of a clever array of gears. They were yelling warnings, trying to make themselves heard above the din of the wheels as they clackety-clacked down the iron tracks.

Gleb stood with his back against the rock as the contraption whizzed past, towing a truck of worthless rock destined to be dumped in an old disused shaft way down the tunnel. It wouldn't be long before they would be heading back the same way for the next load, so he decided to dip into an opening and take the stairs down to the lower levels.

As he walked down, grumbling to himself about the weather, leaving little puddles on the steps, he suddenly grinned at the thought of all the people up top getting soaked through to their skins as they went about their business. What would they pay for a chance to get into the nice dry tunnels and walk to work?

The echo of the pump-trolley came into his mind and the noise filling his brain turned into a vision where it rained, not wet dribbly water, but coins, lots and lots of them, hundreds and hundreds of dollars, all of it flowing into the coffers of the dwarfs.

Reaching the bottom step, he then began to hurry, lest the thought slip from his mind, it being a thought of pure genius, a lightning bolt moment bringing clarity into the darkness of the unambitious: a revelation, destined to make them all rich.

'What?' exclaimed Goodhalgan as Gleb explained his idea. 'You mean you're proposing to let actual people use our tunnels?'

'Well, not only people, anyone really.'

'In our tunnels?'

'Er…Yes. Think about it, all those people wanting to travel across the city. Up there, if they haven't got their own coach or can't afford a cab, then they have to walk. We don't use the top tunnels apart from dumping the crud and we already have some of the tracks. We can make an extra couple of pump-trolleys, bung a few benches on a flat-bed and *charge* the buggers to go across the city. It'd be a licence to print money, lots of it.'

Goodhalgan scratched his head and then stroked his beard in thought. Just the mention of money, and lots of it, had given him pause for thought. 'Run that through me again, Gleb.'

Gleb did, and as he spoke, more ideas began to flitter through his mind. It seemed as if the proposal had taken on a life of its own, a little kernel of corn had popped and now it exploded into a greater thing, a massive thing, something bigger than the sum of its parts. And then Gleb began to add flavours to the popped corn and then colours, a veritable rainbow of colours, each hue a separate strand mixing with the tastes to produce a whole new culinary experience. It signalled a fresh new initiative, a smorgasbord of tastes and sounds and colours. The idea had taken hold and had now grown out of all proportion. No longer just an idea, it seemed as if it had always been and always will be. The idea had come alive.

Goodhalgan sat back in his chair and grinned across the table at Gleb. Gleb grinned back as both their heads filled with the vision. They could already see the hordes of people and animals rushing to take advantage of their new travelling experience, and pay oodles and oodles of cash for the privilege.

'We need the Council's approval though,' said Goodhalgan, now thinking of the practical side, injecting a bit a realism into the equation. 'Even though I agree, something of this magnitude has to be agreed by all of us. I'll convene the Council immediately.'

The Council convened, the Council deliberated, the Council adjourned to get a few snacks and a few more jugs of dwarf beer. The Council reconvened and agreed that a committee should be set up to discuss and analyse the proposal in more depth, the resultant discussions discussed who should sit on the committee and what expertise they would bring, and they discussed co-opting certain dwarfs who had specialist knowledge on certain parts of the proposal. They then discussed the time-frame and to whom the sub-committee should report to in order to consider the report before reporting to the Council with the findings and/or any sub-clauses, amendments, additional clauses, struck clauses, proposals and or anything which would or could have an impact on the direct constitution, or way of life of dwarfdom in general and how the proposal could affect the dwarf/human/animal relationship and whether this would be detrimental to the whole should the proposal be deemed viable enough to proceed.

Goodhalgan had heard enough. 'Who's king here?' he asked in exasperation.

The Council looked up as one.

'Er…You are,' replied Rigroll, the deep tunnel specialist.

'Good, I thought I'd better check. I am of the opinion that we should start work on this immediately. Hands up all in favour.'

The Council looked at each other and then raised their

hands as one, not a few of them relieved that the king had decided to take the decision out of their hands.

'Unanimous then,' observed Goodhalgan. 'Right,' he said, rubbing his hands together. 'Let's get this show on the road.'

An excited susurration swept through under-Gornstock as the news began to spread. Mining defined the dwarfs, they were used to using picks and shovels, breaking rock and forging tunnels but there was a limit to how much fun a dwarf could have swinging a pick at a rock-face which couldn't swing back.

There were several problems to overcome, which wasn't a problem if you were a dwarf. Dwarfs loved problems. Problems were just solutions which decided to go into hiding. When your life depended on keeping several million tons of rock from crashing down on top of your head, it sort of focused the mind a bit, to the point where complicated algebraic equations had become second nature. It also helped that if the chief engineer got his sums wrong and a tunnel collapsed, the relations of the victims would come and have a very serious word in his ear.

Goodhalgan had a problem.

The king stood at the table with the map spread out and mentally began to link all the top tunnels together. He scratched a few lines on the vellum and turned to the chief engineer.

'Seems simple enough.'

'It does,' replied Treacle. 'However, that's the easy bit. The hard bit will be in laying enough track down and making the tunnels big enough for the long-legs.'

'What do you mean? That should be the easy bit. We've got the dwarfpower.'

'Making the tunnels is easy enough, but making the tracks is only easy if you have the ore. We don't have enough ore to make them.' He thumped a digit twice on the map. 'We can start here, but we'll have to stop there.'

'Oh,' replied Goodhalgan. 'That might be a problem.'

Treacle nodded. 'We might have to think the unthinkable.'

Goodhalgan's eyes widened. 'Surely not?'

'It's the only solution I can think of.'

'Well, this is more serious than I thought.'

Goodhalgan stood up and stretched, rubbing his aching back. He stroked his beard and began to pace around the room, coming back to the map every few minutes to see if anything had changed, that the tunnels had somehow become shorter.

Treacle watched him with a degree of sympathy: as chief engineer his job entailed logistics, design and planning, to work out the what, the when and the how; as King of the Dwarfs, it was Goodhalgan's job to give him what he required. He didn't envy him this little problem.

CHAPTER 2

Jocelyn Cornwallis III, shoulder-length dark-brown hair, handsome and better known as Jack, also known as a Lord of Gornstock, as well as an absent member of The Assembly — politics being his least favourite subject, he'd managed to find an idiot to stand as proxy to vote and act on his behalf — also known as a businessman, entrepreneur and private detective, and one of the richest men in the city, peered over the rim of his glass. He watched with interest as his friend and business partner, Frankie Kandalwick, suffered the haranguing and bullying by two ladies of the Gods Quad.

The religious order worshipped the four Twearth gods: the Sun, the Moon, the Fire and the Water. The Sun named his son Fire, while the Moon named her daughter Water. The Sun and the Moon were husband and wife and bickered continually but kept their distance, while the two offspring were always at each other's throats. An interesting version of religion with the family rows taking centre stage.

'All right, all right,' yelled Frankie in defeat. 'Here's yer pennies, one for each of them. Now sod off.'

'What, only one penny each?' said one of the ladies with a condescending expression, while the other chewed lemons. 'You tight-arsed miserable bastard. We need a new gold quadruple for the temple, and I tell you, they don't come cheap, not to mention funding all the feasts; and how are the priests supposed to live on just a penny each? They have to live too, you know, and they are exalted above us so have to have a lifestyle to match. The temple provides and we provide the temple so the gods smile upon us. You, on the other hand, will be lucky if they don't shit on your head. A penny? I ask you.'

Frankie turned, grabbed his two pints from the bar and sauntered away leaving the lady mid-harangue. Fortunately, they spotted another victim as he ordered a drink and arrowed in for the kill.

'You got away lightly there,' observed Cornwallis as Frankie sat down. Frankie, built like an outhouse with light cropped hair didn't suffer intimidation — normally. 'Eddie said they pinned one bloke to the wall last week, talked at him for nearly an hour until he donated everything he had.'

'Yeah, it's the weather. Got a lot to answer for, this weather. Starts raining and that sort just descend, like locusts. Could put a man right off his beer,' replied Frankie taking a long pull of his pint. He smacked his lips in satisfaction. 'Apart from me, that is.'

Cornwallis nodded. 'I noticed that,' he said ruefully. 'Eddie thought about banning them, but then he thought of the entertainment value and decided to let them stay.'

They sat comfortably in The Black Stoat, their regular drinking establishment. Eddie the landlord happened to be the uncle to Rose, the third member of Cornwallis Investigations who also happened to be Cornwallis' girlfriend. Outside, the rain came down hard, bucketing down in fact, which meant that the Gods Quad had a captive audience. The little piazza out front looked more like a lagoon with the squally rain showers that could last for days at this time of year.

Frankie tipped his head in the Gods Quad direction. 'Just listen to 'em. It reinforces my belief that people don't enjoy religion, they just suffer from it.'

'I think they enjoy making people suffer from it,' replied

Cornwallis.

Frankie thought for a moment. 'Hey, you're right; I got it the wrong way round.'

Just then, the front door opened and as ever in the Stoat, everyone stopped talking and looked around to see who had just come in. Interest waned quickly when they saw just a dripping dwarf standing there so conversations resumed, dismissing the interloper with the contempt he deserved.

The dwarf stood for a moment letting the rain from his coat drip onto the floor. He wrung his beard out then took off his reinforced leather hat and gave it a shake.

Eddie eyed the intruder then reached behind the bar where he kept his enforcer, a gnarled old wooden club with lumps of metal hammered into the end. His hand missed the enforcer and instead grabbed a glass.

'Usual Trugral?'

Trugral nodded and then squelched over towards Cornwallis and Frankie. He pulled out a chair and sat down, regarding the two investigators.

'Well?' asked Cornwallis when no form of conversation came forth.

'Hang on, let me get me pint first.'

'Question of priorities then, is it?'

Trugral nodded. 'I'm wet on the outside, just let me get wet on the inside.'

'Equilibrium?'

'Too bloody right. Ah, here we are,' he said as Eddie came over and plonked a glass down in front of him.

The dwarf took a long pull and then smacked his lips in satisfaction. 'Nothing like a drop of Gritblasters fer a bit of equilibrium.'

'No indeed,' replied Cornwallis as he raised his own glass.

'What's an "Ibrium" then?' asked Frankie, thinking a tad outside the box. 'I mean, equals are two a penny, but what about "Ibriums"? How common are they?'

'It's "equil" not "equal", Frankie,' said Cornwallis going back to his schooldays. 'It's spelled differently and it's not two words stuck together, just one.'

'But it means equal on both sides.'

'It does.'

'So why's it spelled like that?'

Cornwallis paused, struggling to think of the answer.

'It comes,' said Trugral, 'from an ancient language. "Equil" means "equal" and "Libr" means "balanced", but actually it's three words because someone bunged an "ium" on the end to make it sound better.'

Cornwallis and Frankie stared at the font of wisdom.

'Yes,' said Cornwallis, recovering quickly. 'Just what I was going to say before you interrupted me.'

'No, you weren't,' countered Frankie. 'You're just as thick as I am, despite your privileged education.'

'Not thick, Frankie, just selective knowledge.'

'So you selected not to know the answer?'

Cornwallis inclined his head. 'Exactly; I have selected not to know the answers to a lot of questions, like how have you survived so long with a knowledge base as low as yours?'

'Eh?'

'You're thinking that I'm taking the proverbial, but you'd be wrong. The system dictated my education, encapsulating a wide range of subjects which pertained to my proper station in life; that is, us nobs, as you like to call us, need to know how to rule and so the tutors taught accordingly. Your knowledge comes from the gutter. You learnt how to sneak in through a window and rifle a bedroom whilst the occupants were still slumbering in their beds, but they didn't teach you how to get out of the charge should Mr Policeman catch you in the act. For that, you need a deep understanding of the finer points of the law and know who to pass the bung to; you have to go to the top, and being in the same club helps tremendously.'

'You may be right, to a point,' defended Frankie stoically. 'But us common folk know that you have to tap up the right person, and our money is as good as yours.'

'Ah, but you're wrong there. A nobs' money is worth more because it comes with obligation and preferment. It's not just the exchange of cash; money is the least of it. A back has got an itch, and someone is working out what sort of scratch will give the most return: what influence can come with it.'

'That's hardly fair though.'

'No, it's not, but that's life under the class system we have in this wonderful city of ours. That is why my education differed from yours.'

'So you know which palm to grease.'

'No, it's *whose* palm to grease, and know what you can do for them, or, what they can do for you.'

'That's all well and good,' interrupted Trugral, 'but my glass is empty and I'm here to do you a favour.'

'A favour?' asked Cornwallis warily.

Trugral nodded. 'Yep.'

'So what is it?'

Trugral tapped his glass and grinned.

Cornwallis sighed and then called over to Eddie for refills.

'So,' said Cornwallis when the refreshments arrived. 'What favour are you going to do for us?'

'Not both of you, I'm afraid, Frankie hasn't got the wherewithal.'

Frankie eyed the dwarf with disdain. 'What do you mean by

that?'

Trugral winked. 'Someone wants to scratch and is looking for someone with an itch.'

Cornwallis and Frankie exchanged a confused look.

Trugral twitched his head and smiled wryly. 'Goodhalgan would like the pleasure of your company. He sent me to find yer.'

Cornwallis followed Trugral down into the dwarf tunnels. He didn't really need a guide now as he had been down so many times, so much so that he was practically an honorary dwarf, considered so by the whole community. He ducked under a low overhang, turned a left and descended the steps down to a lower level.

Goodhalgan continued to study a crude map laid out on the table as Cornwallis walked through the door. He looked up, nodded a greeting and then beckoned the investigator over.

'Look at this, what do you make of it?'

'I think it's upside down,' replied Cornwallis, feeling whimsical after quaffing several pints of beer. 'However, should I peruse it from your side then I might get a better idea.'

Cornwallis walked around the table and peeked over the king of the dwarfs' shoulder.

Goodhalgan sighed and twiddled with his beard. 'Trugral found you in the Stoat, didn't he?'

'Of course. How did you know?'

'The fumes are turning my beard green, and you're trying to be funny.'

'Do you know you're sounding just like Rose? Although she hasn't got a beard, and she's taller, and she's got these two great big—'

'Eyes, yes, I know. I've seen them enough times. Look, this

is… or can be, important. For both of us.'

'Right,' said Cornwallis, stopping his swaying and composing himself. 'Right, I'm all ears.'

'Shall we start again?'

Cornwallis nodded.

'Good. Now, what do you make of this?'

Cornwallis took a deep breath and tried to sober up rapidly. Trugral insisted on having a couple of shots of dwarf whisky before they left and it would have been churlish not to join him: the trouble is, with humans, it can have a mind-numbing effect on the system akin to being hit on the head by a thirty-pound sledgehammer. He jabbed a finger towards a bit of calligraphic script, readjusted his aim and then managed to hit the mark.

'This is the name of one of your entrances, Trafal Square.' He stabbed at another name. 'And this is another, Butchers Street. It's a map of your entrances.'

'It is, well done,' replied Goodhalgan. 'We have loads of them and have come to realise that perhaps they could be put to some use for the benefit of the city. It is our intention to link them all up so that the residents of the city can move easily from one area to another without having to contend with the crowd upstairs.'

Cornwallis let this little nugget of information settle into his brain. 'How?' he asked eventually.

'Carts on tracks: we lay tracks on the upper level and then invite passengers to ride on our carts for a small fee. All underground so they won't get wet.'

'That could actually work,' exclaimed Cornwallis.

Goodhalgan nodded. 'That's what we thought.'

'So why are you telling me?'

'Ah, now we come to the interesting part. We, that is, us dwarfs, would like you to be a business partner.'

19

'Partner?'

'Yes. We can't do it all and a lot of long-legs are ambivalent towards us. Frankly, we need you to put the word about.'

'Why me?'

Goodhalgan took a deep breath. 'For some unaccountable reason, people tend to trust you. I don't know why, but they do. You would give the enterprise a degree of respectability.'

Cornwallis tried to push the effects of the whisky far away as his mind clicked into gear, it whirled, but a cog struggled to knit into the machine as he tried to get his head around it all. He'd had business dealings in the past where alcohol played a major part, but normally the other party suffered marginally more than he did, as he did the buying as well as the pouring: but this proposal could be enormous. He turned his head to look at the grinning king of the dwarfs as he stood beside him: he'd plated the offering, with garnish, and a side order of chips. He did wonder if the shots of whisky were not Trugral's idea, but Goodhalgan's. The king was sober as a plank which put him at a distinct advantage.

Goodhalgan regarded Cornwallis' sober part and saw the glint in the eye, indicating that his interest had been piqued.

'How much?' asked Cornwallis' sober bit.

'How much?' replied Goodhalgan innocently.

'Yes, how much is this going to cost me?'

'Well, since you bring the subject up, it would be remiss of me not to say that a financial contribution on your part would be very much appreciated. It would only be a nominal amount considering the possible long-term revenue that I envisage coming our way. A piffling little bit of small change that you would hardly miss and all for the good of the community. It would hardly dent your coffer and all for a mouth-watering ten percent stake.'

Cornwallis' eyes widened. 'Ten percent? Let's be honest now, I wouldn't get out of bed for just ten percent. Fifty-fifty.'

Goodhalgan looked aghast. 'Impossible. The Council would never accept that.'

The alcohol finally left Cornwallis' head and now he could concentrate as the business brain got into gear. Discussions then began in earnest.

Cornwallis trudged up the stairs and walked into his office. The secretary, Maud, had gone home long ago but she had tidied up and kept the stove going. He put a pot on to boil ready for coffee and then sat down at his desk, now devoid of any paperwork. It had been a long negotiation with Goodhalgan but he felt the end result made it worthwhile. He toyed with the paperweight, mulling over the costs involved. He considered offsetting the investment by offering part of his share to others who may be interested but then dismissed the idea when he thought that the only one he could really trust would be his father and he didn't need the money: nor did he, when he came to think about it, but the plan seemed such a good opportunity and the future returns could be astronomical. He wanted to take the risk. Private investigating could certainly get the pulse racing, but nothing like making a shed load of gold through someone else's honest hard work.

The office door creaked open and a head appeared in the gap. Blonde, beautiful and with eyes to die for, Rose smiled into the darkness.

'What are you doing, Jack? Frankie called round and said you'd gone underground. What was it about?'

'The future,' replied Cornwallis enigmatically. 'The dwarfs and I are now partners in a little enterprise.'

'Oh?'

Rose walked in and began to light a couple of lamps, sending the thoughtful darkness away into oblivion.

Cornwallis turned to watch as she glided across the floor. He never got tired of looking at her and knew full well he received the envy of every red-blooded male in the city. Rose came as close to perfection as a girl could get with blemish-free skin, beauty, brains, honey-coloured hair and a flawless figure. He held his arms out as she lit the second lamp and then came over to sit on his lap, which pleased him no end.

She cupped his head in her hands and kissed his forehead. 'What sort of enterprise?'

'A good one, but one that requires a bit of a risk.'

'Goodhalgan doesn't take risks.'

'He does now and this could be a big one.'

'How, why?'

'He wants… he wants to open up the tunnels to the general public as a means of transportation.'

'Transportation? How?'

She shifted position which pleased him even more.

'He plans to put tracks down and move people through the upper levels on carts. They can hop on and off at the underground entrance of their choice. They stay dry and keep away from the crowds in the street. They won't need to use cabs anymore.'

Rose shifted position again which took a bit of the pressure off.

'You mean it'll put the cabs out of business?' she asked. 'That's hardly fair.'

'It won't put them out of business; it will just give people a choice. At the moment, the only choice they have is either to take a cab or walk. I'm not including those who have a private carriage, just those who can't afford them. Think on it; someone can enter one of the tunnels, jump on a cart, then a few minutes later they'd be on the other side of the city. It will be a revelation.'

Steam rattled the pot, which could have indicated to the more enlightened a new age of discovery and invention, but in this case, it just indicated that it was time for coffee. Rose relinquished her position, leading Cornwallis to sigh in disappointment, and went over to make the drink.

'I can see it working,' she said as she filled the mugs. 'But wouldn't getting something like that off the ground cost a lot of money?'

'Er, yes it would. But we'll be in at the start and as it gets successful, we can offset it in some way. I've already thought about having people advertise their goods and services down there, you know, put up hoardings and posters, that sort of thing. I'm sure that there's a lot more we can do.'

Rose walked over and put the mugs down on the desk before sitting once more in his lap.

'How much money?' she asked. 'I know it's all yours and you can do what you want with it, but sometimes you can be a bit impetuous.'

He gave a wry grin and squeezed her waist. 'Maybe, but I've always made money, in all my ventures, and this is just going to be another. I reckon if we get this right it will be the biggest thing to hit Gornstock — ever.'

'Yes, but how much?'

Cornwallis flapped his hand dismissively. 'Nothing that I can't afford, just trust me. We'll own thirty percent of the whole thing.'

CHAPTER 3

'How much?' asked Frankie incredulously, the shock apparent by the motionless double-beef patty with bacon, extra cheese and relish poised an inch from his mouth.

'Forty thousand dollars,' replied Rose, daintily pecking at hers. 'But that's just for starters. Jack and Goodhalgan cobbled together some figures but the costs could rise. He's in it for thirty percent.'

'Thirty percent of forty thousand?' Frankie tried to count on his fingers but the bun got in the way. 'I make that twelve thousand dollars he's putting in. Bloody hell!'

Rose nodded. 'It's a lot of money but the dwarfs are doing all the donkey work. Jack's money is just to pay for making all the stuff they need.'

'Goodhalgan must have that much stashed away somewhere, so why get Jack involved?'

'Look, there he is.'

'Who, Jack?'

'No, you idiot. We're meant to be working, if you'd care to remember.'

'Sorry, it were the shock. You don't hear that amount of money spoken about often.'

'You do if you live with Jack. We had dinner with his mother and father the other night and you really wouldn't believe the amounts they were talking about, even forty thousand is small change to them. Anyway, you know that.'

'Yeah, I just forget sometimes. So why's Goodhalgan roped him in then?'

'Because... Hang on, let's get a little closer.'

They were in Treadle Street where fashion and music meshed together. Young and upcoming designers and music makers serviced the public from little boutique shops, selling all manner of garments and sheet music to a discerning clientele. If you bought stuff from Treadle Street then you could claim to be "cool," as the young people were fond of saying.

Frankie still had trouble getting his head around some of the words used nowadays. To him, cool meant not being warm, a bit on the chilly side.

Rose elbowed him in the ribs. 'Come on, or we'll lose him.'

They were following a minor government official from the ministry of Arts and Sciences. A man suspected of being involved in the peddling of illegal copies of Morris music, stolen from the register. The government held the copyright of all Morris music, anyone buying or playing Morris incurred a cost and people had to pay accordingly. Recently, though, a flourishing trade in forged and counterfeit copies had come to the surface and the Morris Council, unhappy that money due to them now lined someone else's pocket, engaged Cornwallis Investigations to catch the man.

'Why are we doing this anyway?' asked Frankie. 'It's only bloody Morris music. I can't stand the sodding stuff, like most people.'

'No, I can't either, but it's illegal and we've been asked to catch him. Jethro managed to get out of it by suggesting that the Bagman sort it out but he said he had much more important stuff to deal with, so the minister contacted Jack. Weren't you listening when we were talking about it?'

Frankie sighed. 'No, I fell asleep during that bit. The baby's been having bad nights. Tulip has a touch of colic; so me and Isabella haven't had much rest.'

'Poor Isabella, she said there were a few baby problems.'

'Yeah, I wouldn't mind but she keeps bringing Tulip into our bed; hence my lack of sleep.'

'Er, Frankie. I think you're treading on dangerous ground there.'

'Eh? What do you mean?'

'I mean you should be helping, taking it in turns.'

'Ah, a bit of a problem there; I ain't got the wherewithal.' He indicated what he meant by pointing at bits of Rose. 'Feeding, for the use of.'

Rose pulled a face. 'Tulip doesn't need feeding all the time. A bit of a cuddle sometimes works and you can definitely do that.'

'Yeah, well, mebbee I could,' he conceded.

'Good, I'll expect to hear that you've been doing your bit when I next see her.'

'Yes, Rose,' said Frankie, sighing in defeat.

'Come on,' she said, digging her elbow into his ribs for the second time, this time with a bit more force.

Frankie gave her a wary look and then rubbed the painful bit as they followed the man a little further up the street.

'Here we go,' said Rose.

The man gave a furtive look over his shoulder before stepping up to the door of Clackthorn's Emporium, the addendum beneath the sign saying, "Quality Quivering Quavers," and entered the establishment.

'Quick, we might catch him red-handed,' said Rose, picking up her pace.

'All right, I'm coming,' said Frankie. 'But you still ain't told me why Goodhalgan wants Jack's help.'

'Because... Well, if the dwarfs put up a sign which said, "Come to us and we'll take you for a ride," what do you think would happen?'

'Er, nothing. People would think there was something iffy about it.'

'Exactly. But if Jack said it?'

'Ah, I see. What you mean is that he will lend a bit of, what's the word? Oh yes,' and he clicked his fingers. 'Gravytas to it.'

'Close, but it's gravitas, and yes, he would.'

Frankie nodded in understanding as they got to the shop's window. They looked in and saw the official talking to the kid behind the counter. He passed a brown packet over to the lad who then went to the till.

'Time to move, I think,' said Frankie, becoming business-like for the first time that day.

The door swung open and the two detectives walked in. The official swung his head around at the intrusion but the lad just looked up and smiled a welcome.

'Be with you in a minute, dudes,' he said as he counted out some cash. 'Got some heavy stuff over there if you want to browse.' He pointed to a rack of brightly coloured printed sheets, each one a separate design of artwork. 'They're really real, if you know what I mean.'

Frankie didn't and he looked askance at Rose who wore the same perplexed expression.

'Dudes? Heavy? Really real? What does he bloody mean?' asked Frankie, bemused.

Rose shook her head. 'I'm young, but even I'm lost with that lot.'

Frankie and Rose walked nonchalantly up to the counter and pulled out their handcuffs. The lad and the official had resumed their conversation when the cuffs clicked on their wrists.

27

'You pair are nicked,' said Frankie, grinning.

'Hey, man. What's this?' protested the lad. 'I ain't dun nuffink.'

'You've just given this gentleman some money for those bits of music in front of you, which means you are knowingly receiving stolen goods; this gentleman being the one who nicked them in the first place, which is why you are both nicked,' explained Frankie patiently.

The official groaned and hung his head, it all seemed to be going so well up to this point, and nobody *ever* wanted the sheet music for Morris dancing. The man in the music shop doctored the score by putting a proper beat to the dirge, bringing it up to date and selling it on. How could that be a crime?

Rose held out her hand for the shop key as the lad looked up. They would come back later and search the place for more illicit material.

'What happens now?' asked the official as they walked down the street.

'We bangs you up,' replied Frankie, stifling a yawn. 'Then someone comes to talk to you, then you confess, then you go before a judge, and then you get banged up again. That is if you're lucky. If the Bagman decides he wants a word, which he might, seeing you is an official in the government, then... let's just say it could be a very interesting experience.'

The official's eyes came out on stalks. 'The B... Bagman?' he stuttered, horrified at the thought.

'Oh yes. Now I come to think about it, that's the most likely outcome. Crime against the State, you see. The Warden will definitely hear about it and then the Bagman will have to speak to you. I reckon he'll be pretty annoyed.'

'Frankie,' warned Rose. 'You're scaring the gentleman.'

'Am I? Oh, sorry. I'm sure the Bagman will only use *some* of the methods at his disposal to get a confession from a minor official like what you is.'

The lad from the music shop laughed. 'The Bagman is a myth, there's no such person. Everyone knows that.'

'Do they?' asked Frankie. 'Be sure to tell him that when you meet him.'

'Sorry?'

'Oh, you'll meet him too. You've been receiving government documents, don't forget. But if you say he doesn't exist then you've got nothing to worry about, you can just ignore what he does to you.'

Rose stuck out an arm and a cab pulled up.

'Scooters Yard,' instructed Frankie, still grinning, as they piled in.

Once they deposited the prisoners in the cells, Rose and Frankie headed to the canteen for a well-earned brew. They walked down the corridor, pushed the door open and headed over to the perpetually boiling pot to pour themselves a coffee. A few feelers looked up at their entrance and one nodded a greeting — feeler being the nickname for a police officer, named after their founder, Lord Carstairs Fielding.

'Sergeant,' the lone greeter said to Rose, who held the rank of sergeant in the police as well as being a private detective. Up to a couple of days ago, she'd been instructing some new recruits on how to follow suspects.

'Hello, Cecil,' she replied to Constable Toopins, known to most as Dewdrop. 'I've been thinking about your little problem and I reckon a bunch of flowers and a slap-up meal might be the answer. A girl likes to think she's appreciated, you know.'

Constable Toopins opened his eyes wide in hope and expectation. 'You really think so?'

Rose nodded. 'All couples argue from time to time, you and

Felicity are no different to anyone else. Me and Jack, Frankie and Isabella, we all have rows.'

'What?' asked Frankie, hearing his name mentioned.

'Just that you argue with Isabella from time to time,' said Rose. 'Cecil here has had an argument with his girlfriend.'

'Oh, right; is that all? Isabella sometimes stops speaking to me for days on end. It's worth having the row just to get a bit of peace.'

'Frankie,' admonished Rose. 'You don't really mean that?'

Frankie shook his head and grinned. 'Well, not all of it.'

Rose beetled her brow.

'Well, none of it actually. I was just having a bit of fun.'

'I should hope so to. Isabella has a lot on her hands with Tulip.'

'I do my best,' returned Frankie. 'She's my daughter too, you know.'

'I know, I know,' she replied, holding up a hand.

Constable Toopins decided to make himself scarce. He knew that Frankie and Rose could carry on for hours arguing back and forth, and anyway, Rose had given him a suggestion so as soon as he finished the shift he would book a table.

'Where's he gone?' asked Rose.

'Who?'

'Cecil. I was just talking to him.'

'But you're not talking to him now. He's buggered off.'

'He probably thought you were going to offer your advice.'

'I would've if he'd stayed around long enough. I know a lot of things about women.'

'Hmm, Isabella might be really interested to know that.'

Frankie gave a wink. 'You had a life before Jack, so I had a life before Isabella.'

'From what Jack says yours tended to be a bit more… how

shall I say it? Transient.'

'I don't know what you mean. All my ladies knew what was what and were more than willing.'

'I think we can stop this conversation now, Frankie. I dread to think what you'll come up with next.'

They found themselves a table and sat down. The hubbub of a busy police canteen went on all around them and they studied the constables as they took their breaks before going back out on the streets.

Rose felt a degree of pride as she looked at the mix: both men and women, where before, it had just been men. Now a steady influx of females infiltrated the male domain and she had been part of the revolution.

Commander Jethro MacGillicudy had been enthusiastic when she had first mentioned the idea and after a bit of thought, he had the papers run an ad. He recruited twelve girls then, and now there were thirty, with many more to come.

'So Jack's definitely going ahead with it then?'

His question knocked Rose out of her reverie. 'Oh, yes. He says it's the future, this transport thing. They've just got to come up with a snappy name for it.'

'You mean like the "Underground." Or, as the tunnels are like a cigar container, why not call it the "Tube"? He, he, he.'

'That'll never catch on, Frankie,' replied Rose, sighing. 'We've got to come up with something better than that.'

CHAPTER 4

'Right,' said Cornwallis, rubbing his hands together as the little group assembled on the street. 'You're going to be the very first to trial this. Three sections of The Pipe have been completed and you will get on and off at each of the entrances.'

'The Pipe?' queried Frankie. 'What sort of name is that?'

'It's the name that Goodhalgan and I have come up with, as the tunnels resemble a pipe.'

'Reckon my ideas were better.'

'Yes, I heard about them,' replied Cornwallis.

'And what's wrong with them?' asked Frankie indignantly.

'Nothing, but they don't run off the tongue. The Pipe is short, catchy and easy to remember.'

'So's the bloody flu,' responded Frankie sourly.

Cornwallis took a deep breath but decided not to answer as he caught a look from Rose. She wore a half-smile with a slightly inclined head. The look said things were amusing but to leave it at that, as Frankie felt nervous about the prospect of travelling under the ground with all that rock above his head waiting to fall down right on top of him. It's amazing what a single look could convey.

Commander Jethro MacGillicudy along with Constables Cecil Toopins and Felicity Dill were present for the dummy run. Rose especially invited Dewdrop and Felicity as she had a soft spot for both of them and as some ruffles had appeared recently in their relationship, this may be a way of smoothing some of them out. They were an incongruous couple as Felicity once adorned some of the more downmarket tabloids as a page three woodcut. She was pretty much all that a young man wanted and desired; being blonde, slim, pretty and delightfully formed. Dewdrop had somehow been the one to catch her, much to everyone's surprise, least of all, Dewdrop's. He had a stick-thin body with a dark mop of unruly hair and until recently seemed to sport a near-permanent droplet of snot on the end of his nose; hence the name Dewdrop. Heads shook in disbelief as the pair walked arm in arm down the streets.

MacGillicudy stood with his hands in his pockets as his moustache and side-whiskers twitched, more in trepidation rather than expectation as he waited for the inevitable descent into the dwarf tunnels. A big man, more muscle than fat with hair just beginning to silver, he wore his civilian clothes rather than his normal commander's attire, and at that moment, he wished that he and Cornwallis weren't quite such firm friends.

'Come on, Jack, let's get this over with.'

'Soon, Jethro,' replied Cornwallis. 'We have to wait for the signal.'

'Signal?'

'Yes.' Cornwallis sounded exasperated. 'It's the first run and we want it to go right.'

'Oh, so when it's up and running, people will have to stand out here and wait?'

'No, no, no. They'll be able to go and wait inside, by the track. This time we want your experience on the whole operation.'

'Well, if you want my opinion, I don't need to travel on the thing. I can tell you now—'

'Jethro,' interrupted Rose. 'That's not like you. You sound worse than Frankie.'

MacGillicudy sighed and took a deep breath. He thought about speaking, then he glanced at the two constables by his side and then thought he'd better not, as their commander saying he might be just a tiny bit scared might give the wrong impression. Besides, they may decide to talk back at the Yard and his credibility would go out the window. 'If you'd let me finish, Rose, I was just about to say that this whole thing is a splendid idea and with Jack and Goodhalgan involved, it's certain to be successful.'

Rose opened her mouth to say that she didn't believe him when a smiling dwarf appeared in the entrance wearing a little uniform. The black trousers had blue trimming down the legs and the black jacket had blue lapels and cuffs. A black peaked flat cap perched on his head, a little blue line along the front of the peak. His long unkempt beard threw the smartness out of kilter as he looked like a scruffy child with a false beard going to a fancy dress party.

'Welcome to The Pipe,' he intoned gravely. 'If you would care to follow me.'

Everyone stood waiting as the dwarf looked up at each face in turn. Eventually, Felicity stepped forward, cast a withering glance at Dewdrop then pulled on his arm to get his leaden feet moving.

'I'm coming, Flick, wait a minute.'

'You said you couldn't wait to try it out. It's an honour for both of us. Think on it; we're going to be the very first, Cecil, the very first to try out this new mode of transport. We're pioneers, you and me.'

'Exactly,' said Cornwallis. 'This is Gornstock progressing, moving into the future, modern times just around the corner. Think on what it will mean for the city with transport links to every corner.'

'Jack, stop preaching,' said Rose. 'You don't have to sell it to us. We're already here.'

'What? No, I wasn't preaching.'

'Yes you were. Save it for later when you're selling it to the public.'

Frankie grinned. 'Yeah, Jack, and you can put yer arms down now; you look like a bloody semaphore with them dancing hands.'

Cornwallis stopped mid-gyration and put on a sheepish grin. 'Sorry, just think we're on to a good thing.'

'I'm sure we are, but let's see what it's like first,' replied Rose.

'Are you lot going to shift yer arses?' asked the dwarf. 'We ain't got all day, you know.'

Felicity and Dewdrop were still in front so they were the first of the group to enter the dwarf tunnels. Rose linked her arm through Cornwallis' and they both quickly followed.

'Don't you bloody well hold on to me,' warned Frankie to MacGillicudy.

'No sodding chance,' replied the commander, horrified at the thought.

The six prospective commuters entered the dimly lit entrance. Inside, a barrier stopped their progress with a booth for tickets alongside. Another dwarf, dressed as the first, handed out pieces of paper with a number on each.

'A dollar, please,' said the dwarf as he handed out the tickets.

'What?' asked Frankie, shocked at the charge.

'Don't worry; you don't have to actually pay. I'm just practising.'

'Oh, that's all right then, but a dollar seems a bit steep.'

'Early days,' said Cornwallis. 'We're yet to fix the fares.'

Frankie eyed the dwarf warily who grinned in return before

sniffing and swallowing a gobbet of snot.

'Nice,' observed Frankie as Cornwallis pulled out his notebook and started to write.

'Come on, there is a timetable, you know,' said the dwarf impatiently.

The six intrepid commuters cast a look at the dwarf and then negotiated the gate and moved further into the tunnel, which meandered snake-like, deep down into the underside of Gornstock. Cornwallis held back a bit and watched his five companions closely.

'Could do with a bit more light,' ventured MacGillicudy. 'Black as a chimney sweep's arse.'

As Felicity giggled, Frankie nodded sagely, though the gloom made him difficult to see.

'Hmm,' mused Cornwallis. 'You may have a point there,' he agreed, pulling out the notebook again and scribbling some more.

'A few lanterns along the wall?' suggested Rose.

'Possibly, but the oil will need to be topped up all the time and candles would need to be replaced regularly; it would cost a fortune.'

'Fireflies?' suggested Frankie. 'Bung a load of 'em in a bottle. That'll work.'

Cornwallis shook his head. 'No, we'd need millions and millions of the little buggers. I'll have to give it a bit of thought.'

They moved around a corner into a better lit spot where tracks barred the way ahead. The tracks extended to the left and right, entering and exiting a particularly dark and uninviting tunnel. The dwarf guiding them put out an arm to stop them going further.

Then from the right came a low grumbling noise which morphed into a slow clack-clack which became steadily louder and seemed to be coming closer. They all stared into the deep dark mouth of the tunnel as the noise approached.

Suddenly the noise reached a crescendo and a little contraption with two dwarfs upon it lurched into view. A flat-bed pump-trolley hooked up to a cart with the two dwarfs pumping the handles as if their lives depended on it: the cart looked like a shed on wheels, with cut-outs where windows should be and a little door at the rear on the nearside to allow entrance to the shed.

The two dwarfs ceased pumping and one grabbed a handle, pulling on the brake until the whole thing ground to a stop, adjacent to the six commuters.

Another dwarf appeared at the open door of the cart. 'Tickets please. Step aboard.'

A slight problem now became apparent. There were no steps and the floor of the cart lay about three feet above where they were standing, which necessitated some undignified clambering. Eventually, Cornwallis got on board and he pulled out his notebook.

'Move along please,' said the dwarf guard. 'Take your seats quickly.'

The seats were in rows, along both sides of the cart, enabling it to carry twenty seated passengers. When everyone had made themselves comfortable, the guard stuck his head out of the windowless window.

'All aboard,' yelled the guard. 'Give it a bit of welly.'

Cornwallis eyebrows shot up and the notebook received another scribble.

The pump handle went up and down and the cart began to move, heading off into the pitch dark mouth. Everyone grinned nervously as the contraption entered the maw of doom.

'Bit dark in here,' ventured MacGillicudy after a couple of

moments.

'A bit dark?' returned Frankie. 'I can't see my bloody hand in front of my face.'

'Er, slight technical problem,' said Cornwallis.

A noise of a slap intruded. 'Cecil, don't do that, not here anyway.'

Rose grinned into the dark as she couldn't help but eavesdrop.

'Sorry,' apologised Dewdrop. 'Just wanted to hold on to something.'

'Well, try holding my hand instead.'

MacGillicudy, seated next to Frankie, turned his head. 'Don't you have any ideas about holding on to something, because there's a right-hander here, waiting just for you.'

'Don't worry, Jethro, there is absolutely nothing of yours that I would want to touch.'

'That's all right then,' replied the commander. 'However, I've got a bit of an itch down here if you wouldn't mind helping.'

'Sod off, Jethro.'

'Oh, for the gods sake,' whined Rose. 'You're worse than children.'

'You want to be where I'm sitting,' said Felicity.

'That's not fair,' countered Dewdrop. 'We're an item.'

'No, Cecil, we're a couple. Didn't last night prove that?'

It was dark, nobody could see, but everyone knew that eyebrows shot up.

'Last night?' queried Cornwallis. 'Do I want to know about last night?'

'No, Mr Cornwallis, you certainly don't,' replied Felicity vehemently.

'That's okay, Rose and I didn't happen either.'

'Jack,' exclaimed Rose.

'Bugger,' responded Frankie. 'As if I had the bloody chance, what with Tulip an' all.'

'Thanks for reminding me,' said MacGillicudy, 'that I am somewhat bereft in the happening department.'

'That's your own fault,' countered Frankie. 'I've introduced you to loads of ladies recently.'

'Frankie, your idea of a lady is a very loose term, as is, if I may be so bold to say, their morals. I would even go so far as to say that they came with a price list.'

'Ah, but you have to admit that Clarissa scrubs up well. She even gives a discount to her regulars.'

A bit of a judder came from the cart and then a slight hazy light instilled itself into the dark and over the six virgin passengers.

The guard emerged from the shadows. 'Approaching Tooley Street,' he informed, as the light then came rushing in.

The pump-trolley dwarfs yanked on the brake and the cart slowed to a halt.

'Tooley Street already, eh? That was quick,' said Cornwallis.

MacGillicudy nodded. 'I'll give you that. Would have taken at least fifteen minutes up top.'

'Longer, if it were the rush hour,' added Dewdrop. 'Er, sir.'

'You're quite right, Constable Toopins. We've no traffic down here.'

Another uniformed dwarf helped them down from the cart and guided them up to the entrance where they could breathe the fresh clean Gornstock air.

A few minutes respite and then the whole process began again, back down into the tunnel, onto the cart, clambering not optional, and away, off to Slingshot Row, conveniently situated close to the Stoat, where the inevitable debrief would take place.

'Now that we've all got a drink,' said Cornwallis, 'we can

begin. Who wants to go first?'

The pub started getting busy. Eddie had installed a skittles alley at the back and a team of dwarfs were playing a team of bears. As always, there were plenty of bets flying around, as well as skittles.

'It were too dark,' ventured Dewdrop after a while. 'Looking from a police point of view, if the Commander don't mind me saying…' MacGillicudy gave him a nod to continue, so Dewdrop did. '…it would be easy for a dipper or a groper to operate down there.'

'Well said, lad,' said MacGillicudy. 'They were my thoughts precisely. Anywhere dark like that would be giving the thumbs up to all sorts of undesirables. There needs to be a lot more light.'

Cornwallis scribbled in his notebook.

'The tunnels don't need light, just the carts,' suggested Felicity. 'Then the guard would be able to see what goes on.'

'Good idea,' said Cornwallis, scratching out what he'd just written and replacing it with something new. 'Anything else?'

'Getting on and off weren't easy. Needs steps or something,' said Frankie.

'Or raise the floor a bit,' suggested Rose. 'A platform so you can just step into the cart.'

'Carriage,' amended Cornwallis. 'I've decided to call the carts carriages; it makes them sound posher, lends it a bit of class.'

'In that case,' said Rose. 'You'd better do something about the ride. It was as hard as nails. At least the road carriages have some suspension.'

'And the seats,' added Felicity. 'They were just wooden boards; you'd get a really numb bum if you went any distance.'

'You could've sat on my lap,' said Dewdrop, and then turned a deep shade of crimson as everyone looked at him.

'This is definitely a new side of Constable Toopins coming out, ain't seen this one before,' said Frankie with a grin. 'I'll tell you what son, me and you will have a little word later and I'll give you some tips,' and he gave a little wink.

Rose sighed.

Felicity sighed.

Cornwallis and MacGillicudy laughed.

*

'Gentlemen, thank you for coming. We have a very important issue to discuss. I have learnt that the dwarfs are planning to introduce a new mode of transport to the city.' The Chairman of the Guilds reached forward to take a sip of water from his glass. 'It goes without saying that this office welcomes enterprise, innovation and invention for the good of all our band of brothers. But, and indeed, it is a big but, the dwarfs are not members of the Guilds Hall. Therefore, it poses a bit of a problem. Before, we could ignore them, as they just sort of dug around down there, doing whatever it is that they do, but with this proposal, they intend to impact on us up here; they intend to enter into the world of commerce and business. In effect, they are planning to take the food from out of our mouths. The Guilds can't stand around idly watching while all this happens. We need to stop all this from happening; we need a strategy to thwart their ambitions. We can't let a minority group dictate to us. Thoughts gentlemen?'

'How did you learn about this?' asked the master of the guild of pawnbrokers.

'Ah, a good chairman has eyes and ears everywhere. I heard it from one of my contacts.'

In fact, he'd heard it from someone who had heard it from

someone who had overheard a couple of dwarfs talking a few nights ago, when he had been at his club, dressed in a manner not necessarily pertaining to his sex; his release in times of stress or euphoria, depending which was prevalent at the time. He'd just made a great deal of money, so decided to celebrate with one of his set of Molly boys.

'Reliable contact?'

'Oh, very. You can take what I said as fact.'

'Then we will have to do something. Can't be having those short-arses getting above their station.'

A murmur of general agreement ran through the meeting and then the hard work of working out what to do began. What were they to do?

CHAPTER 5

'There's been a delegation with a protest,' announced Cornwallis senior as he strolled into the office.

Rose and Cornwallis junior looked up as the earl entered, as did Frankie and Isabella. MacGillicudy ignored the slam of the door as it smacked against the wall, as playing with Tulip took priority, bouncing her up and down on his knee; some happy gurgling coming from both participants.

'What do you mean?' asked Rose, a look of consternation briefly visiting her face.

'I mean the Master of the Guilds, and the committee, visited the Warden, and the Warden has asked me to look into it.'

'But you can't, can you?'

'I can and I will. The Warden doesn't trust anyone else to do it. The Guilds think that any new and large enterprise should go to them first for approval, to see if it impacts on any existing guild member. As the guilds pump money towards the Warden, the Warden conceded that they may have a point.'

'But the guilds don't want anything to do with the dwarfs. They've said that often enough,' argued Rose.

'That's not the point,' replied the earl. 'The point is that it may have an adverse effect on some of their members.'

'Who?'

'Er, the cabbies for one. This could have a serious impact on them.'

Rose's eyes blazed with a light that the earl had never seen before.

'Well, at least it might have an effect… in some way… Rose, please don't look at me like that. I'm only doing my job,'

'You're going to help the guilds? You're going to go against both the dwarfs and us?'

Cornwallis interrupted before things took a turn for the worse. Rose had passionate beliefs about a lot of things and one of them pertained to how the city treated the dwarfs as a sub-species. 'Let's not jump to conclusions,' he said. 'There are many ways to look into things and now we have an advantage; we know what's going on.'

'Exactly,' said the earl, taking a deep breath. 'So, please, Rose, can you readjust your gaze to one of undying love and admiration. I'm a politician, so I know what questions to ask to get the answers I want, I can ask the questions that nobody wants to know the answers to, and I can ignore asking the questions where people actually want to know the answers.'

Rose sighed. 'I suppose so, but it galls me that the guilds think that they can dictate to everyone.'

'That's because they can. The guilds are powerful; they have oodles of money to splash around so they can call the shots. Don't forget, in this city, money talks. Well, in reality, it shouts.'

'But that's not fair,' replied Rose indignantly.

'No, it's not but it's a fact of life and, in this instance, it's got its aim on the dwarfs and this Pipe thing. They are going to do everything they can to make sure that they win. The problem is that I have to make sure they don't.'

'You mean that?' asked Cornwallis. 'You'll take our side?'

'Of course I will, my boy. Blood is thicker than water, after all. I'm just telling you how things stand at the moment.'

Tulip made another gurgling sound, this one being more ominous. Her face turned a little puce and MacGillicudy began to look a little worried. He was just about to hand her back when it happened. A foul-smelling, creamy torrent of liquid erupted from between her lips and spurted straight onto the shirt-front of the Commander of Police.

'Oh, bugger,' said the commander who sat resolute and in control. 'Poor little lamb, are you feeling a little iffy?'

The smell took on a persona of its own, a thick, cloying aroma, wholly human in an unhuman kind of way.

Isabella jumped up from her chair and hurried over with her typical mothers' bag full of unlimited accoutrements. She fished out a cloth and picked hold of Tulip, handing her to Frankie.

'Who's daddy's favourite girl then, puking on the good commander? Don't worry, he's used to it.'

MacGillicudy raised a laconic eyebrow as Isabella wiped the offending deposit off his shirt. 'Ah, yes, but normally I can arrest the little shite.'

Frankie wibbled and wobbled her lips with his fingers and Tulip broke out in a smile.

'Ah,' said everyone in unison.

Then everyone went 'Ooo,' as Tulip's face went bright red and her features set determinedly, screwing up her eyes and puckering her mouth, the strain ready to produce.

'Is daddy's ickle girl having a shit?' asked Frankie, cooing proudly.

'This should be interesting,' said Isabella quietly to Rose. 'He was the last one to change her.'

A slim, attractive girl, Isabella had long dark hair, full lips and dark intense eyes; she had once rented a room from Cornwallis to conduct her business of speaking to the dead.

Frankie's broad proud smile began to falter a little; his eyes became slightly larger and developed a hint of consternation. His mouth began to harden in a tight grimace and his nose began to twitch as he felt a nice warm spot develop on the front of his trousers, which had nothing to do with him, but everything to do with Tulip.

He lifted her up.

He had a double whammy.

MacGillicudy howled with laughter.

'Apparently, there has been a bit of a protest,' remarked Cornwallis. 'The Guilds, but my father is going to deal with it.'

Goodhalgan stroked his beard and looked up as he and Cornwallis poured over the notes made on the trial run.

'Really?'

'Yes, they're worried about their members, but I don't think there's need to worry.'

'In that case, I won't,' replied Goodhalgan, dismissing it out of hand. He turned back to his notes. 'All this will take some dwarfpower,' he said tapping the bits of paper.

'Which you have in plenty,' observed Cornwallis, leaving the protest to a corner in his mind. 'We need to get it right from the very beginning, otherwise people won't come back.'

'We've now built three carts, I mean carriages, and they seemed to be better than that first one. Those cushions seem a bit soft to us, but if you really think you need them, I suppose we'd better do them all.'

Cornwallis nodded. 'We're going to need to build lots of carriages and lots of trollies to pull them. These trains of carriages are going to have to run regularly, frequently and on time.'

'We're working on that. All the mining has stopped and we're putting all our energy into this. The Pipe be in operation as soon as we can; just a few weeks at most, as many stations as we can.'

'In that case, I'd better start looking at how to advertise it.'

Goodhalgan grinned. 'I'm glad that's your department; whoever heard of a dwarf doing advertisements?' He pulled out his axe and stroked the blade. 'This is all the advertising we normally need.'

'And I thought that subtlety was your middle name. I've got an idea or two; there are a few agencies who sort of specialise in this type of thing. They're a pain in the arse to deal with and they speak a language that only they can understand, but they love money, especially when someone else is giving it to them to spend. The good thing is that sometimes they actually get results, though not necessarily the result the client wants. Should be fun.'

'Well, just remind them that I can always bring my little friend here to see them and this little beauty *always* gets a result. You can also tell them that we have some *very* deep holes down here.'

Cornwallis smiled. 'No need to worry, that'll be the first thing I'll tell them. In actual fact, I might pop around to the one I'm thinking of now. May as well see what's going to be involved.'

The office of the Garchi brothers was in The Lane, one of the most upmarket streets in Gornstock. The wide, clean, tree-lined avenue dripped with money. Gated entrances were the norm and the private residences all had staff; the pavements weren't exactly made of gold, but the inside of the mansions certainly had enough of the stuff. Cornwallis hated its pretensions, which he could, being better off than most of them put together — his father once owned the whole lot until selling at a massive profit some years ago.

An unobtrusive, small brass plaque screwed to the wall by the door indicated the location of the office, the simplicity lending it the class it thought it exuded. These were the agents who had acted for the Warden when he decided that he needed to create a better profile for himself. The agency's campaign subsequently elevated his approval ten-fold and for the first time ever he was actually popular with the city's citizens. Those lining up to depose him underestimated the power the advertising men wielded and the success threw a devilish curve-ball into the delicate game of politics.

This was the agency Cornwallis intended to recruit to advertise The Pipe, the very best that Gornstock had to offer.

'I would like to see Mr Garchi please,' said Cornwallis to the fashionably young receptionist.

'Which one?' she asked in a clipped confident tone. 'They're busy men and if you haven't got an appointment…' She let the sentence drift off with a knowing twitch of her head, indicating that she didn't need to add anything more and that the door was behind him.

'I'm sure they, him, them are very busy, however, my name is Jocelyn Cornwallis. They, him, them may have heard of me.'

'Oh? And why is that?'

'Because, young lady… just because.'

'Right, one of those, are you? No matter, I'll just go and see if anyone is available to see you.'

She disappeared through a door behind to the back rooms wearing a look of contempt as Cornwallis took stock of his surroundings: a drinks dispenser, dispensing only water, much to his disappointment; there were magazines and papers on the little table in front of him; comfy sofas littered the little reception area. He figured they had to be comfy because of the length of time some people would have to wait; however, the garish decoration with the posters, presumably of past campaigns, would encourage people to leave as quickly as possible; there seemed to be a contradiction there, or could it be his age?

'If you would care to come through, Mr Cornwallis, Mr Garchi will see you now,' said the girl as she returned.

'Thank you,' said Cornwallis, hiding the triumph in his voice. He got up and followed the girl through into a door-lined corridor, plushly carpeted, with more posters stuck on the walls.

She took him to the last door on the left and opened it, showing him in with a smile. Cornwallis inclined his head in thanks and entered, stopping dead in his tracks as he saw what he took to be a schoolboy sitting behind the desk.

'Erm?' said Cornwallis, hesitatingly.

'Ah,' said the schoolboy. 'You must be Mr Cornwallis. From what my brother said, I thought you would be older.'

'Strange that,' replied Cornwallis. 'I thought much the same.'

The schoolboy smiled. 'I am the youngest brother, Mr Cornwallis, but this is a young industry and we can't let youth get in the way of ability, now can we?'

Cornwallis shook his head. 'Indeed not, Mr... er, Garchi?'

The schoolboy nodded. 'Trevor Garchi, at your disposal.' He stood up and offered a hand.

Cornwallis saw the small soft appendage reach across the desk towards him so he took it in his own hand; it felt like shaking hands with a limp rag. 'Jocelyn Cornwallis,' said Cornwallis, introducing himself.

'My pleasure,' said Mr Garchi. 'Though I'm a bit confused as my brother mentioned that he had recently conducted some business with a Jocelyn Cornwallis, who is the Earl of Bantwich; an older gentleman, I believe.'

'That would be my father,' explained Cornwallis. 'We're not very inventive when it comes to names in our family. I'm the third Jocelyn.'

Trevor smiled. 'I can identify with that problem, though it may be even worse for us. I'm Trevor, my brother is Trefor, and

49

my father is Trepor. Our sister's name is Tepil and my mother's name is Trepail. It can prove very interesting in our house when someone calls out.'

Cornwallis had to concede the point on that one. 'It happens to have been my father who recommended you to me after you'd done that very successful campaign for the government; the one where you had all those people standing in a queue, with the tagline "Poverty doesn't work, the Morris does." Fair kicked the dissenters into touch, did that one.'

'Very proud of that, we are; had billboards all over the city with flyers and posters everywhere. We even put it into the newspapers, and there wasn't even an election. Actually, when I come to think on it, I can't ever remember an election.'

'That comes with having a democratically elected dictatorship, Mr Garchi,' said Cornwallis. 'The Morris has always been very fair about that.'

The penny suddenly dropped for Trevor that he was in actual fact talking to a member of the Assembly, family tradition and all that. 'Oh, I don't mean to sound contentious, just stating the fact of the matter. No, no, I would never say anything negative about our government.'

'You wouldn't? I bloody would,' replied Cornwallis. 'Our democracy is about as undemocratic as you can get.'

'I wouldn't go as far as that,' said Trevor, defensively.

'No? Let's be honest, Mr Garchi, Trevor. It's a benign dictatorship. I freely admit that, and I'm a member of the bloody thing. I'm allowed to say that, though I know you're not; well, not in public anyway. But I'm not here for politics; I'm here for what you can give me, which is the power of advertising. You, Trevor, will be advertising The Pipe.'

'The what?'

'The Pipe, Trevor, the brand new mode of transport,

designed, manufactured and run under the city's streets. It's going to be big, Trevor, and I'm offering you the chance to be at the forefront of this brand new enterprise. It will revolutionise the city. It will be wonderful. Think on it, I'm giving you the chance to be the first and only agency involved in this spanking new opportunity in transport development. Between us, we will make this city move. How about that then?'

Trevor's eyes widened and a big grin appeared on his face. 'You're talking my language, Mr Cornwallis. Ever been an ad man?'

CHAPTER 6

Constables Pooney and Trumpington-Smyth patrolled the river beat with a diligence previously unknown to Pooney, his beat partner determining just how watchful they were — that is, very.

Trumpington-Smyth took the job seriously and the constable's insistence on being vigilant went contrary to his normal mode of patrolling, proving irksome, insomuch as he had never worked so hard in his life. They had already made three arrests; caught one burglar in the act, one for picking pockets and one for drug dealing, and it was still only halfway through their shift. Pooney thought that he might have to look for another job if they kept this up.

A steady stream of conversation, most of it one-sided, came from Trumpington-Smyth. Pooney considered most of it banal and trite but nodded regularly as they proceeded.

Feelers rarely walked when they were on duty, they proceeded and Trumpington-Smyth had got proceeding down to a fine art: dignified, deliberate and very definite. If the city's university gave out degrees for proceeding, then Trumpington-Smyth would get a first... with honours... with a knob on the end. Proceeding was walking with meaning.

'I don't think I could ever do anything else,' said Trumpington-Smyth. 'I mean policing. The fact that we are protecting the public, allowing them to get on with their lives, whilst we, unknowing to them, protect them from all sorts of undesirables and occurrences, is something that gives you a great big warm feeling inside. It gives a sense of purpose, of being. Don't you find the same?'

'Wha… What?' replied Pooney, not quite believing his ears.

'We are keeping the city safe. All of this is ours,' and the constable swept out an all-encompassing arm towards the visage before them.

'Ours? It's the docks. Why would I want the docks? It's shite.'

'No, I mean we belong to it, and so, in a way, it belongs to us, as Police Officers.'

Pooney cast a guarded look at his beat-mate and sighed. He had difficulty enough to keep his mind on avoiding working so hard, let alone in the company of someone who actually wanted to do the job. Although rare, that did sometimes happen, but his real trouble centred on working with Trumpington-Smyth. Tall, willowy with long dark hair, she had full wide lips and a cute button nose, which had a very disconcerting effect on bits of his anatomy.

'Tiffany, Tiff. Look, we haven't all got your enthusiasm; you're still pretty new to all this. When you've been here a couple of years, you might find that Gornstock is a total shite-hole, and us feelers are really just the bit of paper that wipes the shite.'

'We are not arse-wipes, Peter, we are custodians of the law,' replied Trumpington-Smyth, a touch of exasperation distorting her normally perfect vowels. 'We have a purpose in life.'

'Yes, to keep our bloody heads down and our lives intact.'

'That's bollocks, that is.'

Pooney's mouth opened but the shock of the vehemence of her reply prevented him from talking.

Lady Tiffany Trumpington-Smyth had joined the force in the very first intake of female constables; a select group of feelers championed by the commander. The fact that she had sprung from the loins of a minor noble and had a title to go with it, gave her a natural-born confidence and an air of authority over and above that of a normal constable. Pooney found her intimidating, which only made his secret fantasy-fuelled desires even worse.

'We have a duty to protect the citizens of this city, Peter, and if by doing so we get hurt, injured or worse, then we will have fulfilled our oath. Nobody joins the force expecting an easy life.'

Pooney thought about replying, because that was precisely why he *had* joined the force, but he caught the look in her eye, the one that boded no argument, so he decided to leave his thoughts unsaid.

They proceeded in silence along the wharf, adjacent to ships berthed alongside which showed their night-lamps, casting an ethereal glow, illuminating their progress. The warehouses to the back of the wharf were dark and menacing, showing that inanimate buildings could take looming to a higher level. There were ropes pulled taught, empty crates, machines used to lift cargo, little metal things that only a select few knew what to do with them; all kinds of detritus littered the wharf as the constables walked their beat. Empty bags blew in the wind, rats scurried, wheels whirled, the occasional clank as something moved; and then something else moved, a little figure came staggering along the wharf just up ahead.

Tiffany stopped and grabbed hold of Pooney's arm. 'Look at that. What do you think is going on?'

'Firstly, I don't want to, and secondly, I don't care.'

'Peter, you're a policeman, you've got to care.'

Pooney shook his head. 'Not on the docks. It's like being in the slum; don't see anything you don't need to see.'

'Well, I see it clear enough and I'm going to find out what

it's about. I won't be long, are you coming?'

Pooney sighed. 'I'll come; the alternative is to stay here.'

The constables moved towards the figure. It had come from between two warehouses and now moved erratically, making its way across the wharf towards the river. Its movement indicated that a large quantity of alcohol could have been involved, as he zig-zagged about, stumbling frequently. The odd thing about the figure was the absence of arms.

'What's he doing?' asked Tiffany.

'Er, tripping, I think,' replied Pooney as they watched the figure fall over a pile of rope.

'Well, he's just head-butted the ground; that's going to be painful,' observed Tiffany with a grimace.

'As long as it's not me, I don't really care,' answered Pooney, indifferently.

'Peter, this is a side of you that I never expected to see.'

'You mean the side that says look after number one because no other bugger will? I've been in this job too long to look at it in any other way.'

'I'm sorry for you, but I think it's a sad indictment of our society if you think that. I care.'

'Do you?' asked Pooney, his hopes rising a little.

'Yes, I do. I don't want any of my colleagues to think that I'm not looking out for them.'

'Oh,' said Pooney, his hopes dipping again. 'I thought for a moment…'

'Sorry? Oh, what's he doing now?'

Pooney looked at the figure scrabbling and squirming about on the ground. 'He looks like a seal, but there's no water and he's got no style.'

The two constables closed in on the figure just as it reached the edge, another couple of moments and it would have plunged out of sight into the river below, probably never to be seen again.

'Hello, hello, hello,' said Pooney. 'What's going on 'ere, then?'

'Mmmph, mmh, hhhmph,' said the seal-like creature.

Tiffany peered closer. 'It's got a sack over its head and body,' she observed. 'And look, there's a rope tied around its middle.'

'That would explain the lack of arms, then, but what about the lack of legs? Definitely a short-arse; looks like a parcel,' said Pooney.

'No, Peter, it's a dwarf. Come on, help me get him free.'

'Nnn, hmmph, uurgg,' said the parcel.

Tiffany knelt down and fiddled with the tricky knot, but she couldn't see how it had been tied; the parcel wriggled and slithered as she worked, compounding the issue.

'Stop bloody moving,' she ordered, getting exasperated. 'We're not going to hurt you, we're the police.'

'Uh?' said the parcel.

'Yes, now stop it.'

The parcel did as ordered.

'Good, now let's get this off you.'

The cessation of movement rendered the job much easier and she managed to get the knot loosened.

'You're not helping much, Peter.'

'I'm keeping watch,' replied Pooney. 'You never know when a hoard of marauding psychopaths might erupt from the stygian gloom.'

Tiffany suddenly stopped what she was doing and looked up. 'Do what?'

'You know, mad bastards; some might want to attack us in the dark.'

'I understood the sentence, Peter; I'm just surprised to hear it coming from you.'

'Thanks.'

'You're welcome.'

'I'm not totally stupid, you know,' he defended.

'I'm sure you're not, Peter,' she said, but she kept the, 'just mostly stupid,' to herself.

She returned her attention back to the parcel and finally, the knot became undone.

Pooney stood with his hands in his pocket as she turned the parcel over and watched as it managed to sit up. Tiffany helped remove the sack by pulling it up and over the head.

The dwarf stared wide-eyed and open-mouthed at the constables and then his hands went to his mouth as he grunted and groaned. His fingers reached into his open orifice and he wretched, removing a wad of soggy paper.'

'Bastards, bloody bastards,' exclaimed the dwarf. 'You wait 'til I gets hold of them bastards. I'll rip their gonads off, I will.'

'Who?' asked Tiffany. 'What happened?'

Even in the dark, the dwarf's eyes blazed with angry fire. 'Got me when me back were turned, they did. Smacked me on the conker, jammed that thing into me gob and then trussed me up. Bastards kept hitting me when I couldn't hit back.'

'And stole your clothes?' asked Tiffany.

'What? Oh shit, give me back that sack.'

'Who did this?' asked Pooney, finally showing an interest.

The dwarf fiddled with the sack, giving him a bit of cover and a degree of modesty. 'How do I know? If I knew that, I'd be doing fer 'em, right now.'

The dwarf sat on the wharf and tested his jaw, moving it this way and that, making sure his drinking muscles were still working. Satisfied that he had suffered no serious damage, he climbed the short way to his feet, holding the sack so that it wouldn't fall off.

'Why were you attacked?' asked Tiffany, deciding to change tack.

The dwarf shook himself and then looked up at her. 'The Pipe: that's why they attacked me. Warned me that if we carried on with The Pipe, then things could get very bad for us dwarfs: close it down, they said, or else.'

CHAPTER 7

The peculiarity of the material allowed it to be folded, then folded again, and then folded yet again until it fitted into a cupped hand, and when released and shaken out, instantly taking the exact shape, without any creases whatsoever, as the design originally intended.

An elven maker's mark explained a lot.

Rose possessed several dresses made by the elves which she proceeded to try on in front of the full-length mirror, preparing for the grand opening of The Pipe. Gossamer thin, the tight ones moulded to the body with an air of seduction and sensuality. The loose ones, flouncy and airy, made the wearer feel fun and frivolous.

Cornwallis watched through the open door as she tried on dress after dress to see which one might be suitable. Even after all this time, he still couldn't believe his luck: out of all the men in Gornstock, she had chosen him. Only he, unlike anyone else, could see, look, touch and kiss…

'What do you think, Jack? Am I putting on weight?' she asked lightly, twisting her head and casting a look into the mirror. 'Now, be honest.'

The warning bell clanged violently in his head as the question forced him out of his reverie.

'I don't think you've put on an ounce since we met,' he replied truthfully, without missing a beat.

'Not an ounce?'

'No, a couple of stone, maybe, but an ounce? Never.'

She hesitated, but only slightly. 'You, Jack, are a bastard.'

'Ooh, I like it when you talk dirty.'

Rose smiled and peeled off the dress that clung to everything. 'You'd better get yourself ready, buster, because a big lump of lard is heading your way.'

A knock at the door disturbed them.

'Jack? We need you downstairs,' yelled Frankie.

'Oh gods, not now,' murmured Cornwallis quietly, and then he called out. 'I'll be down in a minute.'

Rose giggled.

'There could be a problem,' shouted Frankie.

'You're telling me,' said Cornwallis quietly.

Rose giggled again.

'It's about The Pipe,' added Frankie.

'Yes, yes,' yelled Cornwallis.

'There's some news,' tried Frankie again.

'I'll be as quick as I can,' replied Cornwallis.

'No you bloody won't be,' said Rose, chuckling.

Another bang on the door.

'You coming, Jack?' asked Frankie.

'You took your time,' said Frankie as Cornwallis and Rose came through the door. 'Coffee's on the table but it might be cold by now.'

'We'll take that risk, Frankie,' said Cornwallis, ignoring his opening sentence. 'Now, what's all the fuss about?'

Tiffany Trumpington-Smyth rose from her chair, thankful at the interruption as it spared her from listening to Frankie's description of Tulip's latest developments. 'I'm sorry, Mr Cornwallis, Sergeant Morant,' she said, casting an apologetic look towards them. 'But I thought I'd better tell you what happened last night.'

'What do you mean?' asked Rose, grimacing at the touch of the cold coffee on her lips.

Tiffany took a deep breath. 'I don't know if it means anything; Sergeant Boen thought that it wasn't worth pursuing, but I do, I'm afraid.'

'You're going against your sergeant?' enquired Rose.

Tiffany nodded. 'It's about The Pipe. A dwarf got warned about it; he got beaten up down the docks.'

Cornwallis was making a fresh pot of coffee and the pot clanged on the stove as he spun around quickly. 'He what? Who?'

Tiffany nodded and smiled grimly. 'Poor fellow was battered black and blue. They shoved a sack over his head, took his clothes and then knocked seven colours of the brown stuff out of him. He was on his way back from a pub.'

'Who is it?'

Tiffany consulted her notebook. 'His name is Sigiladizi Grouphonatchlyl,' she said, pronouncing his name very slowly.

'Ah, Sigi,' said Cornwallis, chucking his cold coffee out of the window. 'Lead Trolley-Pumper, muscles like concrete, built like a brick outhouse, albeit a small one; I've seen him take on half a dozen men on his own.'

'Hence the sack,' suggested Rose.

Cornwallis nodded. 'Probably. It'd be the only way the attackers could walk away. What was said?'

'I've got the sack and the rope tie here,' said Tiffany rummaging in the bag by her feet. 'The Sergeant didn't want them either.' She consulted her book again. 'They told him to tell the dwarfs to close down The Pipe or worse would happen. Tell the king that this is just the start,' she said, reading.

'Nice, but threats like that will just make the dwarfs more

determined.'

'And then some,' added Rose. 'Was Sigi badly hurt?'

Tiffany shook her head. 'Just bumps and bruises mostly. Very angry, never stopped swearing, but that's not surprising as they stripped him too. I don't fancy picking up the pieces if he ever finds out who did it.'

Cornwallis and Rose shared a rueful grin; a dwarf could hold a grudge for a very long time and could be especially vengeful for anything other than a minor slight.

'Thank you, Tiffany,' said Cornwallis thoughtfully. 'This may change a few things, and you were right to tell us.' He stepped over and picked up the sack and the rope. 'Looks like the sort of bag that carries coal but that rope you can pick up anywhere.'

'Does that mean we get to bang a few heads?' asked Frankie hopefully.

'First, we have to find out whose head to bang,' said Cornwallis, turning back to the coffee pot which now started to steam. 'It might be just someone with a chip on their shoulder about dwarfs making money or it could be something a bit more serious.'

Rose's cold coffee went the same way as Cornwallis', out of the window, but a shout of outrage came up from below. 'Sorry,' she yelled down, putting a hand up to her mouth to hide the grin.

'He's probably had worse,' remarked Frankie, grinning too.

'I'm sure he has,' replied Cornwallis, lifting the lid of the pot in the hope of hurrying it along. 'Especially if he's walked under your window.'

'Been a long time since I dun that,' chuckled Frankie, reminiscing. 'I remember when I were still living at mum's and we had no end of those religious nutters knock on the door. Mum went and stored up the contents of the piss-pots into a big bucket, it had big lumps in it as well, stunk like shit, practically and metaphorically, if you know what I mean. Anyway, we stored it outside so that it could ferment in the heat, marinated beautifully, it did. Then the time of day came when they'd been calling, so when they knocked, mum sends me out to get the bucket. They go and knock again and by this time, we're at the window above the door. Window opens and I fling the whole lot out, bucket and all. Scored a direct hit, I did. Best shot ever. We peeked out and there were two of them puking in the gutter.'

'I don't suppose they knocked again,' reasoned Rose.

Frankie shook his head. 'No, they didn't, but we had to move house.'

'Move house? Why?'

'It weren't the nutters, it were the rent men come to collect.'

Tiffany burst out laughing, a great horsey laugh, baying and snorting as she rocked on the chair.

CHAPTER 8

Cornwallis emerged from the tunnels via a ladder into a warehouse, which stirred a memory and he recalled the last time he came up through here: the dwarfs had agreed to let some men hold someone down in an unused bit of the tunnels for a time before bringing him up to put on a ship. Cornwallis remembered how they had found out about it then followed them all. Things had definitely improved with the dwarfs since then and Cornwallis doubted that that sort of thing would happen now, unless an awful lot of money changed hands, that is. He bought the warehouse from the agents looking after it with the idea of using it for an import, export business, but that idea had yet to bear fruit. There were only a few crates and a couple of bibs and bobs there, most of it empty.

He came out of the warehouse through the side door and walked down and onto the wharf. After a few deep breaths of fresh air, he looked up at the leaden sky and contemplated the downpour that appeared imminent. He turned and looked up at the front of his warehouse, to which, an advertising hoarding had recently been nailed: a group of excited, smiling, happy people stared out of the window of an underground carriage. "The Pipe," it proclaimed. "Tomorrow's future today." He smiled; the agency had got to work at last.

Ships, lined up alongside the wharves, disgorged both people and goods. Newcomers to the city would get off the ships and the first thing that they would see would be the hoarding advertising The Pipe. All the workers, and there were hundreds of them, would see it too, all day long. Cornwallis felt pleased at this beginning.

Tiffany told him where she had found Sigi, so while he went to see Goodhalgan, she showed Rose and Frankie the scene of the attack, before getting off home herself to get some sleep before the next night shift started.

Rose and Frankie waited at the agreed place, next to a crane. They chatted to the polar bear who worked it as he pulled the levers that shifted the weights that lifted the arm that picked up the cargo. Frankie took advantage, when he noticed Chalkie's distraction, by delving into the bear's lunch box.

Cornwallis threw out a wave as he approached and Rose replied with a warm smile. Frankie replied by gagging on a slimy raw fish sandwich that he had just shoved into his mouth.

'Euuughh,' groaned Frankie, spitting out the offending article.

Chalkie turned around at the noise. 'You got a problem there, Mr Kandalwick?'

'You could have warned me.'

'You could have kept your thieving hands out o' my lunch box.'

He has a point there, Frankie,' observed Rose.

'True enough; remind me never to eat something meant for a polar bear ever again. Ye-uk!'

'I see you're up to your normal tricks, Frankie,' said Cornwallis just before he kissed Rose on the cheek.

Chalkie climbed down from his crane and grabbed hold of his sandwiches, taking a great big bite out of the one Frankie discarded, the whole time fixing his eyes on the thieving detective. 'Lovely,' he said with relish.

'Just a normal everyday occurrence in the rich tapestry of life which is Cornwallis Investigations,' said Cornwallis with a grin. 'Now, let's get to business.'

And down to business they got, starting from where Tiffany and Pooney found Sigi, just a bit further along the wharf. They studied the area, close to the edge, where Sigi nearly had a permanent dunking and found a bit of scraping on the ground, where the dwarf tried to get up, but nothing else.

They began to retrace Sigi's journey.

There wasn't much to see along the route, apart from the normal dog turds; fast-food wrappers; the occasional pile of vomit; the odd cast-off boot; old newspapers; battered chairs; a bed with the mattress spewing its insides out; a rusty bucket; some personal preventatives, which did bring a bit of wondering as to the comfort of the experience at the time, or perhaps, desperation; a cartwheel with the spokes broken; a coil of rope; a sack; a manky blanket; a few dead rats, a piss-pot with a hole in it.

'Hang on,' said Cornwallis, holding up his hand. 'Let's reverse up a bit.'

They turned around and walked back to the coil of rope and the sack, lying next to the manky blanket. They were in the lane behind the warehouses, lined with derelict workshops and sheds, emanating a nice whiff of wee and rotting meat.

'They look familiar.'

Rose nodded. 'Yes, the sack that they threw over Sigi, and the rope—'

'Which they used to tie him up,' added Frankie, interrupting. 'Look, someone's cut it,' he said, reaching down and picking up the end.

'It's not proof, but it's likely,' said Cornwallis. 'Sigi said he got jumped on somewhere down this lane. He may have been a bit the worse for wear, but he had enough about him to know where he was going.'

'Which was where?' asked Frankie.

'My warehouse. He thought I wouldn't mind if he used it as a shortcut.'

'And do you?' asked Frankie.

'No, but I don't use it at the moment.'

'That's beside the point,' said Rose. 'He used it, and he got jumped. Someone must have been keeping an eye on him.'

Cornwallis nodded. 'Probably from the pub, The Long Man, which is somewhat ironic, considering he's a dwarf.'

Frankie poked around the detritus with the toe-end of his boot, disturbing a pungent whiff that rose up to assail his nostrils. He recoiled a little then settled back into looking once more. 'The sack is the same as the one used on Sigi and it seems to have been lying here for a while, cacked with muck, but the rope and blanket aren't.'

'Perhaps they were brought here,' said Rose. 'That's perceptive, Frankie, even for you.'

'Oh, thanks, Rose, demeaning my intellectuals like that.'

Cornwallis looked wryly at them in turn. 'Will you two behave, it's like working with a pair of five-year-olds. Just put the blanket and the rope into a bag and we'll take them with us,' said Cornwallis focussing on the task at hand.

'Didn't bring one,' said Frankie.

Cornwallis rolled his eyes. 'Bloody amateurs. Use that old sack then,' he suggested. 'It'll be apt if nothing else.'

Frankie took a deep breath then let it out slowly as he looked around for an alternative — he didn't find one. 'Bugger,' he said to himself, as he resigned himself to the task.

He tentatively pulled the sack out from under the rubbish and gave it a shake to dislodge anything still sticking to it. He looked inside and found it remarkably empty. Rose decided to give him a hand so she picked up the blanket and rope and stuffed it inside as Frankie held the neck open.

'Come on you two, get a move on,' said Cornwallis impatiently.

'Bloody slave driver,' remarked Frankie.

'Yes, he likes that game,' said Rose with a giggle.

'Really?'

'You heard that?' she said, eyes wide. 'I thought I thought it.'

'No, you definitely said it.'

'Oh, shit.'

'Still, gives me an idea of what you pair do when the door's closed,' he said with a big smile.

'You two coming?' said Cornwallis turning and moving away.

'Yes,' said Frankie and Rose together, Frankie giving a wink with Rose pinking slightly in her cheeks before chasing after.

The Long Man had seen better days, a grubby pub decorated with a grey austere outer shell which didn't improve once inside. The bar mirrored the decoration of the outside, basic, with no adornment and frequented mainly by the dockworkers. Despite its closeness to the tunnel, it seemed strange that Sigi had cause to visit it.

'Sigi the dwarf?' replied the landlord to Cornwallis' question. 'Yeah, he were 'ere; playing dominoes.'

'Dominoes?' said Cornwallis. 'Sigi plays dominoes?'

'And what's wrong wiv that?' asked the landlord looking a bit miffed. 'It's a game of skill. Takes a real man to play dominoes.'

'Or dwarf,' remarked Rose quietly.

'Does he play here often?' asked Cornwallis, shooting Rose a quick look.

The landlord nodded. 'We play in a league. Sigi's one of our best players. We was home last night against the Shovel and Bucket, a bit of a grudge match, but we won in the end, thanks to Sigi.'

'The Shovel? Isn't that where the cab drivers drink?' asked Rose.

Frankie nodded. 'Yeah, they do, mind, I 'aven't… Hang on…' a bit of light entered his mind.

Cornwallis felt a smile come to his lips as he looked at Frankie and then Rose. 'Possibly a couple of disgruntled cabbies? Coincidence that The Pipe is about to open and here's Sigi, with a bunch of them — and winning too.'

When certain circumstances dictated, Cornwallis and Co used a cab. They had their own coach, of course, two of them in fact, but with Rose's driving invariably resulting in a trip to the repair yard, an alternative came in helpful. In that case, the detectives frequently turned to their cabbie of choice, Coggs, and if he wasn't on the rank or taking a fare, he would invariably be found propping up the bar in the Shovel, supping pints and passing the time of day with his cronies.

The cabbies were a tight-knit group and each driver knew what another would be doing. Cornwallis spied a lone cabman and walked straight up to him.

'Know where Coggs is?' asked Cornwallis, looking up at the driver as he sat on his bench, reins held loosely in his hands.

'Aye, I do. Want me to take you there?'

'He's in the Shovel then,' replied Frankie, seeing the obvious.

'Didn't say that, did I?'

'No, but you said you'd take us there. If he were on the rank or with a fare, you'd have said that he were working, so by implication, he's either at home or in the Shovel, and it's too early fer him to be asleep.'

69

'Well worked out,' said Rose.

Frankie grinned.

The cab driver sighed and dropped his shoulders.

'Never mind,' said Cornwallis. 'We still need to get there.'

The driver's face brightened at the prospect of a fare and he eagerly jumped down to open the door. 'Where to?' he asked out of habit.

'The Shovel,' replied Cornwallis, shaking his head ever so slightly. 'Via Hupplemere Mews; need to drop this sack off.'

'Right you are, sir.'

The journey turned out to be smooth, comfortable and reasonably quick; it could have been longer but Frankie indicated that the lane the driver took for a short-cut may not be the best option; that is, if the driver wanted to have more children. Once they regained the right road, another five minutes saw them pull into the cartpark at the back of the Shovel.

Considering the city centre's close proximity, the space out back was enormous; room enough for several dozen cabs and carts with the addition of stabling for horses. Some cabbies left both horse and cab there permanently.

Cornwallis paid the fare and the three detectives made their way to the door of the pub, quickly followed by their driver, who, it appeared, had now knocked off for the day.

The place heaved. Cab drivers were eating and drinking as if it were going out of fashion. Plates and jars were being borne by dextrous barmaids as they pushed their way through the crush. Loud and boisterous it may have been, but strangely, devoid of rancour: a cab family get-together where everybody actually got on.

Cornwallis and Frankie had been here before but it took a few moments to get their bearings. It was the first time for Rose so she looked about with interest.

Cab drivers memorabilia littered the place; hardly a space left on the walls where paintings of cabbies sitting atop their coaches, studies of cabbies that had done special service, portraits of cabbies who were elected to represent in the Guild, looked down; there were whips and hats and a collection of fare markers, which were contraptions that when fitted to the wheels of a coach, clicked and turned a dial to show the distance covered, all various types from the ancient to the modern. There were money pouches and licence plates too: anything relating to a cab got nailed up, set on a plinth or locked in a cabinet.

Rose stared in wonder, a transport akin to delight, but which encompassed bewilderment too, back to a time before memory, as ancient cab drivers stared down into the bar of the Shovel, some even holding pint pots as if drinking a toast to their descendants.

Frankie managed to plough his way through to the bar and ordered three pints from the cheerful-looking landlord.

'Coggs around?' he asked as the first pint landed in front of him.

'Aye, that he is; somewhere over yonder,' replied the landlord, pointing a digit to the far corner. 'You here to join the celebration?'

'Celebration?' said Frankie cautiously, before his brain knocked into gear. 'Yeah, we is, joining in the fun.'

'Yeah, he's pleased with himself, you know. He reckons he's going to go places now. A cab driver, going places … eh, get it? Ha, ha,' laughed the landlord.

'Very droll, I'm sure,' said Frankie.

'I thought so, at any rate. This Pipe thing won't know what's hit it. Old Coggs will get his likeness up on the wall before you know it. He'll be the most famous cab driver of this generation, he will.'

Frankie's bemused expression threw the landlord for a moment, until Cornwallis, listening to the exchange, jabbed him in the back with his elbow.

'Yeah,' continued the landlord. 'Good ol' Coggs, eh?'

'Yeah, definitely,' replied Frankie, as he passed a couple of pints to Cornwallis. 'Good old Coggs.'

Frankie turned away and they threaded their way back to Rose.

'Did you hear that?' asked Frankie as they negotiated the crowd.

Cornwallis nodded. 'I did; it sounds interesting. Shall we go and find out why our favourite cab driver has suddenly become famous?'

'Thank the gods for that,' said Rose as she accepted the pint from Cornwallis.

'Uh?'

Rose grimaced. 'I've had six propositions since you've been at the bar, and two proposals of marriage.'

'Aren't you the lucky one, then,' said Frankie. 'Did you accept any?'

'Of course I did. Sorry, Jack, but apparently I'm to be taken to the height of Mount Pleasure, wherever that is.'

'Ah, a good view from up there. You'll like it,' replied Frankie seriously. 'Big hill just on the outskirts of the city. Graze sheep.'

'You mean it's a real place and not a euphemism?'

'Oh yeah, it's real enough. Can't move there sometimes when the rut's on.'

'Rams and ewes?'

'No, gods, no. Couples having a bit of illicit nookie. The problem is that most girls come back down with sheep-shit stuck to their arses. A bit of a giveaway is that.'

Rose expressed a long drawn out sigh, pursed her lips and then took a swig of her beer, deciding not to ask how he knew about the goings-on at Mount Pleasure.

'Let's find Coggs,' suggested Cornwallis quickly, eager to get off the subject in case Rose asked him some pointed questions about the place. 'The landlord said he was over there,' he said, waving a hand in the general direction.

CHAPTER 9

Cornwallis forced a path through the crowd with Rose following close behind, but the sea of bodies just closed behind him and she had trouble keeping up, but she kept her composure despite some interesting brushes with one or two cabmen. Frankie just growled at anyone in his way and miraculously, he forged a path quite easily.

'Randy bunch, aren't they?' said Rose as Frankie closed in on her.

'I think hopeful would be a more apt description,' replied Frankie. 'Some o' them could be your grandad.'

Cornwallis managed to squeeze through to a gap in front of a table surrounded by raucous and cheering cabbies. Beer flowed in vast quantities as the residual glasses indicated. At the head of the table sat Coggs, and he appeared to be the worse for wear.

The three detectives stood behind Coggs until the drunken revellers looked up and noticed them.

'Ay, ay, look 'o we 'ave 'ere,' said one of the revellers, struggling to focus his eyes. ''Tis The Pipe man.'

'An', an… It's the uvver one too,' said another.

'Yeah, an' is that a girl? I can tell that, 'cause o' 'em,' said a third, flapping his hand vaguely and trying to stand up to prove his point.

The cabbie came dangerously close to connecting with Rose, but Cornwallis, fixing him with a steely-eyed expression which could have withered a walnut, intercepted him. The potential prodder returned to his seat duly chastised.

Coggs turned in his chair and cast an unfocused look over his shoulder. He wobbled as the alcohol exerted its influence but then he broke out into a fixed vacant grin. 'Itsh me mates,' he slurred as recognition dawned. 'If it ain't me ol' mates come to help me shella…. celbra… celer bra…' He waved a loose hand. 'Party thing.'

Cornwallis and Frankie reached forward and each grabbed the cabbie under the arm and lifted him up off his chair as Rose pulled the chair away: they about turned and dragged Coggs away.

'Back in a minute, boyssh,' said Coggs as his head lolled.

'Right, Coggs, it's time for an explanation,' said Cornwallis once they were outside and had him pinned up against the back wall.

'Explanasshun?'

'The Pipe. What have you done?'

'Dun? Ain't dun nuffink.'

'You've done something, haven't you?'

Coggs grinned drunkenly. 'Whatsh good fer the chicken is good fer the weasel, or summat like that.'

'What's he on about?' asked Frankie.

'I think we need to sober him up a bit,' said Rose.

'I don't think we have the time for that,' replied Cornwallis. 'I mean, look at him. He's sweating beer as it is.'

'Need a widdle,' announced Coggs with a hint of desperation.

'Not now, Coggs,' said Frankie.

'I think it is now,' observed Rose as the cabbies hands started extracting the means pertaining from his trousers.

'Oh gods: hold me pint, Rose, and don't drink it.'

Frankie propelled Coggs around the corner just as the

splashing began, followed by a lot of swearing and various shouts of outrage punctuating the peace. A couple of minutes later he re-emerged with Coggs.

'Wouldn't put the bloody thing away,' said Frankie with disgust. 'He said he wanted to give it an airing.'

Rose looked down and then leaned in closer. 'It's difficult to tell. I assume you persuaded him to put it away?'

'Too bloody right I did. He might whiff a bit, the little bugger dribbled down his trouser leg.'

'Ooh, nice.'

'We've put up with worse,' said Cornwallis. 'Now we need to find out what he's up to. Would you kindly do your worst, Frankie.'

Frankie bunched up a fist ready to do his quick sobering of potential informants when Rose stepped in.

'Wait a minute. Hold this, will you.' She handed Frankie his pint and gave hers to Cornwallis. 'Coggs: look at me, will you?'

Coggs turned his bleary unfocused eyes upon her and grinned lewdly.

'Just tell us what you're up to.'

'Oh, that? S'not a secret. Done you up like a kipper. We's going to set up in competition. We's going to set up an above ground Pipe thing. Going to get big coaches and carry loads o' people. We's going to call it an ommni… omami… ominunib… a *bus* service.'

'A what?' exclaimed Rose.

'You 'eard,' said Coggs, grinning drunkenly.

Cornwallis raised his eyebrows. 'A bus service?'

'Yeah, gonna apply to the Assembly, we is.'

'And then what?' asked Rose.

'Gonna run it, ain't we.'

'Well,' said Frankie. 'If what he's saying is true, then he's got

76

good reason to want to shaft The Pipe.'

'There's definitely that possibility, but let's find out. Coggs,' he yelled into the cabbie's ear. 'Did you do for a dwarf last night?'

'Do a dwarf?' replied Coggs, sobering up at the thought. 'Wot do yer take me for?'

'No, not that, we mean scrag, kick the shit out of, beat up,' said Frankie, leaning in menacingly. 'Did you beat up a dwarf last night on the docks?'

Coggs pushed both arms out, flapping his hands in denial. 'No, no, no, don't do that sort o' thing. What're you on about?'

'Were you at the Long Man last night, for the dominoes?' asked Cornwallis, changing the subject.

Coggs nodded, his head on a spring. 'Yes, yes, wouldn't 'ave missed that. Good match it were too.'

'Good, now we're getting somewhere. You saw a dwarf playing for the Long Man, remember?'

Coggs nodded again. 'Yeah, I remember 'im. Pulled a double six out o' nowhere; didn't see that coming.'

'So who took a dislike to it, then?'

Coggs shook his head. 'No one I know. We plays fair; it's a serious game.'

'But someone took exception to Sigi,' said Frankie.

'Yes, someone did,' added Cornwallis. 'Someone who has something against The Pipe.'

'What? The Pipe? Oh no. Not me, it weren't me, or any cabbie. None of us, nosirree, weren't us,' said Coggs.

'But you said you're setting up in competition, you've been banging on about it.'

'Competition, yes, but we don't beat people up.'

'Someone did,' reiterated Rose, taking a deep breath and sighing. 'And you were there when it started.'

77

Coggs dragged his eyes up to her face. 'Honest, it weren't us.'

The three detectives stared at Coggs as the cabbie stared back. In the end, Cornwallis broke the silence.

'What do you think, Rose?'

Rose took another deep breath. 'I think he's telling the truth.'

'So do I, but the attackers came from the Long Man. We'll have to go back and have another word.'

'Does that mean yer done wiv me?'

Cornwallis nodded. 'For the moment, at any rate.'

'What about this bus thing?' asked Frankie.

'In truth, good luck to them; fair competition and all that. Actually, it might not do us any harm; it could be good for the city.'

'Really?' said Rose, a bit shocked.

'Yes. It means we will have to keep ahead, develop, innovate; if you don't move forward, it means you're going backwards.'

'That sounds like advertising speak,' observed Frankie distastefully.

'Exactly. Blue sky thinking.'

Frankie grabbed Cornwallis' beer and gave a sniff. 'Sure it's just beer in here?'

Cornwallis grinned. 'We need to be where it's at, Frankie. Shake the tree and see what drops.'

'Yeah, a lot of bloody shite.'

'Can I go now?' asked Coggs, seeing an escape route. He seemed remarkably sober.

'Yes,' said Cornwallis, with a wave of his hand. 'Go back to your celebration and make the most of it while you can.'

'Hang on,' said Rose, peering closely. 'You're not pissed.'

Coggs grinned. 'I'm not bloody stupid either. When you lot came in, being pissed seemed to be a good option. I thought you were going to kick the shit out of me.'

'We still might,' said Frankie, getting ready to do the honours.

'No, you won't, not now. In any case, if you did, I wouldn't tell you what I saw at the Long Man.'

'Wha... what?' exclaimed Cornwallis. 'You just told us you didn't know anything.'

'I didn't, I said it weren't us.'

Cornwallis took a deep breath in order to keep his temper in check. 'In that case, we'll start again, Coggs, and this time you can tell me everything, including the answers to the questions that I haven't asked. Is that clear?'

Coggs suddenly found himself going backwards at a rate of knots until he was once again pinned to the wall, his head bouncing nicely on the bricks as the wall stopped his momentum. Cornwallis and Frankie had their hands on his shoulders and they weren't being gentle.

'Now, Coggs,' said Cornwallis menacingly. 'I have one hand holding a glass and one hand holding you, Frankie is likewise. If either of us decides to hit you we will have to use the one holding the glass and it will be carnage, understand?'

Coggs couldn't nod fast enough, his adam's apple bobbing up and down his neck as he swallowed hard.

'Now, tell us what you saw.'

'There were two young fella's,' said Coggs hurriedly. 'They just kept an eye on the dwarf.'

'Who were they?'

'Dunno,'Coggs gulped. 'They weren't with us and I don't think they were local. One of 'em wore a leather apron thing, loads of scorch marks on it, the other wore a leather hat, the type that 'as an extra bit that rolls down to protect yer neck. That were burnt too.'

'Blacksmiths?' suggested Frankie.

'Could be,' replied Cornwallis. 'Though I can't for the life of me think why they would want to close down The Pipe.'

'Doesn't have to be blacksmiths,' said Rose. 'Could be anyone working with fire. Glassblowers, foundrymen, wheelwrights, barrel makers. The list can go on.'

'Yeah,' said Frankie. 'But we want the list to stop. Who do you think they were, Coggs?'

'The leather seemed to be for big stuff, iron working, I reckon. Oh yes, they had a blanket tied up with rope too.'

'A blanket?' asked Cornwallis as he looked at Frankie.

'Yeah, dunno what that were for.'

'I think we do. Anything else?'

Coggs shook his head and Cornwallis and Frankie eased their hands away. Coggs took the opportunity to scarper as rapidly as he could.

'Ironworkers?' said Frankie, bemused. 'What would they want with the dwarfs?'

'Who knows, but it's somewhere to start,' said Cornwallis thoughtfully. 'We'll go to the Stoat and chew things over,' he added, coming to a decision. 'It'll be quieter without the cabbies and we'll get a decent pint.'

Frankie turned the pint in his hand contemplatively. 'I didn't think this were that bad.'

'No, but it's not Hammerhead's Scull Breaker and Eddie has just put on a fresh barrel.'

'Ooo,' replied Frankie. 'You've persuaded me.'

'It doesn't take much,' said Rose laconically.

CHAPTER 10

The desperate high-pitched scream rent the thin air, threading the nerves and mangling the senses like a saw-toothed bow scraping the string of an out of tune second-hand fiddle. The noise exploded without warning in the dead of night. The pitch, high as a banshee's and designed for maximum penetration: strident; needle-like; sharp and extremely painful, silenced everything around it. It didn't know mercy, it just signalled the absence of hope — it was just plain bone-chillingly evil.

'Zzzz,' snored Frankie, oblivious.

'Frankie,' hissed Isabella, elbowing him in the ribs. 'It's your turn.'

'Gnnerh?' groaned Frankie. 'Wassersermmasser?'

'Tulip needs you.'

'Urrgh.'

'She might have a bit of wind.'

'Wind?'

'Yes, I fed her an hour ago, so she's not hungry.'

'Shit.'

A pause ensued.

'That's definitely a possibility,' agreed Isabella in the end.

The wail paused during the conversation, but now it started again anew and this time it had knobs on.

'Frankie,' implored Isabella.

'All right, I'm going,' replied a reluctant Frankie.

He flung off the blanket then rolled onto his side and then continued the roll with the help of Isabella's foot until his knees landed with a bump onto the floor. He stood up slowly and groggily and then yawned, stretching his back and scratching his bits.

'There are two ladies present, Frankie, so please put something on. I can see your hairy arse lit up by the moonlight.'

'Ain't you the lucky one.'

'No, not at this time of night, I'm not.'

'It's a thing of beauty, my darling.'

'Bugger off,' she replied, rolling over. Within seconds, he heard her snoring gently.

'Heathen,' he said quietly.

He scratched again, just because he could and then sniffed before pulling on his gown and padding over to Tulip's cot.

'Come on little princess, what's the matter with you then?'

He lifted her up and gave a sniff down below, thankful that there had been no activity. He put her against his shoulder and began to pat her back, waiting expectantly for the expulsion of trapped air. Tulip continued to wail, so he began to pace around the room, cooing and speaking gently to calm her down, feeling her snot-filled nose rub against his neck. He looked at Isabella and felt a twinge of sympathy as the wailing increased in volume, so he flicked the door handle and walked out onto the landing and over to the other room. He walked around patting her back and, despite the hour, couldn't help feeling the pride and love, as the pure baby smell flowed up his nostrils. He glanced out of the window and saw a couple of people in the street. He turned and began another circuit of the room and this time the reward came with an almighty belch emanating from his daughter. Tulip gave another couple of blasts and then began to settle. He breathed a sigh of relief, kissed her forehead and began to head back to his own room, now that the Kandalwick household had regained some peace.

A crash, the tinkling of broken glass followed closely by a thump gate-crashed his domestic idyll.

Frankie paused for half a second before rushing in to find Isabella sat up in bed with her hand at her mouth, the squeal of anguish dying in her throat as she saw him come through the door holding Tulip.

Shards of glass lay scattered on the floor, the moonlight making them sparkle like diamonds: the result of the window being smashed.

'Are you hurt?' asked Frankie urgently, as Tulip lay snug and snoring against his neck.

Isabella shook her head. 'No, no, I'm fine.'

Frankie hurried to the window and looked out. He saw nobody but he could hear running footsteps slapping on the cobbles in diminishing volume.

'Bastards,' exclaimed Frankie.

He went over to Isabella and handed Tulip to her. Then he lit the lantern by the side of the bed, cranking up the wick until a blaze of light lit the room. He then turned and looked over to Tulip's cot and saw a half-brick resting on her pillow, a note tied around it.

It took a moment before the full import of what he saw assaulted his brain.

A half-brick, laying where Tulip's head would have been had she not started screeching — his daughter's head would have been mashed to pulp.

With deliberate slowness, in order to contain the rage that coursed through his veins, he bent forward and picked up the offending object. Isabella's eyes were like flint as she and Frankie exchanged glances. She held Tulip protectively, thankful that she was unaware of the drama surrounding her.

'Feckless evil bastards,' seethed Isabella. 'What did they do that for?'

'Dunno; whoever did it has gone now. I thought I saw a couple of people when I burped her, but I didn't pay much attention. By the gods, I wish I had; I'll wring their bloody necks if I get hold of them. Why would some little scrotebag go and do something like that, eh? Why? It must have been them. I'll be doing for them as soon as I get hold of them — bastards.'

'Who? What did they look like?' asked Isabella leaning forward with urgency.

Frankie shook his head. 'I don't know. I just noticed they were there.' He started to unwrap the brick. 'But I now know what it's all about.'

He handed Isabella the note.

'What's this? "Stop The Pipe," ' she read and then dropped the note on the bed. 'The bastards.'

'That's putting in mildly, you wait 'til I gets hold of them, they'll wish they'd never been born.'

Both of them stared at the window, no need for words: the rage, the anger, the relief, palpable. Frankie sat down on the bed next to Isabella and folded both her and Tulip into his arms.

For the first time ever, his work had followed him home.

Cornwallis and Rose stood watching the man as he glazed the window. They were shocked speechless at the mindless thuggery of a brick through the window where a baby lay sleeping. It was beyond comprehension.

First thing in the morning, Frankie had sent a boy around to the office with a note briefly outlining what had happened during the night. Luckily, Maud had arrived early and rushed upstairs to wake Cornwallis and Rose who then hurried over to see for themselves what had happened.

The note hung limply in Cornwallis' hand. "Stop The Pipe," it said, his Pipe, the one he and the dwarfs were going to open. Not Frankie's or Isabella's. So why were they targeted with the brick and not him?

'Association,' ventured Rose when he voiced the question. 'Our place is too high so they looked for an easier target.'

'You're probably right,' agreed Cornwallis. 'This is an attack on us just as much as Frankie and Isabella.'

Rose nodded. 'First Sigi and now this: I'm wondering what's going to happen next?'

Frankie walked back in. 'Isabella's giving Tulip her breakfast. I've been told to stop fussing so much, but I can't help it. I keep thinking about what could've happened if I hadn't got up.' He wiped his meaty hand down over his face. 'Oh gods, she could've been torn to ribbons.'

Rose lay a hand on his arm. 'But she wasn't, Frankie, and it won't happen again. You can all have my old room at the Stoat until this thing's resolved. Eddie won't mind.'

'He won't?'

'No, of course not and you'll only fret if they stay here.'

He nodded and sighed. 'That's true,' he said and then gave an embarrassed grin. 'I bet you never thought you'd hear me say something like that? Big tough Frankie, eh?'

'Oh, you're big and tough, but not to those who love you.'

'Whoa,' said Cornwallis. 'Steady on there, that's taking it a bit far.'

Rose rolled her eyes. 'Men, why can't they be honest once in a while.'

'Rose, if only you knew,' said Cornwallis casting a glance in Frankie's direction. 'We can't stand the sight of each other.'

'Too bloody right,' agreed Frankie. 'The little shite never

85

pays me enough.'

'Oh for god's sake, I've had it with you two.' She flung her arms into the air and walked out, heading downstairs to speak to Isabella where she might find a bit of sense.

The glazier gave a wipe to the new window with a bit of cloth then began to pack up his tools. Cornwallis fished out some money and handed it over. As the man left, Cornwallis turned to Frankie.

'We'll find the bastards, don't you worry. This is now very personal to both of us.'

'Yeah, it is. To top it all, the bloody cat has gone missing too.'

CHAPTER 11

Constables Toopins and Dill looked up into the night sky and saw a few stars twinkling far away in the distance. The moon peeked around a bit of cloud, briefly, before disappearing once more, back into obscurity. A dog barked at something unseen, the noise echoing through the streets until it finally petered out with a yelp and a whimper.

Gornstock resumed its slumber.

'Romantic, isn't it?' said Constable Dill, sliding up close to Constable Toopins and linking an arm through his. 'There's just you and me with the whole city before us. Just streets and streets of empty, where in the daytime, you can hardly move for the crush. But at night you can get all this,' she said, waving a hand in demonstration, 'and there's only you and me to see it.'

'That's because all the sane people are tucked up in bed. It's the lot of a feeler to do the things no one else wants to do, and do we get any thanks for it?'

'We get paid, and we keep the streets safe, and we never get bored with our job.'

'True.'

'And we get to go to bed when everyone else is getting up to go to work.'

'There's that too.'

'And, Cecil.' She leaned in close and whispered in his ear.

Dewdrop began to grin. 'Day shift? I thought you said she was off?'

'Overtime.'

'Then we can…?'

'All day if you want.'

'We'll have to get *some* sleep.'

'In-between.'

They turned a corner and came face to face with another pair of feelers patrolling the adjoining beat.

'In-between what?' asked Tiffany, a bit of a smirk on her face.

'Just between,' replied Felicity. 'We were talking about fitting things in, how to rise to the occasion and that it should be done whenever an opportunity arose.'

'The opportunity to do what?' asked constable Strew innocently.

'Polish the truncheon. The Sergeant is very hot on that at the moment,' replied Felicity, straight-faced. 'I hope you've polished your truncheon, Wilf.'

'Oh, yes, all the time. A bit of oil and I give it a good old rub. Does wonders for it.'

'So I hear. I polish Cecil's for him now and again. He's really happy when I do that for him.'

Strew nodded in understanding. 'I'm not surprised; my arm don't half ache afterwards.'

Tiffany coughed. 'Well, perhaps that's enough of that. Shall we see if we can find us a brew?'

They all nodded in approval.

'Then, if the two gentlemen would oblige, there's a baker back there and he just went into his shop.'

Dewdrop and Strew began to walk down the street to where a little light had just appeared in a window.

'Is he really that innocent?' asked Felicity. 'I mean, Wilf.'

Tiffany nodded. 'I thought it was hard work with Pooney,

but Wilf comes from another world. It must be a nice one because it bears no relation to the real one.'

'He's sweet though.'

'He is, but he doesn't know the meaning of the word "innuendo." He's just so… you know.' She held up her hands.

'Hmmm,' agreed Felicity. 'Cecil was a bit like that to start with, you know.'

'Until you polished his truncheon?'

Felicity laughed. 'You could say that.'

'Well, I'm not offering to polish Wilf's.'

'Whose then?'

'Now that would be telling.'

Felicity raised a quizzical eyebrow. 'Oh, come on,' she encouraged eagerly.

Tiffany shook her head. 'No, not yet; even he doesn't know about it yet.'

'Really? Now, here's a mystery; but you'll tell me first, won't you?'

'I'll let him know first, you can be second — if it happens.'

'You mean when; I can't see anyone turning you down.'

'I'm an old girl now, don't forget, I'm thirty-two.'

'Yes, but you look ten years younger.'

They chatted some more as they waited for the boys to return, speaking quietly so as not to disturb the peace of the streets. A few minutes later, the boys walked back up carrying four steaming mugs of tea.

'We have to take the mugs back when we're done,' said Wilf. 'He says he keeps losing mugs to feelers.'

'Come on, there's a bench over there by that green bit. We can rest our feet,' said Dewdrop, marching determinedly over.

The others joined him and they all sat in a line on the bench, slurping at the hot thick brew.

Felicity sighed. 'You know, life as a feeler ain't that bad.'

'Pay could be better,' said Dewdrop.

'Well, yes, it could.'

'And it would be better if we weren't spat on, thumped, kicked and generally sworn at.'

'Yes, there's that.'

'And if we were allowed to arrest all the bad people we know.'

'That would help.'

'And if people didn't distrust us when we ask a question.'

'That too.'

'And—'

'Yes, yes. We know all about it, but in general, it's better than when I used to have to flash my bits just to get a bit of money.'

A short tense silence settled on the little group, most of it coming from Wilf as Felicity's words penetrated his brain. She'd forgotten that Wilf didn't know about her previous job as a page three woodcut model.

'Flash your bits?' asked Wilf hesitantly.

'No, no,' replied Tiffany quickly. 'She said, "Fish for nits." She used to go around schools checking the kids' hair.'

'Oh, I see.'

'Yes, no bits being flashed here.'

Felicity smiled her thanks at her friend and the tension disappeared.

Wilf put a finger in his ear and dislodged a piece of wax. 'I could have sworn she said—'

'Oh, what's happening here, at this time of night?' asked Dewdrop, as he heard the patter of feet turn the corner.

Two lads came jogging along and immediately slowed to a walk as they saw the four feelers sitting on the bench. They walked past quickly, trying desperately to avoid eye-contact as the feelers watched their progress, all of them slurping at their mugs.

'What do you think?' asked Dewdrop.

'Could be going to work, could be up to no good,' replied Felicity,'

Dewdrop nodded and then stood up. 'Excuse me, gentlemen, can we have a word?' he called after them.

The two lads looked back over their shoulders and hesitated before breaking into a sprint in the general direction of away.

'Oh, bugger,' exclaimed Tiffany. 'I was enjoying this tea as well.'

Just then, a cat ran past, a ginger cat, looking mean and moody.

'C'mon, after 'em,' said the cat as it raced after the two lads.

'Wha…?' said Wilf in astonishment. 'Did that cat just talk?'

'Yes,' replied Dewdrop. 'And I think I know whose cat it is too.'

'It's Mr Kandalwick's, isn't it?' said Tiffany. 'It's called Fluffy.'

The lads turned the corner and ran down towards the baker's, the cat following and the four feelers close behind it.

'Mugs,' yelled Dewdrop as they passed the baker's.

A neat line of mugs immediately appeared on the windowsill, a startled baker looking out as Tiffany waved a thank you as she hurried along.

Boots slapping on the pavement, they ran after the lads, who had the advantage of knowing where they were going. The suspects turned a corner into an alley with the cat skidding after, immediately a bang and a crash echoed into the night. The four feelers followed and saw a bin bouncing towards them, having first bounced on the cat.

Fluffy seethed from his flattened position then scrambled up and resumed the chase, now having lost a significant amount of ground.

The four feelers had to slow down, all the light disappearing in the maze of alleys that snaked ahead, but the cat had good night-vision and sprinted off into the gloom.

Dewdrop finally managed to get his night-light out and then it seemed to take an age before a little flame appeared. The arc of light only extended a few feet in front, giving a narrow field of vision, but enough to see where they were going.

Up ahead, another bang pierced the peace and then an ear-splitting feline type of wail followed by a screech and a hiss of anger. A door slammed and then the feelers could hear a loud desperate scratching coming from just a little way ahead.

Tentatively, they crept on, all clustered around Dewdrop's little pool of light and eventually, the cat entered the weak beam.

Fluffy sat staring menacingly at a door. 'They's went in 'ere,' said the cat out of the corner of his mouth. 'The bastards.'

'Who are they?' asked Tiffany, squatting down to cat level.

'Bastards,' reiterated the cat. 'The bastards wot broked the winda.'

'What window?'

'My winda.'

'What? Do you mean Mr Kandalwick's?' she asked, the surprise evident in her tone of voice.

'O' course I do, 'oo did you fink I meant?'

Wilf tried to follow the conversation but the shock at hearing a cat speak and the shock that his companions were treating it as normal, stunned him.

'Why did they do that?' asked Felicity leaning forward.

'Buggered if I's know?' replied Fluffy. 'All I knows is that they chucked sommat through the winda and legged it. Bastards kicked me as well, just 'cause I managed to get me teeth into a leg.'

'That's criminal damage, that is,' observed Dewdrop.

'Wot, eating a leg?'

'No, smashing a window.'

'Which means we can arrest them,' said Tiffany.

'Oh, I don't know. On the say-so of a cat?' argued Dewdrop.

'Hmm, there is that, but this is Mr Kandalwick we're talking about. His window.'

'Youse saying I's not telling you the truth?'

'No, but you're a cat and the sergeant will go mental if it isn't done properly.'

'Sergeant Morant always says we should use our initiative,' said Felicity. 'She would arrest them and argue afterwards, especially if something had happened to Mr Kandalwick.'

Dewdrop nodded as the thought of having to explain why he hadn't done anything to Sergeant Morant, Cornwallis and Frankie, filled him with dread. 'Maybe you're right. Let's bang on the door; if no one answers we'll go in.'

Felicity stepped up and hammered on the door.

They waited and then tried again.

When there was still no answer, they had to make a decision, so Tiffany made it.

She stood back up and grabbed the door handle, depressing it at the same time. The door swung silently open and she swallowed hard, seeing a great black void beyond the portal.

'Who wants to go first?' asked Tiffany, nervously.

CHAPTER 12

The four feelers searched every room in the house but couldn't find a sign of the window breakers. Sparsely furnished, the house had long seen better days, a house whose occupants didn't possess much in the way of money.

They toyed with the idea of staying and waiting but they had their beats to finish and the sergeant would be far from happy if they told him they had sat and waited for two lads to appear, all because of a broken window. Eventually, they left, and three of them agreed to meet up after the shift and tell Frankie what they had done.

Fluffy waited until the dawn light broke, then sauntered off home, defeated.

The cat and the feelers arrived at the same time, just as the glazier walked down the street, whistling tunelessly.

'Empty?' asked Cornwallis, leaning forward and listening eagerly. 'And you say there was no back door?'

Dewdrop nodded. 'Well, no people, no door neither. They just disappeared.'

'They can't have just disappeared, so they must have been hiding or got out another way.'

'Anything's possible, Mr Cornwallis, but we searched and couldn't find them,' said Tiffany. 'Sorry,' she added, disappointedly.

'No, it's not your fault at all,' said Rose, giving a sympathetic smile. 'At least we know where they went.'

'Can you remember what they looked like?' asked Frankie earnestly.

'It was dark and we didn't get a good look at them,' said Felicity. 'Two young men, in their twenties, about Cecil's height wearing dark clothing and caps. Maybe your cat got a better look.'

'Bloody well hope so,' replied Frankie gruffly. He looked around. 'Where's the little bugger gone now?'

The little bugger had gone out to the back yard, to the wood-store, trying to find a bit of peace for a nap, but Frankie soon found him and dragged him back into the house, the nap disturbed.

'A 'uman, two o' 'em,' replied Fluffy to the interrogation.

'Yes, we know that but what did they look like?'

'I jest tells yer, 'uman.'

'I mean distinguishing marks, colour of hair, facial features.'

'Jest 'uman.'

'You're bloody useless, you are.'

Fluffy sniffed.

'He's got a point,' observed Rose as she helped Isabella get some things together. 'Describe Fluffy.'

'Wot?' responded Frankie.

'Describe him.'

'Well, er, a ginger tom; looks mean and demented.'

'Is that it?'

'Yeah, pretty accurate, if you ask me.'

'Describe his finer features.'

'He ain't got any.'

'Oi, steady,' snarled Fluffy, flicking out a claw.

'You see, Frankie, cats look at us just as we look at them. We can't see what other cats see in other cats, so cats can't see what we see in other people. However, I bet Fluffy would recognise them again.'

Fluffy bobbed a head. 'O' course I would.'

'There you go, job done. All we have to do now is find them.'

'Yeah, but that means we'll have to take the cat with us,' said Frankie, casting a mean look at the fur-ball.

'Youse got a problem with that?' asked the fur-ball.

Frankie hesitated.

'They do like each other really,' said Isabella to the feelers, bouncing Tulip on her hip. 'They just don't tend to show it very much.'

Cornwallis sent the three feelers home, they were looking tired and they had done all they could, and besides, they had another night shift to do and they needed to get some rest.

A short while later Rose took Isabella and Tulip to their new accommodation at the Stoat to see them settled in, whilst Cornwallis, Frankie and Fluffy went to the house to see what they could find out.

The townhouse, in the middle of a terrace, had definitely seen better days. The paint flaked off and the sills and window frames showed signs of rot.

'Classy,' said Cornwallis as he surveyed the property. 'Now, let's go inside, and Frankie, don't forget that if they're here then we need to speak to them, not batter them to oblivion.'

'You sure?'

'Yes.'

'Can we speak to them first, and then batter the living shit out of them?'

'Possibly, but I'm making no promises.'

'Me neither.'

'Perhaps it would be best if you stayed out here.'

'No bloody chance, they nearly did for Tulip.'

Cornwallis sighed then pushed down the handle and cautiously opened the door.

The house matched up to the feelers' description: dark, dank, dishevelled and definitely the worse for wear. It had an unlived in feel and a quick look in the store cupboards confirmed it; they were empty. The house itself had three floors with two rooms on each floor, windows only to the front, the back wall connecting to the house behind. It didn't take long to search it and Cornwallis and Frankie stood scratching their heads as Fluffy still maintained that they hadn't come out.

'This is a rum 'un,' said Frankie, his eager anticipation now evaporating. 'You sure, Fluffy?'

'Wot do youse fink?' replied the cat disdainfully. 'I ain't gonna get that wrong now, is I?'

Cornwallis shook his head. 'No, but they're not here, nor is there any sign of them. Where did they go?'

Fluffy sat and licked his paws, wondering whether to state the bleeding obvious or let the detectives work it out for themselves.

'We've got the wrong house, ain't we?' said Frankie, eyeing the cat with contempt. 'You got it wrong.'

Fluffy stopped licking and looked up, shaking his head, before once again carrying on with his task.

'Hard as it is for me to defend the animal,' said Cornwallis. 'But it seems he's adamant that this is the place, so let's look again.'

Frankie swore, a lot, as they began to search again. Fluffy got to his feet and then padded slowly up the stairs to the top of the house, then lay down on the landing, waiting patiently for the detectives to catch up.

Cornwallis and Frankie delved into all the corners of every room, checking the walls for secret doors and the floor for loose floorboards and hidden chambers, they were determined to leave nothing out; if the house did hide some means of escape then they were sure to find it. But they found nothing, zilch, not a sausage. Every room seemed normal and they were getting to the point of exasperation when they came out to the top-floor landing and saw the cat still sitting there.

Fluffy cast them a withering glance and then looked up at the ceiling, in actual fact, not at the ceiling, but at the trap door in the ceiling which led to the attic.

Cornwallis and Frankie followed his gaze wordlessly and then they looked at each other.

'Ummm?' said Frankie.

'Exactly,' returned Cornwallis.

'Maybe we missed the obvious.'

'A bit tired.'

'Not thinking straight.'

'Getting ahead of ourselves.'

'But we got here in the end.'

'We did.'

'And now?'

'Notice a ladder?'

Frankie shook his head.

'In that case, you'd better cup your hands and give me a lift up.'

'If you've stepped in shit then I'm not going to be happy, you know,' said Frankie, leaning forward and making a stirrup with his hands.

'Don't worry; you can always stroke the cat.'

Fluffy looked up at that. 'No, he bloody can't.'

Cornwallis grinned and then placed his foot. With one hand on the wall and the other on Frankie's shoulder, he pushed up.

'Hold it there,' instructed Cornwallis, as he let go of Frankie and reached up for the trapdoor. He pushed it a little and it tilted up.

'C'mon, hurry up, you're heavy.'

'Hang on.'

'I am bloody hanging on.'

Cornwallis manoeuvred the trapdoor with little bumps until he could get his hand in properly and give it a shove, sending the whole thing away into the dark.

'Right, I've done it. Now lift me higher so I can grab hold.'

Frankie grunted and gave a big heave up.

'Ow,' exclaimed Cornwallis as his head hit the wooden rim.

The human missile had neglected to aim himself and the propeller didn't look.

Cornwallis crumpled and fell onto Frankie, with both tumbling to the floor.

Fluffy sat unimpressed. 'Bloody amateurs,' he grumbled quietly.

Cornwallis saw stars briefly and then felt a momentary pain behind his eyes. He rolled over and sat up, rubbing his head.

'Now, shall we try that again? And this time do it properly,' he asked patiently.

'I bloody did,' answered Frankie. 'It weren't my fault you missed.'

Cornwallis rubbed his head again, relieved that no blood dripped down but knowing that there might be a bump there before long.

They both scrambled to their feet and got into position, this time both checking the trajectory.

'Ready?' asked Cornwallis.

Frankie nodded.

'Then…'

Frankie heaved up and Cornwallis shot into the air and flew

through the trapdoor without even catching the sides. As he went through the hole, he flung his arms out and as the momentum decreased, he caught his elbows on the rim, holding him fast.

'Push me feet,' ordered Cornwallis.

Frankie pushed and Cornwallis scrambled inside.

'Thank the gods for that,' he murmured as he found safety.

'What can you see?' asked Frankie.

'Nothing, it's too dark. It's an attic.'

'Oh yeah.'

'Hang on; I've got a match somewhere.'

A few moments later a scratch came and then a brief flash of light.

Cornwallis quickly looked around only to find it empty, not even the obligatory box of junk from an unknown age. 'Plenty of cobwebs but not much else,' he called down. 'Except, of course, this very nice convenient ladder, which happens to be right behind me.'

Cornwallis dropped the ladder down and Frankie climbed up with Fluffy clinging to his shoulder. By expedient use of a few more matches, they managed to explore the attic. To each side were two walls, which rose up to the roof, but the joists went back a fair way, indicating a double attic, shared with the house behind.

'Well, well, well,' said Cornwallis, looking at the trapdoor, the twin of the other. 'I think we've found the answer to our little conundrum.

Frankie pulled open the cover and they knelt down, listening intently for noises of occupation. Satisfied that he could hear nothing, Cornwallis eased over the edge and dropped down. Frankie waited for a moment then went back and pulled the ladder up from the other house.

Shortly the two detectives and the cat were exploring the second house.

It appeared as empty and dilapidated as the first, with no signs of occupation. Frankie sighed in disappointment as he had hoped the lads were stupid enough not to go far.

'The front door's locked,' said Cornwallis thoughtfully. 'Meaning that they used a key.'

'But the other one was left open.'

Cornwallis nodded. 'Yes, but I somehow think that with four feelers running after them they neglected to lock it.'

'Ahem,' said Fluffy petulantly.

Cornwallis looked at the cat.

'Four feelers and a cat,' corrected Cornwallis.

'Better,' growled Fluffy.

'So if they have a key then I reckon they use it a lot. What do you think the chances are that they will use it again, pretty soon?'

'Quite high, I reckon.'

'So do I, Frankie, so do I.'

CHAPTER 13

MacGillicudy's office in Scooters Yard didn't mirror the methodical commander. Paperwork littered the place, strewn around, either on or in all the surfaces, cupboards and boxes, but the method was in the knowing and fortunately, MacGillicudy knew.

Cornwallis sat opposite the commander cradling a mug of Scooters best, a coffee with personality: rich, dark and with a tendency to shout.

'So, you don't think that this will just peter out?'

Cornwallis shook his head. 'Sigi's scragging could have just been someone with a grudge, but a brick through Frankie's window would indicate that it isn't. Someone directed it. I'm involved with The Pipe, but Frankie isn't, so whoever did it went for the easy target. I reckon things will ramp up.'

'Any idea who?'

'Not a clue, which is why I want to borrow some of your constables.'

'Shouldn't be a problem; who do you want?'

'Just the three who spoke to me this morning.'

'Then they're all yours. What do you want them to do?'

'At the moment just to spend the night in that house, see if those louts come back. I don't want Frankie to do it for obvious reasons.'

'You mean you want to be able to speak to them?'

'Exactly, plus your three saw them. The cat will be there too, we left him looking after the place.'

'Where is this house exactly?'

'Loom Lane, it's got a number eighteen scrawled on the wall.'

'Ah, yes, I know the area well.'

Cornwallis drained his mug and stood up. 'I'm off to see Goodhalgan. Rose will speak to your feelers; in actual fact, she should be doing that now.'

'Do what?'

'Knew you'd agree. I'll buy you a pint at the Stoat later.'

'Cheeky bloody sod.'

*

Rose tried hard not to smile as Felicity eventually answered the door, wearing a slightly red face and a thin almost transparent gown. After she explained the reason for calling and who else she had to call on, Felicity hesitated.

'Er, you might just stick to Tiffany, Sergeant, Cecil won't be there.'

'Then…?' A pause. 'Oh, I see.'

'Don't worry though,' said Felicity quietly. 'We'll be there,'

'I'm sure you will,' replied Rose, and then she couldn't resist it. 'Bye, Cecil,' she called.

Another pause, a slightly longer one this time.

'Goodbye Sergeant,' responded Dewdrop weakly from behind the other door.

Rose winked at Felicity and then strolled on, heading over to Tiffany's and wondering what she would find there.

Nothing, as it happened. Tiffany had no visitors to disturb, much to her disappointment.

Things had definitely moved on in the short period of time since he last graced the tunnels. The dwarfs had laid down more tracks, linking two more entrances, and platforms made and put into position for easy access to the carriages.

The entrances still required a bit of work to make them more inviting, but on the whole, he couldn't complain with the progress.

Noises of dwarfs at work echoed throughout the tunnels and chambers: there were bangs; rustles; swearing; thumps; hammers hammering; more swearing; shouts; yells of pain; even more swearing. Cornwallis weaved his way through the detritus that littered the place, thankfully just moving out of the way in time as a pump-trolley came hurtling around the corner. He dived into an alcove where a flight of steps led down to the lower levels and breathed a sigh of relief; at least he had gained safety now.

He found Goodhalgan in the Council chamber with reams of scrolls and parchments scattered around. Flames flickered from the wall-sconces sending writhing shadows streaming across his haggard face. He looked up as Cornwallis approached and nodded a welcome.

'Whose bloody idea is this, eh? Paperwork, paperwork, paperwork. Look at it. You can't move for the sodding stuff. Most of this pile of rubbish has come from the Assembly and the Health and Safety; I've got risk assessments; structured implications; taxes; revenue projections, you name it, I've got it. What am I to do with it all?'

'Er, to be honest, do what the rest of us do, ignore it.'

'Yeah, and we'll get closed down. We're an ethnic group, so that lot up there will try and throw as many spanners into the works as they can.'

'Just put everything aside when this sort of stuff comes in

and leave it for me to deal with. Remember that I am an Assembly member, and so is my father.'

Goodhalgan looked relieved.

Cornwallis picked up a few random bits of paper and scanned through them. He knew that most of it originated not from the Assembly, but from the guilds. He gathered everything up into a pile and smiled at the King of the Dwarfs. 'I'll file it later; you just concentrate on getting The Pipe ready. This lot,' and he tapped the pile, 'is my department.'

Goodhalgan stroked his beard thoughtfully and his facial muscles twitched, indicating a smile. 'That'll be one less thing to worry about, I must admit.'

Cornwallis grinned back. 'Paperwork is my speciality.'

Goodhalgan grabbed hold and then unwound a very large scroll which turned out to be the plan of The Pipe. Dwarfs like to complicate things when humans were involved but liked to keep things simple when just dwarfs were involved. Privy now to a very simple plan, Cornwallis felt privileged that Goodhalgan trusted him so much.

'There's a sort of beauty to this,' Cornwallis observed. 'Nice straight lines where there should be bends and curves. This is more of a map though.'

Goodhalgan nodded. 'That's precisely what it is. We've ironed out a few things from our original map and added some bits here and there. All these dark blobs are the entrances, you see we've put the names above them, and the lines are the tracks where they join up with the entrances. We've put down the ones we've already done, and the ones we think we can do in the future.'

'Why are the lines coloured differently?'

'They indicate different tracks; we can't link every entrance on just one continuous track; we will have to have a few to cover everything. It's just a rough plan at the moment.'

'An underground map then. I like it.'

'It's just so we can see things at a glance.'

'Yes, but we will have to have something so that people will know when to get off. This is perfect for that.'

Goodhalgan shrugged. 'Mebbee, but I thought a more detailed map would be needed.'

Cornwallis shook his head. 'No, it may go against the grain, but we'll stick to this. Even Frankie would be able to follow it. Can I have a copy?'

Goodhalgan moved over to another table and picked up a scroll. 'Here, have this one. We've got a couple more,' he said, handing it over.

'Thanks, I've got an idea: we make it smaller, then print it and stick it up in the carriages. By the way, has anything else happened? I mean like Sigi's encounter.'

Goodhalgan shook his head. 'No, not yet, but I'm not optimistic about it continuing like that.'

'Why?'

'Because of these.' He turned back to the table and picked up some scrunched-up bits of paper. 'They keep getting thrown into the entrances.'

Cornwallis unscrambled a bit and read. "Stop The Pipe."

'And this,' said Goodhalgan handing over another.

"Scummy Dwarf bastards." Cornwallis read.

'And this.'

"Short arses go home."

'Nice,' observed Cornwallis. 'Not exactly eloquent. I thought you said nothing had happened?'

'Nothing has. We get these sort of things all the time, but it seems to have increased a bit over the last few days.'

'You think because of The Pipe?'

'Yes, but that ain't going to stop us.'

'No, but maybe…?'

'What?'

'Well, the cabbies are setting up in competition. They plan to start an above ground sort of Pipe. They're going to call it a bus service.'

'Oh yes?'

'We might have an interesting couple of weeks ahead of us.'

CHAPTER 14

Rose made her way through the streets accompanied by the catcalls, whistles, suggestions and downright lewd comments that generally followed a girl in Gornstock. Strangely enough, it didn't happen as often when accompanied by either Jack or Frankie.

Long ago, she decided to embrace her femininity and appearance and not hide under layers of clothes or to stay behind locked doors only venturing out when she had a chaperone. It wasn't her fault that she looked the way she did; she knew other girls had the same problem, all of whom suffered from the sexist one-dimensional attitude of an egocentric narrow-minded bunch of imbeciles whose minds and thoughts originated from just below the waistband of their trousers. It wasn't her fault that society had taught male superiority over females since the founding of the city or even further back than that, despite proof to the contrary. The system continued to teach boys to be bastards, while the girls were still taught to be meek and compliant; but that should be ancient history now — rising from the ashes of the past, modern Gornstock should flower and embrace the changes in society.

Since the police force had recruited women, society had begun a sea-change. More and more women were asserting themselves, and the right to be themselves, demanding the long-overdue respect that they deserved; Rose could feel it in her bones that the change would actually happen; it might take a while but in the end, women will get there, treated as equals with men.

She headed for the Assembly, the place where she hoped to find the information she sought: the owners of the two empty houses.

With a great deal of willpower, she managed to ignore the temptations wafting on the air as she went past Sal's Sizzler. Frankie's mum owned the best street stall in the city and she rarely passed up an opportunity to indulge, but this time she just gave a cheery wave from the other side of the street and promised herself she'd make use of it on the way back.

Two Morris guards stood sentinel at the ornate entrance to the Assembly, resplendent in traditional uniform of knee-breeches with white shirts and dark waistcoats. Bells tied to their knees tinkled and they wore dark hats with colourful ribbons dangling and catching in the wind. They held their batons upright, ready to defend the Assembly from attack by a rampaging populace. Onlookers paused, looking on admiringly, waiting for the next ceremonial changing of the guard.

However, being female, she couldn't use the main entrance; she had to go around to the side to an unobtrusive door.

The side entrance may have been unobtrusive, but it was made of stout oak with an inner lining of solid iron, belying its appearance: this door was not for the faint-hearted, it was the women's entrance.

The hatch slid open at her knock and two beady eyes scrutinised her. Somehow, she managed to suppress the urge to poke an eye with her finger and waited until they had seen what they wanted to.

'Cook, clean or the other?' the male voice enquired.

'None of the above,' replied Rose evenly.

There were a few seconds of contemplative silence. 'I grant you don't look like a cook or a cleaner, but you look pricey.

Inner Circle?'

Rose sighed. 'If you must know, the Earl of Bantwich.'

'Ooo, lucky old earl.'

'If you say so.'

The hatch slid shut and the door began to rattle as the locks were drawn. The door swung open and Rose stepped inside.

Unlike the guards at the front of the building, this one dressed in plain dark garb with a short, presumably sharp, sword hanging from his waist.

He looked her up and down, several times.

'Look, I'm off in half-an-hour, when yer finished with his earlship, perhaps… you know? I've done a bit of overtime an' can afford to splash out a bit. What do you say?'

'I'd say no,' replied Rose, knowing that to reply in her normal manner would prevent her from seeing the earl. 'Besides, the earl can be *very* demanding.'

'Oh, oh well, perhaps another time then.'

Rose just smiled and waited while the seconds ticked by.

'Right, I'll send someone up,' the guard said eventually.

'Perhaps that's the best thing to do,' replied Rose sweetly. 'Can't keep him waiting, you know.'

The guard poked his head through the connecting door. 'Oi, Dobbie, there's a girl out 'ere for the Earl of Bantwich: blonde and expensive. Go give 'im the nod, will yer.'

The guard turned back and renewed the leer.

Rose returned the look evenly and felt her hackles begin to rise.

'Now, sweetheart, you'll be waiting here fer a few minutes, so…'

Dobbie returned a while later and let her through.

'Oh, what happened here?' he said looking towards the floor.

Rose regarded the guard lying prostrate with his legs drawn up, moaning softly. 'Nothing really, must have the gripes.'

'Yeah, lot of it about,' he replied, looking at her warily. 'Come wiv me and I'll show you up,' he added as he cast a last look at the guard on the floor.

The earl sat in his office surrounded by paperwork, a flunkey darted in and out adding to the piles as Rose stood at the door. The title "Minister without Portfolio" meant, in his case, that he was the Wardens deputy, just one step away from supreme power in the city.

'Ah, come in, my dear. I wondered who wanted to see me. The description passed to me gives no justice to your finer points.'

Rose raised an eyebrow. 'They being?'

'Beauty and intelligence, as well as a fair degree of brute force and artifice.' He smiled and indicated that she should sit down.

'Thank you,' she said sweetly.

'Now, what can I do for you?'

Rose pulled out a piece of paper with the two addresses on it. 'I need... we need, to find out who owns these places.'

'Do you? A bit of detectoring is it?'

'You could say that. Two young men ran into them. The same two men who had just lobbed a brick through Frankie's window, which landed in Tulip's cot, a brick which had a message attached which said, "Stop The Pipe." Frankie had just lifted Tulip out of the cot, as she couldn't sleep. You can imagine what would have happened if he hadn't.'

The earl looked aghast. 'Oh gods,' he exclaimed.

'We think the two men had keys to the houses.'

'Willy,' he yelled at the door.

A head appeared shortly after. 'Yes, sir?'

The earl proffered the piece of paper. 'Find out who owns these places, but first, get some coffee in here.'

'Yes, sir, right away, sir.' He disappeared back out the door and then a few moments later he returned. 'Will that be coffee for two, sir?'

'Too bloody right it will. Now, shift your arse, this is important.'

'Yes, sir.'

The earl leant back in his chair. 'He'll get onto it right away. Willy is very good at ferreting stuff out.'

Rose raised an eyebrow.

The earl grinned. 'It can be fun when you get someone to shout out that they need a Willy quickly.'

Rose smiled. 'I'm sure it's very appropriate sometimes, especially in this place.'

'You can be sure of that. Won't be a minute, I just have to sign this pile and then I'm all yours.'

The earl began to scribble away and Rose took the opportunity to regard him for the umpteenth time. Suave, sophisticated, debonair and handsome; he was definitely Jack's father. She looked at the man that Jack would become in thirty years' time and hoped she would still be around to see it. Jack would become the earl and if by then they had married then that would make her... what? A countess? It didn't bear thinking of; Jack hated titles, he should be a Lord, by rights, but he said life is easier when he just stays an Honourable. She studied the earl's face as he concentrated. The salt and pepper hair still luxuriant and shiny, sun-tanned face with character lines etched in; a striking-looking man, she could see how women fawned over him. She knew he took advantage of that, but only up to a point. He'd flirt, but he never took it further than that nowadays.

'Right, that's all done now. Where is that coffee?' said the earl looking up.

The rattling of the cups wafted through the air and shortly a woman appeared pushing a wheeled trolley.

'Here we is, me dearie, nice pot of your strongest. Can't let you fall asleep on the job now, can we?'

Rose raised her eyebrows: A woman, in the upper offices, working?

'Thank you, Mrs Piperly, that would be most welcome and do I see a few little accompaniments?'

'Of course, sir. I knows how you like a little nibble now and again.'

'Oh, I do, I do, Mrs Piperly.'

'Same as my Stanley, sir, 'e especially likes it in bed, always wants a nibble, does Stanley.'

'Does he indeed,' said Rose, a hint of a smile on her lips.

'Oh, yes, ducks, but the bloody crumbs get everywhere, if you know what I mean. Some days my arse looks like it's been sandpapered.'

'Thank you, Mrs Piperly,' said the earl jumping in. 'If you just leave everything on the desk you can go and see to the others.'

'Thank you, sir. You're my favourite gentleman, you is, sir.' She turned to face Rose. 'You be gentle with 'im, miss, you know how the old 'un's think that they're still young 'un's.'

She turned and wheeled the trolley back out, the cups rattling nicely.

'Er…' said the earl. 'She sometimes gets the wrong end of the stick,' he explained quickly. 'Let's be honest, most of the members here take advantage of their position and there's a fair rate of grunting coming from behind locked doors. I reckon the Assembly could count itself the biggest brothel in all of Gornstock.'

'You do surprise me,' said Rose laconically. 'I suppose, looking at some of them, they'd be hard-pressed to get it any other way.'

'Too true,' replied the earl. 'The irony is that it all goes down on expenses, so the bloody city ends up paying for it all.'

'I thought you had put a stop to all that some time ago?'

'I did, for a while, but it creeps back and there has to be some things which you have to turn your back on. This is one of them. We know it goes on so we can control it and we use it to exert a little pressure now and again. A bit of lee-way makes them more pliable when certain occasions arise. This is politics, you know.'

'Glad I'm not involved then.'

'Sometimes I wish I weren't'

'And Mrs Piperly?'

The earl smiled. 'She's the result of the good commander recruiting women to the police force. The Warden decided to allow some of your gender to rise up from the basement. We now have tea-ladies on all the floors, instead of them making it downstairs and letting a man bring it to the offices, which is an improvement because now it's hot.'

'A revolution then.'

'It is for this place, but the good part is that there are going to be discussions on allowing some women to actually be more than just cleaners and tea-ladies. There might be women secretaries and assistants soon.'

Rose's eyes widened. 'Well, that will cut down on expenses, then.'

The earl thought for a moment and then twigged the implication. 'Possibly, but that will probably bring me more problems to deal with. As I said, some members think that they're entitled to do what they want to women, up to now they've got away with it. I hope things will change when we actually employ them in responsible positions.'

Rose barked a short laugh. 'That remains to be seen, but I wouldn't hold my breath if I were you.'

'Little acorns, don't forget.'

'I hope it's going to be crushed nuts, actually.'

The earl pulled a face. 'Ooh, that sounds quite painful.'

'Nothing less than they deserve.'

'True, too true. Now, tell me what else has been happening.'

The next twenty minutes brought the earl up to speed with the latest developments and state of play with regards to The Pipe. The cabbies starting a bus service was new to him, though sometimes things took a while to filter down, especially if it's only a proposal. The guilds only ever sounded out those who were likely to agree with them.

Willy knocked briefly and then entered, handing over the sheet of paper in his hand.

'That will be all for now, thank you.'

'Yes, sir,' replied Willy as he retreated.

'Now, let's see what we have here,' said the earl, unfolding the sheet with a flourish.

CHAPTER 15

Big George, the brown bear, pedalled furiously, turning the fan which wafted the fug of alcohol and stale tobacco out of the open door of the Stoat. The miasma had been building up for days now and although many welcomed the atmosphere, the arrival of Isabella and Tulip had forced Eddie's hand. Dwarfs, animals and older humans could breathe the fetid air without it affecting them, but he couldn't force a baby to breathe in the stench, it went beyond the pale. It had to go and George made sure it went.

Frankie sat on a stool at the bar with a pint in one hand and flicked some beer mats with the other, stacking the mats one by one until the layers built. He flicked a seven stack and lost concentration, shooting the mats in all directions at once. Millie, the barmaid, wasn't impressed as she fished out an errant stray from the front of her blouse.

'Sorry,' apologised Frankie with a weak smile.

'You're bored, aren't you?'

Frankie nodded. 'Not used to sitting on me arse doing nothing. I mean, I do enjoy sitting on me arse doing nothing when I have something to do, but it's this hanging around that gets on me nerves, doing nothing when I've got nothing to do.'

'There must be something not to do?'

'Nope, I ain't allowed. Isabella won't let me help sort everything upstairs and Jack won't let me loose out there. So for once in me life, doing nothing is what I gots to do.'

'There's a load of glasses to wash behind here—'

'Hang on, steady, girl,' replied Frankie, interrupting her and holding up a hand. 'There are limits, you know.'

Eddie walked in from outside and took a deep breath, one that turned his chest into a big round ball. 'Ah, that smells better. Shame about the piazza though, like walking through a lace curtain out there. Never mind, it'll waft away soon, hopefully towards the Duke and then they can't complain I never give them anything.'

The Duke was the pub on the other side of the little square.

'They'll always find something to complain about,' said Frankie, taking a slurp. 'I were in there a couple of weeks ago, had to, because of work,' he added as he saw the look on Eddie's face. 'They looked at me as if I were a dog turd on the end of a boot, then I looked down and found there *was* a dog turd on the end of me boot. I wondered where the smell came from.'

'So they were right,' said Millie.

'Gods no, I mean they *looked* at me as if I were the turd. They ignored the actual turd itself.'

'No accounting for some folk, is there,' said Eddie. 'What did you do?'

'Wiped the shit off on their rug, the good one, you know, then ordered a pint and then pinned a shyster up against the wall.'

'Bit radical just because they looked at you funny.'

'No, 'e were the one I were after; didn't reckon on getting caught with his hand in the till, so to speak. He were syphoning off money from his employer to fund the lifestyle he wanted to aspire to; hence I were in the Duke.'

Big George climbed off the seat of his pedal fan and stretched the aching muscles away. He slowly walked over to the bar and downed the pint that Millie had poured for him in one.

'Needed that, Mr Kandalwick, works up a thirst, does that.'

'I just have to walk in a pub to get a thirst on. Don't need to do all that pedalling just to get nowhere; beats me why someone would invent something like that.'

'It clears the air, Mr Kandalwick. Does a grand job, it does.'

'Ah, Frankie,' said Cornwallis as he stepped over the threshold. 'One pint pronto, if you please, and by the way, have you farted out there? Stinks like shit and you can't see your hand in front of your face.'

'Blame George here, he just fanned the pub clean.'

'Ah, that would explain it. Evening George, you're doing a fine job, so you are.'

'Thanks, Mr Cornwallis, I try my best.'

Frankie and Cornwallis sat with their beer and chewed the cud, chatting amiably as punters came in and punters went out until Isabella eventually came downstairs carrying Tulip, the girl's little fingers scrabbling at her shirt.

'Tulip's come to say goodnight to daddy,' said Isabella, walking towards Frankie.

Frankie looked up, his face ablaze with parental pride.

Cornwallis regarded his friend, always amazed at the look of wonder on his face every time he set eyes on his daughter.

Frankie let go of his pint and held out his arms ready to accept his little bundle of joy.

'Me, first,' demanded George, flinging his cloth down and sauntering over. He gave an understated low growl which set the floorboards humming and a look of contentment wafted over Tulip's face.

The little girl chuckled as George bent down low and brushed his hairy face against hers as his big meaty paws engulfed her tiny head. His tongue lashed out and he licked her from chin to forehead; Frankie noticed that the snot from her nose had now disappeared. George didn't seem to notice.

Minth joined the queue, an aged dwarf with a long grey beard stretching all the way to the floor. He wore a permanent scowl and had the reputation of being one of the fiercest fighters in the city. Isabella held her daughter low as Minth came close and Tulip leant forward with both hands and grabbed his beard. She giggled and then jerked her head forward, landing a perfect Gornstock kiss right on the dwarf's nose. He roared with laughter and then planted a gentle kiss on her forehead. Then Millie the barmaid took a turn and then several other punters pushed in as Frankie waited patiently, basking in the glow surrounding him.

Finally, Tulip came to Frankie and he accepted her gratefully with great big calloused hands that could mete out retribution just as easily as a gentle stroke. Isabella watched proudly, as did everyone else, most never having seen this side of the big detective before.

Rose breezed in through the door just as Frankie handed Tulip back to her mum.

'Oh, just in time,' she cooed as she hurried to complete the ritual. 'I'd have never forgiven myself if I'd left it too late. Come to Auntie Rose, you little dumpling,' she added as she held her arms out wide.

'Your new nickname, Jack?' asked Eddie, whimsically.

Cornwallis smiled. 'Just one of many, Eddie, though my favourite is still Billy Big Boll—'

'Jack,' exclaimed Rose. 'Not in front of the children.'

'Child,' amended Cornwallis.

Rose swept her eyes around the pub and considered for a moment. 'No, I think I was right the first time.'

As Isabella and Rose disappeared through the door leading upstairs with Tulip, the pub resumed its normal demeanour:

noisy, sweary and very beery.

'Let's hope she found something out,' said Cornwallis as Millie placed a couple of pints on the bar in front of them.

'Wha…?' replied Frankie, miles away with the soft sweet scent of his daughter still clinging to his nose.

'Rose,' explained Cornwallis. 'Let's hope she found out who owns those places.'

'Oh yeah, definitely,' said Frankie absently.

Cornwallis sighed and then pushed the fresh pint right under Frankie's nose.

The smell of the beer brought the smitten father back to his senses. 'Sorry, Jack. You say something?'

'Never mind, we'll find out soon anyway.'

'Find out what?'

'What Rose found out.'

'She find something out?'

'I don't know yet.'

'Then why did you say she has?'

'I didn't.'

'Didn't you?'

'No.'

'Oh, I thought you said something about "the places." '

'I did, but I was just vocalising my hopes and thoughts.'

'Right, so she hasn't found anything out?'

'I don't know yet,' said Cornwallis, now getting exasperated.

'All right, all right, keep yer hair on. If anyone should get upset it should be me; it were my house that got bricked, after all.'

'I wasn't getting upset.'

'Wha…? You're not upset my house got bricked?'

'Yes, of course I am. Frankie, clean your sodding ears out.'

Frankie held up his palms. 'Okay, okay. Can't say nuffing

nowadays.'

They both reached for their drinks and took a gulp.

'Nice pint, this. New on?' asked Cornwallis, changing the subject.

'Yes, Millie just put it on. Murglebaggers Moth Spit, but I don't reckon it's as good as Gliblamers Knobbler. Shame that the Hammerhead Skull Breaker has finished, though.'

'Oh, I don't know, it's not far off, but I agree about the Skull Breaker: good pint that.'

Frankie nodded his agreement, their taste for beer being very similar. 'However, Wartblurgers Special is the one for me, but Eddie don't seem to have a barrel at the moment.'

Cornwallis inclined his head sagely. 'Supply problems, I hear. They're only a small brewery and someone nicked their water.'

'What? How can someone nick the water?'

'Apparently, the pipe to the spring got diverted by the local Morris for their new water feature. A bit of a legal wrangle going on, I hear.'

'Oh, how come I ain't heard about it?'

'You have, you just haven't listened.'

'Cheeky bloody sod. When did I hear this then?'

'Last week. In here. Just after Eddie threw out that orangutan for spitting peanuts at everyone.'

'Oh, yeah. Tulip weren't well that night, I had me mind elsewhere.'

'No matter, but that's why there's no Wartblurgers.'

Cornwallis grimaced as someone poked him in the back. He was just about to turn around to remonstrate with them when Rose leaned across and whipped his pint away.

'Nice to see you're being observant as always,' she said, holding the glass against her lips.

Cornwallis eased himself up from the slouch he had adopted

and regarded her seriously. 'We were having an important discussion, if you must know, on how to attain a higher level of being with regard to consumption of locally produced libations.'

Rose thought for a moment. 'You mean you were talking about beer.'

Cornwallis nodded. 'Has Eddie heard anything about the Wartblurgers?'

Rose licked the residual beer from her lips, which always sent a shiver down Cornwallis' spine as he watched.

'Haven't a clue,' she replied. 'But I hope it's sorted soon.'

Frankie sighed. 'So do I,' he said, a touch of yearning in his voice.

'Well, now we've got the important stuff out of the way,' said Cornwallis. 'You can tell us what my father told you.'

Rose put the pint down and signalled to Millie for another. 'He got his Willy working for me.'

Cornwallis had just taken a slurp which was somewhat unfortunate as it hit the back of his throat and went down the wrong way. He spluttered, coughed and then wheezed. 'He did what?' he asked breathlessly, wiping the droplets from his nose.

Frankie guffawed.

'Willy is his secretary, Jack.'

'Thank the gods for that, I was wondering there for a moment.'

'I don't know what you're on about, your father is a perfect gentleman,' she replied innocently. 'Anyway, to get back to business, he found out who owns those two houses for us. They are owned by the Ironworkers Guild.'

CHAPTER 16

Entertainment and diversion in a practically empty house, in the dead of night, when you were listening out for the slightest of noises, could be somewhat lacking. The birds on the wallpaper had been counted several times as were the knots in the wooden floor.

The three plain-clothed police officers had made themselves as comfortable as possible in the downstairs front room. The place stank of damp and mildew and the two battered armchairs reflected the state of decay. Fortunately, there were four wooden chairs around a wooden table that seemed to have escaped the ravages of neglect, which at least allowed them to sit down.

Light was impossible, it would just filter out through the thin, flimsy bit of cloth that acted as a curtain and indicate that the place was occupied.

They sat in the dark and spoke together, the whispered conversations that they had begun soon developing into the volume of normal conversation.

Fluffy, the de facto leader of the surveillance team, was not impressed. 'Youse wants the whole city to know youse 'ere?' he asked with a hiss, as he jumped up onto the table. He eyed each in turn. 'Yeesh,' he added with a shake of his head before jumping back down and padding softly out of the room.

Tiffany, Felicity and Dewdrop looked suitably chastised as each looked at the other.

'He has a point,' said Tiffany quietly, after a pause.

'He does,' agreed Felicity.

Dewdrop nodded. 'I think we may have to rethink our strategy.'

The two girls turned to face him.

'How?' asked Tiffany.

'Well, we're all here sitting nicely around this table,' he whispered. 'We haven't thought this through. We need to spread out.'

Felicity nodded. 'You're right. We're not here for a chat and Sergeant Morant is trusting us to do the job properly.'

'Exactly, so I suggest I go upstairs to the room next to the attic. One of you stays in here and one goes over to the room next door. We'll leave Fluffy to do what he wants, as he will do that anyway. If anyone comes in from the attic, I can follow them down and we can nab them from three sides. Unless one of you can come up with something better?'

'No.' Tiffany shook her head. 'We'll go with that.'

'Right, in that case, I'll get upstairs,' he said as he slid the chair back, stood up and marched out through the door.

The authoritative egress only spoilt when he tripped over the cat as it sat by the stairs.

'Bugger,' exclaimed Dewdrop, ever so quietly as his head hit the wooden stair.

'Keep your noise down,' called Felicity, but quietly and with emphasis.

'I'm bloody trying to,' responded Dewdrop, 'but the sodding cat got in the way.'

'Bloody 'umans,' said Fluffy huffily.

Dewdrop regained his feet and rubbed his head, grimacing ruefully.

The cat looked up at him, his eyes glinting menacingly in the faint ambient light.

Dewdrop gulped and then did the only thing he could do under the circumstances. 'Sorry,' he said. 'My fault,' he added as he tore up the stairs.

Fluffy's nose twitched and then he stood up and followed after, slowly, meaningfully and with deliberation.

The girls soon sorted themselves out, deciding that Felicity should stay put while Tiffany decamped to the other room.

Boredom soon set in.

Having tripped over the cat, Dewdrop felt wary as Fluffy followed him up. The feline may be small but he packed a punch far greater than the sum of his parts, and the feeler had seen the damage the cat could do in the past. He had wondered how vengeful the cat felt, but he sighed in relief as he just lay down next to him and appeared to fall asleep. Appearances though, could be deceptive; you couldn't take this cat for granted.

The initial excitement of gaining entrance to the house unseen and then the anticipation of quickly apprehending the felons had dissipated rapidly once they were on their own. Felicity and Tiffany could just about communicate with one another by flapping their arms and hands around, but upstairs, Dewdrop had just Fluffy for company, but a cat revelled in doing absolutely nothing for long periods of time — one of the many things he excelled at.

The night wore on, the late hours turning to the night hours and then the night hours turning to the wee small hours and then finally, dawn began to break.

With nothing to show for the night's work except aching muscles cramped through immobility, the three feelers and the cat stirred and stretched as the light insinuated its way into the dank dark house.

Peeking out of the front door, they waited for a couple of early workers to clear the lane, and then emerged to greet the morning, disappointed but even more determined to bring a successful conclusion to the task; they hoped they would be given another chance to repeat their surveillance in a few hours time.

An overriding urge to avail themselves of certain facilities suddenly came to them, and luckily, there was a communal necessity at the end of the lane which received three more deposits in quick succession. Dewdrop and Felicity then headed off, leaving Tiffany to report back to the sergeant.

Fluffy, with nothing else to do, tagged along behind her.

Tiffany smiled to herself as she watched her two friends walk off into the distance. She surmised that they might not be too tired for an hour or so when they reached Felicity's lodgings; if her flat-mate happened to be doing some more overtime, that is.

Fluffy hissed a warning just as she set off.

'Stays still, don'ts move.'

'Wha…?'

'Twos of 'em 'ave just come frew the door. They's coming this way. Now, give us a fuss.'

Tiffany felt her heart hammer in her chest as she fought the urge to turn around and stare. A flush flittered across her face as she crouched down and began to tickle Fluffy's head.

"Ere they comes,' warned the cat out of the corner of his mouth.

He wasn't wrong. Two sets of feet kicked up the dirt of the lane as they went past, inches away from her. She looked up briefly and saw the backs of the louts as they jostled playfully with each other, each wearing a backpack. They were unconcerned as they sauntered along, oblivious that a feeler watched them closely.

Tiffany got her mind sorted. 'Run after the others, get them back while I follow these two,' she said quietly to Fluffy. 'They're up to something, I know it.'

The cat cast a quick glance at Tiffany and then pelted away, leaving her hand hovering in the air.

Tiffany stood up and took a deep breath. The louts turned into Nobble Row but they didn't appear to be in a hurry, which would give the others a chance to catch up. The thought crossed her mind transiently that she could soon be on her own if Fluffy couldn't find Felicity and Dewdrop, but then she dismissed it as being a minor inconvenience.

Fortunately, the street bustled with people in a hurry, hiding her in plain sight as she sat doggedly on the tail of her quarry. She did think that she should be following cattedly, considering the circumstances, but the whimsical thought flew out of her mind as the two louts reached the end of Nobble Row and turned into Collider Square.

A couple of minutes had passed since Fluffy had scampered off, so she took a quick glance behind in the hope that Dewdrop and Felicity would make an appearance, but they weren't in sight, leaving her no choice but to continue to follow on her own. All she could do now was to keep her fingers crossed and hope that somehow Fluffy would find her and bring reinforcements.

The louts elbowed their way through the crowded square and Tiffany had some difficulty in keeping them in sight, but she breathed a sigh of relief when they stopped at a stall selling hot oatcakes from a griddle. A smell of bacon wafted up her nose from another stall and she wondered about the louts taste in food; she knew which one she preferred.

Tiffany waited, the smell of the bacon teasing her taste buds. The louts finished their breakfast and then scrutinised a piece of paper which had miraculously appeared in the hand of one of them. She frowned, neither of them had fished it out of a pocket,

127

she was certain of that. They were reading what seemed to be a note and the two of them hunched over it as they read. She began to feel anxious, feeling sure that the note was important and then it dawned on her that she had witnessed a meeting, which would explain the choice of food, but whomever they met had now gone and she berated herself for her lack of observation.

Something brushed her leg and the touch broke her concentration. She flicked her hand out at the unwanted intrusion and half turned to remonstrate with the opportunistic pervert when she heard a familiar refrain.

'Bastards, can't they sees me down 'ere?'

Tiffany smiled and then she sighed. She turned her head quickly and there were Felicity and Dewdrop hurrying to her side. Fluffy, trying to escape the feet that were crunching down a fraction from his head, dived between her legs for protection.

She looked down and then crouched, sweeping the cat up in her arms. 'Better?' she asked as she stood up.

'Too soddin' right, it is. Bloody dangerous down there. Youse try being a foot tall in this place. Yeesh!'

'I'll try to avoid that, if I can.'

A couple of the people passing close increased their pace accordingly, to get away from the mad cat woman, believing that the nutter talked to herself in different voices. Another, braver man, stuck his head close and put his hand out to touch the cat, but Fluffy hissed with dynamic intensity, startling him into changing his mind.

'You're brave,' said Dewdrop when he drew alongside her. 'I mean, holding him.'

'Not really. He's a sweetheart,' she replied, the relief evident as the tension left her face.

Dewdrop cleared his throat and bit back the reply as he

caught the look in Fluffy's eye.

Felicity appeared on her other side. 'What's happening?' she asked urgently.

'Those two are happening,' replied Tiffany, surreptitiously pointing a digit at the two louts just starting to move off. 'They're the ones. They came out just as you turned the corner. If we'd waited just a couple of minutes longer we would have had them. I think they've just been passed a note, but I didn't see who passed it.'

Felicity sighed. 'Sods law,' she observed wryly. 'But we can get them now.'

'We could,' answered Dewdrop, engaging his brain. 'But maybe we should follow them for a bit longer. See what they're up to.'

'Good idea,' replied Tiffany. 'Suddenly, I'm not that sleepy.'

CHAPTER 17

'I wonder what sort of night our three friendly feelers have had?' mused Rose as she put a mug of coffee down on the bedside table.

Cornwallis lifted himself up on one elbow and reached out for the mug. 'Hopefully, we'll find out soon. Oh, you're already dressed.' He sounded disappointed.

'I am; so no morning exercises for you, tiger. I'll wait downstairs; Frankie and Maud should be in soon.'

Cornwallis sighed a wistful moan as he put the mug down and rolled back over, staring at the ceiling. As Rose walked out, he lifted the blanket and shook his head ruefully.

Maud had already begun work but Frankie hadn't yet made an appearance. The secretary fiddled with some files, trying to make some sense of them after Cornwallis had tried to search for something. She tried not to sound exasperated as she transferred various sheets of paper back into their correct location.

'I really wish he'd ask me for what he needs. It'll make things so much simpler.'

'Tell me about it,' responded Rose sympathetically. 'You try living with the man, he's worse than a two-year-old. Never puts anything back; then moans he can't find things when he needs them.'

Maud nodded and smiled knowingly.

'Isabella has the same problem with Frankie,' continued Rose. 'I'm not sure whether they do it on purpose so that we have to do everything for them.'

'Tradition has a lot to answer for,' said Maud. 'The Morris were bastards for that and they perpetuated the ethos of male superiority.'

Rose raised her eyebrows at Maud's swearing. She never swore as a rule. 'But you go to a Morris re-enactment club.'

'I do, but it's a bit of light relief and I meet some nice people; doesn't mean I agree with what they did and stood for. We're moving into modern times now, throwing off the yoke of oppression, leaving the old ways behind and moving forwards. The trouble is, we're having to drag the male of the species through the mire that they made. We give in now and they'll never get out of the habits of old.'

'There is that to it,' said Rose. 'Perhaps I'll have another word with Isabella.'

'It'll do Mr Kandalwick good, and Mr Cornwallis, if you don't mind me saying. They both need a bit of a kick up the arse.'

'Morning,' cried Frankie, as he breezed into the office. 'I see most of us are up and ready for the day, where's his nibs?'

'His nibs will be here shortly,' replied Rose, turning to look at him.

Maud did likewise.

'What?' asked Frankie after a few moments, their expressions indicating that he had done something wrong. 'I haven't done anything.'

'No,' said Rose pointedly. 'That's the problem.'

Frankie looked from one to the other. 'You've lost me there.'

Rose sighed. 'It doesn't really matter. Maud and I were just talking about some things and you came through the door at the wrong time.'

'Oh, and what were you talking about?'

'Men.'

'Oh, I see.'

'No, you don't, that's the problem.'

Frankie scratched his head and looked confused. 'Which problem's that?'

Rose sighed again. 'Empathy, consideration, equality, understanding, thoughtfulness. Do you want me to go on?'

'Yeah,' said Frankie. 'You're listing all my good points.'

'For your information, I'm listing all the points that you, and men in general, lack.'

'Never,' responded Frankie. 'I got it all in bucket-loads. You just ask Isabella.'

'We have,' said Rose and Maud together.

Another few moments of silence.

'You're ganging up on me, ain't you? I seem to recall having similar slights made against my person in the past.'

'Yes, but you didn't listen.'

'I always listen.'

'Maybe, but you never *hear.*'

'That's what I like to see,' said Cornwallis, stepping in. 'Healthy debate and a friendly exchange of views first thing in the morning, sets you up nicely for the day ahead. Get the arguments over with early, is what I say.' He clapped his hands and rubbed them together in a brief display of enthusiasm.

'Bloody hell, Rose,' said Frankie in shock. 'You slipped those happy pills into his coffee?'

'No,' replied Rose. 'But maybe I should give him the other ones.'

'Just trying to relieve the tension that obviously pervades this establishment this morning,' answered Cornwallis, walking over to the coffee pot and showing his disappointment by pulling a face when he found it empty. 'There's no coffee.'

'No,' said Maud, picking up a sheet of paper and giving it a short sharp shake.

'Why?'

'Because you haven't made it yet.'

'I've only just walked in. The agreement is that the first one in puts the pot on.'

'And who is the first one in, most of the time?'

'Er, you are, Maud.'

'Exactly, Mr Cornwallis. If it's not me then it's Miss Morant. It's never you or Mr Kandalwick. Today I am putting my foot down. I'm going on strike.'

'Strike?'

'Yes, at least as far as the coffee is concerned.'

Cornwallis scratched his head. 'I've never heard of the thing. Rose?'

'Don't look at me, I'm with Maud.'

'What's brought this on?'

'You have, the pair of you,' replied Rose, suppressing the grin. 'I'll tell you what, I'll show you how to make the coffee; then you'll have no excuse.'

'Wha...? I make the coffee, sometimes, and so does Frankie.'

'Emphasis being on the sometimes, and *never* in the morning.'

Cornwallis sighed. 'Great; Frankie, put the coffee on,' he ordered.

'Whoa, Jack.' Frankie held his hands up in defence. 'I think Rose indicated that as you is the last one in, you should, and anyway, I'm the one who had to get out of me own house.'

'And where have you relocated to?'

'That's beside the point.'

All four took a moment of contemplation.

'Okay,' conceded Cornwallis in the end. 'I'll make the bloody coffee and then perhaps we can get to work.'

Rose and Maud exchanged grins of victory.

'One point to the girls,' said Rose triumphantly.

'I heard that,' said Cornwallis warningly.

With the coffee sorted, the focus turned to the main business of the day. The cat and feelers were yet to report in, which meant that something must have happened. The initial morning banter ground to a halt as the time wore on and a few worried frowns began to appear, not least from Rose, who felt that she should have been with them on their night-time vigil.

'I feel guilty,' she announced. 'I shouldn't have gone down the pub with you.'

'Nonsense,' said Cornwallis. 'They're feelers, they know the streets. They will have been in worse situations, plus they have the cat with them.'

Frankie nodded. 'Yeah, I hate to admit it, but that cat is worth more than two young yobs any day. He'd rip 'em to shreds if they gave him even a little trouble.'

'See,' said Cornwallis. 'No need to worry. They're just a little late; they could even be at the Yard processing them. We'll hear soon.'

'That's not good enough,' said Rose sighing. 'I'm going to look for them,' she added, coming to a decision.

Cornwallis and Frankie exchanged a look as Rose stood up.

'We'll all go,' said Cornwallis as she began to walk towards the door. 'Just hang on a minute.'

Rose stopped, turned and crossed her arms, her impatience indicated by the tapping of a foot. Cornwallis ignored the obvious signs and finished the dregs in his mug before standing up and adjusting his trousers. Frankie mimicked the actions which elicited a deep sigh from Rose.

'They're doing it on purpose,' observed Maud. 'In retaliation for earlier.'

'Yes, I know,' agreed Rose. 'They're just being petulant little brats. However, if they keep this up, then one of them will be sleeping in the spare room.'

Cornwallis' head shot up. 'Er…?'

'You heard.'

'Come on, Frankie, can't take all day, you know,' said Cornwallis, afraid that rationing might come into play. 'Hurry up.'

'I'm coming; I'm just waiting for you.'

Cornwallis flashed a big beaming smile and walked towards Rose.

Rose shook her head sadly and then reached for the door. She snatched the handle and the door flew open revealing a little ball of fluff sitting on the mat.

'Bloody hell,' said Fluffy. 'I ain't even announced my arrival.'

The three heads of the detectives stared down at the ginger menace.

The brief moment where nobody moved and nobody spoke flittered by, like a tableau, caught in a lightning strike.

'What's happened?' asked Rose, the first to react. 'Where are the others?'

Fluffy held up a paw. 'Nuffing, they're keeping an eye on the little bastards, that's all. I'm 'ere to get youse lot, so stop buggering about and come wiv me.'

'Really,' exclaimed Maud from inside the office. 'That cat's language just gets worse.'

CHAPTER 18

He hammered the last nail in with a flourish, sighed heavily and then began to climb down the ladder. He'd now erected the shed and even if he said so himself, he could feel proud of it: it was a shed built to last; a shed of elegance; a shed that anyone gazing upon it could look at it and nod knowingly, knowing that nothing could compare to this shed; a shed built with his own hands, designed and constructed with the finest of materials; the shed of sheds, he even may go so far as to say, the king of sheds; just one more thing to do and it would be finished. He bent down to the precious object nestling in a soft blanket and lovingly unwrapped it. Solemnly, he ambled over to fix it to the side of the shed. He pulled the last nail from his pocket and placed it in the little hole he'd drilled earlier. He raised the hammer and smacked the head of the nail, driving it into the wood. "Tikits," said the plaque he'd just nailed up, written in fine squiggly writing. The poshest of signs now adorned it, setting the shed off perfectly.

And then the arsonists decided to strike.

The oil-soaked ball of rags bounced down the steps from the entrance and rolled forwards, flames were already licking and flicking, but unaware, the dwarf looked upon his shed with pride. The ball rolled on remorsefully, its momentum carrying it along until it came to rest in the little gap between the floor and the shed. It fizzed and sizzled, hidden from plain sight.

The dwarf sniffed as he opened the door to gaze at the

shelves and cubby holes; there were cheering sounds coming from upstairs but he ignored these, instead, he just gazed lovingly at the thing he had created. He'd taken time to carve the intricate shapes of the various drawers and had greased the runners so that they would slide silently and smoothly. He sniffed again as he stepped inside and opened up the hatch where folk would stand to buy their tickets. He tried the little seat with the soft cushion and sighed as he lowered his backside down to test the upholstery. He grew concerned that the smell could be coming from somewhere close and he scratched his head in puzzlement as his nose twitched at the acrid whiff.

A frown creased the dwarf's brow as he looked down. Little tendrils of wispy smoke rose up from between the planks of wood, turning corkscrew as they wafted up towards the roof. He stroked his beard, bent down and peered closer, just as a lick of flame shot out of the gap, catching the hairs, singeing them, turning the ends into crispy frazzles. His eyes widened.

'Fire!' he bellowed as the realisation dawned that a dwarf's worst nightmare could be coming to pass: an uncontrolled fire in the tunnels.

'Fire!' he yelled again, then shot out of the shed and knelt down, peering into the gap.

The little ball of rags blazed nicely, getting up to maximum temperature with the fire grabbing hold of the wooden fuel. Draughts of air wafted through the gaps, sending flames shooting out of the side.

'Fire!' shouted the dwarf again, and then shortly he could hear the patter of tiny but heavy feet.

'What's that you yelling,' said a dwarf, coming around the corner.

'I said "Fire." You brought any water?'

'No, just wondered what all the fuss was about. Looks like

your shed's on fire.'

'Really? I would never have known. Perhaps we should get some *water* on it, in that case.'

'Now, no need to get like that; where am I goin' to get enough to put that out, eh?'

'I hoped you weren't on yer own. Bucket chain would be good.'

'Everyone's too far away; anyway, looks like yer shed's had it.'

The fire gave a roar and the base of the shed collapsed bringing the sides down with it. With the absence of the sides, the roof collapsed too, in an almighty crash and a shower of sparks and flames.

Another dwarf came jogging around the corner and this one carried a bucket of water.

'Heard someone yell "Fire," he said as he skidded to a stop. 'Oh,' he added as he looked at the shed. 'Might be a bit late now.'

The dwarf gazed at the bucket then looked again at the shed and sort of shrugged his shoulders. He threw the bucket over the fire, which hissed momentarily as a bolt of steam shot up and then carried on burning regardless.

'Oh, well, I tried,' said the dwarf with the bucket.

'You tried?' exclaimed the first dwarf. 'That was my sodding shed!'

'Yeah, nice bit of filigree on that bit there. Take you long to do that?'

'Take me…?' Like his shed, the dwarf steamed nicely.

*

Cornwallis, Frankie and Rose rushed through the streets chasing after Fluffy, his little legs pounding the pavement as he skidded and dodged the legs of the crowds.

'C'mon,' yelled Fluffy, to the bemusement of the pedestrians, who looked everywhere but down as they tried to discover the origin of the calls. 'This way.'

The three detectives followed the cat as he dived into an alley. They pounded down the unsavoury looking thoroughfare and emerged at the bottom, unscathed but with their noses twitching.

'Nice place for a toilet,' observed Rose.

'Makes you proud to know the citizens like to keep the turds out of the midden,' replied Frankie. 'That'll be blocked off soon by a wall of shite.'

They emerged into Collider Square and then elbowed their way through the massed ranks of ne're-do-well's, spongers, beggars and the occasional honest burgher going about their daily business to the far side where they found Felicity hopping impatiently from foot to foot.

'What's happening?' asked Cornwallis as he stood next to her.

'They've gone down there,' she said pointing to Pickalilly, 'I can just see Tiffany.'

The three turned to look and could just see Tiffany's head bobbing up and down like one of those toys you get where you hit a figure on a spring with a mallet.

As they walked towards Tiffany, Felicity brought them up to date with what had happened during the night and so far this morning, all the while keeping an eye on the bobbing head.

'Where's Dewdrop?' asked Frankie, scanning the crowd when they came up to Tiffany.

'Over there,' said Tiffany, indicating another crowd of people by the dwarf entrance. 'I think there's something going on.'

Cornwallis saw the body language of the crowd and felt the hairs prickle on his neck. 'There's definitely something wrong there, can't you feel it?'

Rose nodded. 'Yes, they're up to no good. Look at them; they're spoiling for a fight.'

'Then let's give them one,' suggested Frankie. 'Especially if those two little shits are in there.' He flexed his fingers before balling them into a fist. 'A nice little ruck will do me no end of good, the way I'm feeling.'

'I think it would be best to find out exactly what's happening first,' said Cornwallis, casting an eye Frankie's way. 'There could be an innocent explanation.'

'There could be, but I doubt it.'

'Emphasis on could. Now, where's that bloody cat gone now?'

'He's over there,' said Rose taking a step towards the crowd. 'I think he's looking for Cecil.'

A cat disappeared beneath the feet of the gathered crowd, wriggling through a gap until the tail vanished from view with a determined flick.

'Oh, great. We're going to have a flat cat to deal with now,' observed Cornwallis.

Frankie chuckled. 'I thought you knew that feline. If anything's going to get flattened, I tell you, it ain't gonna be Fluffy.'

A hoarding caught Rose's attention out of the corner of her eye: an advert for The Pipe. A happy rosy-cheeked family holding baskets as they sat in a carriage pulled by an equally rosy-cheeked dwarf wearing a big wide smile with a rope attached to his waist. "Tomorrow's future today," proclaimed the headline, with the subtext saying, "The Pipe, coming soon."

'Your man is starting to earn his dollars then,' said Rose,

jabbing Cornwallis in the ribs and indicating the ad.

'Yes,' agreed Cornwallis as he turned his head and gave a self-satisfied smile at the hoarding. 'They're going up all over the city.'

'Oh yes?' said Frankie, now grinning. 'They all got that extra bit too?'

'What extra bit?'

'That bit,' said Frankie, pointing to the dwarf's nether regions. 'He's normally got that bit tucked away in his trousers.'

Cornwallis took another look. 'That's only been up a couple of days, it doesn't take the artists long to add their additions, does it?' he said ruefully.

The noise of the crowd rose up a few decibels before dropping away to an unsure murmuring. A hesitation then seemed to drift over it as if someone had thrown a blanket of uncertainty over it all.

'Let's go now,' said Cornwallis. 'We need to put a stop to anything that's happening.'

Three detectives and two police officers set off in determined fashion, each of them eyeing up any potential threat as they closed on the throng.

'Jack,' said Rose. 'Look.'

A scuffle had broken out amongst the crowd, then a gap appeared and Dewdrop emerged from the mob with a big grin on his face and the two yobs handcuffed together. Fluffy followed close behind, spitting out bits of trouser. Both appeared a little battered but triumphant.

CHAPTER 19

'Arson? Definitely. Criminal damage? Yes. Attempted murder? No. Not unless you're referring to the transfer of the subjects to this here establishment and the treatment they received on the way, Frankie. I understand that one of them may have trouble begetting children in the future and the other can only look at a steak from now on, knowing that the wherewithal for chewing is lying somewhere on the streets of Gornstock.'

Frankie grinned. 'Yeah, and given a bit more time, they would've matched injuries too.'

'Yes, but the trouble is neither of them are in a fit state to talk.'

'Oh, they'll talk all right,' countered Frankie. 'Just give me a few more minutes.'

MacGillicudy sighed, wiped his forehead with his hand and cast a withering look at both Cornwallis and Frankie who were sitting on the opposite side of his desk. 'I'm surprised at the pair of you.'

'They resisted arrest,' explained Frankie.

'They did not,' replied MacGillicudy. 'Dewdrop had already arrested them.'

'Well, they looked like they were going to resist again. I just pre-empted it.'

'Jack, help me out here.'

Cornwallis took a deep breath. 'We're talking about Tulip, Jethro, and what they nearly did to her.'

'Yes, I know. But there are rules.'

'There never used to be.'

'But there are now.'

'Perhaps Frankie forgot them for a moment. He only hit them once.'

'Yes, once too often. Oh, well, perhaps nothing will come of it. I'll suggest that Dewdrop forgets that bit in his report.'

'No need,' said Cornwallis. 'So too with Tiffany and Felicity. They didn't see a thing.'

'Really? You surprise me with those girls.'

'Actually, they didn't see it, neither did Dewdrop.'

'What?'

'Yes. The girls were tending Dewdrop's cuts and bruises at the time, so I had the privilege of looking after the, er... suspects,' admitted Frankie

'So technically, my feelers are in the clear?'

'Yep,' replied Frankie.

'That's all right then,' said a relieved commander. 'You two are big enough to look after yourselves if the shit ever hit the fan. What about Rose?'

'Same as the others; Dewdrop being the centre of attention of course,' said Cornwallis.

'The cat?'

'Buggered off; think he was hungry.'

'Then all the boxes have been ticked.'

'Apart from the one telling us who hired those louts to do what they did.'

'Should have thought of that before *you* did what *you* did.'

'Yes, all right, I'll grant you that one,' said Cornwallis with a frown. 'But you know what Frankie's like when he gets the urge.'

'Don't I just.'

Frankie grinned.

A knock at the door interrupted the conversation.

'Come,' yelled MacGillicudy.

The door swung open and a feeler appeared carrying a tray with three mugs of coffee on it.

'Thank you, Constable,' said MacGillicudy.

'Pleasure, sir. Er… them prisoners that were brought in; I thought you'd like to know they's stopped screaming now, just whimpering a bit.'

'Oh, that's good.'

'Custody sergeant asks if you would be kind enough to do them over a bit more, as they is encouraging the other prisoners to be a bit talkative, like.'

'Every cloud, eh?' said MacGillicudy, breaking into a grin. 'Toenail Teddy?'

'Yep.'

'Good.'

'Toenail Teddy?' asked Cornwallis. 'Haven't heard of him.'

'Chiropodist,' explained MacGillicudy. 'Cuts toenails and then steals the old folks' money when they ain't looking.'

'Nice.'

'Mind, have you seen the state of some peoples' feet? Part of me feels like he deserves a bit of extra for the trouble.'

With the coffee finished, the three ambled down from the relative peace of upstairs to the hustle, bustle and confusion of downstairs. They headed for the canteen at the back of the building where they found Rose and the three feelers huddled around a table and cradling hot mugs.

'Go home and get some sleep,' ordered MacGillicudy to his three feelers. 'You can finish off your reports later.'

Three pairs of bleary eyes looked up in gratitude; the only thing keeping them going now was the thick black concoction that the feelers called coffee.

'Thank you, Commander,' said Tiffany giving a jaw-cracking yawn. 'I'm looking forward to seeing the inside of my bed.'

'Then be off with you; and you two…' He paused as he looked at Dewdrop and Felicity. 'Stick to sleeping.'

'Don't worry, Commander,' replied Felicity. 'I'm too bloody knackered for anything else.'

Dewdrop flashed a disappointed look, hope disappearing like a wisp on the wind.

As the three feelers disappeared through the door, Frankie turned to MacGillicudy. 'Well?'

MacGillicudy nodded. 'Yes, but later; give the prisoners a bit of time to recover first. Technically speaking, Frankie, you shouldn't even be here, seeing as you are, as it were, pertinent to the case.'

'Pertinent, my arse: they nearly did for Tulip.'

'My point exactly. You've already given them a tap and we don't want your enthusiasm to get the better of you again.'

'How about if I promise not to be enthusiastic?'

MacGillicudy shook his head. 'It's hands-off, Frankie.'

Frankie's face took on the lost boy look.

MacGillicudy eventually relented. 'All right, we'll go for the subtle approach and you can come in with me. Any trouble and you're out of it; agreed?'

Frankie reluctantly agreed, with the proviso that if the subtle approach didn't work, then he could help when they used the unsubtle approach.

The two louts were waiting for them, each in their own little interview room; separated by another room which was kitted out with a punch-bag, a wooden bench, a whip and a couple of solid truncheons. Two grinning feelers were waiting to get stuck in.

MacGillicudy strode up to the door and flicked the handle,

the door swinging open silently and ominously; he looked in, winked and gave a thumbs up to the two feelers, who got to work.

A rhythmic series of noises began to permeate the corridor of rooms. Thumps and scrapes, cracks and snaps were intermingled with groans and yelps and screams and sobs as the two feelers laid into their imaginary suspects.

MacGillicudy waited for a few minutes and then signalled for them to stop.

A pause as the commander waited for the display to take effect. He looked along the corridor at Cornwallis and Rose and then nodded and then each pair went into their designated room.

'Bring it in,' ordered MacGillicudy to the feeler standing guard in the interview room.

'Yes, sir,' replied the feeler.

Two doors down, Cornwallis and Rose followed the same process.

The commander and Frankie stood silently contemplating their suspect who looked up, the concern and apprehension etched on his features as he looked from one to the other while still protecting his gonads after Frankie's little tap earlier. Frankie flexed his hands making the knuckles of his fingers crack and grinned evilly. The consternation cranked up a gear as the feeler returned, pushing a trolley with a squeaky wheel, a crisp white sheet covering the contents. The bumps and indentations looked anything but innocent.

'Name?' barked MacGillicudy.

The lout looked from the trolley back to the commander, his mind realising that it really didn't want to know what the cover hid.

'Er...'

'S'not a difficult question,' growled Frankie.

The lout hung his head after looking at the trolley again. 'Herbert,' he replied quietly. 'Herbert Wince.'

'Good, now we're getting somewhere. And his?' asked the commander throwing a thumb at the wall.

Herbert looked up and cast a glance where MacGillicudy's thumb indicated.

'Yes, we already know, but we want you to confirm it.'

A few cogs clicked into place having heard the noises a few minutes ago and his eyes widened considerably. 'Norris, sir. Norris Hangweight.'

MacGillicudy smiled grimly. 'Well done, Herbert. Young Norris there thought that he could keep his mouth shut, and he did for a while, but we showed him the error of his ways, didn't we, Mr Kandalwick?'

'We did indeed, Commander. You might of heard young Norris, Herbert, as he realised his error.'

Herbert gulped as he cast another look at the wall.

'You tell us what we want to know, Herbert, and the trolley can be wheeled back out, unused. Do you want to tell us what we want to know?'

Herbert nodded, vigorously. Whatever had happened to his friend, he certainly didn't want it happening to him.

Frankie scowled in disappointment. 'Any chance of ignoring that, Commander?'

MacGillicudy hesitated, and as the commander hesitated, Herbert took full advantage of the lull. His mouth opened and he didn't stop talking until he had talked himself dry.

'That went better than I expected,' said MacGillicudy as he sat back down on his chair. 'Criminal damage, arson, incitement to riot, aggravated assault. He ticked off each charge on his fingers as he spoke. 'Those two won't see the light of day for a while.'

'It's a shame,' said Rose sadly. 'They're very young.'

'They may be young but they knew what they were doing,' replied the commander. 'More than knew, they actually relished causing trouble.'

Frankie nodded. 'A spell in the pokey will do them a world of good, and I reckon they'll know what pokey is all about within a couple of days.'

Rose raised a questioning eyebrow.

'You don't need me to spell it out, surely, Rose? Deep dark cells, no women, incarcerated lags, no women, few guards, no women.'

'Oh,' said Rose raising a hand to her mouth. 'I'd forgotten that sort of thing happens there.'

'They won't. It serves them right for lobbing bricks at Tulip.'

'That's going to be their problem,' said Cornwallis. 'Our problem is going to be finding this man they mentioned.'

'What about their families?' asked Rose. 'Perhaps they said something at home.'

'Unlikely,' replied Cornwallis. 'But we'll have to speak to them anyway, let them know where the fruit of their loins have ended up.'

'Another trip to The Brews then: half of our investigations seem to draw us to that slum, and we always have to go and see Gerald.

'It'll make his day, Rose. I swear he instigates most of it, just so you can visit him.'

'Sometimes I think you're right.'

'And we've still got to go to the Ironworkers Guild, but I'm sure they're not involved, seeing as this unknown man gave our yobs the clothes of an ironworker and the keys to ironworkers' houses and told them to pretend to be ironworkers.'

'A bluff?'

'No, it seems to me someone is telling us to look there, and not somewhere else.'

MacGillicudy nodded. 'We were bound to pick them up sooner or later. Scragging the dwarf, even the brick through Frankie's window and the bricks chucked down the tunnels, they could have got away with all that, but that note told them to send a fireball into the tunnel, which is arson, and in front of all those people too. Now that's something they had no chance of getting away with.'

'And it's all to do with The Pipe,' said Cornwallis ruefully. 'I'm wondering if someone has decided that these lads have come to the end of their usefulness, get rid of them

and plan to do something else.'

CHAPTER 20

The dark, dank streets and alleyways oozed through the slum area known as The Brews. Light rarely filtered down to ground level, making walking a precarious occupation with the pavements hidden under layers of filth and decay: caked in dirt and muck, both animal and human, rancid flesh, rotting veg and last night's dinner, little streams of gunge, with a piquant waft of ammonia, dribbled its way slowly as it fought its way through the peaks and troughs, making its unerring way towards the river which swallowed it with a noise very much like "Glop". Occasionally there would be a drift, which meant that an unfortunate tenant would need a bucket and a shovel to reach their front door.

Frankie and Rose squelched along, keeping a beady eye aloft in case of airborne deposits, heading for two addresses deep in the bowels of The Brews. Normally, outsiders were quickly relieved of their valuables and many a curious, and sometimes lost, tourist had reappeared at the edge of the slum devoid of everything apart from their skin, modesty preserved by a well-placed bag previously containing something with special fried rice.

The two detectives were safe from interference due to the arrangement with Gerald. The King of The Brews and Cornwallis had a long-standing understanding that what happened in the slum, stayed in the slum and only that which happened outside of the slum, where leads pointed to the perpetrator living within the slum, could be investigated in the slum. MacGillicudy had reached a similar agreement, but only for a few named officers.

Gerald liked to keep things nice and tidy and always kept the slum on a tight leash. A few years ago, Gerald tried to burgle the Universal Collider — a device for seeing into other universes, a rent in the fabric of time and space which manifested in a kind of portal, now contained in a building just outside the city. Very rich people could pay a lot of money just to see what was happening somewhere else; with a bit more money, more levers and knobs allowed the possibility of seeing into a potential future. Gerald had fallen into the Collider but unlike most people who fell in, he managed to get back out. It changed him, because now, when the mood took him, he could manipulate his atoms and kid them that he wasn't really there. People found it very difficult to cause Gerald harm so consequently, they generally did as he demanded, especially when he demonstrated his party trick.

Frankie and Rose knew that they had to pay him a visit, but only after they had seen the two families of the accused and informed them of their present situation. It probably wouldn't come as much of a surprise, considering the general lawlessness of most of the slum's inhabitants.

'Ain't been down this way for quite a while,' said Frankie as they took a left into a particularly noxious alleyway.

'I've never been here,' replied Rose, wrinkling her nostrils. 'It looks worse than the rest of the place.'

'It is. This is the slum of the slum. They call it The Palace.'

'Bit of irony going on?'

Frankie shook his head. 'Legend has it that the old Morris built a palace here to get away from the scum of the old city across the river. Fell into wrack and ruin, then the roof fell in. We are supposedly walking along the palace's corridors and the

151

houses here are where the old rooms once were with various additions and roofs.'

'Some palace,' said Rose as she stepped over a particularly nasty looking pile which appeared to be steaming.

'Yeah, nice, innit.'

They turned right into an even narrower tunnel-like alleyway, with only a slim slither of light visible from above.

'Here we is,' said Frankie stopping at a door. He pointed a digit. 'Look at the lintel.'

Rose did. A mason must have carved the ornate lintel long ago, a talented man, according to the evidence before her eyes. However, the rest of it paled into insignificance, a mish-mash, hastily put together. The walls crumbled and the door, if you could call it a door, was several strips of leather nailed to a manky wooden frame. Frankie tapped on the frame.

'Don't knock too hard or the whole thing'll fall down.'

They waited for a few moments and then some shuffling noises from beyond the leather indicated that someone had heard the knock. A few moments later, the door scraped open and a screwed up face appeared.

'Whatyouwan'?' barked the face.

Rose recoiled from the stench escaping the confines of the room inside as she stared at the visage, having difficulty in determining whether it was male or female.

'We're here about Norris,' said Frankie, ignoring the smell.

'Oh, yeah? Wot about 'im?'

'He's at Scooters Yard. Been nicked.'

'His own fault then. Sod off.'

The wonky door rammed shut in their faces and the scuffling noises behind it returned. The smell began to dissipate in the already fetid air.

'Good start,' observed Rose, wafting as much good air as

she could under her nose.

'Much as expected,' said Frankie. 'Let's try Herbert's; his is just a couple of doors down.'

This time a proper door confronted them in that it was made of wood and filled the aperture, but the outside of the house appeared just as run down and decrepit as the other.

Frankie knocked again and they waited patiently until the door clicked open. A face appeared, which to Rose's relief, was definitely female, with the bonus that no extra smell came with it.

'Come about Herbert,' said Frankie.

'Who are you?'

'Detectives.'

'Oh, what's 'e gone and dun?'

'Are you his mother?' asked Rose softly.

The woman nodded and then flung the door open fully. 'Ye'd better come in then.' She turned and wandered back inside.

Rose and Frankie exchanged a look and then followed after.

Rose gawped at the neat and spotless room with not a bit of dust anywhere. A weak light filtered through from the scullery out back but the main light came from two tallow candles fixed to a shelf on the wall. A small table with two chairs took up the middle of the room with two old upholstered armchairs positioned to either side of a small fire grate. A chest of drawers and an old bureau completed the sum of the furniture.

'Sorry, missus,' said Frankie as he stood by the table. 'But Herbert's been nicked. He's down at Scooters Yard.'

The woman nodded acceptance of the fact. 'With Norris, was 'e?'

'Yes,' answered Rose, taking a moment to study her. Thin mousey hair, a pinched, haggard face, small and skinny, wearing threadbare old clothes: she could have been any age between thirty and sixty. Rose thought she looked more like sixty but suspected her age nearer thirty. Life did that to you in the slum; it sucked all the youth out of a body like a leech.

'Tried to tell 'im that one were trouble, but would 'e listen? No, would 'e f—'.

'Anyway,' interrupted Frankie. 'He's down at the Yard; thought you'd like to know.'

'What 'e do?'

'There's quite a list, I'm afraid,' said Rose not unsympathetically. 'The main one being trying to set fire to the dwarf tunnels. We believe Herbert and Norris were being used by a mystery man who they met down a pub; he's been giving them money to cause trouble.'

Herbert's mother sighed and then flopped down in an armchair. She sighed again as she drew her hand down her face. 'I 'ad 'im followed, I did,' she said quietly, staring off into space.

'What's that you say, missus?' asked Frankie, his ears straining.

'I said I 'ad 'im followed: my Herbert. I knew 'e were up to no good as 'e 'ad cash in his pocket and 'e never 'as cash. Twenty dollars. I counted it when 'e were asleep.'

Rose and Frankie shared a glance, twenty dollars was a lot for someone living in The Brews.

'What did you find out,' asked Rose, trying to keep the eagerness out of her voice. 'It might help Herbert if you know something.'

'I tried to bring 'im up 'onest, I really did, but it's 'ard round 'ere. The likes o' Norris don't 'elp; 'e's always 'ad sticky fingers, 'as Norris.'

Frankie nodded his agreement. He'd come from The Warren, a better class of slum, but had at one time lived on the wrong side of the law. When you had nothing there wasn't a decision to make. 'I'm sure you did, missus, but he's old enough to know right from wrong, unfortunately, he picked wrong. Same as I did when I were his age, but it don't mean you can't change.'

Herbert's mum looked up, a little bit of hope in her eyes. 'Really?'

'Yes, really. Now, about you following young Herbert. What happened?'

The light that momentarily flared died and she looked down once more, contemplating her hands in her lap. 'It weren't me, it were a man I knows. 'E followed Herbert to the Bull and Badger. 'E sees 'im and Norris talking to a man in the snug. They laughed a lot but the man weren't laughing in 'is eyes. 'E gave 'em a bag o' coins and then left. My friend decides to tag the man, as 'e didn't seem to be right, if you knows what I mean. Anyways, 'e follows 'im across the bridge and blow me, didn't 'e just walk straight into the Assembly. My friend couldn't follow 'im in there, so 'e comes back to tell me.'

'The Assembly? You sure he said that?' asked Rose, shocked at the revelation.

The woman nodded. 'Straight through the front door.'

'And this friend of yours, who is he?'

'Phil,' said Herbert's mum. 'Phil the Flick, on account of the knives he carries.'

'Oh, *that* sort of friend,' said Frankie.

The little group of hard-nosed bruisers looked up from their game of dice as Rose and Frankie approached the front door. One climbed to his feet and flashed a toothless grin before banging a fist on the door. The door opened revealing another heavy, but this one sported a full set of tombstones, indicating that maybe he was a little better at the job than the one outside, his array of weapons confirming the judgement.

Frankie nodded a greeting but needn't have bothered

because, as normal, all eyes were on Rose, or to be more precise, on the bits of Rose which tended to get the most attention.

"E's upstairs,' said the man with the teeth. "Eard you were visiting 'is turf and is expecting you.'

Rose smiled back and briefly brushed his arm as she walked past, causing a little stir in certain regions.

Crinning, Gerald's assistant, a thin dapper-looking man dressed very much like a butler, appeared at the top of the stairs and beckoned Frankie and Rose to come up to the lair of the King of The Brews

'Mr Gerald will be with you shortly,' he said as Frankie and Rose joined him. 'He's just making an enquiry into an occurrence that, er, occurred.'

He led the detectives into the inner sanctum with a throne-like chair placed on a dais at the far end of the room. As always, Frankie and Rose winced at the décor. Sumptuous and comfortable, but the array of clashing colours and styles left the brain wondering what spectrum it was in. Crinning ushered them to a set of chairs below the dais and bid them sit to await the king's pleasure.

An open window, fronting onto the river, let a gentle breeze waft into the room, rippling a fine silk wall hanging behind the throne-like chair. Frankie and Rose sat down whilst Crinning hovered attentively close by, waiting.

A muffled thump came from the room next door, closely followed by a whimper. Some muted conversation and then another thump and then a howl which descended in volume through the wall only to resume a moment later from outside the window, but this time at full volume, until it ended abruptly with the noise of a splash.

A door rattled and Gerald appeared clad in a collarless white shirt with the sleeves rolled up to his elbows. Braces kept the trousers up which showed bare sockless ankles. A small man with salt and pepper hair he wore a cheeky and mischievous grin.

'Well now, me darling, where you bin 'iding?' he said to Rose as he bounced towards her holding out his hands.

Rose stood and welcomed him in an embrace, the top of his head reaching just above her chest. He smiled again in gratitude as his head bowed and rested there, cushioned as it were.

'As if I would hide from you, Gerald,' replied Rose with a smile on her face. Even though he delved so deep into lawlessness that he would need a shovel just to get up to the level of criminal, she rather liked him.

'Me offer still stands,' responded Gerald. 'Soon as yer done wiv Cornwallis, then come to me an' I'll treat yer as me queen.'

'I'll bear it in mind,' said Rose, the offer being the ritual of their frequent meetings.

Gerald reluctantly broke the contact and stood back. 'Now, what brings yer 'ere, eh?'

Frankie indicated the window. 'Bit of trouble?'

Gerald shook his head. 'Not fer me. Let's say 'e wasn't fully open an' 'onest, as it were. I'll 'ave me cut, fair and square, that's the rools. 'E wanted to give a bit of square, but keep the fair — bit of a dunking will learn 'im.'

'I take it he can swim?'

A bit of a pause ensued as Gerald thought, then he walked over to the window and looked out. 'Crinning,' he yelled.

'Yes, Mr Gerald?' replied Crinning, making a rapid appearance.

'Send someone dahn t' fish 'im out, will yer.'

'Right away, Mr Gerald.'

Gerald turned and rubbed his hands together. 'Right, where was we? Oh, yeah, what's you doing 'ere?'

Over tea and biscuits, Frankie and Rose explained about

157

Herbert and Norris, and what they had been up to over the last few days. Gerald listened attentively, just in case he learnt something he didn't already know. There wasn't much that happened in Gornstock that he didn't hear about from his many sources, normally about ten minutes after they happened. A crime Tsar had to keep his finger on the pulse of the city.

'So, you want's to speak t' 'erbert's mum's friend, then?'

Frankie and Rose nodded.

'No problem. Crinning,' he yelled again. 'Get Phil the Flick 'ere pronto.'

'Right away, Mr Gerald,' replied Crinning, dipping his head formally.

'Just be a tick,' said Gerald with a wink.

CHAPTER 21

There were never enough hours in the day, reflected Cornwallis as he headed off to the Guild of Ironworkers: so many balls to juggle, so many things to do and people to see. He'd taken his eye off The Pipe because of the attacks and disruption, leaving all the day to day organising down to Goodhalgan. He really wanted to be involved now as the opening was just around the corner, but he still had so much to do.

Anyone wanting to find the Guild of Ironworkers would naturally go to either the Guilds Hall or the iron foundry on the outskirts of the city where the foundry belched smoke and steam; another reason why the Sterkle glooped instead of flowed as it swallowed up all the detritus that came from the foundry, but they would be wrong. Most of the guilds had offices away from the Hall and away from their main area of work in order to hold meetings that could be deemed "sensitive," if anyone found out about them.

The Ironworkers Guild had its offices down a back alley off of Chancers Lane, above a shop selling second-hand clothes, or pre-loved vintage, as the sign said, enabling them to charge three times what an item cost when new.

Cornwallis rattled the knocker on the door next to the plaque which indicated the Guild's presence and waited. Perusing the shop window brought to mind the clothes worn by his grandmother, which they had dumped when she passed away;

now, he learnt, they had inadvertently given away hundreds of dollar's worth of legacy.

The door cracked and a nervous face appeared. 'Can I help you?'

Cornwallis whipped his head back to view the man standing there. A small man wearing a dark suit, he had a small round head and wore spectacles, wisps of hair were playfully covering a bald dome, a hopeful attempt to prove a full head of hair; sadly, it didn't work.

'I'm looking for the Ironworkers Guild,' said Cornwallis, looking down at him.

'In that case, you've found it.'

Cornwallis waited.

The small man looked up expectantly.

'Now that I've found it,' said Cornwallis. 'Do you think I can come in?'

'Oh, yes, I suppose so.'

'Obliged,' replied Cornwallis stepping in.

He followed the man up the narrow dark staircase to a small office above the shop, cluttered with bits of iron in various stages of manufacture, most of it rusting nicely. A small desk with a chair behind backed up against the tiny window, shining a little dreary light on the surface. Another two chairs sat in front of the desk.

Cornwallis took one of the two chairs and sat as the little man squeezed behind the desk and eased down into his, looking up expectantly.

'How may I help you, Mr... er?' enquired the man.

'Cornwallis,' replied Cornwallis. 'I'm an investigator, presently attached to Scooters Yard and I'm investigating a crime.'

'Oh, my; that's sounds serious.'

'It is, Mr… er?'

'Tredding, Ernest Tredding. Master of the Guild of Ironworkers.'

Cornwallis inclined his head in acknowledgement. 'Mr Tredding, I wish to know who uses two of your properties. One is in Loom Lane, number eighteen, and the one it backs on to in Fetter Street.'

Mr Tredding nodded. 'Yes, we own a number of properties there. Most are empty, I believe. We use them as temporary accommodation for foundry workers.'

'So you have keys for them?'

'Oh yes.'

'Here?'

Mr Tredding shook his head. 'Not enough room. We keep them at the Guilds Hall.'

Cornwallis raised his eyebrows. 'So who has access to them?'

'Just us. Safe as houses there,' said Mr Tredding, not realising he'd made a pun. 'No one would ever think about using something from another guild. It wouldn't be proper.'

Cornwallis opened his mouth to reply, but a look at the guileless master prevented his rejoinder. Mr Tredding believed what he just said. 'I'm sure you're right, but if you could humour me for a moment. Why don't you and I take a little stroll down to Guilds Hall and take a look at the keys, just to check that all is as it should be.'

'Oh, do you think that's necessary?'

'I'm sure we'll find everything in order, but it will help my investigation. Shall we go now?' said Cornwallis, rising from his chair.

The walk to Guilds Hall took ten minutes. On the way, Cornwallis tried to gauge the master's views on the imminent opening of The Pipe, whether it would have a positive or negative impact on the iron business. Mr Tredding appeared to not only approve of the enterprise but believed it would be beneficent to his guild. The dwarfs and he had come to an agreement where the foundry would turn ore into iron for them in return for supplying extra ore at a discounted rate.

This was news to Cornwallis but Goodhalgan had told him that he would take care of the iron and that he could organise it all. Evidently, he had.

Cornwallis filed that bit of knowledge in his mind for later perusal. He'd never been to the Guilds Hall before, so the opulence of the entrance lobby took him aback as they entered through the massive doors, guarded by gigantic columns of marble, supporting a decorative portico.

Festooned with colourful bright banners and flags hanging from the walls, each one representing a guild from the city, the vast rectangular space of the lobby spread out before them. Above them, the ceiling, ornate with panels of frescoes painted by a master artist. A lattice-work of polished wooden cubicles skirted the walls, furnished with benches and low tables. The floor, covered by slabs of marble, gleamed as if polished within an inch of its life. To the right, a dozen porters and flunkies pandered to the enquiring members behind a long shiny wooden counter.

'I'll just sign you in, Mr Cornwallis,' said Mr Tredding as he stepped up to the counter.

Tredding clicked his fingers and a liveried flunkey stepped smartly up. The master explained Cornwallis' presence and the flunkey reluctantly signed him in, distaste at a non-member of the guilds evident by the look of derision that shot Cornwallis' way.

Cornwallis ignored the implied insult, instead just winking and grinning until the flunkey went back to his work.

Mr Tredding guided Cornwallis across the floor to a nondescript door at the far end, flanked by a couple of guards. Once through the door, the Guilds Hall became functional: no adornments, no decoration, no nothing — just plain and simple austerity.

Mr Tredding headed up the steps to the second floor and then along a corridor hosting a number of doors, each one with a little plaque and a tiny flag next to it, indicating which guild resided there. The Guild of Ironworkers had its office towards the end of the corridor, next door to The Guild of Socks and Hosiery Makers.

'How many guilds are there?' asked Cornwallis.

'Hundreds,' replied Mr Tredding. 'The founding members are on the first floor, you know, like the carpenters, the masons, butchers, bakers—'

'Candlestick makers?' said Cornwallis interrupting.

'Precisely,' said Mr Tredding. 'And of course, the ladies.'

'Ladies?' asked Cornwallis.

'The oldest profession, of course; they have to be on the first floor.'

Cornwallis acknowledged the sense of that. 'You're on the second floor,' he continued.

'Indeed. We were not original members but gained approval shortly after. There are seven floors and the newest member is up the top. That's how it works.'

Cornwallis nodded and followed the master into the ironworkers' office; he noted that the door was unlocked.

The large office contained a finely carved desk and chair. Around the walls were intricate cabinets, some glass-fronted, to show off pieces of finely wrought iron. There were drawers; loads of them, containing only the gods knew what. The Chain of Office draped from a lump of wood fixed to a stand to show it off with other bits of regalia on a table beneath. A posh office, and therefore, Cornwallis could see that it was all for show, like looking at a bottle of the finest whisky, but not being allowed to try it.

Mr Tredding went to a set of drawers below the display of some strange bendy bits, which Cornwallis couldn't fathom out at all. He pulled one out; inside were little compartments, each containing a set of keys. A piece of card below the keys indicated where and what they belonged to.

Mr Tredding scratched his head. 'Oh! The keys to those two houses are missing, Mr Cornwallis, and I haven't the foggiest idea why.'

'Not another member of your guild?' asked Cornwallis, looking at the empty spaces.

Mr Tredding shook his head. 'I've been the only one coming here. I saw the porter writing down my name in the guild book. There's only been my name for months.'

'Any other keys missing?'

Mr Tredding opened other drawers, checking the contents in each and it dawned on Cornwallis that the ironworkers guild owned an awful lot of properties.

'Is the guild wealthy?' asked Cornwallis a little uneasily.

'No more than any other guild,' said Mr Tredding, still checking the drawers, ever more frantically. 'We have to safeguard our members in case of hardship.' Finally, Mr Tredding stood up. 'No, no other keys are missing, just those two. How very strange.'

'Maybe not so strange,' said Cornwallis. 'Tell me, has there been any trouble between your guild and another?'

'Trouble? Between the guilds?' asked the master; his eyes widening. 'How could you suggest such a thing? The guilds are like a family, Mr Cornwallis.'

Which meant, thought Cornwallis, that everyone would be at each other's throats. Someone in the guilds wanted to point a finger towards the ironworkers; he now had the problem of finding out which guild. At least it indicated progress; he could now narrow it down to several hundred suspects.

'Tell me, Mr Tredding,' said Cornwallis, a thought coming into his head. 'With the dwarfs prepared to sell you ore for your foundry, who would be the biggest loser?'

'Loser? I don't think anyone would lose. We take all the ore we can get. A city like this gobbles up ore like there's no tomorrow.'

CHAPTER 22

Phil the Flick looked around nervously as he came through the door flanked by two of Gerald's heavies, his eyes never resting on anything long enough to notice what he could see — self-preservation being high on his agenda. He had never been invited into Gerald's lair before and he knew that many didn't get a second invitation, namely because you can't invite someone who is no longer there. He decided to be conciliatory, innocent, ignorant and compliant. He wanted to walk back out the same way he came in.

Tall and skinny as a boot-lace with a gaunt drawn face and a mop of dark unkempt badly cut hair, Phil got nudged from behind and stumbled forward to where Gerald sat with Frankie and Rose, drinking tea and nibbling biscuits.

'Er…?' began Phil as he looked at the three of them sitting there. His eyes rested on Rose; he'd seen her about the slum before, but only at a distance and that hadn't prepared him for seeing her up close. 'Er…?' he repeated as she put the mug down and stood up. She smiled at him. 'Er…?' he said again, now getting the full front-on experience and he couldn't handle the things that were happening to various regions of his anatomy.

Gerald waved him to come close. 'You've gone an' followed a couple o' lads; 'erbert an' Norris. Tell us abaht it.'

'Er…' said Phil, still staring at Rose, his tongue hanging out.

'We ain't got all day,' prompted Gerald, now noticing the way he looked at Rose and deciding that it was a look too far, especially here in The Brews where only *he* could look at her like that. 'Right, sod it, you're getting a special.'

Gerald stood up and took a few steps towards Phil, who with eyes still staring at Rose, hadn't noticed. He still hadn't noticed when Gerald stood right in front of him and then when he did notice, quite suddenly, and in a way that he wouldn't have thought possible, he realised that he should have been paying attention earlier. He'd heard of Gerald's special talent, now he experienced it, fully and undiluted.

Phil suddenly had the breath sucked out of him as Gerald stepped forward and merged into him. He let out a wail as his body protested at the feeling of being turned inside out, he shuddered and shivered and then an icy finger seemed to rip up from his toes to his head and nausea hit, as though his breakfast wanted to make a bid for freedom. Then Gerald did what he only did to special people. Instead of walking right through a body, he sometimes stopped and turned around. This made for an especially excruciating experience, not painful, but weird beyond weird.

Rose and Frankie had seen this before and they always wanted to know what Gerald could see. For some reason, neither of them had the nerve to ask.

Gerald re-emerged from Phil wearing a big wide grin of satisfaction. Phil, to the contrary, wore a big wide grimace of having been scared shitless — though Gerald may have an opinion on whether that was, in fact, true or not.

Phil shuddered again and decided not to fight the cringing feeling that swept over him as he sank to his knees and sort of folded in on himself.

Gerald turned and nudged him with his boot. 'On yer feet, lad, we got a load o' questions to asks yer.'

Phil raised his head and climbed unsteadily to his feet, his face like a bowl of jelly with a fart running through it. 'What do you want to know,' he asked hesitantly, now not looking at Rose at all.

'That's better, me lad. Norris an' 'erbert. You followed 'em. We wants to know all abaht it.'

Phil began to relate the story from when Herbert's mum approached him with her concerns, offering him a freebie should he decide to help her.

'Freebie?' asked Rose interjecting.

'Don't be naive, Rose,' answered Frankie quietly. 'How do you think she puts bread on the table?' He indicated to Phil to carry on as Rose shifted uncomfortably in her seat, thinking about daily life in the slum.

Phil explained how he followed the two lads to the Bull and Badger and sat in the corner as he watched them engage in conversation with the mystery man and then receive a bag of money from him.

'So this meeting seemed pre-arranged?' asked Rose, getting her mind back to where it should be.

Phil nodded. "E were already there and 'e seemed to be expecting 'em.'

'What did he look like?' asked Frankie.

Phil shrugged. 'Dunno really. A man.'

Rose sighed. 'How old? How was he dressed?'

'C'mon, spit it out,' ordered Gerald. 'You want me to do me little trick again?'

'No, no, no,' replied Phil holding up a hand, horror flooding his face. "E were about forty, light hair, a bit long, big red nose like he drinks too much, good clothes like a tailor makes, dark suit it was, nice cut. 'E 'ad a really irritating laugh, like an 'orse being kicked in the goolies.'

'And he didn't have anyone with him?' asked Rose.

'Not that I could see. I follows 'im when 'e left as I were a bit curious, an' I reckoned I could get a few more freebies if I found out who 'e were.'

'Did you?'

Phil shook his head. 'No, 'e just went straight to the Assembly. Walked in bold as brass as if 'e owned the place. I left it there and went back to get me reward.'

'You didn't ask one of the guards who he was?'

Phil laughed. 'Yeah, they really gonna tell me that, ain't they?'

'No, I suppose you're right.'

'But you'd recognise him if you saw him again?' probed Frankie.

'Yeah, but I ain't likely too, am I.'

'Oh, I don't know. I reckon you'll be seeing him very soon now. I think a little wait at the Assembly is in order.'

The Stoat was packed but unusually subdued by the time Rose and Frankie arrived. It had been a very busy day and they needed a little light refreshment to bring succour to the soul. They had arranged to meet Cornwallis there and true to his word, he'd already bagged a table and lined up the pints.

Sliding into her seat next to him, Rose reached over and cuddled his arm, planting a kiss on his cheek. At the same time, Frankie eased into the chair opposite and wasted no time on pleasantries but just grabbed the pint in front of him and downed a good half of it.

'Ah, lovely stuff,' he opined as he crashed the now half-empty glass onto the table. 'Curdles the toes good and proper.'

'Glad you appre—' began Cornwallis until a ruckus at the bar interrupted the flow.

Two gentlemen were having a disagreement, presumably,

from the general ebb and flow of the conversation, concerning the correct order of attention from the maid behind the bar. Elbows were prominent as were fists and feet as the duo launched into one another. Grunts and swearing ensued until Big George put down the empties and sauntered over, grabbing each of them by the scruff of the neck and dragging them to the front door, both still trying to lay into one another. A kindly patron opened the door and George gently threw them out. He turned and retraced his steps, picking up the empties then carrying on as if nothing had happened.

'George must be in a bad mood,' surmised Frankie. 'He normally lets 'em go on for a while first.'

'He's not in a bad mood. He's doing you a favour, trying to keep things quiet...ish because of your Tulip having a doze upstairs,' replied Cornwallis. 'That's the third fight he's stopped since I've been here. Eddie reckons he's turning into an uncle and he won't stand any disturbance when she's sleeping.'

'Ah, that's lovely,' said Rose. 'A bear that really cares.'

'That also explains why this place is so quiet,' said Cornwallis. 'George has warned everyone not to disturb her.'

'Do you think he's getting broody?' asked Rose seriously, looking over her shoulder at the big brown bear. 'Is there a missus George at all? I know he hadn't got one not long ago.'

Cornwallis shook his head. 'I asked Eddie that same question not a quarter of an hour ago. Apparently, he's been like this since you came yesterday, Frankie; and no, Rose, there is no missus George.'

'Then we should do something about that, can't have George going without,' suggested Rose. 'There must be a lady bear somewhere in this city for him.'

Cornwallis grinned. 'There probably is, but how can you tell a good looking one from a... a... a not so good looking one?'

'Easy, I'll ask another bear.'

Big George dumped his empties and then strolled over to pedal the fan to get rid of the smog that had built up, unaware that three detectives had just taken an interest in his love life.

Isabella came down and joined them, leaving Tulip in the care of Trudi the barmaid, who looked forward to an hour or two of peace and quiet.

'Budge up, big boy,' she said as she nudged Frankie. 'Let a lady take her ease.'

Frankie shuffled up leaving a space for half a buttock, then flung an arm around her shoulders and pulled her to him, giving her a big soggy kiss.

'Urgh, get off!' she said, waving a hand in distress.

Frankie went and found a free chair from the far side of the bar and slid it in next to Isabella, in that time Rose and Cornwallis had informed her of the intention concerning George.

'I'll ask some of the girls here,' said Isabella. 'They probably know George better than anyone. They might have an idea of how to proceed.'

With that item ticked off their agenda, they turned to the more pressing issue with regard to the day's activities, namely how to catch the one who wanted to do for The Pipe.

It became obvious that there was more to the sabotage than just the disgruntlement of a couple of malcontents as they talked through what they'd learnt. The Guild Hall and Assembly indicated that powerful people were involved, which made things, paradoxically, easier but harder — and this Phil the Flick could identify one of the saboteurs.

'In a way,' said Cornwallis. 'I'm quite looking forward to tomorrow.'

CHAPTER 23

While he waited, Cornwallis again pondered on the ever-increasing list of things to be done. A note to Goodhalgan explaining his absence would hopefully mollify that aspect of the things that wouldn't get done; he had hoped to devote more of his time to getting The Pipe up and running. However, finding the man behind the attacks was probably more important because at least then The Pipe would have a chance.

He stood outside Sal's Sizzler waiting for Phil the Flick. Located in a prime position close to the House of Assembly, the constant stream of hungry mouths queued to sample the food on offer. Saying that it was lucrative didn't do it justice, it minted money and in exchange, you got the street food of angels.

Cornwallis waited impatiently with the waft from the stall tickling his taste buds and making him feel hungry. He had a hard time resisting temptation as punter after punter strolled by cramming the delights into their mouths. Cornwallis felt his saliva thicken and he decided that he would only wait for another five minutes and then he would indulge — Phil the Flick, or no Phil the Flick.

'Er... Mr Cornwallis?' said a voice in his ear.

Cornwallis whipped his head around quickly to confront the person addressing him. He looked him up and down and it took a few moments to register that the man he was waiting for had arrived.

Phil the Flick stood before him having been transformed

from a Brews street thief to a middle-class man about town. Gerald had done wonders in producing a man that could go anywhere, be anyone.

'Phil?' queried Cornwallis.

The man returned a hesitant smile. 'Yep, Mr Cornwallis.'

'How did you recognise me?'

'I didn't. That man over there did it for me.'

Phil indicated someone loitering down the street and Cornwallis nodded as he saw Crinning standing by a street lamp. Crinning inclined his head and then turned and walked away.

Cornwallis turned to his new best friend. 'Well, Mr Phil, let's hope you can spot the man for me. Ever been inside the Assembly before?'

'What?' replied Phil, his face suddenly draining of colour.

'How else are you going to point the man out? Why do you think you are dressed as you are?'

'I don't know. Mr Gerald just made sure I were clean and respectable. I fought maybe I were to stand here and watch the door. That's what your mates said I were to do.'

Cornwallis grinned wryly. 'Change of plan. You could end up standing here for days on end. No, we're going to poke around inside. Just remember to keep your hands to yourself. You get caught thieving in there, you won't know what'll happen tomorrow because for you, there will be no tomorrow. Understand?'

Phil gulped. 'Yes, Mr Cornwallis.'

'Right, we got that sorted. Hungry?'

Phil nodded. 'I live in The Brews, Mr Cornwallis. I'm always hungry.'

'In that case, before we start, we'll have one of Sal's specials. Don't worry, I'm paying.'

Phil's taste buds did somersaults and his stomach growled

like a lion in anticipation. He'd been trying to fight the aroma attacking his senses ever since he first approached Cornwallis, but now, with this revelation, he could let the smell do its worst.

Shortly two buns the size of dinner plates passed across the counter, each filled with rashers of bacon, several sausages, loads of ham and all covered with eggs and a thick brown sauce. Two hands were required to hold it all and a fair degree of time and contemplation to eat it. For Phil, breakfast had never been this good.

The House of Assembly, a red granite edifice, loomed large and permanent. At the top of the steps by the front entrance, the Morris guard protected the House from riots and attacks. They stood menacingly in their dark waistcoats and trousers with their white shirts and dark wide-brimmed hats. Their little bells tingling as they stood to attention with their batons held high. Thankfully, the ceremonial opening of the House had finished a while ago, the tourists seemed to have liked it, but the locals of the city considered it cringe-worthy.

Cornwallis led Phil up the steps and past the protecting guards without acknowledging their presence and in through the door to the foyer beyond. Perkins, the ever-present porter, standing in his customary position behind the highly polished desk, looked up and beckoned him over.

'Ah, Mr Cornwallis, sir. Haven't seen you around the place for a while, sir.'

'No, indeed not, Perkins. I'm just showing Mr... er... Flick here around as he may decide to join my staff here. I trust Mr Speckleby is in the house today?'

'Yes, sir. I believe he's in the office, sir.'

'Good, good, Perkins. Thank you.'

Conrad Speckleby acted as Cornwallis' understudy, holding the seat on Cornwallis' behalf, saving him the job of actually having to attend the Assembly himself.

'Will that be all, Mr Cornwallis, sir?'

'For the moment, yes, Perkins.'

Perkins then appraised Phil and obviously found him wanting, not of the required class, so dismissed him instantly from his mind. However, as Cornwallis saw the dismissal he knew that word of Phil's appearance with him would soon filter down to the man that nobody wanted to know or mention — The Bagman, the head of Gornstock's secret police.

Cornwallis gently tugged Phil's arm and dragged him through the foyer and into the ornate lobby beyond.

The enormous lobby had green marble flooring with four rows of white pillars rising high to the intricate ceiling above, where a few massive chandeliers dangled menacingly, ready to drop on any miscreants below; some say the journalists were especially targeted, but that was only a rumour put about by a disgruntled member embroiled in a legal wrangle with the press. People packed the lobby: reporters and members telling secrets and doing deals, all for the good of themselves. Nothing was sacrosanct, apart from the money changing hands.

'Keep an eye out,' instructed Cornwallis quietly. 'Give me a nudge if you see our man.'

Phil couldn't trust his voice at the moment so he just nodded as he looked around and studied the opulence; never in his life did he imagine how richly built the Assembly was: where did all the money come from? And then he realised the money came from poor bastards like him, who had their wages docked so that chunks of it could go to the Morris to pay for stuff like this, to keep them in the style to which they wanted to become accustomed. All these rich bastards were screwing all the poor bastards so that the rich bastards didn't have to pay for anything. Being a thief did have some advantages as he didn't pay taxes, but then he thought that he did spend the money he stole, which meant that that money, spent in legitimate places, was liable for tax, which meant that he *did* contribute in some way to the taxes which paid for all this. He seethed at the injustice of it all, his hard stolen money, gone, to this!

'Any joy?' asked Cornwallis.

Phil shook his head. 'No, can't see 'im in 'ere,' he said through the gritted teeth of resentment.

Cornwallis shot him a look. 'A problem?'

Phil shook his head again. 'No, it's just that all this costs a bloody fortune. When half the city's eating the leather off their boots, this lot in 'ere live like this; it don't seem right, somehow.'

Cornwallis couldn't help but agree. 'No, it doesn't, but that's how society works. The Morris happened to be the biggest crooks around some years ago and they built things like this from the money they stole from the people. As a thief, I would have thought you'd appreciate the fact that they were better crooks than the rest of the population.'

'You mean all this is from ill-gotten gains?'

'Oh, yes, same as all the churches; you ever had a look inside some of them?'

Phil nodded. 'Yeah, I've nicked a few bits.'

'Then you know what I mean; same applies to them, only instead of stealing your money, they get you to give it to them. It's a great big confidence trick when you boil it down. They're promising you something that they can't deliver: when you find out, it's too late because you're already dead.'

'But there are gods,' countered Phil. 'Loads o' 'em.'

'Yes, but there are more gods than churches. Who built those churches? Who asked for money to build those churches? Who asks for money to keep those churches going? The churchmen who decide to worship one particular god, that's

176

who. They don't worry about the rest of the gods, because they're earning from one. One god has just the same amount of power as the next one, but the churches just focus on one god each and frighten the people into giving them money and hope that the people will forget the other gods.'

'Oh.'

'It just means that some churches are better than others at extorting money.'

'I take it you're not a fan of churches?'

'No, I'm bloody not.'

'You do surprise me.'

Cornwallis sighed, feeling better now he'd got that off his chest. 'Now, let's get back to doing what we're here for, see if you can spot our mystery man.'

The chamber beyond the lobby was out of bounds for non-members, but fee-paying citizens could watch the Assembly conduct business from a gallery. The enthusiasm for observing the government in action was such that it was frequently empty, devoid of onlookers, and the queue to watch, conspicuous by its absence. The populace of Gornstock couldn't be arsed.

Cornwallis guided Phil up the stairs and deposited a couple of dollars into the hand of a surprised looking official, roused from contemplating either the meaning of life, or the inside of his eyelids, and went into the gallery.

Dust covered the benches and spiders had free rein as the cobwebs indicated. The windows at the back of the gallery could have done with a bit of a polish and the floor hadn't seen a broom for weeks.

Cornwallis pulled out a clean hankie and wiped a bench down and then they sat, leaning over the rail above the Assembly.

'Take your time,' said Cornwallis quietly. 'There's only about half of them here, but one or two may wander in from time to time.'

Phil began to scrutinise the members, looking keenly trying to spot the one they wanted. Cornwallis spotted his father, sitting next to the Warden, stifle a yawn as another member droned on about something to do with the law regarding sheep escaping from the slaughterhouse; they were arguing that the finder assumes ownership because the slaughterhouse would be proven negligent, or some such waffle which was neither interesting nor important, except maybe for the sheep.

The earl received a nudge from behind and a whisper in his ear then looked up at the gallery, giving a nod of recognition, he then mimed raising a pint. Cornwallis smiled and then shook his head, pointing a finger at Phil. The members' bar was for members only, but the bar next door was available to all so Cornwallis mimed a flick with his fingers and raised his own pretend pint. The earl gave a small nod and then patted the Warden on the shoulder as he got up to leave, the droning continuing without a break.

'E ain't 'ere,' said Phil quietly once he looked at all those assembled below. 'An' listening to that lot down there I'm surprised that anyone's 'ere.'

'Tell me about it,' replied Cornwallis. 'That's about as exciting as it gets. The real business is done in the members' bar and down in the lobby, same as all governments everywhere. This is all for show, though very few ever turn up for it. Come on, we'll go and have a drink in the free bar.'

'Free bar?'

'Not what you think, you still have to pay. It's just free of restrictions, meaning anyone can go in.'

Cornwallis had wondered on the wisdom of bringing Phil into the Assembly, into all this wealth and privilege where an astute thief could wreak havoc, especially one who could quite rightly hold a grievance against everyone there. Phil had, in the space of an hour, gone from the worst sort of poverty to rubbing shoulders with the highest in the land, a transformation that must be addling his mind.

A surreptitious look as they left the gallery convinced Cornwallis that Phil had put his resentment aside, unless of course, he hid his fury well and the reaction was going to come later when the realisation hit home that to these people he was just a dog turd on the boot of humanity. He wasn't going to count his chickens just yet, but so far, the flick-knife hadn't made an appearance.

The free bar adjoined the members' bar and its clientele comprised of all those working at the Assembly, but who were not members of the Assembly. Members could go to the free bar to entertain visitors and hangers-on, or journalists and campaigners. It was the busiest bar in the house and the place where many members preferred to be.

The bar heaved at this time of the morning. Cornwallis and Phil used their elbows to force their way through to the bar where the earl waited alongside three freshly pulled pints of Splodge, or "best bitter" as a non-member might say.

'What on twearth are you doing here in this godforsaken place, my boy?'

Cornwallis smiled at his father's welcome. 'Business, actually.'

'Oh?'

'Yes, let's find somewhere to talk.'

'Little chance of that in here, but there are places where nobody listens, if you know what I mean.'

The earl eyed Phil the Flick a little warily as the trio again deployed elbows to move over to the far side where talk was at its loudest and where a small group could converse in private.

'What's this all about then?' asked the earl, once they had found a suitable spot.

'The Pipe,' replied Cornwallis, his words disappearing into the hubbub of conversations going on all around them. 'This is Phil and he saw one of the saboteurs walk in here.'

'Saboteurs?'

'Rose told you some of it; since then there's been an arson attack on The Pipe by those two lads. Phil here saw the man who seems to be arranging these little diversions with them, he saw him pass money to them and then he saw him come in here. Ergo, he works here.'

'I just seen him,' said Phil quietly.

'That's not good,' said the earl. 'I've been looking at the pros and cons of The Pipe, whether it'll be good or bad for the city, as you know, and now I have concluded my analyses, deciding it'll be good. The Warden agrees and is happy for it to go ahead.'

'"E's over there,' said Phil.

'That's good news, but have you heard any rumours about some people wanting to stop it, regardless?'

'No, there are a few who aren't keen, but none of them particularly vociferous. The Guilds don't like it, but with the Warden going along with it, there's nothing they can do.'

Phil grabbed Cornwallis' arm.

'What?' snapped Cornwallis.

'I've been telling you, he's over there.'

Cornwallis' head whizzed around. 'Where?' he asked urgently.

'There, that bloke over there.'

'Which bloke?'

'The one next to that other fella.'

'Which other fellow?'

'The bloke's next to the fella who's talking to the geezer.'

'Geezer? Which geezer?'

'The one talking to the fella.'

Cornwallis' mind began to scramble as he tried to make sense of it all, but realising that it was impossible to distinguish a bloke from a fellow or a fellow from a geezer he gave up. 'Go and stand next to the bloke,' he ordered in the end.

Phil shuffled forward, after raising his eyebrows and sighing heavily at Cornwallis' inability to understand plain Gornstockian, to stand next to a man with his back turned towards them. He raised a finger and then jabbed it towards the bloke, nearly ramming it in his back in his eagerness. He then twitched his head in the bloke's general direction, emphasising the jab of his finger.

Cornwallis signalled his understanding with a slow nod of his head and then beckoned Phil to return to them.

'Who's that then?' asked Cornwallis, turning towards his father.

'That, young Jocelyn, is Fletcher Phimp. His master is Celwyn Brooksturner, the relatively new Minister responsible for Dwarfs and Bipeds.'

CHAPTER 24

Goodhalgan stood with his arms braced against his waist with his elbows jutting out, looking much like an ancient urn, with a look of contented pride etched on his face as the dwarfs raced along like ants in their nests, scurrying between the chambers, hurrying this way and that, up and down, here and there. Activity was everywhere and there was no respite as the day of The Pipe's opening fast approached. The king of the dwarfs pulled a piece of paper from his pocket and perused it.

The chief engineer sidled up to the king of the dwarfs with a roll of plans gripped in his hands, just as Goodhalgan finished reading Cornwallis' note.

'Nearly there now,' said Treacle. 'All we need is a queue of people ready to pay and we'll be good to go.'

Goodhalgan grinned. 'Won't be long. Any more sabotage?'

'None at all, seems to be quiet today on that front.'

'That's a relief; it was starting to get tedious. Mr Cornwallis thinks he's on to something, which is why he won't be joining us down here for a day or two.'

Treacle acknowledged this by a dip of the head. 'We've still got the tunnel under the river to finish widening. Good job it's mainly clay, makes it easier to dig out, but easier for the wet to get in if it all squidges down.'

'The solution?'

'Bricks and metal plates. Lot's of 'em. Make an arch with the bricks and then line it all with plates. Got to make it fit snug, otherwise we'll have the river down here.'

'It wouldn't be the river I'd worry about, it'd be the shite that'd come down with it.'

Treacle unrolled the plan and laid it down on a bench then both dwarfs scrutinised it. All the tunnels were there as well as all the entrances, the whole network, including the tracks that were yet to be laid. It would encompass the whole of the city. To Goodhalgan, it looked beautiful.

The king of the dwarfs puffed out his chest in pride and slapped the plan with his hand. 'This is going to change Gornstock, and, I believe, the way that dwarfs will be viewed in the future. We will be seen as innovators, investing in the future of the city, a forward-thinking species with the ability to integrate within society.'

'Yeah, all those long-legged bastards up there will have to look up to us, else we'll close down The Pipe and they'll have to walk everywhere again. We'll be able to drink in all those posh places where they ban folk who ain't got money because *we'll* be the ones with the money.'

'Money isn't everything, you know. We will have respect. We will have done something nobody else could do. I believe The Pipe will become the arteries of the city, carrying all those people to all those places to make the money that keeps Gornstock alive. The money we make is incidental to that because respect breeds respect.'

'But the money helps, right?'

'Too bloody right it does. Let's go and see how our money-making machine is doing; hopefully no last-minute problems to sort out.'

Treacle rolled up the plan as Goodhalgan yanked on his belt to hoik up his trousers, setting them so he wouldn't trip over the leg-ends, and set off on the inspection.

The original idea to have just three or four streets covered by The Pipe had changed; things had moved on at a pace and now there were ten streets covered with ten more nearly completed. Going at the rate they were going, it wouldn't be long before the whole city was connected.

*

'We seem to be coming close now,' said the well-dressed gentleman sitting back in his chair. 'The Warden is prepared to let The Pipe go ahead as long as there is no cost to the city, despite my, ahem, best endeavours to persuade him otherwise.'

'I trust you didn't try too hard?' said the other gentleman.

The man puckered his lips as though in thought. 'Hard enough: I sometimes had to counter my own arguments but it needed to be done, and I had to counter the Master of the Guilds too; toothless, he was, which was all to the good.'

'The Master has always been lacking in that area, he's never hated the dwarfs enough.'

'Unlike us, eh?'

'Indeed not, my friend. Those little bastards will get what they deserve.'

'Oh yes, that is for certain; it's about time we stood up for the superior race. The people will thank us in the end.'

'What about those two who got arrested?'

'Doesn't matter, they were just fodder anyway, and nothing can be traced back to us. Phimp was the only one they saw and they never knew his name; it's hardly likely they'll see him again. They were just gullible, greedy and very very stupid; I mean, thinking Ironworkers go to the pub in their leathers, eh? Anyway, if necessary your man can deal with Phimp.'

They looked at each other, both forming grins on their faces as the two glasses of wine received a refill.

'Yes, I did mention the possibility and he does like that type of work.' He held up his glass and studied the colour.

'Reliable?'

'Oh, yes, the good thing is that he's not a resident here, so no one knows him and he can move around freely.'

'Do you mean he couldn't move around freely where he comes from?'

A shake of the head indicated that he couldn't. 'He had a little problem, had to be looked after for a while.'

An eyebrow raised in question as the other man drained the glass and proffered it for another refill.

'He hates dwarfs.'

'That's a plus. What did he do?'

'He dispatched seven dwarfs with his bare hands and injured a few more.'

'Oh?'

'One at a time,'

'Ah.'

'All within an hour.'

'Really? Where?'

'Up north. They sent him into a place for help, although he didn't think he needed it.'

'But he can still be trusted?'

'Yes, he'll do what is required, especially now he knows what's going to happen. He doesn't like people much either, to be honest, but then again, neither do I.'

'Sounds like our type of man. I'm sure we can find him a suitable position once all this is over. Clothes fitted all right?'

'Perfect fit, he just blends in.'

'I do like it when a plan starts to work.'

'The end justifies the means.'

'Doesn't it just.'

Both held up their wine in a toast.

'To success,' said one, as they drained the glasses.

CHAPTER 25

Frankie and Isabella had taken Tulip into town to take advantage of the slack morning to get their daughter a new cot, seeing as the last one received a brick and several chunks of glass, leaving Rose to twiddle her thumbs until meeting up with Cornwallis when he finished at the Assembly. Eddie would find her something to do.

That something turned out to be her old job, helping out behind the bar and waiting on tables, though thankfully not helping out in the kitchen which she knew from previous experience could be a fraught affair with a constant barrage of abuse and low-flying spoons and plates. A prickly character, the chef ruled his domain with a rod of iron, and woe betide anyone who transgressed or criticised his culinary expertise. Some bar staff had never even seen him, they just poked orders through a hatch and waited for the ding of the bell to tell them that the magic had occurred and the food was ready. It suited everyone involved.

When Cornwallis finally turned up, Rose had been on the go for several hours and fatigue had definitely set in. Working as a detective was making her soft. When she worked at the Stoat before, she could keep going all day and most of the night, but now she flagged, desperately needing a rest, and then the excuse she needed walked through the door.

'Sit down,' she said as she kissed him on the cheek. 'I'll get us a drink.'

A minute or so later, she flopped down next to him and sighed in relief.

'Busy?' asked Cornwallis with a hint of mischief.

She shot him a sharp look. 'Yes, very.'

He grinned in reply and she had to exercise a serious amount of self-control not to pick up the pint and tip its contents into his lap.

'Jack, if you want to play hide the sausage at anytime in the future then I suggest you recompose that look on your face to one of concern, sympathy and understanding. Smug condescension is only going to work if you intend playing solo.'

'Ah.'

'I have been running around like a blue-arsed fly and am not in the mood for clever repartee. Possibly in a little while, but definitely not now.'

'I take it Eddie has taken advantage.'

Rose breathed out slowly and heavily. 'In truth, no. I just forgot how hard I used to work and how unfit I've become.'

'Then it's just as well you have a new career and new responsibilities.'

'Responsibilities?'

'Yes: me.'

'I'd hardly put you down as a responsibility. Irresponsible, perhaps.'

A smile spread across Cornwallis' face, a warm contented one, one that showed that indeed he was a lucky man. The bad moods never lasted for long.

'Anyway, what happened at the Assembly?' she asked taking a pull on her pint.

'I thought you'd never ask,' he replied aping her action. 'It worked out better than I expected.'

'You mean you found the man?'

'Oh, yes.'

He paused.

'Jack, stop pissing about.'

Cornwallis chuckled. 'Just trying to inject a bit of drama into the conversation.'

'Don't bother, you're a ham actor.'

'That's nice; there's me perched on the edge of danger risking life and limb, while you stay here taking it easy, relaxing in a pub... Ooof! Ow, that hurt,' he added as her elbow dug into his ribs.

'Serves you right, Jack Cornwallis. As if you ever perch on the edge of danger, you normally leave that to Frankie and me.'

'The art of management is delegation. As the head of the company, it's down to me to make certain the appropriate person is delegated the appropriate task.'

'Whoa, big boy. Are you saying that my welfare comes second to the job?'

Cornwallis' eyes widened as he stared into the hole he'd just dug. 'Er, no. I just wanted to know if you'd bite, and you did.'

'Too bloody right I did. If I thought for one moment that you didn't care about what happens to me and Frankie then that would be the end — of everything.'

Cornwallis' face drained of colour as he stared into the abyss. 'No, no, no. NO. I do, you know that. Look, I'm sorry I tried to be funny. It didn't work. You know how I feel about you, and I'm panicking now. I'll say something nice.'

'What are you going to say?'

'What do you want me to say?'

'Jack, has anyone told you that you can be bloody useless at times?'

'Er, yes.'

'Well, you've just confirmed it.'

Silence descended between the pair of them, tumbleweed rolled through the pub, but only two people noticed. Each picked up their pint and took a swig, the slurps highlighted by the lack of interaction. Rarely were there moments of silence between them, except companionable silence, and this certainly lacked the companionable bit. The eeriness heralded a row and both of them knew it. It had just flared up out of nothing, a spark igniting where a spark shouldn't have flashed. An innocent occurrence that could have serious consequences; Cornwallis became more worried now than he had ever been. Rose was his world and he wasn't going to lose her for anything.

'Er… has something just happened?' he asked, a worried cadence to his voice.

'Yes,' replied Rose. 'It has.'

'Do you mind telling me what?'

'Work it out.'

'I'm trying.'

'Not hard enough, that's obvious.'

'What do you mean?'

'You're being a dick.'

'What?'

'A prime one at that.'

A sigh. 'If I said I'm sorry, would that work?'

'Possibly, if you meant it, really meant it.'

'I do mean it.'

'What are you sorry for?'

'For being a dick.'

A silence came again but the tumbleweed had rolled into the distance now, but still just visible, as both pints were drained to the sludge at the bottom of the glass.

'Okay, I'll forgive you, but only if you promise not to look at me and Frankie as part of the furniture, ever again.'

'I never have done,' he defended.

'No?'

'No, never. Look, I just tried to be light, tried to be funny, tried to lighten your mood after the busy day you've had. I know who bribed those lads to do what they did and thought to tease you a little. It's all gone wrong. I'm sorry.'

Another silence.

'Get the pints in, Jack, and I might, just might, forgive you,' said Rose eventually, a little sparkle coming back into the corner of her eyes.

Cornwallis didn't hang around, returning with two brim-full pints and a packet of roasted nuts, a large packet, knowing how she liked them.

'Ooh, nice,' she remarked as they plonked on the table. 'Did you order some chips too?'

Cornwallis' mouth opened to make a smart reply but managed to stop himself just in time. 'Not yet,' he replied instead.

She painted on a hurt look.

'I'll just go and order some now, shall I?' his backside still poised above the chair seat.

Rose nodded and then smiled. 'You know how to spoil a girl, Jack.'

With chips ordered and nuts demolished, resumption of the day's business could recommence.

'So, who is it?' asked Rose, rinsing the nuts away with a slurp.

'Fletcher Phimp,' replied Cornwallis. 'He works for the minister responsible for Dwarfs and Bipeds.'

'What?'

'Yes, exactly. At face value, it would seem the minister's heart is not exactly on the job. However, even if Phimp is involved, it doesn't mean the minister is too, but it does seem likely.'

'That's a turn up for the books. Do you know this minister?'

Cornwallis shook his head. 'Not personally, but his name is Brooksturner. We'll have to keep an eye on the pair of them, especially Phimp, but it's going to be difficult.'

'Your father?'

'He'll do what he can, but he's got all his work to do as well.'

'In that case, why not just have a few words with Phimp; see if imminent arrest can work its magic.'

'If the opening of The Pipe was tomorrow, then I think we would. But I want to know if the minister is involved and I also want to know who in the guilds is in on it because there must be some.'

'Phimp would tell us.'

'Maybe, but what if he doesn't? Pulling him in would just alert everyone else and then they'd go to ground. No, I think another day or so might lead us to whoever is orchestrating it all. At least we've got another link in the chain. Ah, here comes our defective detective,' he added as Frankie walked in.

'Afternoon,' bellowed Frankie as he approached the table, Isabella and Tulip in tow. 'Strewth, have you ever looked at the price of baby beds in town?'

Cornwallis and Rose shook their heads slowly.

'No problem for your pocket I suppose, small change to you, but us mere mortals—'

'Frankie,' interrupted Isabella. 'Shut up. You're not poor. You were once, I grant you, but not now and anyway, only the best for our daughter.'

'Yeah, but they were taking the piss for a bit of wood and a mattress.'

'But you bought it and I don't remember you moaning at the

time.' She turned to Rose.' But he's certainly made up for it, whining all the way back here.'

'No, I was being polite, and of course, I were still in shock at the price.'

'Let's be honest here, Frankie. You moan about spending half-a-dollar on a kebab.'

'No, I don't moan about the half-dollar, but I do want a kebab that's full.'

'Full of what?' asked Cornwallis.

'Whatever shit goes into a kebab. How the hell should I know what goes into them things? I just want it full of the stuff.'

'As long as there's extra chilli sauce, eh?'

'Too bloody right, which is why I'm moaning about what you gets fer yer money. You gets the extra chilli sauce with a kebab, but not with a sodding baby bed. No extra bits there, just a bed and a mattress.'

'But it's just a bed,' reasoned Rose.

'Yeah, but they could give you some ribbons or something. At that price, they could afford to.'

'Frankie,' shouted Isabella. 'Will you just bloody well shut up, will you.'

Everyone turned and stared in muted silence.

'Isabella,' said Frankie when he recovered from the shock. 'You just swore in front of Tulip.'

'Yes, and if her first words turn out to be "Bugger" or "Bollocks" or 'Shit", then you know who to blame because it won't be me.'

'Do you mind, I don't bloody swear in front of my daughter.'

'What did you just do?'

'What?'

'You just swore.'

'No, I didn't.'

'Yes you did. Rose, Jack, tell him.'

'Er,' said Cornwallis, not wanting to get involved in their argument having just settled his own.

Rose pursed her lips. 'Frankie, you are an arse. You swear all the time; you just don't know you're doing it.'

'What do you mean? My language is nowt but clean Inglionish, albeit with a smattering of Gornstockian thrown in.'

Frankie, just shut up and get some drinks in. It's your round.'

'No it bloody isn't, we've just got here.'

Rose and Isabella shook their heads slowly, as if to a naughty schoolboy.

'He tries my patience sometimes,' remarked Isabella.

'Mine too,' agreed Rose. 'Not sometimes though, all the bloody time.'

Cornwallis and Frankie shared a look of their own. 'Come on,' said Cornwallis. 'You're not going to win. Let's get the drinks in.'

Cornwallis and Frankie headed over to the bar, Frankie mumbling discontent all the way. As they ordered the drinks, Cornwallis began to rub his chin in thought.

'Have you seen your cat recently?'

'What, Fluffy? Yeah, 'e went back to the house.'

'Oh good.'

'Why?'

'There's a little job he can do for us.'

Rose yelled over. 'And find out where those bloody chips have got to.'

CHAPTER 26

He didn't like it at all. The meanest, crabbiest thing on four legs this side of the river suffering the ignominy of being unceremoniously carried through the austere surroundings of the house to only the gods knew where, crammed into a dark, smelly and rank leather holdall, which at present bounced and battered him as the holdall hit doors and walls and scraped along dusty floors and corridors. Forced into compliance with a promise, just on the off chance that something might happen. They were in the inner sanctum of the Assembly and his porter for this enterprise was none other than the Earl of Bantwich himself.

Fluffy didn't care who did the carrying, but the conveyance itself degraded a cat of his eminence. If the story ever got out it would take an age to live it down: being carried, in a bag!

Muffled words hit his ears, filtered as though through cotton wool. Fortunately, he didn't need to hear properly at the moment, just wait until the earl released the little flap in the bag so he could get a tiny view of the man he needed to follow.

The bag thumped to the ground and Fluffy swore under his breath as he lurched to the side and came up against the soft springy leather; a few seconds later, a little light appeared through a gap. The earl had opened the flap and Fluffy could now see a pair of legs covered in black trousers. It was a start, but he would have to see a bit more than a couple of cloth-covered sticks in order to keep an eye on a man.

He eased himself as far forward as the constraints of the bag allowed and then gazed up, catching a look at Phimp for the first time.

'…Of course, the cab drivers are setting up in a service of their own, but I'm sure the minister will put all his efforts into supporting the dwarfs.'

'Of course, sir,' replied Phimp smoothly. 'I will inform the minister of your interest in the matter.'

Fluffy didn't like Phimp. Bucket-loads of animal instinct kicked in as the secretary spoke. Phimp emanated. What he emanated, Fluffy couldn't say, but it emanated towards him and he didn't like it one iota. His hairs stood out like prongs as he viewed the thin, oily, hawk-like secretary to the minister.

Phimp had a thin face with a protuberant nose; light mousy over-long hair flopped about his face accentuating his slit of a mouth. His whole demeanour indicated poised calculated subservience, hiding his natural demeanour of confident arrogance; he was the type of person who sidled. Though at the moment only a secretary, he hoped to someday bridge the divide.

'You do that, Phimp,' replied the earl. 'Just let him know that the Warden and I are interested spectators.'

'Spectators, sir? I believe your son has a healthy interest in The Pipe.'

'Oh, he does, Phimp. But his businesses and mine rarely come into contact.'

The earl touched Phimp's arm and steered him around, allowing Fluffy time to creep out of the bag and dive beneath a chair close by. The earl continued talking whilst at the same time looking over his shoulder at the bag on the floor. He just saw the end of a ginger tail disappear from sight and figuratively breathed a sigh of relief. He could now make his excuses and get away from the odious Phimp, his job now done.

Phimp narrowed his eyes as he watched the earl disappear

196

down the corridor, it was unusual for someone of the earl's rank to converse with just the mere secretary of the minister, and it raised a slight suspicion in the back of his mind, but only for a moment. He worked hard to be willing and compliant, so he assumed the earl was sounding him out for a possible promotion to a higher ministry in the near future. The Assembly had its little ways and he knew that this was one of them. Nearly all the members had inherited their seats, but just occasionally, a vacant one came up. Could it be possible that something might be in the offing? If only the earl knew how duplicitous he could be, he thought, suppressing the grin that wanted to break out; now he had both bases covered.

A couple of minutes later, Phimp followed the earl out of the reading room and fairly skipped down the corridor, followed closely behind by a little ginger fur-ball.

*

'Didn't you say you were not staying long?' asked Maud from behind her fortress of a desk. 'I mean, three detectives on an active case shouldn't be sitting around twiddling their thumbs and drinking coffee, leaving a little pussycat to do all the work for them, should they?'

'In these circumstances, yes,' replied Cornwallis. 'We are anticipating developments, and anyway, describing Fluffy as a pussycat is a bit like describing dwarf whisky as flavoured water: there is only a vague resemblance, though admittedly based on fact.'

'Yes, well…'

'I think Maud would like us to vacate the premises,' said Rose, smiling at the secretary. 'We're in the way.'

'In the way?' asked Frankie from his position of slouching in the chair. 'How are we in the way in our own office?'

'Because,' answered Cornwallis. 'When Maud is in the office, then it's her office, we are just the furniture. She's right though, we should be getting our arses into gear. I need to see how The Pipe is doing and you two should be down at the Assembly, keeping our police officers company.'

'Dewdrop and Felicity,' said Rose nodding agreement. 'You told them we'll be down later?'

'I did. Sal will keep them fed, so they won't go hungry and Sal knows both Phimp and Brooksturner; quite regular customers from what she said.'

'Special rates,' explained Frankie. 'She feeds ninety percent of the Assembly on a regular basis. No one does a special quite like mum.'

'You need to be there for the lunchtime rush,' said Cornwallis. 'Dewdrop and Felicity are there just in case, but it's unlikely that Phimp will leave the Assembly until then. My father has ensured that the minister, Brooksturner, has work all morning and will need Phimp to help him.'

'Let's hope they let slip a few nuggets of information and that Fluffy is there to hear it,' said Rose.

'That's the hope,' replied Cornwallis. 'I'll walk down with you, I can get in at The Trand entrance; I'll come and join you when I'm finished with Goodhalgan.'

Cornwallis watched with interest as he stood outside the entrance, observing as the ladder went up. The grand opening was just two days away and the dwarfs were busy applying the finishing touches. One dwarf climbed the ladder as another passed up the sign which he then hammered into place. "The Trand" proudly displayed in a bar across a white roundel with a blue rim; a solid black circle filling the middle. They had agreed the logo a few days ago: the black circle denoted the tunnels and the rest because it looked nice. It seemed to work though.

The grinning dwarfs greeted Cornwallis as he entered the gleaming station. He walked past the ticket office and across the foyer to the steps which led down to the platform where the trains would stop. Everything looked the business and he visualised advertising posters that could adorn the walls giving the place a bit of colour and breaking up the expanse of bare wall.

All that was in the future, at the moment, it was more important to get The Pipe working and get people to use it. He hoped all the advertising around the city was going to bring paying customers flocking to use it.

Cornwallis looked up as he heard a noise coming through the tunnel: a clack-clackety-clack noise indicating the imminent arrival of a train.

A four-dwarf powered train trundled into the station with four carriages, all packed with dwarfs, standing room only. It eased to a halt and then the doors burst open and everyone inside piled out, all eager to be somewhere else. The platform swarmed with dwarfs, all of them running in different directions. Cornwallis stood wide-eyed in the centre of it all as the crowd engulfed him, pushing, shoving and jostling him here, there and everywhere. The dwarfs all shouted at the top of their voices, a deafening noise, made worse as the walls bounced the noise back to the ears. A whistle blew two short blasts and then all the dwarfs did an about-turn and rushed back towards the carriages. It was a scrum as elbows and feet were used to the utmost advantage to get through the doors in order to bag the few seats available. The melee ensued for a few more moments, leaving Cornwallis spinning on his spot, totally bewildered and bedraggled. Another whistle and the doors smacked closed and then the train moved off, front wheels screeching as they slipped and spun, trying to gather momentum. Then the back of the last carriage disappeared into the gloom and peace and tranquillity returned to the platform.

Cornwallis shook his head wondering whether he had just imagined the whole thing, whether his mind was playing tricks, whether he was suffering from a hangover that he didn't know he had.

'Hello, Mr Cornwallis,' said a dwarf, emerging from the shadows. 'Testing seems to be going well. I did call you but you didn't hear.'

'Wha… what just happened?'

'Rush hour: we've been replicating different scenarios, seeing how it will all work. Doing well so far. Shame you got caught up but you actually helped as you kept getting in the way.'

'Glad to be of help,' he replied through thin lips.

'You just wait for another couple of minutes and you can do it all again.'

'No bloody chance. Where's Goodhalgan?'

'You just missed him, 'e were on that train that just left. He gave you a smack on the leg just as the whistle blew.'

Cornwallis rubbed the bit that ached. 'Considerate of him.'

'Yeah, he likes to keep things real, does our king.'

'Too bloody real sometimes. If he comes back, tell him I'll be in his chamber, writing out a compensation claim.'

The dwarf grinned and then ticked off another item on his list: "Disgruntled Passenger," whilst waiting for the next train to arrive.

Cornwallis limped off to the steps that led down to the lower levels and then limped through the tunnels towards Goodhalgan's chamber. It was eerily quiet as it would seem most of the dwarfs were upstairs playing with their trains instead of hammering away with picks and shovels.

It took a few minutes for the numbness to evaporate and the leg to return to normal but in that time, he flipped through the bits of parchment and paper that festooned the table in front of him.

It was all there, the plans, the maps, the timetable, income projection, expenditure, the dwarfpower required, everything, even down to the amount of ore needed.

He turned over another pile and there were letters and forms from the deliveries of ore that had come from up north on the ships owned by the dwarfs. Next to them were more letters but these were complaints and threats, some of them from the guilds.

Cornwallis began to read through them and set aside those from the guilds.

'Ah, looks like we have a thief in the underground.' Goodhalgan bounced into the chamber wearing a big wide grin. 'Caught in the act, as it were.'

Cornwallis looked up from the letters and nodded a hello. 'So it would seem, but then again I blame the assault I suffered but a short while ago.'

'Ah, yes, sorry about that; you were in my way.'

'Hmm,' mused Cornwallis. 'I'll let you off this time. What about these,' he asked waving a letter in the air. 'You've kept these quiet.'

Goodhalgan shuffled over and took a look. 'Yes, didn't think it was worth bothering you. Nothing new, we've been getting those things for years.'

'But these are specifically to do with The Pipe.'

'Yes, but they're full of piss and wind. Anyway, things have gone quiet since you arrested those lads.'

'That's something. By the way, we believe Brooksturner, the

minister for dwarfs, might have something to do with them.'

'Now that wouldn't surprise me; odious man: been down here a few times and couldn't get rid of him fast enough.'

'Do you mind if I take these?' he asked, tapping the pile.

'No, I were going to hang them on a nail in the privy but if you want them, feel free. The paper ones are a bit thin with a tendency to split though.'

'Urgh,' replied Cornwallis, a picture forming in his mind.

They discussed things for a little while longer and then Cornwallis took his leave, everything appeared to be covered and everything appeared to be working. He just hoped that that would be the case in a couple of days' time when The Pipe opens for business.

CHAPTER 27

Rose and Frankie sat on a stool at the back of the stall and chewed contentedly on their respective culinary delight. Frankie had a special and the egg yolks were already running down his chin. Rose didn't feel up to a special so just made do with a sausage held in a delicate napkin, her second of the day so far. The sausage flopped and the punters on the other side of the stall watched in leg-clenching fascination as she held one end whilst nibbling at the other. Several respectable gentlemen had to walk awkwardly away.

'Causing problems again?' asked Cornwallis as he eased himself down next to Rose, observing the customers strained visages.

She turned to him and winked.

'You could cause serious death amongst those with a delicate constitution,' he replied.

'Wash voo ornaboot?' asked Frankie with his mouth full.

'What?' said Cornwallis thinking that someone had just plugged his ears with cloth.

Frankie swallowed and tried again. 'I said; what are you on about?'

'Rose,' answered Cornwallis. 'The damage she can do with a sausage.'

'Oh, yeah; noticed that. Mum always says she's good for business. A while ago Felicity were doing the same. You should have seen the poor bastards out there with two of them going at it.'

Cornwallis closed his eyes and sighed as Rose giggled. 'And you call *me* juvenile.'

He opened his eyes when he felt a shove in his chest and found Sal thrusting his usual at him, half the size of Frankie's, but still big nonetheless.

'Thanks, Sal.'

'Pleasure, my boy. Yer looking a bit on the thin side, if you don't mind me saying.' She turned to Rose. 'You need to fatten him up a bit, my girl; thought that when I saw 'im yesterday.'

'I'll send him to you a bit more, Sal,' said Rose smiling.

'You do that, girl. Soon get a bit o' lard on 'im, I will.'

'Exercise, Sal,' defended Cornwallis. 'I'm a lean mean love machine.'

'Bollocks,' replied Sal. 'In yer dreams,' and then she looked at Rose. 'Well, mebbee not bollocks after all,' she added quietly, almost to herself.

Rose raised an eyebrow and smiled knowingly.

Frankie finished his special and licked his fingers clean. 'Ay up, the feelers are back.'

Dewdrop and Felicity came around the back of the stall and reported.

'No, it wasn't him,' said Felicity. 'We thought it was, but it wasn't.'

'Fluffy,' explained Rose to Cornwallis' enquiring eye. 'A ginger cat, over by the Assembly.'

'Oh, so no sign of anything?'

'Not yet but there's plenty of time; you said they were liable to be busy until lunch.'

Cornwallis nodded and then checked his watch. 'It's after lunch now, so with a bit of luck…'

'What do you want us to do, Mr Cornwallis?' asked

Dewdrop.

'Wait, with us,' replied Cornwallis. 'The hope is that there will be two to follow; the minister and Phimp, so whoever they meet might be in on it too and we'll need to follow them. Although there are five of us, we might end up light-handed.'

'Oh,' replied Felicity. 'Er, Tiffany should be here soon, we banged on her door when we were coming down. She said she would join us, but she wanted to let the commander know what we were all doing.'

'Probably wise,' said Rose. 'Jethro does like to—'

'Hang on,' said Cornwallis, leaning forward. That's the minister coming down the steps.'

'Is it?' asked Rose. 'You mean that short fat shifty looking man with a comb-over and wearing a suit two sizes too small?'

'Yes,' answered Cornwallis.

'Looks a bit like a gnome.'

'Funny you should say that as that's what people call him behind his back. Not a popular man, which is why he got the ministry for dwarfs, according to my father, anyway.'

'I thought your father helped appoint ministers?'

'He does normally, but the Warden seemed particularly keen for Brooksturner to take on this ministry because he hates the man, and he liked the irony of a short man taking the ministry for dwarfs. The aim is to get rid of him when he cocks it all up, which he will. Not fair on the dwarfs and the others, but it's politics.'

'Let's hope we can help get rid of him, then.'

'Oh, here he comes. I'll turn around, I don't think he knows me but let's not take the chance.'

Cornwallis swivelled around and obscured his face as Brooksturner approached the stall. He didn't wait in the queue.

'Make way there, minister on important business.'

The crowd around Sal's looked down on him with contempt, but with him being so short, he never looked up to notice. The crowd were used to ingrates from the Assembly anyway and another one wouldn't make a difference. The barbs and insults just bounced off him as those of that ilk never believed that a citizen would have the temerity to belittle a member of the upper classes.

Sal served him quickly, mainly in order to get rid of him so she could serve her better-behaved customers.

Brooksturner turned with his purchase and sniffed impatiently as someone blocked his way. 'Oh, I say, you there. You are in my way,' he said mustering his imagined authority.

The blockee turned and looked down at the little man. 'Sod off, short arse.'

It took a moment for the comment to penetrate Brooksturner's mind. 'Are you addressing me, sir, perchance?'

'Yeah, what of it?'

'I am a member of the Assembly, Morris Council, Inner Circle. By obstructing me, you are obstructing the law. The penalty, I believe, is death. Let me through or I will summon the guards,' said Brooksturner, trying to look down his nose with disdain and up at the same time — a strange sight, especially has he had hold of a Sal's delight with extra cheese and sauce.

Reluctantly the blockee took a step back which allowed Brooksturner to move forward and someone else to nip ahead in the queue.

'Bugger,' exclaimed the blockee as the gap in front of him disappeared.

Brooksturner took a bite of his lunch and hurried off, oblivious to the looks aimed at his back

'C'mon,' said Frankie. 'He's off.'

Cornwallis spun back around. 'Frankie, he's yours. Take

Cecil and Felicity with you. We'll wait for Phimp.'

'All right; good job I've finished me lunch, don't want indigestion.'

'What about Tiffany?' asked Felicity.

'Don't worry about her, we'll sort that,' replied Rose, urging them off.

Frankie, Dewdrop and Felicity set off and almost immediately were lost from view as the crowd around Sal's surged forwards as a couple of spaces became available.

'Just Phimp, now,' said Cornwallis. 'Hope he makes an appearance soon or Sal will start feeding me again.'

'Oh, look,' said Rose. 'Here's Tiffany and she's got Jethro in tow.'

'The more the merrier,' replied Cornwallis.

The commander and Tiffany came up and MacGillicudy raised a hand to Sal and then slipped behind the stall.

'What's going on?' asked MacGillicudy lowering himself onto the stool just vacated by Frankie.

Cornwallis brought him up to speed as Sal once again dished out free food. Cornwallis and Rose declined the offer, but an old policeman never refuses food, especially when he doesn't have to pay for it and Tiffany was learning too.

'So,' said Cornwallis. 'That's about it. We're waiting for Phimp to show his nose and then we can see where he goes.'

'We could be waiting a while,' said the commander, having demolished his lunch in short order.

'I don't think so, especially now that Brooksturner has left. You staying or going back?'

'Oh, definitely staying. When Tiffany requested that the three of them help you out again I looked at the four walls of my office: like a bloody prison that place is sometimes, and thought that I really needed to get out on the streets. Left Wiggins in charge, he can run the force for a day.'

'I think I just saw a cat over there,' said Tiffany, still only halfway through her bun.

'Probably the one that Cecil and Felicity saw a while ago,' replied Rose, standing up and trying to peer through the crowd. 'Look's a bit like our one, apparently.'

'Was it hanging off the arm of a guard?'

'Er, no.'

'Well, this one is: hanging by its teeth.'

'Where?'

'There,' she pointed with the half-eaten bun. 'At the top of the steps.'

Cornwallis and MacGillicudy looked at each other then stood up too.

'Oh, yes,' said Rose. 'I can see.'

'Me too,' said Cornwallis. 'Looks like ours.'

'The guard has now grabbed Fluffy by the scruff of his neck and is getting his baton out,' observed Tiffany. 'He's going to hit Fluffy,' she added in alarm.

'He is,' agreed Rose.

There was a pause for a few moments.

'Ouch, that's nasty,' said MacGillicudy wincing.

'Painful,' added Cornwallis.

'Unfair to do that, he's defenceless,' said MacGillicudy.

They watched as the cat dropped to the slabs on the ground. It spun a bit and then quickly scampered off, heading in the direction of Sal's Sizzler.

'He should have known better,' said Rose. 'It's his own fault.'

'That's unlike you, Rose,' said Cornwallis. 'You're normally a bit more sympathetic than that.'

'Yes, but he was going to hit Fluffy.'

The guard stood on the top step in shock, his baton held loosely in his hand, the whole front of his shirt, waistcoat and trousers were ripped to shreds by the cat's claws; blood speckling the tatters. He'd made the mistake of holding the cat too close to his body, dangling from the scruff of its neck. Four sets of claws were in easy reach and Fluffy made the most of his opportunity. The guard looked like he'd been through a mincing machine.

Fluffy appeared from under the counter wearing a look of extreme satisfaction on his face. 'No biddy kicks me up the arse,' he said affronted, and if he had fingers, one digit would be thumping into his chest. 'No, siree, no one.'

'What happened?' asked Rose bending down and scooping him up in her arms.

'I's got caught, wiv a lady.'

'A lady?'

'Yeah, loads of 'em in there.'

'You were meant to be working,' interjected Cornwallis, exasperated.

'I were, but...' he sort of shrugged. 'Youse know 'ow it is.'

'No, I don't.'

'Ferrymoans, youse calls it. When a cat's in season they gives 'em off, and I tells youse, this one were really giving it off. Gives me the wink, she do, if youse knows wot I mean.'

'So you stopped working for a—'

'Jack, don't be crude.'

'Yeah, Jack, don't be crude. It were luurve,' explained Fluffy.

'I was going to say, dalliance,' said Cornwallis eventually.

'We definitely dallied,' said Fluffy. 'But it weren't when I was working. I'd stopped and were on me way 'ere. Anyways, there we was, dallying around all nice and private, like, when I gets a boot up me arse and then got grabbed by the neck and pulled off. It fair put me off it did, I can tells youse. How would youse like it being pulled off halfway through, eh?'

'Umm,' said Cornwallis.

'He wouldn't,' replied Rose quickly jumping in.

MacGillicudy and Tiffany exchanged a look and then both looked at Rose, a half-smile on their faces.

Rose coughed and then changed the subject. 'Why were you coming here, then?' she asked.

"Cause youse told me too if I found anyfing out.'

'And?' encouraged Cornwallis.

'I did,' said Fluffy triumphantly.

'You're doing it again,' said Cornwallis.

'What?'

'Winding me up. C'mon.'

'Okay, okay, keep youse hair on. Well, I keeps an eye on the man like youse asks. Phimp, youse says. First 'e didn't do nuffing, jest walked around wiv bits o' paper telling other people to do stuff. Then a short fat man came an' told this Phimp to do stuff and then 'e said they'll discuss the other matter later. Phimp called him sir.'

'The minister, Brooksturner,' said Cornwallis. 'Go on.'

'Anyways, 'bout an 'our ago this Phimp goes to the other fella's room but theys shuts the door before I can get in. I listens but it's a bit muffled. I 'eard a bit about dwarfs and The Pipe thing an' a bit about a solution. Then the short-arse says that Phimp 'as to go and meet someone but I couldn't 'ear where. Then Phimp asks what short-arse were doing and short-arse says he's got a meeting too, wiv someone else, summat about a guild.'

'Which guild?' asked Cornwallis eagerly. 'What solution?'

'Dunno to both questions, 'e didn't say.'

'Bugger.'

'So I fought you'd want to know, so 'ere I is.'

'Somewhat delayed though.'

'I'm a cat; youse takes it when youse can. Anyways, we don'ts take long, not like youse lot.'

'I can assure you, Fluffy, humans can be pretty quick too,' said Tiffany sadly.

This time a long pause ensued while Rose, Cornwallis and MacGillicudy wrestled with the information.

'Right, well,' said Cornwallis, breaking the silence. 'At least we know Brooksturner is going to see one of the guilds, so Frankie, Dewdrop and Felicity should find out which one. We should then be another step closer and all we want now is for… Oh, look, and here he comes. With a bit of luck, we'll get to see who Phimp is going to meet.'

CHAPTER 28

Brooksturner scuttled off down The Trand away from the Assembly, chewing the last of his lunch. He threw the used napkin carelessly onto the street, knowing that some poor unfortunate on a dollar a day would be along shortly to clear up his mess. He considered littering to be his civic duty, creating work for those needy people at the bottom of the social pile.

Frankie, Dewdrop and Felicity followed discreetly at a distance; they had spread out, all three seemingly to be walking on their own, but each keeping everyone in view. They kept to Brooksturner's pace, wary in case he turned around and spotted them.

They needn't have bothered.

The minister walked along oblivious to the goings-on behind him. As he passed one of the dwarf entrances, he took a moment to pause and a knowing smirk tickled his lips, which, Frankie, walking nearest to him, noticed and wondered what the minister knew that they didn't.

Once beyond the entrance, he took a left turn up a side street and then turned right at the top. There were fewer pedestrians here so the three following became more cautious, increasing the distance from the target.

Frankie stopped and waited for Dewdrop and Felicity to catch up.

'You're a couple, now,' he said staring into a shop front of kitchenware. 'Get closer and I'll tag along behind.'

Dewdrop and Felicity linked arms and carried on, increasing their pace slightly to catch up with the minister.

Brooksturner paused at a row of shops before quickly opening a door and stepping inside.

'What's that he's gone into?' asked Felicity, frowning.

'I don't know,' replied Dewdrop. 'Let's find out.'

They walked forward a bit and looked up to read the sign of a shop selling balls of wool and knitting accessories.

'Uh? What's he interested in that for?' asked Dewdrop.

'Hang on, he's coming out again.'

Brooksturner exited the shop and rubbed his hands with glee before moving off and into the next shop in the line: this one being a small grocery.

The two feelers were standing by the first shop and turned to stare into the empty window: no merchandise, no goods for sale and a dark dispirited interior of nothing.

Frankie quickly approached them. 'Go and buy a ball of wool, find out what he wanted in there.'

'What?' asked Felicity.

'Ask some questions, friendly-like.'

'Okay,' she replied, a bit uncertain.

Dewdrop and Felicity entered the wool shop and saw the man behind the counter with his head in his hands; he peered at them through the digits of his fingers and tried to compose himself.

'Can I help you, miss?'

'Er, I'd like a ball of wool, please.'

'You've come to the right place, then. It would help if you could expand a bit on that, as it will give me a clue as to what you want.'

'Oh, right, sorry. It's for my cat.'

The man nodded and reached beneath the counter. 'Will this

one do? Popular amongst the cat fraternity, is this.'

'Is that what the other man got?' asked Dewdrop, warming to the task. 'I mean the one that just left.'

The shop owner's eyes narrowed and his mouth twitched. 'Gods, don't mention him. That was my landlord.'

'Landlord? You don't seem happy with him.'

'Would you be happy if he wants to double the rent?'

'Er, no. That doesn't sound fair.'

'It's not. He owns this whole row and wants us all out, so he can redevelop it. That one there,' he threw his thumb in the direction of the empty shop, 'has already left.'

'But you're going to stay?'

'Been here fifteen years: it's my life. I'll stay as long as I can, but… you know?' and he shrugged helplessly.

Felicity and Dewdrop nodded in understanding.

'Bit of a bastard, then?' said Dewdrop.

'Not a bit of one, a total one.'

Felicity put on a sympathetic look; she didn't have to try very hard. 'Just my wool then, please. I'm sorry for you. Let's hope he has an accident or something.'

'I can assure you, I keep hoping.'

They left the shop and looked around for Frankie who seemed to have vanished off the face of the twearth. Brooksturner emerged from the last shop in the row and headed purposefully off in the general direction of away.

Dewdrop and Felicity were in a bit of a quandary; follow Brooksturner or look for Frankie?

They followed Brooksturner.

Felicity left Dewdrop and crossed the road. A couple of carts trundled by and a few pedestrians managed to give enough cover for both of them to blend into the background. Up ahead, the minister continued on his way, moving quite smartly for a short fat man, his waddling gate propelling him along at a pretty decent rate.

Felicity had just passed a doorknob emporium when she sensed a shadow behind her, a big looming shadow.

'It's only me,' assured Frankie, stepping up and alongside her.

Felicity breathed a sigh of relief.

'What's he up to?'

'He wants the whole row out so he can redevelop it,' she answered. 'He owns it.'

'Ah, typical of that kind: always wants more, never happy with what they've got; rich bastards always want to be richer.'

'Oh, er… but Mr Cornwallis is rich, though?'

'He is, but he doesn't really care if he's rich or not. No, tell a lie, he likes being rich but it's not exactly what he is, if you get my drift. He's the exception.'

'Ah,'

'Not like that bastard over there: now, I wonder where he's going to take us next?'

The answer to that question came just two streets further on when he went into another shop: this one an agent for travellers to distant lands.

'What's he gone in there for?' asked Felicity as Frankie stood next to her.

Across the road, Dewdrop looked at the agents and shrugged, just as flummoxed as they were.

'Another place he owns?' suggested Frankie, scratching his head. 'Wants to go on holiday somewhere?'

'No, I don't think so,' replied Felicity, who had better eyesight than Frankie did. They were on the opposite side of the road to the shop and looking from a distance. 'There's a guild plaque by the door and didn't you and Mr Cornwallis say that you thought a guild was involved?'

'Yes, we did say that,' answered Frankie, furrowing his brow and trying to focus on the blurred outline of the plaque.

'What do we do now?' she asked.

'Let's go and see which guild it is.'

They took their lives in their hands crossing the busy street, full of people and traffic going about their business and Dewdrop waited patiently as Frankie and Felicity dodged a couple of carts and came over to join him.

'You two don't fancy a trip to faraway lands, do you?' asked Frankie.

Felicity and Dewdrop raised their eyebrows.

'You paying?' asked Dewdrop hopefully.

Frankie's eyes narrowed. 'Bollocks to that,' he answered forcefully. 'Look, you don't have to book, just make an enquiry.'

'But we don't look like we could afford something like that.'

'You don't need to; people do it all the time. Anyway, just say you've got an inheritance coming. Some rich eccentric granny has snuffed it and left you a shed-load of cash.'

'Okay,' said Felicity hesitantly. 'But where do we want to go?'

'Oh, I dunno. What about seeing the apes in their natural habitat, or go see the dragons out east, or go and see that land out west, which is a bit wild and where they think they can speak inglionish? You know, the city they call the Big Banana or something. Some explorer found it years ago when he took a wrong turn trying to find the dragon route. What do they call it?'

'Merca,' replied Felicity. 'Unified States of Merca.'

'Yeah, that one. I 'ear lots of people want to go there for some reason.'

'They call it the land of the free.'

'Well, there you are; shouldn't cost you a penny, then.'

'No, not that type of fr...' she limped to a stop, not sure if Frankie intended the joke or not. 'Er... We'll check the prices for Merca, then. Come on, Cecil.'

'Uh?' replied Dewdrop who had lost concentration.

'We're going to pretend to go to Merca. You're paying.'

'Great; better do a bit more overtime, then.'

'Yeah, you do that Dewdrop, and while you're in there, see if you can hear what Brooksturner is up to.'

'And what will you be doing?'

'I will be looking at the plaque and waiting for you to come out.'

Frankie grinned as Dewdrop and Felicity once again linked arms and aimed for the agent's shop. He watched them glance at the plaque as they went past and hesitate, briefly, before stepping forward and pushing open the door. At least Felicity looked like someone who might have a bit of money and could afford to take a trip across the sea, he thought, as he watched them go inside.

He sidled up to the plaque and leant forward, peering at the inscription. What the buggery have *they* got against The Pipe, he thought, as he read the name of the guild.

CHAPTER 29

Phimp didn't look a happy bunny. He even ignored Sal's Sizzler, not giving it even a glance, as he pounded down the steps of the Assembly and hit the pavement. He stood there a moment taking big deep breaths as he blocked the path of the crowds of people who were eager to look at Gornstock's seat of power. Eventually, he got the message, being the recipient of a few nudges and a fair bit of jostling, that he was in the way and stalked off with a frown of discontent painted on his face.

Cornwallis elbowed MacGillicudy as Rose and Tiffany stood up. 'You with Tiffany, me with Rose,' he said, indicating Phimp with a jerk of his head. 'Fluffy will do what he wants.'

'There's gratitude for youse,' growled the cat from ground level. 'Put's me life on the line and what fanks do I gets? "Do what youse wants," I asks youse.' If he could have, he would have thrown his paws into the air.

'You come with us,' said Rose. 'I appreciate what you do for us, even if misery-guts here doesn't.'

'What?' said Cornwallis. 'I'm not miserable and I do appreciate what Fluffy does for us. You're maligning an innocent man. I'm just being dynamic, making a decision and while we stand around yacking like this, Phimp will be gone and out of sight.'

He had a point as Phimp had already walked a good few yards down the road, increasing his pace as he stomped along in determined fashion.

'Quick, let's go,' ordered Cornwallis.

They hurried after, splitting into the designated pairs with Fluffy trailing after Rose and Cornwallis. They needed to get closer to Phimp as the bustle along The Trand kept obscuring their view. People were everywhere and the carts, cabs and coaches jammed the road: everyone wanted to get to somewhere and it seemed that everyone wanted to get to the somewhere, now. It was gridlocked and a poor unfortunate feeler would have to come along and sort out the mess. Tiffany and the commander, both thankful they weren't in uniform, tried not to look at the chaos.

Cornwallis and Rose quickly gave up trying to follow on the opposite side of the road; they found a gap between two carts and slid between, finding themselves a few yards back from Tiffany and the commander. Fluffy, tail in the air, followed on behind.

Phimp turned off The Trand and travelled down a slightly less busy street, but here he started being accosted by street vendors selling all sorts of Gornstock tat to unsuspecting tourists from out of town: there were flags; little models of the Assembly; hats with the legend "I love Gornstock" written on; boxes of matches with a picture of a Gornstock cab on the top; toy batons and jingly bells; any amount of Morris paraphernalia; little toys for little hands; shirts with clever and witty sayings on the front; all of it guaranteed to fall apart within five minutes of use. It was proper Gornstockian enterprise and Phimp sailed through it all with an expression of disdain on his face.

Rose watched from behind as Tiffany and MacGillicudy tried to blend in; it seemed to her that the commander walked a little bit more proudly with his chest puffed out and his head held high as they tried to appear as if they belonged together. Tiffany seemed to be playing along, possibly even instigating the illusion as she and the commander negotiated the crowds of people.

'Jethro seems to be enjoying himself,' observed Rose. 'Look at him.'

'Uh?' said Cornwallis, the statement catching him off balance.

'Well, he is. It's not everyday he walks down the road with a pretty girl on his arm.'

'Jethro hardly knows what one looks like,' said Cornwallis. 'The Yard takes up all of his time.'

'Yes, but he's still a man, and he's not exactly old, is he?'

'Middle forties, I think, but he eats, drinks and sleeps the service; he's got "feeler" stamped on his soul. Anyway, we've been through this before; he's had plenty of opportunity, but, as he says, he's got other things to worry about.'

'I know, it's just seeing him, albeit on a job, with a girl. It doesn't seem fair.'

Cornwallis sighed. 'It's his choice, Rose. I hope you're not thinking of trying to pair him up with someone, Frankie has introduced him to no end of women.'

Rose snorted. 'Yes, and we know the type he's been introducing.'

Cornwallis grinned wryly. 'That's true, however, you've already got Big George in your sights, trying to look for a lady bear; Jethro would be a tougher assignment than that.'

'Maybe,' conceded Rose, whimsically.

'Rose,' warned Cornwallis. 'He won't thank you for it.' He paused a moment. 'Who do you have in mind?' he asked, feigning indifference.

She giggled. 'There's one or two rattling around inside my head; I'll think some more on it.'

'It's going to have to be someone normal. He's a bit rough

around the edges though, so no one who likes dainty little tea-parties, etc.'

'You mean like your class of people: Ladies who lunch or ladies of leisure; ladies with a title or ladies who aspire to a title? No, Jethro has got his standards; he prefers the common type, like me.'

'Exactly, but maybe someone not quite as common as you, I mean, we don't want to go *that* low,' he replied with a wink. 'We want someone who actually apologises when they fart.'

'Wha...? I don't fart,' she replied indignantly.

'You do.'

'No, I don't.'

'Rose, sometimes you put Frankie to shame.'

'Bloody cheek. I'll have you know I was brought up properly.'

'That doesn't mean you don't fart, you just blame it on someone else. Anyway, I've seen you wafting.'

'Wafting?'

'Yep.'

'Oh.'

'One point to me, I think,' said Cornwallis triumphantly.

Rose pondered for a moment. 'All right, I'll give you the point, but I can get it back.'

'Er, how?'

'What's the brush in the privy for?'

'To give the bowl a clean.'

'Exactly. At least you know what it's for; now you just need instruction on how to use it. One point to me, I think. Now we're even.'

Cornwallis opened his mouth to deny the accusation and then realised that he had no grounds for denial. 'I forget sometimes, okay? Used to have a long-drop until not long ago;

didn't need a brush with one of them, and anyway, that's what the staf…'

'No excuses, Jack. What's more, you were about to say, "That's what the staff are for", weren't you?'

He hesitated.

'I rest my case,' said Rose, thinking that she had gained at least two points. 'One point for not using the brush and one point for considering me as staff; you're one point down and if you try to think of something else then—'

'Hang on,' interrupted Cornwallis, relieved to find an excuse not to delve into some of his other habits. 'Where's Phimp going now?'

Rose frowned. 'It looks like he's heading for the river.'

'I wonder what he wants down there?'

'Hopefully, we'll find out, but those streets and alleys are like a maze, we might lose him.'

'No, we won't. Fluffy?'

They could hear the cat sigh from behind them. 'Wot?'

'Run ahead, will you. Keep an eye on the man Phimp, just in case we can't keep up.'

'Wot, again? Keeps doing your bloody job, I do.'

'Assisting, Fluffy, assisting.'

'Assisting, my arse.'

'I'll assist your arse in a minute, with my boot.'

'Jack, be nice to him. He's helping.'

Cornwallis sighed. 'Fish,' he said. 'Two crates.'

'Deal,' replied Fluffy immediately and then quickly scampered off with a big satisfied grin on his face.

Cornwallis shook his head slowly in resignation whilst, beside him, Rose grinned.

'He can twist you around his little claw,' she said. 'Knows just which button to press.'

222

'Yes, and he's got you to help.'

'Really, Jack, he's just a cat.'

'Is that what he is? I wouldn't have known unless you told me.'

Rose pouted and blew him a kiss.

Ahead of them, Phimp had just turned into a narrow cobbled street, the wood-framed buildings dark with muck and damp from the river mists which seemed to hang around in a permanent shroud; MacGillicudy and Tiffany hesitated to follow. There were no carts and very few pedestrians so they would stand out like a sore thumb. Fluffy skittled past them and ran after Phimp with barely a glance at them.

'I grant you,' said MacGillicudy. 'A cat does come in handy sometimes.'

'What do we do, Commander?' asked Tiffany.

'Wait a bit; let him go a bit further.' He turned his head as Rose and Cornwallis joined them. 'Unless you've got a better idea, Jack?'

'I think we should all go together now. Four of us: two men and two girls should look less suspicious than just one or two — a little group heading for the river for a walk on the docks.'

'Good idea, you can buy the ice-creams.'

'This weather, more like a hot toddy.'

'That'll do, but you're buying.'

'Let's see what Phimp's up to first.'

The four headed down the street, walking slowly as if they hadn't a care in the world. The rough cobbles turned slimy, where carts, hauled up from the river, had spilt their loads of perishable goods, coating the street with a gooey mess.

Between the four detectives and Phimp, Fluffy padded along softly, eyeing out tantalising and interesting things stored in the sordid alleyways: future investigation foremost in his mind.

Oblivious to the goings-on behind him, Phimp never looked back, not even suspecting that four detectives closely followed him — confident or reckless? The depressing thought passed through Cornwallis' mind that perhaps Phimp's intents were all legal and above board and the chase they had embarked upon would lead them to a dead-end. It could be possible that they were wasting their time.

'He's turning right,' observed Tiffany, keeping her eye on Phimp.

Cornwallis acknowledged with a nod.

'And so's the cat,' added MacGillicudy.

Another nod.

'There's too much happening on this side of the river,' said Rose. 'All those ships tied up at all these wharves. The likelihood is we'll lose him in the crush.'

'We might, but I don't think the cat will.'

They quickened their pace and came to the end of the alley then poked their heads around the corner looking at the direction that Phimp went. A track led behind the warehouses and although Phimp had gone out of sight, they could still see the cat. Fluffy looked over and made sure that the detectives were following and then carried on with the pursuit.

Cornwallis and the others rushed forward and were quickly behind the warehouses. Moving forward they paused at the end of one and looked towards the river. Fluffy sat at the end, waiting for them.

'Where is he?' asked Cornwallis as they approached the cat.

Fluffy twitched his head. 'Over there; he's standing and looking down into the wet.'

Cornwallis looked to where the cat indicated and could see the back of Phimp standing on the edge of a wharf. He seemed to wait for a few moments and then stepped forward and gradually his head disappeared.

'Steps,' said MacGillicudy. 'He's going down some steps.'

'Thank the gods for that,' said Cornwallis. 'I thought my eyes were playing up for a moment. C'mon, let's see what he's up to.'

The four and the cat moved forward and spread out, dodging the carters and dockers working along the quay and the wharf. They went and stood at the edge, looking down as surreptitiously as they could. They saw Phimp sitting in a wherry, back straight and staring ahead, over the head of the wherryman as the boat moved out onto the river.

Cornwallis moved close to MacGillicudy. 'We can't follow him now,' said the commander.

'We can,' answered Cornwallis. 'There's a water-cab there,' and he pointed at a small boat bobbing against the side.

'Hang on a minute,' said the commander. 'I think Phimp is aiming for that ship over there. The one anchored with those funny looking bits on the side, opposite your warehouse.'

'So he is,' answered Cornwallis, looking keenly at the ship in question. 'I wonder what those bits are for?'

CHAPTER 30

Tiffany felt a little out of place as she took another sip of her glass of best bitter. She was adept at feeling at home in most social situations, from the boisterous atmosphere of the feelers local, The Truncheon, to afternoon tea with the ladies of Gornstock's aristocratic social elite. She could turn from Lady Tiffany Trumpington-Smyth to just plain Tiff in the blink of an eye, discoursing on a whole range of subjects from "Who got it in the nadgers?" to "Where did you buy those delightful curtains?" She never got lost for words. However, sitting in the Stoat that evening, the protocol confused her: is it work or is it a social occasion? In other words, who did she have to be?

The problem rattled around inside her head as she listened to her commander and her sergeant discussing Cornwallis' latest idea.

'Just need to use the facilities,' announced MacGillicudy, pushing his chair back. 'I'll order some refills on the way.'

Rose turned to Tiffany as the commander battered his way through the throng to the privy at the back of the pub. 'You're quiet, is there something on your mind?' she asked, a hint of concern in her voice.

'Um, er,' replied Tiffany hesitantly. 'To be honest, I'm not sure I should be here.'

'Rubbish,' answered Rose. 'Er… unless you don't want to be here?'

'That's not the problem, no, but I'm here as a feeler, with

my commander and sergeant. I'm not here with Rose and Jethro, am I?'

'Oh, I see what you mean: rank or perception of rank. We've put you in an awkward position.'

'A little bit of one,' she admitted.

'If it helps, I'm only Sergeant Morant when I put on the uniform; it's more an honorary rank anyway. At all other times, I'm just Rose, a poor country girl who got lucky.'

'So at the moment, you're Rose?'

'Yes, look, you respect the uniform, whoever's in it at the time; when they're not in uniform you can respect the person, or not, as the case may be. You're here to help us, but not as a feeler, but as Tiffany who happens to be a feeler. As far as I'm concerned, you're just a friend who's helping. In truth, it should be me feeling awkward, as socially, you far outrank me. You're Lady Tiffany; I'm just plain Rose Morant from the sticks.'

'I'm only that when I go home,' replied Tiffany. 'I left all that when I joined the force.'

'Like Jack; does he swan around as Lord Jocelyn Cornwallis III?'

'No, no, he doesn't.'

'In actual fact, if the question arises he says he's just an Honourable. He hates titles, he even prefers just plain mister.'

Tiffany sighed. 'I know what he means. I used to be a stuck-up snotty little cow who used the title like a sledgehammer to get what I wanted. Now I've learnt that it's people who matter. When I meet up with my old friends, I see how vacuous their lives really are. I don't want to be part of that anymore. Mr Cornwallis, Jack, showed that I could do it. I never met him, but all my type knew of him, how he elbowed privilege away.'

'Really? He'd be pleased to hear that, however, he hasn't given it all up; he's still stinking rich.'

'So am I, but only a whiff, not a stink.'

They shared a look and then a laugh just as MacGillicudy returned.

'Beer will be over shortly, they're a bit busy there. You taking advantage of my absence in order to take the piss?'

'As if we would, Jethro,' said Rose sincerely. 'We were just talking about social rank.'

'Ah, I haven't got any. Plain old farming stock I am; by rights, I should have my arm stuck up a cow's arse; mind, there ain't much difference being Commander of Police: I'm still up to my neck in cack most of the time.'

'You like that part of the job; you say it keeps you on your toes. But what we were on about is this: who are you now, sitting there?'

MacGillicudy looked a little confused so Rose expanded.

'Are you Commander MacGillicudy, Mr MacGillicudy or just plain Jethro?'

'Oh, I see, one of them games; depends who I'm with.'

'You're with us.'

'I know. I'm just getting to that bit; I'm all three.'

'What?' exclaimed Rose, surprised.

'Yes, I have to be, whether I like it or not. I think I know why you're asking the question.' He looked at Tiffany as he spoke. 'I want to be Jethro, but Felicity and Dewdrop will be here soon: what will happen if Constable Toopins calls me Jethro? What if he goes back to the Yard and lets slip that he sat in a pub with me and can now call me by my first name? I'll tell you what; his life wouldn't be worth living, that's what. Everybody in that place will make his life a misery. What I want, doesn't come into it, it's what's expected. I can't be seen to have favourites.'

'But I just told Tiffany that it's the uniform that matters, not the person.'

'Yes, that's true, but I have to wear the uniform all the time now, even when I'm not wearing it. It goes with the job. If I still had my sergeant's stripes, then things would be different.'

'He's right,' agreed Tiffany, butting in. 'Commander MacGillicudy has to represent the police force all of the time.'

'Yes, well,' said Rose indignantly. 'Anyway, you call me Rose, despite what he says.'

'Unless you're in uniform,' added the commander.

'All right, Jethro.'

MacGillicudy grinned and looked back at Tiffany. 'M'lady,' he said as he doffed an imaginary cap.

'Commander,' replied Tiffany, with a regal inclination of her head.

Rose looked from one to the other. 'Now who's taking the piss?'

The door flew open and in walked Frankie with Dewdrop and Felicity in tow.

'Three pints, Eddie,' he bellowed at the heaving bar.

Eddie raised a hand in acknowledgement.

'You don't do beer,' said Dewdrop quietly to Felicity.

'No, but don't you dare tell him.'

Frankie sat himself down and grinned at the three already there. 'You not drinking?'

'We're waiting,' replied Rose. 'Jethro ordered them a couple of minutes ago.'

'Oh, right. Jack not here?'

Rose shook her head. 'No, but he'll be back soon, he's got a little task to do.'

Felicity and Dewdrop squeezed in with a scraping of chairs.

'What task?' asked Frankie, bouncing up and down, eager for his pint.

'To find whoever it was who Phimp met.'

'Er, is that a proper sentence?'

'It is now. Phimp met someone and Jack had to wait for darkness so he can put Fluffy on board.'

'On board? On board what?' asked Frankie bemused.

'The ship.'

'What ship?'

'The ship on the river. Phimp went to this ship, but obviously, we couldn't. So, we decided that Fluffy might like to be a ships' cat for a night.'

'Oh, right, I'm with you now. A ship, you say?'

'Yes.'

'Oh, that's strange.'

'Why?'

'Well, Brooksturner went and visited a place… What was it again, Dewdrop?'

'An agent for travellers,' replied Dewdrop. 'They sell holidays across the sea.'

'Yeah, one of them. Anyway, there were a guild office above it, and… C'mon, guess which guild.'

Rose shook her head. 'I don't know, but knowing you and the way you're setting it up, it could be anything.'

No, fairly obvious,' said Frankie, grinning. 'Go on, guess.'

Rose sighed. 'Fish merchants?'

'Oh, come on, try a bit harder. Why do you say fish merchants?'

'You mentioned an agent for overseas travel. Fish live in the sea, so…'

'Nope. Go on, try again.'

'Can't be the coach drivers,' said MacGillicudy. 'The clue being travel, they've got their offices in Peabody Street, over a pawnbroker's.'

'Eh?' said Frankie. 'If you know where it is, why did you say it?'

'Just playing along: coach drivers, travel, you know.'

Frankie shook his head. 'Right, I'll make it easier for you; how do you travel across the sea?'

'Boats,' answered Rose.

'Nearly,' said Frankie. 'Ships. It were the Guild of Ship Masters.'

'Ship Masters?'

'Yeah, said it were strange that you mentioned a ship. Ah, about bloody time,' he said as a barmaid appeared with a tray of six pints. 'Thank you, my darling,' he said as he swiped one off the tray.

'Give her a chance,' said MacGillicudy as the pints wobbled.

Frankie grinned. 'As it's a bit busy, my darling, could you get us another round, save us dying of thirst. Better get one in for when Jack gets back, and another one in case Isabella pops down and I'm a bit peckish so could you get us a bowl of nibbles too. Better make that two bowls, just to keep us going for a while. Is cheffy still here, because I wouldn't mind something a bit more substantial?'

'Sorry, Frankie,' said the barmaid. 'Chef buggered off as someone asked for a steak, well-done. He hit the roof and stormed out. He'll probably be back tomorrow, though.'

'That's annoying, I fancied a kebab; now I'll have to go and queue up out there with the rest of the drunkards.'

'So what happened?' asked Rose.

'Chef walked out, didn't you hear?'

'No, not that. I mean the Ship Masters Guild.'

'Oh, that? Nothing.'

Felicity cast a withering glance at Frankie. 'Except that Brooksturner went into that shop specifically. He went upstairs to meet someone from the guild and then went back to the Assembly. We couldn't get access to the door at the back of the shop as the agent wouldn't leave us alone.'

'No, he were too busy trying to sell us a trip to Merca,' added Dewdrop. 'We must have been convincing because he kept shoving all these woodcuts of the place at us, saying we had to visit this place and that. Did you know they got this big statue stuck on an island in the port? Got its arm up, holding a big ice-cream cone; dunno why, it seems a strange thing to hold up, it'd melt in the sun, would an ice-cream cone.'

'The agent said it represents freedom,' added Felicity, with a sharp look at Dewdrop.

'Yeah, he did; but what's it got to do with a banana?'

'Banana?' asked MacGillicudy.

'That's what they call the city. The Big Banana. It looked more like an ice-cream cone to me.'

'No, they don't,' said Felicity. 'And it was a torch, Cecil. The Big Banana is a nickname for the city which is really called New Tork.'

'Then why do they call it the Big Banana?' asked MacGillicudy.

'No one really knows,' answered Felicity. 'The agent said it had something to do with horse racing: could have been the shape of the track or a prize. Anyway, the name stuck, so now everyone calls it the Big Banana.'

'Bloody expensive to get there,' said Dewdrop. Weeks on a ship, apparently.'

'Wouldn't fancy that,' said MacGillicudy. 'Stuck on a ship with nothing to do but wait for the bloody thing to sink.'

'I think it could be quite exciting,' ventured Rose. 'A new land to see and experience.'

'That's all right for you,' replied MacGillicudy. 'You can

afford it.'

'I can't, but Jack could.'

'Frankie did,' said Dewdrop.

'Sorry?' exclaimed Frankie, his head whipping around. 'What did you say?'

'You told us to behave as if we were buying a trip, so we did. Bought two tickets in your name.'

'You did what?' exploded Frankie, eyes out on stalks.

'Yep, three thousand dollars, but you need to pay the deposit for us.'

'You little bastard. You'd better start praying now, 'cause you're about to meet your gods,' said Frankie, standing up with a face turning crimson.

'He's joking,' interjected Felicity with her palms up in supplication. 'We didn't really.'

'You didn't?'

'No.'

Frankie eyed Dewdrop menacingly. 'That ain't gonna stop me knocking seven shades o' shit outa you, Cecil bloody Toopins.'

'Sit down, Frankie,' said Rose laughing along with everyone else. 'He's having a bit of fun.'

'Fun? That's not what I call fun.'

'Oh, I don't know,' said MacGillicudy. 'You should have seen the look on your face.'

Frankie shot him a venomous look.

'Puce, nice colour,' observed Rose.

'All right, all right, I'll take the joke,' said Frankie in the end. 'But that doesn't mean I can't get my own back at some point. You have been warned, Toopins,' he added, pointing a wagging finger. 'This is war.'

Dewdrop just grinned at his success in winding up Frankie,

it had been a long time coming and the promised retribution would happen in the future, so he'd worry about that another time.

Cornwallis appeared as if from nowhere, stood behind Rose then rested his hands on her shoulders before bending down and planting a kiss on top of her head.

'I hope that's who I think it is,' she said, tilting her head back.

'No, it's his younger, better-looking brother,' said Cornwallis. 'Nice to see everyone here.'

'What've you been up to, Jack?' asked Frankie. 'I asked earlier but Rose decided to be oblique; just said you had a task and something about Fluffy and a ship.'

'Exactly, now is there a pint for me?'

'Coming,' replied Frankie.

'Oh good: us seafarers need our tot.'

'Seafaring?'

'Sort of: Fluffy is now a ships' cat. Took him over in a boat and chucked him on board: we'll pick him up in the morning; unless he decides to stay.'

'Ah, right.'

'I told you all this,' said Rose, looking pointedly at Frankie.

'No, you didn't. You didn't say we had to pick him up in the morning,' replied Frankie grinning. Anyway,' he added turning back to Cornwallis. 'Brooksturner went and saw the Guild of Ship Masters. Reckon the two are connected?'

Cornwallis hardly hesitated. 'They've got to be. I have a feeling we're getting close to things now.'

CHAPTER 31

Cornwallis settled himself on the back thwart and held on to the rope with a half-smile on his lips, watching Frankie as he stepped into the wherry. Last night's escapade flailing around with a couple of sticks showed he has severe limitations with regards to rowing and once or twice it had been a close call as he nearly pitched the whole thing over, cat and all, into the deep, dark and very unpleasant waters of the Sterkle. He had no intention of repeating the performance, especially in front of his friend.

Frankie just slowly shook his head as he sat down and fitted the oars onto the thole pins, indicating with a nod for Cornwallis to cast off.

Within the first few moments, Cornwallis realised that Frankie knew what he was doing; where he had acquired the skill did not concern him at the moment, suffice to say that he had no intention of owning up to his own lack of skill.

The ship that they were aiming for loomed up in the darkness, the ship's lights guiding them in. It was well before dawn, and thankfully, their advance shielded by the impenetrable gloom.

Cornwallis had rented the wherry from the owner last night, no questions asked, leaving the man with the distinct impression that they were up to something decidedly illegal. He'd chuckled as he counted the coins, a week's pay for no work and no risk, which, he felt, was a good return.

As they got nearer the ship, Frankie shortened his strokes, controlling the approach. Cornwallis guided him from his position at the back of the boat, speaking quietly or indicating left or right by pointing with his hand.

The cat and Cornwallis had agreed the pick-up point to be the stern of the ship, or as Cornwallis liked to think, the flat end. Frankie manoeuvred the boat and then backed oars against the flow of the river to hold position.

They looked up and found no sign of the cat.

All was silent on board the ship apart from the creaks and groans and the occasional slap of a rope against a mast as the wind blew. There were no lookouts, no patrols, just a sleeping ship in harbour.

Cornwallis pointed to the anchor and Frankie nodded then guided the boat over to where they could grab hold of the cable to stay put.

They waited and then waited some more and still the cat hadn't shown.

Slowly, almost imperceptibly, the dark of night began to roll back; dawn was coming and the ship began to emerge from out of the shadows. A silvery light eased into the night's sky heralding the coming of a new day.

Cornwallis caught a movement high up by the stern rail, it appeared to be a blob against the lightening sky, but it moved and then it launched itself into the air towards them. Then they heard a splash, a small one, close by, but then nothing as the river closed over whatever had made the splash.

Frankie and Cornwallis exchanged looks and then looked at where they thought the splash had occurred, but wavelets washed over the spot hiding any evidence of ripples.

'Was that him, then?' asked Cornwallis quietly.

'Dunno,' replied Frankie. 'Can't see a bloody thing.'

'I'm sure it was, can't think what else it could be. Look harder.'

They both leant further forward, peering into the watery miasma, intently staring at the spot a few feet from the boat. Suddenly something shot out of the water like an eruption, sending spray flying into the air. They saw a brief moment of two flailing paws and two frightened eyes before the apparition disappeared again beneath the surface, this time just in reach of the boat.

Frankie plunged an arm in and leant even further forward, half-in and half-out of the boat, rocking it alarmingly. Cornwallis had to grab his legs and lean back to counter the imbalance, just before he toppled over into the murky depths of the river.

'Got the bastard,' said Frankie as he hauled his arm out, his other arm bracing against the gunwale.

Fluffy emerged arse first as Frankie grabbed hold of the first thing he found: his tail. The sodden fur-ball, dripping wet and filled with malice, spat copious quantities of the Sterkle back into the river.

'Bollocks, bugger, shit,' hissed Fluffy as Frankie swung him unceremoniously over the gunwale and lowered him into the bottom of the boat. 'Buggering bastard,' he continued as he spat the remnants out. 'That don't taste nice.'

'Let's go,' ordered Cornwallis.

Frankie caught the oars and began to pull as quickly as he could.

'Shush,' said Cornwallis as Fluffy continued to rant. 'They might hear us.'

'Bollocks to them,' said Fluffy as he sat in the bottom of the boat like a washed-up ginger rag. 'Wot 'bout me?'

'Soon, just keep yer gob shut,' said Frankie. 'You're alive, ain't yer?'

'Only sodding just,' came the angry response.

Frankie continued to row, pulling hard for the shore as the obscene muttering carried on with barely a pause.

A few minutes later, the boat glided up to the jetty and Cornwallis jumped out and tied the mooring rope to the pole, leaving the boat parked up as if it had never been away. Frankie picked up the half-drowned cat and stepped out.

'Well, that went well,' observed Frankie, holding Fluffy at arm's length.

'Well?' exclaimed Fluffy. 'Youse wants to see it from *my* end!'

'You missed the boat, that's hardly our fault.'

'Youse should've been closer.'

'You want me to wring you out?' asked Frankie, the question holding just the right amount of threat. 'Just say the word.'

'Steady, you pair,' said Cornwallis with a wry grin on his face. 'It's all finished now, so no harm done.'

'No harm?' ranted Fluffy. 'Youse seen my fur? Youse know wot a dunk in the river can do to sommat like this? Try it sometime, buster, and see if youse likes it.'

'All right, all right. I'll pay you double,' said Cornwallis, holding up his hand. 'Just after we find somewhere to give you a wash.'

'A wash? I've jest had one.'

'Er... A clean one. You stink worse than an overflowing privy.'

'Yuk, you're right, Jack. I think that's a turd hanging off his ear.'

'A turd?' yelled Fluffy. 'A bloody turd?'

'Frankie, I don't think you should have told him that.'

They soon found a horse trough and Frankie cleaned up his sodden arm, then Fluffy received his second dunking of the morning. Thankfully, this time, he came up cleaner and smelling decidedly fresher; however, the horse trough suffered terribly as a result.

As the silvery dawn light flooded the sky, the two detectives and the cat headed for the nearest eatery, a rough-looking place but one that had a high reputation amongst the fraternity of dockers and the occasional hungry feeler. Already workers were arriving to begin their labour for the day and many were intent to load up with food before starting their shift.

Big Bobs Diner hadn't quite got into full swing as Frankie pushed open the door and traipsed in. There were a couple of empty tables but within a few seconds, there was only one left as Cornwallis and Frankie nabbed the nearest. A couple of seconds after that, there were no tables left, leaving a group of workers incandescent with rage as they had first stopped to talk to another group before taking their seats.

Frankie grinned as the group railed at him, letting all the insults fly over his head, as he knew that a bum on a seat beat any number that were still in the air.

The bald-headed waiter sauntered across to take their order, his once white apron billowing over his vast stomach.

'Yes, sirs, what'll it be?' he asked, pencil poised.

'Ah, two coffees, please,' said Cornwallis. 'And—'

'Ahem.'

'And a cup of milk.'

'Wot?'

'Er, could you make that cream, please.'

'Of course, sirs,' said the waiter wondering where the cough had come from.

'And we'll have two fried breakfasts with extra sausage please, and a kipper.'

'Ahem, ahem.'

The puzzled waiter looked around again.

'Make that two kippers, if you will.'

'Of course, sir,' answered the waiter with a frown. 'Anything else?'

'No, that's enough for now.'

'Right you are, sir; be with you in a moment.'

The waiter moved away, waggling the end of the pencil in his ear.

Fluffy sat on the floor under the table, between the two chairs. Fortunately, the noise the dockers made with their idle chatter drowned any words coming from a ragged looking, bad-tempered ginger tomcat.

'Well?' asked Cornwallis once they had settled. 'What happened?'

'Ah, well, not a lot 'appened, as it were, except fer the rats. They 'appened, but there's a few less now. The cat that's already there is bloody useless, lets 'em run all over the place, it does.'

'What about why I put you on there in the first place?'

'Oh, that. Yeah, found the bloke 'oo spoke to that other fella. Nasty piece o' work too.'

'What did he do?'

'Nuffink, 'e didn't need to. 'E exuded.'

'Exuded what exactly?'

'Malice; suppressed rage; mean type o' bastard.'

'A bit like you then?' suggested Frankie.

Fluffy looked up slowly, a questioning look on his face.

'All right, maybe not quite like you, then,' added Frankie quickly.

'Better,' growled Fluffy.

'Did you hear what's being planned?' asked Cornwallis.

'Not exactly, but the fella kept yacking to 'imself.'

'Saying what?'

"E kept going on about bastard dwarfs, that 'e 'ates the little runts, I think it were runts 'e said, anyways, 'e were going to do fer 'em. Kept looking out that little winda they's got on that ship, staring at the city; bit ironic, really.'

'Ironic? Why?'

"E were like a dwarf 'imself: a short-arse, very short but as wide as 'e were tall. Ugly bastard too, no beard but big staring eyes; reckon 'e's a right nutter, I do.'

'Nobody spoke to him?'

'Nah, everyone kept away from 'im. I 'eard a few saying that they'll be glad to be rid of 'im.'

The waiter returned with two mugs of coffee and a mug of cream.

'Saucer,' said a voice from below.

'Can I trouble you for a saucer, please?' asked Cornwallis and pointed to the floor.

'Ah,' said the waiter, noticing the cat for the first time. 'Didn't see that there; nice pussy,' he said patting Fluffy on the head.

'Pussy?' said Fluffy indignantly.

'Oh,' said the waiter. 'Sounds like it hissed; doesn't like being patted?'

'Loves it, loves it,' said Frankie. 'He'll start purring in a minute,' he added as he gave Fluffy a tap with the end of his boot.

'Purr,' said Fluffy.

'See,' said Frankie. 'Loves it, he does.'

Satisfied, the waiter turned and walked off to fetch the breakfast.

'Bastard,' said Fluffy.

Frankie chuckled as Cornwallis poured the cream into the saucer and put it on the floor. A few seconds later the waiter returned with the food and put two plates on the table, and now wise to the cat, placed the plate with the kippers on the floor. With a big beaming smile, he patted Fluffy again and then turned and walked off.

'You didn't even say thanks,' admonished Frankie.

'Sod off,' said Fluffy, eyeing the smoked fish and savouring the smell.

The two detectives ate in silence, relishing the artery busting globules of fat and grease sticking to the bacon and sausages; beneath the table, Fluffy chomped quickly through the two kippers, demolishing them, heads and all.

Cornwallis ordered more coffee and they sat back full and satisfied with Frankie undoing his belt a notch to relieve the strain.

'That weren't bad,' opined Frankie.

Cornwallis nodded. 'Especially after all that exertion in the boat.'

'Exertion? You did bugger all. It were me who did all the rowing and me who got me arm wet dragging the cat out.'

'Yes, but I did all the thinking. Stressful thing thinking, and I had to steer you.'

'Steer?'

'Yes: I had to tell you to go left or right and that's hard when you're facing each other. I want you to steer left and I had to think right, your right, so that you didn't go left, my left. Not easy that.'

'You're full of bull, Jack.'

Cornwallis grinned. 'One does one's best, Francis.'

Frankie shook his head ruefully, picking his teeth with a fingernail in order to dislodge a bit of bacon.

'Oh,' said Cornwallis as something leapt into his mind. He looked down at Fluffy. 'Did this dwarf-like nutter have a name?'

Fluffy looked up slowly and gave a satisfied burp. 'Yeah; someone called 'im Clarence.'

'Hmm,' said Cornwallis, thinking. 'I reckon another day of waiting is in order.'

'Oh, great,' said Frankie. 'You mean me, don't you?'

'For a time, yes. I'll get Dewdrop to come down later and maybe one of the girls. I've got to see Goodhalgan as The Pipe opens tomorrow. We've also got Phimp, Brooksturner and the Ship Masters Guild to worry about too. I'll give it a think and get Dewdrop to let you know what's happening.' Something else then occurred to him. 'Fluffy?'

'Yeah?' replied the cat.

'Did you find out what those things on the side of the ship are for?'

'Not really but the ship 'as something to do wiv making bridges.'

'Bridges?'

'Yeah, they's go wherever a bridge needs to be built.'

A thoughtful look appeared on Cornwallis' face. 'We don't need another bridge here, one seems to work well enough; so what's it doing here?'

'Beats me,' said Frankie, finally getting the bit of bacon out.

CHAPTER 32

Cornwallis thought hard as he made his way up from the docks through the early morning traffic. One thing about being up and about at this time of day was that you could see the city come to life as people emerged from their little brick cocoons to throng the streets with life and activity. Cabs were parked up ready to take folk off to work or to the shops or to a meeting and Cornwallis thought how that might change once The Pipe was up and running. He thought briefly about Coggs and his idea of a bus service and wondered if that had died a death, as he hadn't heard a whisper of its progress for a while now. Time would tell, but at the moment, he had a more pressing thing to consider — what on twearth was being planned to disrupt The Pipe?

He turned into Hupplemere Mews, pushed open the street door and hurried up the stairs to the office. Inside, they were all sitting waiting, and all but one had a face furnishing a wry little grin.

It took a moment for him to see why.

Jethro MacGillicudy had had a shave. The moustache and side-whiskers were gone and a rosy-cheeked fresh-faced commander sat in the chair. His hair had received some attention too as well as his dress-sense because he now wore a new suit in the latest fashion.

Cornwallis looked at him and scratched his head and then he too smiled. 'Morning, Jethro, you're looking a little, er…

different today.'

'Morning, Jack,' replied MacGillicudy, unfazed by the grins. 'You'd have thought this lot have never seen a man after a shave,' he said waving an arm around the room.

'I think it's probably more the fact that it's *you* who's had the shave, Jethro. The whiskers seemed somewhat attached to you.'

'I thought they were a bit old fashioned, to be truthful, so this morning on the way here, I called into a barber's, then next door a tailor just opened up so I got some new togs off the rail.' MacGillicudy stood up and gave a twirl. 'Not a bad cut considering they're ready-made.'

'No, I grant you that, but you didn't say anything last night.'

'And why should I? Just thought I could do with updating my image. A Commander of Police can't look like yesterday's man.'

Maud sat at her desk leaning forward with her chin cupped in her hands wearing a dreamy look, sighing slowly and looking at the commander as if he were an icon of the theatre.

Cornwallis was caught off-stride as she sighed. 'Maud, you should know better.'

'Yes, Mr Cornwallis, but he looks so much younger and I never realised he is so handsome.'

'What?' exclaimed Cornwallis.

Rose laughed. 'It's true, it's such a transformation. You've got a bit of competition now, Jack,' she warned. 'I'm really liking the new look.'

The three feelers sat there not daring to say anything. Felicity and Tiffany shared a glance but Dewdrop just stared at his boots as though he had something really interesting stuck to them.

MacGillicudy sat back down and rubbed his hands together. 'Come on, Jack. What's happened?'

'You mean apart from the unsettling experience of walking in here?'

MacGillicudy rolled his eyes. 'Yes.'

'All right then: Phimp went to see a man called Clarence, who, apparently, hates dwarfs for some reason. This Clarence is, according to Fluffy, a short-arse himself, though not technically a dwarf. Fluffy described him as a nutter. Couldn't find out why he's here but Frankie and Fluffy are keeping an eye on things down there. The ship is normally used in the construction of bridges but that's as much as we know.'

Cornwallis sat down at his desk and Rose handed him a mug of coffee. He screwed up a bit of paper and tossed it towards Maud, breaking her close inspection of the commander. 'Down girl,' he said playfully.

'Mr Cornwallis,' replied Maud indignantly. 'I'm hardly a girl.'

'You could have fooled me. Do something mean and nasty, Jethro.'

'That might make it worse,' answered Rose, smiling.

'You're just jealous, Jack,' countered MacGillicudy, raising an arm and wafting it regally around. 'As Rose just said, you've now got competition. You're running scared.'

Tiffany and Felicity stifled a giggle and Dewdrop seemed to be having trouble keeping his shoulders still.

'Ha!' Cornwallis threw his hands into the air. 'Running scared, am I, Jethro MacGillicudy? A penniless policeman or a suave sophisticated man about town: you decide, Rose. Which of us would you choose?'

'That's unfair,' said MacGillicudy. 'You've already corrupted her.'

Rose burst out laughing. 'You two can stop now or I might cause myself an injury from laughing too much. There's only one real man here but he's already attached, and that man is Cecil.'

'Wha…?' said Dewdrop, looking up quickly.

'So you two can start behaving as grown-ups.'

'Did you hear that, Jethro? We've both been cast aside,' said Cornwallis, aghast. 'Women! Ha!'

Dewdrop, eyes wide, wondered how to respond as everyone looked towards him. Er…' he said, hesitantly.

To save his blushes Cornwallis grinned at him. 'I think perhaps we should return to the problem at hand. Cecil, you and Felicity can go down to the docks and meet up with Frankie; you'll be after this Clarence fellow and we need to see what he's doing and where he goes.'

'Yes, Mr Cornwallis,' replied Dewdrop, relief evident in his voice.

'In the meantime, I have to see Goodhalgan again as it's opening day tomorrow. Jethro, if you're still willing to help?'

MacGillicudy nodded with a slight smile on his face.

'In that case, can you see if you can find out a bit more about the Ship Masters Guild, you should be okay as no one will recognise you now.'

'And me?' asked Tiffany.

Cornwallis thought for a moment. 'Actually, you can go with the commander. You might be able to keep him out of trouble.'

'Thanks, Jack,' said MacGillicudy ruefully.

'That just leaves me,' said Rose.

'It does. I think you should stay here for now, coordinate between us all.'

'Oh goody, there's a few things I need to do here anyway.'

Cornwallis gave a greeting to the dwarf guard and then headed further down onto the platform below. This station still had a deal of work to do, to get it ready for when The Pipe expanded its network, which wasn't too far into the future. He knew the route through the tunnels now and it wasn't long before he entered one of the chambers, he even remembered to duck as he passed beneath the overhang. He expected this chamber to be empty so he walked across and then into another tunnel which branched into various destinations. Goodhalgan's office-cum-chamber was just down on the right off the middle tunnel.

'Ah, Mr Cornwallis,' said Goodhalgan as he pushed open the door. 'Wondered when we'd see you.'

Cornwallis smiled. 'Never one to disappoint; no problems at all?'

'None whatsoever. Everything is ready to go. I've sent the invitations to the Guilds and the Assembly and the booze is ready and waiting. Everyone gets a free drink, a nibble or two and a free ride.'

'Just wish I felt as easy about it as you do. We haven't found out what's being planned to disrupt it yet.'

'Maybe there's nothing,' replied Goodhalgan confidently. 'I promise you, we can take care of anything should it happen, so you're worrying needlessly. We are dwarfs, Mr Cornwallis, and down here we have total control.'

'I hope to the gods that you're right. If it's any help though, Brooksturner is definitely involved with the disruption and so, we believe, is the Guild of Ship Masters. What they don't like about you, I don't know. We're trying to find out.'

'Interesting,' remarked Goodhalgan. 'I've had a letter from the minister; it's here, somewhere.' The king of the dwarfs rummaged in the drawers of his desk until he withdrew an official looking missive with the seal of the Assembly adorning it. 'He thanks me for the invitation and gladly accepts. He informs me he will be bringing with him several guests including his secretary, Mr Phimp, as well as a few guild members including the Master of the Ship Masters Guild.'

'Let me see,' said Cornwallis, holding out his hand.

Goodhalgan held out the letter and Cornwallis nearly snatched it out of his fingers. He read quickly, scanning the obligatory banal bit at the beginning until he came to the meat of the letter, the names of those who would be joining him.

'But you said you'd invited all the guilds.'

'I have, but I sent a blanket invitation to the Guilds Hall as there are so many to invite individually, same as the Assembly. It would take weeks otherwise; far easier to do it this way.'

Cornwallis nodded. 'But Brooksturner decided to invite these guild masters, presumably before the guild got the invite.'

'Possibly, I did send to the Assembly first.'

'So, we have: Frederick Wantlebury, Master of the Ship Masters; should have come here earlier, would have saved Jethro a bit of time; Gobber Stippins, Master of the Guild of Signwriters; Brisco Nugent, Master of the Guild of Lamplighters; Johnston Crew, Master of the Guild of Labourers; Micah Standish, Master of the Guild of Coal Merchants. Plus you have Phimp and a Clarence Fogg. I wonder if this is the same Clarence from the ship?' He looked at Goodhalgan to explain. 'There is a Clarence out on a ship on the river and Phimp went to see him; by all accounts, the man is a nasty piece of work, hates dwarfs.'

'Nothing unusual there,' said Goodhalgan. 'Half of Gornstock hates dwarfs.'

'Yes, but what is unusual about this one is that he is extremely short.'

'Then I shall look forward to meeting this man, eye to eye, as it were.' Goodhalgan chuckled at his little joke. 'Eye to eye; haven't done that with a long-leg for a long time.'

CHAPTER 33

'You what?' said Frankie, the incredulity apparent by the high-pitched last word.

'Shaved,' repeated Dewdrop. 'New clothes too.'

'But why?'

'He said he wanted to freshen himself up.'

'That doesn't sound like Jethro; he's always been old school. Half of him has always lived in the past.'

'It suits him,' chimed in Felicity as she gazed over the docks. 'He doesn't look half as intimidating as he did with a face full of fungus.'

'He's had that ever since I've known him. Bet he feels the draught now, eh?'

'I wouldn't know, speaking as someone who doesn't need to shave.'

'No, I don't suppose you do. In that, you mirror Dewdrop here.'

'Oi, I do shave; every couple of days,' protested Dewdrop.

'Could have fooled me, young Toopins. My Tulip's got a hairier arse than your rosy-red cheeks.' Frankie looked at each of them for a few moments then he grinned. 'So, Jethro's gone for a new look,' he added thoughtfully. 'I wonder what's brought that on?'

'You'll have to ask him,' replied Felicity, sitting herself down.

Frankie chuckled at the thought of a clean-shaven

commander.

'So,' said Dewdrop, changing the subject. 'What do you expect to happen?'

'Dunno,' said Frankie with a shrug. 'We is watching and we is learning; as it happens, I've already learnt something.'

'What's that then?'

'Look at the ship we're watching.'

'Yeah?'

'Those bits on the sides, they're used fer drilling into the river bed. What they do is drill down into the rocky bit, then put a metal sheath over it, then pump the water out. They then sends some poor bastard down with a shovel and they make the foundations and put some poles in to reinforce things. They then build upwards until they get to the height they want. Clever, eh?'

'How did you learn that?'

'Fluffy just 'eard it. A couple of blokes were talking out there.' He pointed out towards a wharf.

'Does that help with why we're here?'

'Probably not, but the little bastard we've got to follow is on that ship, so I suppose anything we learn could be helpful.'

Cornwallis' warehouse acted as their lookout point, sitting by the front door and looking out through the hatches, one in the door and another in the front wall; some old empty crates utilised as chairs. Fluffy prowled outside on the wharf, hoping to pick up a morsel of food or a snippet of information.

'Did you know,' said Frankie, to no one in particular. 'That this place used to belong to The Great East Company, stored tea here until they went bust. Back there,' and he threw a thumb over his shoulder, 'is a trapdoor which leads down to the dwarf tunnels. He, he, we had some fun with that a while ago.'

'Oh, yes, I remember,' said Dewdrop with a glum expression. 'That bloke who got his head ripped off; you bastards made me dive down to get it.'

'What?' exclaimed Felicity. 'You mean you actually retrieved an actual head from the river?'

Dewdrop nodded. 'I did: not nice that. I mean, have you ever *swum* in that river?'

Felicity stared at Dewdrop, her mouth hanging open, a respect bordering on adulation flitting across her face.

'Made a man of you, boy,' said Frankie. 'I mean, not many people survive a ducking in there.'

'But a head?' said Felicity, still staring at her hero.

'That were the easy bit,' replied Dewdrop, smiling ruefully.

'You can tell me all about it later,' said Felicity reaching over and patting his hand. 'It would seem there's still a lot I don't know about you, Cecil Toopins.'

'Ay up,' said Frankie, straightening his back. 'Looks like something's happening over there.'

A man waved from the ship and shortly a wherry pulled off from the jetty and began to row towards it.

'Let's hope it's going to bring this Clarence geezer over to the shore as my arse is getting a bit numb now,' said Frankie, standing up and rubbing the affected area.

The three watched as the little boat pulled alongside the ship and the figure of a man climbed down a ladder, a diminutive figure, somewhat lacking in height, but certainly not lacking in breadth.

'Yes.' Frankie punched the air in delight. 'About bloody time.'

Fluffy appeared at the warehouse door at the same time.

'Yer little man is on 'is way over,' said the cat, scratching his neck with his paw.

'So we noticed,' answered Frankie, adjusting himself in the trouser department. 'You sure that's the one?'

'Yeah,' replied Fluffy.

'Fair do's,' said Frankie.

'And yer other man is 'ere too.'

'What? Who?'

'The one youse calls Phimp, over by that crane.'

Frankie peered through the hatch, trying to get an angle to see. Felicity just pushed open the door a tad and got the better view.

Fluffy eased through the gap, looking up expectantly at the three. 'Any rats in 'ere?' he asked hopefully.

'It's a warehouse,' replied Frankie. 'Of course there's rats.'

'Oh good, time fer an early lunch.'

Fluffy tore off into the darker depths of the warehouse and within a few moments, various bangs and curses floated over, signalling a successful beginning.

'I suppose that's him done, then,' said Dewdrop.

Frankie nodded. 'Yeah, won't see 'im again today.'

Another bang and then a series of furious scratching noises.

'Gives 'im something to do,' said Frankie, almost to himself as he kept his eyes on Phimp.

Phimp stood by a crane with his hands buried deep in his pockets, looking out, watching the progress of the wherry as it approached the shore. As soon as the boat hit the jetty, the passenger stood up and stepped out. He tossed a few coins into the bottom of the boat and strolled away without a backward glance, the wherryman eyeing the little man in a way that did not indicate a future friendly relationship.

'He does look a mean bastard,' observed Dewdrop with distaste. 'He's just elbowing everyone out of his way.'

'Not a good thing to do, down here,' said Frankie. 'These dockers are not exactly known for timidity. He carries on like that then he's gonna get a right-hander.'

'Let's hope so,' said Felicity. 'It looks like he's got a big small man problem.'

'Phimp doesn't look happy,' observed Dewdrop.

'Not surprised,' said Frankie. 'He's gonna have to get that Clarence out of here pretty quick or there'll be a riot.'

'Now he's running forward with his hands up,' said Dewdrop.

'Yes, we know,' said Frankie. 'We can see him.'

'And now he's waving his arms and saying something to the dockers.'

'Yes, that's pretty obvious.'

'And now he's bending down and speaking urgently to the little man.'

'Dewdrop?' said Frankie.

'Yes?'

'Shut the f—'

'Cecil?' interrupted Felicity quickly. 'I think Frankie would like you to knock off with the commentary.'

'Oh, right, sorry.'

'No worries,' said Frankie. 'Oh, look, they're walking off now.'

'Yes, we can see,' said Dewdrop and Felicity together, not quite hiding the triumph in their voices and the grins on their faces.

Frankie snapped his head up. 'Oh, right. I see what you did there; that was very nearly funny.'

'We thought so,' said Felicity, flashing a smile at Dewdrop.

'C'mon,' said Frankie, with a shake of his head and wearing a wry grin. 'Let's get after them, they're off now.'

Phimp and Clarence hurried away, Phimp still speaking urgently into space about a foot above Clarence's head, towards the streets and alleys leading up from the docks and into town.

CHAPTER 34

Billboards and posters adorned the city with adverts of The Pipe and people were taking note of them, Cornwallis observed. He watched as several people stopped and looked and pointed and spoke in hushed whispers at the prospect of an underground transport system. He could tell that they were excited and he hoped that that excitement would shortly be turning into dollars for him and Goodhalgan. With his hands deep in his pockets, he continued watching, then lifted up his head to look at the sky; dark clouds floated above and he hoped that it wasn't a portent of things to come.

Brooksturner and Phimp were a bit of a problem, he acknowledged to himself. They were planning something and he surmised that tomorrow would see the result of that planning when The Pipe opened for business: but what and how and where? If he knew either the what, the how or the where then they might be able to do something about it; perhaps they should have pulled Phimp in after all, and squeezed him until something trickled out. Maybe they could still do that, they still had a bit of time left and it would be sensible to use that time wisely. They would pull Phimp in, he decided; see what he had to say for himself.

With that decision made, he strode off determinedly, heading back to the office to see what had been happening whilst he had been underground with Goodhalgan.

He chewed the cud; cogitated, worked on scenarios, drifted

between the possible and the probable, the expected and unexpected. As his mind dwelt on the problems, he didn't notice the non-descript coach pulling-up ahead of him and the door swinging open and hanging there ominously, like the broken wing of a bat, creaking as it bounced against the hinges.

'Mr Cornwallis.' It was a summons, not a question and it emerged from the depths of the body of the coach like a blow from a hammer.

Cornwallis had heard that voice before and he had no wish to hear it again, but the cool calm tones of it penetrated his mind through his ears. A fairly benign voice as voices went; it didn't threaten but it did insinuate. You ignored this voice at your peril, worse still, trying to ignore the owner of the voice could have unforeseen catastrophic results; if you did, then it was likely to be one of the last voices you heard.

He stopped walking and turned to face the open maw. 'Yes?'

'Would you kindly step inside, join me if you will.'

'Do I have to?'

'Yes.'

'Ah, since you put it like that, then it would be a pleasure.'

'I do hope so, Mr Cornwallis; it has been too long since we've had a conversation.'

Cornwallis sighed, stepped onto the running board and entered the portable den with a sinking heart.

'Door,' said the occupant.

Cornwallis reached back and pulled the door to, sealing him off from reality and the world outside, leaving him at the mercy of the man sitting on the bench.

'Take a seat, Mr Cornwallis,' said the man indicating opposite.

Cornwallis duly obliged.

The man raised the cane he held and tapped the roof, two

short, sharp taps and the coach lurched into motion. Cornwallis studied the cane, certain that a slither of very sharp and pointy metal, deadly, much like the owner, lay inside.

'Mr Hawk, so nice to see you again,' said Cornwallis, heart dropping into his boots.

'The pleasure is all mine, Mr Cornwallis. It's been too long.'

'And you just happened to be driving down this particular road just at the same time as I happened to be walking down it?'

'Just so; a coincidence, a fortuitous circumstance because your name just sprung into my mind as we turned the corner and I thought that we should become reacquainted, and then suddenly, there you are. A most pleasing turn of events, don't you think?'

Cornwallis smiled ruefully knowing full well that the Bagman didn't believe in coincidence; he did believe in manipulation, fact and various persuasive techniques though.

The Bagman, slim, almost skeletal with a bald head and little wire glasses sitting on his large protuberant nose, perhaps wielded even more power than the Warden did. The head of the secret police, feared by all, his name whispered quietly in the hope that he didn't get to hear you talking about him, knew what you were thinking before you had even thought of it. Nothing happened in Gornstock without his knowing; his network of spies and informants were legendary. He was a man in the know and you just had to hope that he knew that you weren't worth the bother.

Cornwallis waited, consciously stopping himself from talking as he knew the Bagman liked silences as people tended to want to fill them up with words, some of which, the Bagman liked to hear.

The impasse continued as the coach rocked and rolled down the streets, each regarding the other like two combatants vying for position and control. Cornwallis determined not to be the one to break the deadlock.

'Well,' said the Bagman, eventually. 'This is nice.'

Cornwallis acknowledged with a tilt of his head, but in his mind, he punched the air with his fist in delight. He'd scored a point. 'It is, Mr Hawk. However, pleasant as it is to see you again, I do have things I must do.'

'I'm sure you have, Mr Cornwallis. Your main priority, I understand, is to find out what is due to occur tomorrow when your enterprise opens to the public. The Pipe must be allowed to succeed or fail on its own merits. It will be good for the city, either way.'

Cornwallis wasn't surprised that the Bagman knew something was going to happen. 'So, you're going to tell me what Brooksturner and Phimp have planned?'

'Alas, no, because I don't know,' replied the Bagman.

'Then what is the point of this conversation?'

'A good question, Mr Cornwallis. It is perhaps a warning. What they are planning is not just a mere disruption of The Pipe; it is the total destruction of The Pipe.'

Cornwallis' eyes widened. 'Then why don't you do something: take Brooksturner and Phimp down to those little rooms you have where certain gentlemen are trained in certain arts and ask the certain questions that will give you the answers that you want?'

The Bagman returned a thin smile. 'I would like to, but my hands are tied. This has to be a public humiliation — again, I'm afraid.'

'You mean like Kintersbury?'

The Bagman nodded. Yes, I'm afraid so. The Warden put Brooksturner in as minister so he can fail, because he is a danger to the city. His views are somewhat archaic, but that in itself is not the problem. He wants to be Warden. He wants a return to the old brutal ways of the Morris where life was a little less free, shall we say. He wants to crush the populace and milk the juice and he is persuading some of the guilds to go along with him. Freedom is anathema to him.'

'You mean he's deranged?'

'Some might say that, others, sadly, agree with him.'

'I'm surprised. My father—'

'Your father doesn't yet know,' interrupted the Bagman. 'This is between the Warden and me. I decided that the Earl should not be told, I'm afraid.'

'But you're telling me, now.'

'Yes, because you need to know what's at stake, things have, er… changed.'

'Thanks, considerate of you.'

'You're welcome.'

'No pressure, then.'

'Depends on how you look at it.'

Cornwallis looked at it and he decided he didn't like the view. 'Why me?' he asked after a while. 'Why don't you use all your resources?'

'If it wasn't for The Pipe, then I would have, but that would have taken, will take, a lot of time to build the evidence. You're Johnny on the spot. It's an ideal situation. The Pipe has drawn him out a lot faster than it would have done and you will be there to spoil his plans.'

'So you want me to do your dirty work for you?'

'Yes.'

'Again?'

'Yes.'

'Great!'

The Bagman smiled. 'The city will be grateful.'

'I bet. You know, I just decided that we should pick Phimp up and speak to him at the Yard.'

'Hmm,' mused the Bagman. 'I wouldn't do that, if I were you. Might put out the wrong message to Brooksturner. Phimp is an oily little devil, but he's a go-between and thus integral to their plans. It is my understanding that what they plan to do is going to happen tomorrow when The Pipe opens to the public. You will have all the dignitaries partaking of refreshment after the first ceremonial runs in the dwarfs' main chamber whilst The Pipe begins catering to the paying public. It will be carnage, from what I hear.'

'Carnage?' exclaimed Cornwallis. 'You mean you're going to just let it all happen?'

'Oh, no. We will have some representation down there too. I don't want anything to happen to anyone, now do I?'

'But you'll have all those ministers and guildsmen down there. If Brooksturner succeeds then he will wipe out practically all the government and the guilds masters.'

'Yes,' replied the Bagman calmly. 'Paving the way for Brooksturner, who will undoubtedly survive, to take control of the city. I must say, it's rather a clever ruse, don't you think?'

Cornwallis' face drained of colour as he stared back at the Bagman, sitting there, talking so matter-of-factly, that it sent a shiver down his spine. 'How do you know all this?' he asked, a slight waver in his voice.

'Ah, yes; that brings me to another point.' The Bagman raised a finger in admonishment. 'As you must be aware, I have one or two operatives who are placed in certain positions within society and that includes the Assembly. One of my most trusted and, dare I say it, productive operatives, suffered some unwarranted attention which could have put their cover at risk. Unfortunately, they were unable to fully convey their reason for being where they were when this thing happened.'

'And what has this to do with me?'

The Bagman narrowed his eyes. 'You are not the only one in this city who can call upon the services of an intelligent feline.'

'Wha…? Oh, bugger, you mean Fluffy, don't you?'

'I do, indeed. I understand the phrase in common parlance is, wham, bam, thank you, ma'am.'

Cornwallis shut his eyes hoping that when he opened them again, the Bagman would have just disappeared and he would find that he just dreamt it all. He opened them again and found the Bagman still sitting there. 'He said they were both as eager as each other.'

'So I understand, but it lacks professionalism. You should not be, er… on the job, when you were on the job, as it were. I have spoken to Tiddles regarding her conduct. I suggest you do the same to, er, Fluffy.'

'Oh gods!'

'They won't help, Mr Cornwallis. I understand a guard caught them at it and removed your cat from the scene. I hope there's no real damage done, because if she should have kittens in the not too distant future, then your Fluffy will certainly say goodbye to his furry little bollocks. Ah, here we are, back at your office. Remember, Mr Cornwallis, the city's future is in your hands. Good day to you.'

CHAPTER 35

'Do you know, I actually think this is going to work.'

'I do believe you may be right. Is everything ready?'

'Oh yes. Phimp and our friend Clarence are out checking the entrances at this moment.'

'Why?'

Brooksturner grinned at the Ship Master. 'Escape routes. When everything has happened we have to stop things happening.'

'You mean after and not before?' asked Frederick Wentlebury, the Master of the Guild of Ship Masters.

'Of course, we don't want to spoil everything. I imagine we all may be a touch thirsty and hungry and we don't want to miss out, do we?'

'No, no. Timing is everything though.'

They sat in the little office above the travel agents and discussed the plans they had put in place. Wentlebury opened a drawer in his desk and removed a bottle of the most expensive wine he could find in Gornstock, together with two massive cigars.

'Rolled on the thighs of dusky maidens, they are,' he said as he handed one over. 'Tuban Cigars are the best you can get and I have the contract to import them.'

'Dusky maidens, you say?' replied Brooksturner, wafting it beneath his nose and breathing in the heady scent, imagining the scene in his head.

The Ship Master grinned. He hadn't told a lie, just not all of the truth. In his younger days, he had seen the girls outside the stores doing just that, rolling the tobacco leaves on their naked thighs. Inside the factory, it was a different story. Child labour in abysmal sweaty oven-heated conditions working fourteen hours a day for just a few pennies each. Marketing sold the cigars but poverty made them.

'I'm looking forward to getting the Guilds into line,' ventured Wentlebury.

'So you should, same with me and the Council. Between us, we can return to a better time, reopen the prisons, squash the radicals and put the women back where they belong. An opportunity to fill our pockets and we'll take up our rightful place at the head of the city. Trade and Council, working for a better future.'

'I'll drink to that,' said the Ship Master, raising his glass.

*

'Well,' said Frankie dejectedly, 'might as well go back and see if anything's happened.' He stared at the Assembly as the door closed behind Phimp after he had entered the building. 'Even me mum's packed up fer the day and gone home,' he added, staring at the bare bones of Sal's Sizzler. He sighed discontentedly.

'It can't be helped,' said Felicity. 'It's not our fault they didn't do anything.'

'Oh, they probably did something; the trouble is we don't know what that something was.'

'They were just looking at all the entrances, checking them out, I assume,' added Dewdrop.

Frankie nodded. 'That's what it looked like, but something tells me there was more to it than that.'

'Places to attack?' asked Felicity, trying to think of the reason.

Frankie shrugged. 'Possibly, but without us hearing what they were on about… Oh, well, let's go and get a wet. With Clarence on the ship and Phimp in the Assembly, there's nothing we can do now.'

They traipsed back through the streets and alleyways as darkness descended; most people had already gone home, leaving just the stragglers and the occasional early reveller. It had been a largely wasted day as far as detectoring was concerned, apart from wearing out the boot leather.

The walk back to the office at Hupplemere Mews took only a few minutes and they were soon bounding up the stairs, anticipating a quick catch-up before decamping to the Stoat for a longer one.

Frankie pushed open the door and met six sombre faces staring back at him. 'Cor, look at you lot; somebody died?'

'Not yet, Frankie,' replied Cornwallis. 'But I'm glad to see you three back.'

'Why? What's happened?'

'The Bagman happened.'

Frankie stared. 'Oh, bollocks!'

'Concise and to the point as always, Frankie. Yes, our friendly neighbourhood Bagman took me for a ride, literally, and imparted certain nuggets of information of a somewhat serious nature. Hence…' Cornwallis pointed to his father, chatting quietly to Tiffany. 'I thought it best, considering.'

'Ah,'

Cornwallis took a deep breath. 'What happened with Phimp and Clarence?'

'Nothing, diddly-squat, nada. They just walked around looking at all the dwarf entrances, ticking off something on a pad.'

'No clue there then?'

'No, we going for a pint?'

Cornwallis flashed a short grin. 'Not this evening, we need to keep all this between ourselves, so we'll have to make do with a couple of bottles of wine from upstairs.'

'Wine? Oh, goody,' said Felicity, brightening up a little.

'Splendid,' said the earl looking up. 'Another girl with taste and sophistication.'

'Nothing wrong with beer,' defended Frankie, stoically. 'Nectar, it is; nature's restorative. Anyways, I've seen you drink enough of it, M'lord.'

'Of course I have,' replied the earl, smiling. 'But that doesn't mean I only drink beer. When I want an evening of conviviality and refinement I generally turn to the grape, alas, when I happen to be in the Assembly or in your company, conviviality and refinement go out the window, so I drink beer.'

Frankie looked to Rose. 'Did he just insult me?' he asked, brow furrowed in thought.

'Yes, but he did it nicely.'

'Oh, that's all right then. So I don't need to tell him that he's a stuck-up, prissy-faced bastard of a snob?'

'No.'

'In that case, I won't,' said Frankie, grinning at the earl.

'That's all we need,' said Cornwallis with a sigh. 'The imminent destruction of the government and you two decide to go off on one.'

'You what?' asked Frankie, aghast, the grin instantly disappearing from his face.

'Yes, it's what the Bagman told me. Come and sit down, all of you, and we'll go through it again.'

Frankie, Felicity and Dewdrop made themselves

comfortable, with Maud making herself useful with the coffee pot.

Frankie eased down next to MacGillicudy and looked at him, pointedly. 'Who's the new boy?' he asked, jabbing a thumb at the commander.

'Very funny,' said MacGillicudy. 'Laugh? I nearly did.'

Frankie turned his head towards the commander and winked. 'C'mon, give us a kiss, gorgeous,' he said, puckering his lips.

The elbow jab lacked force when it came; more of a glancing blow and Frankie just sat chuckling away to himself.

Cornwallis wiped the smile from his face and got down to business. 'Oh, Frankie, have you seen the cat recently?'

'No, why?' he asked, still grinning.

'I'll come to that in a minute,' he said. 'But first…'

Cornwallis went through the Bagman's revelations again and everybody listened in silence edged with apprehension. The earl knew how things worked in the Assembly, so the fact that the Warden and the Bagman had kept him in the dark meant nothing to him; standard practice he informed them, as any secret could only remain a secret as long as nobody knew what the secret was. He'd been in politics too long to let things worry him. Then Frankie fully appraised them of Phimp's and Clarence's activities with help from Felicity and Dewdrop. There wasn't a lot there to help raise the spirits; the enormity of the challenge, and the responsibility ensuing, put a damper on the morale of them all.

'Thoughts, ideas, suggestions?' asked Cornwallis when they had all finished. 'It's open house, everyone gets a go.'

They all took a deep breath and got lost in their thoughts; for the first time in an age, total silence insinuated its way into the offices of Cornwallis Investigations as each tried desperately to come up with a plan, a workable plan, one that would keep

The Pipe open and nail Brooksturner and all to the wall.

Eventually, Cornwallis sighed. 'This is no good; coffee isn't working. We need a better type of lubrication.'

'Ooh,' said Frankie, hopes returning. 'Pub?'

'No, Francis, we ain't moving from here until we come up with a solution. Cecil, come with me, we're getting the wine out.'

Dewdrop got up and followed Cornwallis out of the office and up to the flat where he came face to face with the kind of lifestyle that he could only dream about having. He wouldn't have been surprised if the flat had featured in the centre-pages of one of the periodicals that Felicity frequently read: chic, sumptuous and bang up to date in the latest fashion for homes. He knew that money did not necessarily mean stylish, but this was, it oozed it: understated in an overstated kind of way. It was quite simply, classy.

'Come on, Cecil,' ordered Cornwallis. 'Come through.'

Dewdrop closed his jaw and followed the voice to a room at the back. 'Nice home you have here, Mr Cornwallis.'

'Thank you. You should have seen it before Rose got hold of it, had to get a cleaner in just so that I could find the chairs. Typical bachelors pad, but I'm sure you know what I mean, mess everywhere. Now look at it. You'll do well if you let your young lady loose on your place.'

'I've only got one room, Mr Cornwallis. Not a lot you can do with that.'

'Ah, sorry, but maybe things will improve for you.'

Cornwallis then turned and opened another door, entering the room. Dewdrop heard some clinking noises and then shortly a crate came skidding across the floor filled with bottles of wine.

'Grab hold of that, will you. I'll bring the glasses.'

'Yes, Mr Cornwallis.'

A couple of minutes later they were back downstairs,

Dewdrop dumping the crate on the desk.

'Where's the beer,' asked Frankie looking bereft at the lack of a proper drink. 'I know you've got loads up there.'

Cornwallis sighed and threw Frankie the key. 'Go get what you need.'

'And take your boots off first,' ordered Rose.

'I didn't,' said Dewdrop, quietly but anxiously to Felicity.

'That's because you're not Frankie, I suspect. She trusts you a bit more with the carpet.'

Frankie returned with his arms full of beer wearing a big grin on his face. 'You're getting a bit short up there, Jack.'

'I wasn't, but I suspect I am now. Right, you lot, now you've all got a drink, I want a plan and nobody leaves until we've got one.'

'You ain't told me why you want to know about the cat?' said Frankie as the bottles clanked down on the desk. He picked one up, knocked the top off and upended it, taking a long swig.

'Oh yes, I'd forgotten about that. Well, you remember I said that he got caught doing the business with another cat in the Assembly?'

'Yerse.'

'Her name is Tiddles.'

'Nice.'

'You know Fluffy is what's called an intelligent cat?'

'Yes.'

'So is Tiddles. She works undercover so didn't disclose her intelligence.'

'Oh, that's a turn up for the books; Fluffy will be well pleased.'

'Maybe not.'

'Why?'

'Guess who she works for?'

'How should I k…? Oh, bugger! You don't mean? You do, don't you? The Bagman?'

'Yep, and he's promised that should there be kittens, Fluffy will suffer the ultimate fate.' Cornwallis mimed a pair of scissors.

'Ooh, painful,' replied Frankie, and then grinned. 'You wait 'til I tell him, it'll make his day.'

CHAPTER 36

The coffee pot had the distinction of being the most utilised piece of equipment as each tried to chase the cobwebs away after a scant night's sleep. Cornwallis issued a jaw-cracking yawn and then finished the dregs of his mug before immediately pouring a refill. The day of reckoning had arrived: the end of which would see the annihilation of the government and the eradication of the dwarfs… or not, as the case may be.

'Maud,' said Cornwallis. 'I say again, you are definitely not coming with us.'

'Mr Cornwallis,' said Maud. 'And I say again, that I definitely *am* coming. You issued me an invitation which I accepted.'

'Yes, but that was before; it may be dangerous now.'

'I don't care.'

'But *we* do.'

'Mr Cornwallis, it may well be, but I see it like this: most of the government and most of the guilds and lots of civic dignitaries will also be there. If anything happens to them then it will also happen to you. If that happens then I'll be out of a job anyway, besides, I like a bit of excitement occasionally.'

'Excitement? It's hardly that.'

'Jack,' said Rose. 'She can help your father.'

'Whose side are you on?'

'Maud's, in this case.'

Cornwallis started to fling his arms into the air, but then remembered he had hold of a full mug of hot coffee so contented himself with a grunt of exasperation instead.

Rose turned to Maud and winked. Maud squared her shoulders and sat up straighter in her chair, a soft smile of satisfaction on her lips.

A scratching at the door indicated that something on the other side wished to gain entrance.

Frankie perked up and a big wide evil grin flashed onto his face. 'I wonder who that can be?'

Dewdrop, closest to the door, got up and padded over, suppressing the joy he felt that for once, Frankie had something else to take the piss out of.

Fluffy walked in with a confident swagger, eyeballing the occupants as if they were the lesser beings. 'Wot youse lot looking at? Would've been up earlier but some nameless bastard shuts the front door on me,' he turned and looked pointedly at Dewdrop, who, with Felicity, were last in. ''Ad to wait fer summon else to go in,' he added before sitting down in the middle of the room licking his paw.

'Oh, dear,' said Frankie, faux concern. 'What a shame.'

Fluffy stopped licking and cast an evil cat stare in his direction.

'Where you been anyway? Met any nice pussycats lately?'

'Wot youse on abouts? I's bin 'ere and there, doing a bit of this an' that.'

'Ah, that explains it then. The trouble is, you ought to be doing a little less of this and that in the future.'

Fluffy looked confused. 'Wot youse mean?'

'I mean your activities have come to the notice of the Bagman.'

'Yeah?'

'Yes.'

Fluffy's features took on a definite smug look; he sort of

preened and sat up a little more. 'Know's a good 'un when 'e sees it, then?'

'Possibly, then again, possibly not.'

'Uh?'

'What I mean is the Bagman doesn't like his workers interfered with. That cat in the Assembly worked for him: you know, the one that you, er...'

Fluffy's eyes widened.

'Yes, Tiddles is her name but she had to pretend to be a normal cat. The Bagman knows what you did and has promised that should there be kittens then your gonads will be decorating his office, you, however, will not be with them.'

'Oh, bugger!' said Fluffy as he crawled up into a ball.

Cornwallis rummaged in his desk and produced a packet of biscuits. 'Gingernuts, anyone?' he asked innocently.

'Sod off!' moaned Fluffy into his fur.

Maud hadn't been down in the dwarf tunnels before and to find how light and airy some of the chambers were surprised her. Cornwallis' explanation about the crystals in the walls reflecting the light back from the torches, making everything twice as bright, impressed her no end. She watched mesmerised at how organised the dwarfs were as they brought out food and drink to place on the tables and benches that lined the chamber, ready for the soiree a little bit later. There was bustle but very little hustle as each dwarf just got on with what they had to do.

Rose, Felicity and Tiffany each carried a little bag containing a dress and a pair of posh shoes. Following a little discussion last night, which Cornwallis lost, Rose and the two girls headed upstairs to the flat where Tiffany and Felicity picked out one dress each from Rose's collection to wear for a short time until the soiree got properly underway, then they would decamp to

Goodhalgan's chamber to change back into their working clothes in case something occurred. The thought process being that nothing untoward would happen until all the nobs' noses were deep into the trough of free food and drink. All the dwarfs who were not running The Pipe were guarding the tunnels and entrances; it was difficult to see how there could be an attack on The Pipe with all the protection. Everything appeared to be locked up solid, nothing could happen underground, nothing could get in or out without the dwarfs knowing.

'Clear head,' warned Cornwallis as he saw Frankie move towards the beer barrels.

'Just need to check that they're up to scratch.'

'Frankie,' exclaimed Rose. 'It's still early in the morning. You are in actual fact having beer for breakfast.'

'Yeah, great, innit? Anyway, it's just a drop, it's not like I'm planning on a session.'

Rose's head still shook as Goodhalgan ambled in. He had already dressed for the occasion and he'd had his beard specially plaited into two horn-like stalactites dangling from his chin. He wore a chain of office around his neck and his long grey hair hung loose down his back with just a thin golden crown resting on his ears, the emblem of the King of the Dwarfs.

'There's always one,' observed Goodhalgan watching Frankie load up a tankard. 'But he's not the first to try a sample this morning.'

'See,' said Frankie triumphantly.

Cornwallis rolled his eyes and then turned to the king. 'Everything ready, no last-minute mishaps?'

'None whatsoever, and yes, it's all ready.'

'That's good, only…'

'Yes?'

Cornwallis pulled Goodhalgan to the side. 'Only, yesterday I spoke to the Bagman, or to be precise, he spoke to me and I listened. Apparently, Brooksturner and his little gang of criminals are not just planning a disruption today; they're planning destruction of the tunnels and everyone in them. How? I don't know, but whatever is going to happen it is going to happen when the paying public start paying.'

'Oh, that's a bit inconsiderate of them.'

'Inconsiderate?'

'Yes, it means we're going to have to keep all our guards in place and keep an eye on everyone.'

'But they plan on destroying the tunnels.'

Goodhalgan chuckled. 'They're hardly able to do that, even using that explosive gonepowder. There are miles of tunnels down here and we have dwarfs at every entrance. Nothing can get in without us knowing.'

'You seem very relaxed about it.'

'Nothing to get concerned with, we're safer down here than you are up there. I believe the modern expression the youngsters use is "chill out." ' Goodhalgan patted Cornwallis' arm. 'So I suggest you do just that. Everything is under control.'

Cornwallis still wasn't quite so sure. The Bagman didn't give out information lightly, so, therefore, anything he did say, they should take seriously. Despite Goodhalgan's reassurances, he couldn't be so dismissive of the threat. Something was going to happen; he felt it in his bones.

The three girls disappeared down a side-tunnel, heading for Goodhalgan's private chamber, giving Cornwallis time to think things through yet again. He kept an eye on Frankie who seemed to be satisfied with the quality of the beer, seeing as he had hold of a second tankard.

A short while later the girls walked back into the chamber totally transformed. All eyes turned towards them and conversation limped to a halt. They were wearing elven dresses: gossamer thin, they kind of flowed around and over the three lithe bodies like a continuous stream of water, revealing nothing but suggesting everything. They moulded to their contours with jaw-dropping precision. They were demure but alluring and judging by Cornwallis', the earl's, Frankie's, MacGillicudy's and Dewdrop's reactions they were like nothing else on twearth. The intention of these dresses was to provoke and they did this in bucket-loads.

'Do we pass muster?' asked Rose sweetly, giving a slow pirouette.

Cornwallis recovered his decorum. 'You'll do,' he said dismissively.

Rose raised an eyebrow and Cornwallis winked in return.

Tiffany wore posh frocks fairly regularly due to her being Lady Tiffany when not being Tiff the feeler, but this dress eclipsed anything she had worn before, and although Felicity once displayed herself in all her glory in her days of being a page-three woodcut model in some of the more downmarket tabloids, she had posed in the privacy of a studio, not in a chamber full of dignitaries and their wives. Both girls were unused to the sensation of wearing clothes but feeling as if they weren't wearing clothes. They struggled at first with the elven fabric until they began to relax and then they wore them as they should be worn, like a second skin.

Cornwallis pulled Rose to the side. 'Are you sure about this,' he said quietly, cocking his head towards the girls. 'You know what some of these politicians and guildsmen are like, they don't need much of an excuse to go leching and leering.'

'I don't think you'll have to worry about that, they're feelers and can take care of themselves.'

'Yes, but...'

Rose shook her head. 'Really, Jack. Stop being protective; I notice that you left me out of that concern though.'

'No, I didn't.'

'You did.'

'All right, I did, but you're used to it.'

'And you think Tiffany and Felicity aren't? Really, Jack, you should try dressing up as a girl sometime, it'll open up your eyes to what we have to suffer.'

'Um, maybe not. I haven't got the legs.'

Rose raised her eyebrows and then nodded. 'You have a point, horrible bloody things they are too.'

'Cheeky bloody sod.'

CHAPTER 37

Trugral rushed into the chamber, eyes scanning until he glimpsed a golden reflection coming from Goodhalgan's head. He hurried over and pulled up breathlessly. 'They're here,' he announced, as the king turned around. 'Outside, all queuing up.'

Goodhalgan looked at Cornwallis then grinned, rubbing his hands together in anticipation. 'Time to see if all our hard work is going to pay off.'

They trooped upstairs to the foyer of the entrance hall of The Trand underground station where all the dignitaries were starting to gather. Each had to queue up at the ticket office and get a free ticket to ride. Once through the gate, the dwarfs ran around like blue-arsed flies supplying complimentary drinks to them. Like in most walks of life, the government and the guildsmen took full advantage of the free offerings available, just in case at some point, free turned to pay, in which case they would pour as much free booze down their throats as possible in the time allowed.

Goodhalgan greeted the Warden formally, who had a bit of difficulty returning the gesture as he had his ticket in one hand and a glass of something dark and potent in the other.

Cornwallis stood back with Rose on his arm and waited as the official welcome run its course, eyeing the crowd and looking for likely suspects.

'There's your father,' said Rose, indicating with her head. 'Who's he talking to?'

'I'm not sure; I think it's one of the guild masters.'

'Nice one or nasty one?'

'Probably nasty, knowing my father.' He turned his head and looked behind. 'Maud, could you put Frankie down and go and join his nibs, keep an eye on him; make sure he doesn't do anything he shouldn't.'

'Mr Cornwallis, I'm sure the earl knows what he's doing,' replied Maud.

'He should do; we went over it enough times, but he might forget he's a politician and start asking the wrong type of questions.'

'Like what?'

'Like "are you the bastard who's planning to destroy The Pipe." That sort of question.'

'Sounds like a good question to me,' remarked Frankie.

'But not at the moment,' countered Cornwallis. 'We'll ask that one later.'

As Maud wandered off to join the earl, Cornwallis turned to the rest of them. The time to mingle had arrived so they all began to move off into the crowd in their respective pairings. MacGillicudy with Tiffany, Dewdrop with Felicity, Frankie with Rose; they spread out, but immediately Cornwallis noticed that surreptitious listening could be a problem as the girls' attire drew many admiring glances and in some cases, blatant ogling. He shrugged, still hoping that with the booze flowing, somebody may let slip a snippet of information.

When Goodhalgan had finished welcoming the Warden, he came over to join Cornwallis. 'Good turnout,' said the king. 'Just a pity we're not charging them.'

Cornwallis grinned wryly. 'Let's hope we get the chance later. Nothing from any of the guards?'

'Not a thing, so far. I still think you're worrying about

nothing.'

'We'll see, but I hope you're right.'

The pair then surveyed the crowd from their position on the edge of the platform. Everyone who was anyone was there along with their wives and partners, all dressed up in their finery. Competition appeared fierce, especially amongst the wives, but there were enough peacocks amongst the men to give the women a run for their money.

Cornwallis spotted Brooksturner along with Phimp and that short-arse with them must be the mysterious Clarence Fogg, if the guest list could be trusted: he looked exactly like the mean bastard described by Frankie; something in his manner indicated it, in the way he held himself, tense, like a tightly coiled spring, ready to uncoil at a moment's notice. His eyes, fixed on the dwarfs, were devoid of everything but malice.

As the moment of boarding the spanking new transport system approached, a subdued excitement rippled through the crowd. At a signal from Goodhalgan, a bell rang and a few seconds later the first train came rattling out of the tunnel and drew to a halt alongside the platform.

A hush descended on the milling throng.

Cornwallis jumped up onto a couple of crates, cunningly disguised as a small podium and began to wave his arms. 'My Lords, ladies and gentlemen,' he bellowed. 'Your attention, please.'

The eyes of everyone immediately turned towards him, just as a couple of dwarfs ran a red ribbon from one side of the platform to the other.

'I will shortly ask the Warden to step up and cut the ribbon to mark the opening of The Pipe, the very first underground transport system in the whole world; and it has happened here, in our great city of Gornstock.'

A ripple of applause.

Cornwallis held up his hands again. 'The benefits that The Pipe will bring to us are going to be many: quick and easy movement throughout the city; no queues on the roads and streets to worry about; it will be convenient and a station will be close to everyone; it will be cheap and reliable; it will be regular and dry. My Lords, ladies and gentlemen, I will now ask the Warden to step up and cut the ribbon and then we can all board the carriages for the very first underground train.'

The Warden stepped forward as another ripple of applause echoed through the station and Goodhalgan handed him a pair of scissors. The smiling head of government proceeded to snip at the ribbon which split into two, then a surge as the first group pressed forward, eager to board the carriages which sat gleaming in front of them.

Cornwallis stepped down from the podium just as Frankie strolled up.

'That was a load of bollocks, wasn't it; speechifying like that?'

'Needs to be done, Frankie. Nothing gets opened without a load of vacuous bullshit to help it on its way. Besides, this lot are used to it; they spout it every day of their lives.'

'Too bloody true, that,' replied Frankie with feeling, looking at all the nobs gathered. 'Too bleeding true.'

Brooksturner and Phimp followed the Warden to board the first train out, behind them came Clarence Fogg, easing himself into the queue so that he could join them.

'Frankie,' said Cornwallis. 'Keep an eye on your friend Clarence, see what he does. Join the Warden and Goodhalgan, but don't say anything controversial.'

'Me?' replied Frankie, grinning. As if I would.'

As Frankie joined the queue, Rose managed to disentangle

herself from the clutches of a particularly ardent admirer to come and stand with Cornwallis, linking her arm through his as the jilted lothario looked on with envy.

'All seems to be going well,' she said, pressing close.

'So far,' he replied, patting her hand. 'Looks like you're not doing so bad yourself.'

Rose rolled her eyes. 'Really, Jack, this lot are so blatant; they think money is all they need.'

'You mean you're not tempted?'

'Of course I am, but I'll make do with you until something better comes along.'

Cornwallis pulled a face which made her smile. He then turned his attention back to Frankie as he entered the carriage and sat down opposite Phimp and Clarence, it had begun, and he just hoped it wasn't the beginning of the end of The Pipe.

Another train trundled in hot on the wheels of the first, the dwarfs pumping and smiling, as they brought the contraption to a halt. The carriage doors flew open and the carriages filled up, the earl and Maud first in, their faces showing a subdued excitement, despite impending doom.

The third train had MacGillicudy and Tiffany on board, and as that departed, Cornwallis felt a shadow at his shoulder.

'All very exciting, isn't it, Mr Cornwallis?'

Cornwallis' hackles rose.

'And for you too, Miss Morant, I shouldn't wonder.'

Rose turned her head and scrutinised the man standing there.

'Three young female police officers all dressed up in the finest of elven thread, all ready to go to a soiree that would grace the highest in the land; alas, it's just the dark dank dwarf chambers, but I suppose beggars can't be choosers.'

'Mr Hawk,' said Cornwallis, sighing heavily. 'So nice to see you… again.'

'The pleasure is all mine, Mr Cornwallis.' He inclined his head a fraction as he looked at Rose. 'And a pleasure to meet you too, Miss Morant; let's hope it's not going to be our last.'

Rose looked at Cornwallis for confirmation.

'Mr Hawk invited me into his carriage yesterday. I think I mentioned it.'

Rose had never met the Bagman before, though she had heard a lot about him. He looked a bit like an accountant until you saw his eyes, which were flint-hard and dangerous. 'My pleasure, Mr Hawk,' she returned, an icy edge to the words.

The Bagman smiled; at least his mouth did.

'I must say, I'm surprised to see you,' said Cornwallis. 'I thought you said you were going to send some men to the opening?'

'No, I merely said that I would have some representation, I am part of that representation.'

'Aren't you worried after what you told me?'

'Oh no, merely curious. Ah, I believe this is my train; I'm sure we'll speak later, Mr Cornwallis.' He doffed his little hat at Rose and swiftly moved off.

Rose watched him as he boarded the train with a strange feeling running up her spine. It took her a moment to realise that Cornwallis' hand nervously stroked her back.

'You know, if I passed him in the street I wouldn't give him a second glance, but now knowing he's the Bagman, I just feel an icy chill running through me.'

'Just as well Dewdrop and Felicity don't know him, because they've just sat down next to him.'

'Oh, gods.'

CHAPTER 38

Cornwallis and Rose stepped into the last train, leaving the station bereft of passengers. They watched through the window as the dwarfs straight away began to erect the barriers that would funnel the paying passengers towards the ticket office, where they could spend oodles of cash in order to traverse the city quickly and easily and in a certain degree of comfort.

Anticipation built quickly as the train prepared to leave the station, the buzz in the conversations heightened through the sheer excitement of being amongst the first citizens to try this new mode of transport.

The dwarf guard, resplendent in his uniform, slammed the door and then shoved his head out of the window. 'All aboard,' he yelled and then perched on the little ledge designed for just that purpose.

The train moved off and the guard flashed a grin at Cornwallis and Rose as the contraption gathered momentum.

Inside the carriage, the thrill continued and one or two people stood up and caught hold of the grab-handles dangling from the roof, swinging and lurching as the train negotiated a corner. Then darkness engulfed the train as light from the station behind disappeared, indicated by an increase in the volume of exciting chatter within the carriage.

Rose gripped Cornwallis' arm tighter as the lantern inside flickered as the carriage hit a join in the track. A few moments later, they emerged out of the tunnel and began to slow to walking pace as a bright station hove into view, giving them a fleeting glance of the new station from a different perspective, then the pace picked up and they entered another tunnel.

People looked on in awe as they noticed the names of the stations, in big lettering, as they went through. It was so quick, so easy and so convenient to get to all those places so fast and without hindrance.

Cornwallis watched their reactions with more than a passing interest. It was everything he hoped for and more. The Pipe was actually going to work.

The last station disappeared in a slow wink and a few moments later the train slowed and finally stopped. It wasn't a station, but an avenue of torches all leading down further into the depths of the dwarfs' realm.

The guard stood up. 'Ladies and gentlemen, would all passengers care to alight and make your way down to the King's reception. Help is at hand to guide you down.'

Passengers milled about once they had stepped out of the carriage, uncertain and with a degree of trepidation as they were in, what amounted to, a foreign land: the land of the dwarfs, a land which few humans had ever visited. A low murmur buzzed as the train began to move off, leaving them isolated and above all lost. They hadn't a clue where they were or how to get out.

The dwarfs were polite which went against their nature and instinct as they began to lead the herd down, away from the temporary platform and through the avenue of fire.

Cornwallis and Rose hung back, watchful of the pack, suspecting that at least one amongst them one of Brooksturner's cronies, one of those anticipating the end of The Pipe and possibly, the end of the dwarfs and everybody else currently below ground. The thought sobered him and then it suddenly dawned on Cornwallis that Frankie had been with the first train which meant that he would be first to the barrel of beer, which meant that by now he could be well on his way to getting pissed. He voiced his concern to Rose.

'Oh, don't worry about him,' she replied cheerily. 'He promised to be a good boy.'

'I hope you're right; you know what it's like when there's temptation like that. A free bar, I mean, who wouldn't?'

'Sometimes, Jack, I think you underestimate him.'

Cornwallis shook his head. 'No, not where beer is concerned. Anyway, why are you so bloody cheerful when we have impending doom ahead of us?'

'Well, we only live once so we may as well enjoy ourselves whilst we're here; besides, we have you and Jethro and Cecil and the girls and we have your father, all of us seeking to find out what's meant to happen, and anyway, the Bagman is here. If he's here, then you can be as certain as the nose on your face that nothing is going to happen to him.'

'It's not him I'm worried about.'

'Then think of Brooksturner, he's down here too: now, you know nothing's going to happen to him.'

'Yet,' said Cornwallis. 'I can assure you that something will definitely happen to him.'

They passed the last of the torches and entered the upper reaches of the vast chamber. A blaze of light from thousands of candles and torches illuminated it all. They looked down at the crowd below and saw that if they weren't quick, all the food and drink would be gone.

The last passengers from the last train had already reached the chamber and were already getting their noses stuck in to the free food and drink, leaving Cornwallis and Rose the last to descend the steps, which they did slowly, in order for Rose not to trip over the hem of her dress; but it took on the appearance of a regal descent.

It wasn't difficult to notice Rose, at anytime, in any circumstance, but now, wearing an elven dress, made with elven woven thread, stitched together by elves with all their ethereal abilities, it was impossible not to stare, and the crowd, one by one, began to stop talking and turned to watch.

Oblivious to the attention, Rose concentrated solely on not falling flat on her face. She looked up as she neared the bottom of the steps, amazed to see every eye focused upon her.

The Warden, quick to spot an opportunity for further enhancing his reputation, hurried forward with a big beaming smile and offered her his arm.

Cornwallis looked on with a bemused expression on his face as the Warden whisked her away towards his little circle. Rose looked demurely over her shoulder and gave a little wink.

The noise rose as if someone had turned a control knob, as the Warden and Rose got lost in the crowd.

MacGillicudy sauntered over to Cornwallis and handed him a pint. 'Thought you might need this, Jack.'

'Thanks, Jethro, I do.'

'Nice entrance.'

Cornwallis rolled his eyes. 'In truth, it wasn't intentional. It sort of just happened.'

MacGillicudy grinned. 'If they didn't know Rose before, then they certainly do now,' he chuckled. 'The whole government were standing there, salivating.'

'Great. Thanks.'

'No worries, old son.'

'Anyway, where is everybody?'

'Your father is with the Warden's crowd, so now Rose is there too.'

'Yes, okay, don't rub it in.'

'And Frankie is over by the buffet trying to sound intelligent.'

'Talking to?'

'Anyone who'll listen, I think.'

Cornwallis shook his head slowly. 'And the rest?'

'We're over there,' he said, pointing. 'I got collared by several ministers wanting to discuss various ideas they have for policing the city, none of whom have the faintest idea of the problems involved. Dewdrop and the girls are eavesdropping as much as they can, but the girls are only getting slightly less attention than Rose did. I think it might have to do with the elven dresses. They're a sort of firecracker to the senses, you know.'

Cornwallis held up a hand. 'Yes, I worked that out a while ago. I suppose we're so used to them now that we don't see them how others see them.'

'Maybe you do, I don't think I'm that narrow.'

Cornwallis raised his eyebrows. 'Rose wouldn't let me take her for granted; I'd be history if I did. I mean there's no mystery for us, we know them too well.'

'All women like to keep something back, something mysterious, and I for one appreciate that.'

Cornwallis scratched his head; the commander hadn't spoken about the girls like that before. He changed the subject. 'What about Brooksturner and Phimp?'

'They're hovering around the Wardens group, but as far as I could tell, everyone seems to be ignoring them.'

'Clarence?'

'I saw him a few minutes ago, just staring at the tunnels.'

Dewdrop hurried up to them. 'Mr Cornwallis, Commander, sir. I think I know what they're planning.'

'You what?'

'Yes, me and Flick, I mean, Felicity, heard some people talking.'

'Who?'

'Them over there,' and he surreptitiously pointed at a little group.

Cornwallis shook his head. 'Don't know them but they look like guildsmen; what did they say?'

'Erm, they said something about making sure they get wet inside before it starts to get wet outside.'

'Wet?'

'Yes, then one of them laughs and says that he hopes they're out of here before then, that he doesn't fancy eating the Sterkle. Then we starts thinking, me and Flick, and we reckon they're going to use short-arse's ship to drill, because that's what Frankie said it does, into the dwarf tunnel that runs under the river. The ship is right above that tunnel.'

'Oh shit!' exclaimed Cornwallis. 'I think you're right.'

Tiffany and Felicity came over.

'Mr Cornwallis,' said Tiffany. 'I just saw the cat.'

'Cat?' said Cornwallis, his mind now spinning.

'Yes, Fluffy. We both just saw him running after that little man, Clarence, who has just disappeared into one of the tunnels.'

'Oh bugger.'

'And Frankie's gone after them both.'

CHAPTER 39

Cornwallis paced, he looked up and then paced some more, finger tapping his chin; suddenly he snapped his head around, coming to a decision. 'Right, look, here's what we'll do; Jethro, you take Cecil, Felicity and Tiffany and get to that ship and stop them doing whatever it is they're doing; as quick as you can.'

'Of course, Jack.'

'You'd better hurry.'

'But Mr Cornwallis,' said Tiffany. 'We need to get out of these dresses.'

'No time,' said Cornwallis as he stopped a passing dwarf. 'Do you know my warehouse?' he asked; he'd seen him around but couldn't remember his name.

'Yes, of course I knows it.'

'Good, could you guide these people there, I mean now, urgently? They'll explain on the way.'

'Yeah, all right.' He had hold of a tray which he now handed to Cornwallis, which proved a bit awkward as the detective still had hold of his pint.

'Not so fast,' said Tiffany as they rushed away. 'We need to pick up some bits from Goodhalgan's chamber first.'

'Ah, good thinking,' said Felicity.

The dwarf slowed down, shrugged his shoulders and then aimed for the tunnel that led to Goodhalgan's chamber.

'Let's be quick,' said Tiffany when they arrived. 'I'm not going on the river dressed like this.'

They barged into the chamber and then skidded to a stop. Inside were Treacle, the chief dwarf engineer, two ministers and three guildsmen going over the plans for The Pipe.

A couple of minutes later the two girls left the chamber.

'Well,' said the senior minister, wiping a hand across his forehead. 'I must say I didn't expect that.'

The guildsmen nodded their agreement as the junior minister staggered to a chair and sat down clutching his chest.

'You all right?' asked the senior minister to the junior. 'Not too much for you?'

'No, no, I'll be fine. Just need to sit down for a moment.'

'Oh, good. I mean, it's not everyday you see something like that.'

'Do you think we'll see it again?'

'Unlikely; however, we can but hope.'

'They were in the nuddy!' exclaimed one of the guildsmen.

The senior minister nodded his agreement at the observation. 'Yes, oh yes indeed; two of them!'

'Do you think we should have done that?' asked Felicity as they ran up the tunnel.

''We didn't have time to ask them to leave,' replied Tiffany, being practical.

'Ask who?' said Dewdrop.

'Er, there were some men in there,' explained Felicity. 'But don't worry, they were old men.'

'You mean... you mean you...?'

'Yes,' answered Tiffany. 'They looked a bit surprised.'

Cornwallis slammed the tray down on a table and took a last swig of his pint before it too joined the tray. He looked for Rose and eventually spotted her talking to his father and Maud.

'It's starting,' he said as he walked up to them. He had a quick look around to make sure no one could hear. 'We think they're going to try and flood the place by drilling through from the river. Jethro, Dewdrop and the girls have gone to stop it.'

'What about Brooksturner?'

'He's still here, I think, but that Clarence has disappeared and Frankie and Fluffy, yes Fluffy, have gone after him.'

'Oh shit!'

'That's what I said. Hurry up and get changed, and I mean quickly.'

Cornwallis turned to his father when Rose rushed away. 'Have you seen Goodhalgan? We're going to need his help.'

'Yes, he's over there,' he said, pointing. 'Oh, at least he *was* over there,' he added limply.

The earl pointed to a little gap, which, not long before, had been filled by the king of the dwarfs.

'Oh, bollocks. Why is it that everyone disappears when I want to talk to them? Trugral,' he yelled as he spotted his friend.

Trugral trotted over with a smile on his face. 'Going well, this. It seems you're wrong about some people wanting to do for it.'

'Unfortunately, I'm right about some people wanting to do for it, because right now they're doing it.'

'Uh?'

Cornwallis quickly explained and the smile disappeared from the dwarf's face.

'Shit,' said Trugral. 'I'd better get some lads over there quick, but I don't know what we can do if the whole of the river drops in?'

Cornwallis patted him on the shoulder. 'You'll think of something.'

'Gonna need a bit more than a bloody shovel an' a bucket!'

As Trugral ran off, the earl turned to his son. 'What do you want us to do?'

Cornwallis took a deep breath. 'I think we need to get everyone out. The Bagman wanted it all to run its course, but it's time now to stop playing his game.'

'To him, it is a game,' replied the earl seriously. 'Therein lies the dilemma. He never plays unless he knows he has all the trump cards; we are his pawns and he's moving us around the table for a purpose.'

'You're mixing your metaphors.'

'I am, and I don't give a toss; the end result's the same: the Bagman will win.'

'In some respects, I hope you're right but I intend to move some pieces around the board myself, starting with getting this lot out of here.'

Rose raced over to Goodhalgan's chamber, and as she turned the corner, she could see MacGillicudy's back disappearing down the tunnel towards the warehouse. She slammed open the door and rushed in, pulling her dress over her head as she ran to the corner. She kicked off her shoes and then bent down, rummaging in the bag next to Tiffany's and Felicity's, and pulled out her working clothes. She balled up the dress and stuffed it inside along with the shoes. Hurriedly, she began to dress and then noticed something out of the corner of her eye. She stopped and turned. Five refined gentlemen and a dwarf had their mouths open with eyes bigger than saucers. She hesitated for only a second and then carried on dressing.

As she fastened up the last button on her shirt, she smiled at them. 'Sorry to disturb you,' she said sweetly and then dashed out.

Five men and a dwarf stared at the door.

'Er...' said the senior minister to Treacle. 'This seems to happen a lot; what have you got that we haven't?' he asked, hoping he could use the answer.

The junior minister fainted.

CHAPTER 40

He noticed Clarence Fogg edge himself closer towards the tunnel, looking around surreptitiously, until finally, darting in. It seemed as if he knew where the tunnel led, which Frankie knew couldn't be possible; and then, out of the corner of his eye, he saw a ginger blur, small and imperfectly formed and he wondered briefly what the cat was doing there. He caught a look from Tiffany who nudged Felicity and then he dropped his steak sandwich, destined for enjoyable mastication, and legged it into the tunnel.

Within a few short seconds, he couldn't see a bloody thing as after a few turns, the light decided to go on strike. He stubbed his toes and then smacked his head on the low roof, eventually having to crawl to a stop, listening for any clue to where Clarence had gone; if he carried on, he would end up knocking himself out. He could hear the faintest noise of the reception back in the chamber, but nothing else, so he continued hesitantly down the tunnel, feeling his way as he didn't have so much as a match about his person.

Now he felt a bit of a fool, feeling his way tentatively down the tunnel, hands touching the stone-cold rock, hoping that he would come across one of the locals. It was a hopeless situation and one that only an amateur would make. Frankie sighed, then grumbled and then swore, a lot, into the black depths ahead of him.

Unfortunately, nobody swore back.

He gave up and reluctantly turned around and very slowly, hand over hand, made his way back, muttering obscenities all the while until he spied a chink of light in the distance; thankful that now he had something to aim for.

Breaking out of the tunnel, he gazed about, amazed to see utter chaos around the chamber. People were running around with no sense of why they were running around: it was posh peoples' panic.

He caught a glimpse of Cornwallis with Rose, in the company of Jethro, the earl and Maud, together with a few dwarfs and another man whom he did not recognise, but from Cornwallis' description, could only be the Bagman. They were standing there all gazing in the same direction: a little oasis in the whirlpool of humanity.

Frankie forced his way through the milling crowd and came up to Cornwallis' shoulder. 'Bastard got away, that Clarence, he went down one of the tunnels. What's going on here?'

'Got away?' asked Cornwallis, still gazing forward. 'You need to find him.'

'I know; just need a lantern and a dwarf: too many passages down there. What *are* you looking at?'

'Up there, by the steps. Brooksturner has got hold of the Warden. We were just organising an orderly exodus when Brooksturner went into a panic. Now everybody's at it.'

'Not us,' said a dwarf.

'No, not you,' replied Cornwallis. 'Can one of you help Frankie?'

'What, and miss all the fun?'

'I'm pretty certain you'll have all the fun you want with Frankie.'

'You sure?'

Cornwallis nodded. 'Pretty sure.'

The dwarf sighed. 'All right, just hope I don't miss much.'

Frankie grinned. 'I'll tell you what: you can have first swing at the bastard.'

As Frankie and the dwarf left, Cornwallis turned his attention back to Brooksturner and the Warden. The initial panic had now subsided and the two seemed to be arguing which turned into a bit of a tussle and then Brooksturner lobbed a right-hander which caught the Warden squarely on the chin, knocking him down the steps to land sprawling at the bottom.

Behind Brooksturner, a few figures emerged from the avenue of torches, including the little scrote Phimp, just as the Warden completed tumbling down the steps. The crowd that had hushed at the punch now began to voice their opinion on what had just transpired and Brooksturner was certainly not the object of adulation.

'Seems that a bit more than a political argument has occurred,' remarked Cornwallis.

The Bagman grinned wryly. 'A defining moment certainly: not only has he nailed the Warden, but also, I believe, he just nailed his colours to the wall.'

'Who are those behind Brooksturner?' asked Rose.

'The cabal, Miss Morant,' replied the Bagman. 'Finally, the scum has risen to the surface.'

Brooksturner grabbed hold of Phimp and spoke urgently in his ear. Phimp shook his head vehemently and held up his hands in protest, but Brooksturner just pointed down the steps and then pushed Phimp hard so he had to take a few steps down before turning and looking back. Brooksturner shook his head and pointed again and then Phimp gave a last murderous glance in his direction before turning and running down the steps and back into the chamber.

People and dwarfs watched with interest as no one really

had a clue as to what was happening, except that Brooksturner had landed one on the Warden.

'I suggest,' said the Bagman. 'That Phimp is yours, Mr Cornwallis, and you can leave me and your father to deal with Brooksturner and his associates.'

Cornwallis glanced quickly at Rose who nodded, just as Phimp reached the tunnel that led to Goodhalgan's chamber.

'Let's hurry,' said Cornwallis urgently. 'Before we lose the bastard.'

Phimp grabbed a torch from the wall before sprinting off, down the tunnel to only the gods knew where.

Cornwallis grabbed the nearest dwarf. 'You're coming with us,' he ordered as he set off in pursuit.

'Am I?' replied the dwarf.

'Yes,' said Rose. 'They're your bloody tunnels.'

Seeing that she had a point and it wouldn't do for some long-legs to go rampaging through miles of what he termed home, he set off with the two detectives.

Cornwallis grabbed another torch and with the flaming brand held high, they entered the mouth of the tunnel.

Up ahead, Phimp's torch cast a strange silhouette as Cornwallis, Rose and the dwarf charged after. He appeared to grow huge like an avenging angel as his shadow fell on the walls and roof as he ran forward.

Suddenly a "Whumpth" noise intruded and the ground shook making Rose and Cornwallis stumble. The noise came from both behind and in front as though filtered through the passageways of the tunnel.

'What was that?' asked Rose with a high degree of concern.

'Tunnel collapsing,' replied Bracic the dwarf, knowledgeably, as though it was something that happened every day.

And then a sort while later, another came, but this time

louder and closer and it came from directly behind them, from the chamber they had recently left.

'And there goes another,' said Bracic, but this time he wasn't quite as nonchalant, as his worried frown indicated.

Ahead of them, Phimp disappeared around a corner and the silhouette vanished, leaving just a dull orange light flickering off the wall.

'He's turned off,' observed Rose. 'How the hell does he know where to go?' she added, confused.

'Beats me,' replied Cornwallis. 'We've both been down here loads of times, and neither of us know our way around, apart from the few tunnels we use regularly.'

They ran on and then turned the corner that Phimp had taken and saw the torch once more, this time a little closer; it seemed to lower for a few seconds before rising up again. A spark, then a small flame appeared from lower down near the floor.

'Come on, we can catch up with him,' said Cornwallis, putting on a spurt.

Suddenly Phimp's torch disappeared; it sort of winked out leaving no ambient light to indicate that he had taken a turn. It had just vanished as if snuffed out.

'Where's he gone?' asked Rose, hot on Cornwallis' heels.

They slowed down to where they thought they had last seen the torch but the tunnel was devoid of life.

'He must have gone somewhere,' said Cornwallis turning to Bracic. 'Any ideas?'

Bracic put his finger to his cheek and tapped it in thought. 'There's a cut-through back there a bit—'

'Hang on,' interrupted Cornwallis, noticing something.

He bent down towards a gap in the rock and peered closer. He studied in silence for a couple of seconds and then...'Shit!' he yelled. 'Run! Quick! Gonepowder!'

'Wha…?' exclaimed Rose.

'Gonepowder,' repeated Cornwallis, pushing her back.

'Shit!' said Bracic.

They turned and ran and a moment later, it happened: all hell on twearth erupted from behind them; a deafening crack, a whoosh of air and a cascade of tumbling rocks came crashing down to cover the floor of the tunnel.

CHAPTER 41

MacGillicudy poked his head out of the trap-door, crept into the office, moved to the door and peered around. There were only a few crates scattered about, the odd box and a couple of sacks littering the warehouse floor, so he scrambled back and beckoned those below to join him.

Dewdrop still tried to convince himself that they had heard correctly and that they had come to the right conclusion. If they were wrong, then this little foray to the ship would not only be a waste of time, but it would take them away from where they were most needed. The fact that the commander agreed with the assessment wasn't helping very much, he thought that it would be his fault if they were wrong, even though the girls had heard it too. Felicity and Tiffany weren't concerned at all, they were certain; he just wished he felt as confident as they did.

Once through the side-door to the warehouse they walked quickly onto the wharf, Zepi, the dwarf, returned to the tunnels, eager to see what was happening below.

'There's the ship,' said Tiffany, pointing.

MacGillicudy nodded. 'That's the one. Now, all we have to do is get to it,' he said, taking a quick step back as a heavily laden barrow, pushed by a demented looking dock worker with his cap on backwards, rushed by, weaving through the packed throng. 'That is, if we stay alive long enough to reach it.'

Their timing could have been better. The docks swarmed with workers as cargo spewed from the holds of the ships lying alongside. Dockers rolled barrels, dragged carts and pushed barrows; cranes pecked out nets crammed with goods and swung them over to land at the feet of the workers. A tumult of noise assaulted their ears as the feelers dodged all this as they threaded their way through to the water's edge.

There wasn't a wherry, a rowboat or any form of small river transportation in sight.

'Now we're stuffed,' observed Dewdrop disconsolately.

'Not necessarily,' replied Tiffany. 'Look over there,' she said, pointing. 'A sight-seeing boat is pulling in.'

'Oh yes,' said MacGillicudy, craning his neck. 'That'll do.'

It was a mystery as to why people would spend their hard-earned cash to travel on the Sterkle, up the sludgy river to view the countryside, which could easily have been seen from the back of a horse or to go downriver to see the tanneries, the smelters, the alchemists' village; the paddles of the craft churning the river like a farmer churns the soil with fertiliser, the river swallowing up all the stuff that had washed down from the streets giving off the tell-tale whiff of a city with a serious bowel problem. But they did, presumably because people were interested to see where their bowel movements ended up.

The two-bear paddle boat hooked up to the jetty and the people on board began to pour off, hoping to get a whiff of cleaner air, as MacGillicudy strolled up.

'Police,' stated the commander as he dodged around the last passenger to disembark then thrusting his warrant card under the nose of the crewman.

'Where?' came the urgent response, the crewman looking around warily.

'Here,' replied MacGillicudy. 'I mean me.'

'Oh,' said the crewman. 'We ain't dun nuffink,' he added, the response automatic, indicating that despite what he may claim, there was certainly something.

MacGillicudy ignored the implication but stored it away in his mind for future reference. 'I'm not worried about that at the moment. I'm commandeering this boat and its crew for city security.'

'You what?'

'Take me to your captain.'

'Er...'

'Your captain, the man who, er, captains the boat.'

'You mean Nosher. 'E's gone fer a wazz.'

'A what?'

'A wazz, a piss. 'E were first off, a bit desperate. 'E'll be back before we gets going again. 'Bout half an 'our.'

'Bit of a long piss, that.'

'Yeah.'

The crewman didn't elaborate.

'Never mind, you'll do instead. Get this thing going. You're taking us over to that ship out there.' He pointed to where they wanted to go.

'Can't do that,' said the crewman, looking at where MacGillicudy pointed. 'Gotta 'ave Nosher on board. 'E's the only one 'oo can drive.'

'The only one...?' MacGillicudy was incredulous.

'Commander,' said Tiffany. 'If it's any help, my father has a boat and I used to take control of it. I know what to do.'

'You did? Then the boats yours, Captain Tiffany.'

'You can't do that,' said the crewman.

'We just have,' replied MacGillicudy. 'Get the bears to start paddling.'

'Can't do that neither. Tea break.'

'Can't...? Toopins; down below and get those bears moving. Felicity, you help Tiffany and you,' he said waggling his finger at the crewman, 'can unmoor this thing.'

'But Nosher…'

'We are going, Nosher or no Nosher.'

*

Gigali the dwarf ran ahead of Frankie down into the vastness of the dwarfs' domain. It was a city beneath a city with another city beneath that and another city beneath even that. It went down several levels and the only maps were inside the dwarfs' heads. Frankie felt lost within a few minutes of entering the mouth and now all he could do was to follow and hope that Gigali had some idea of where this Clarence had gone.

'What's this man meant to be up to?' asked Gigali as they ran.

'Dunno,' said Frankie. 'But we think he's part of the plan to flood this place.'

'Flood? That's going to be difficult.'

'Not when yer've got a bloody great river above you.'

'Ah,' said the dwarf. 'That could make it easier. How they planning on doing it?'

Frankie gave a quick explanation of what they had surmised.

'They'll have to block off a few places to do that. Water tends to go down and there's a lot of down in here.'

'Then maybe that's what he's going to do. He seems to know this place a bit; how, I don't know? But he must know enough. How would you do it, what tunnels would you block?'

Gigali slowed to a stop and then began to look around in thought.

Frankie caught his breath as the dwarf pondered the situation.

'You reckon they're after flooding and drowning everyone

back there?'

Frankie nodded. 'Reckon so.'

'In that case, I would block two places which would funnel the water this way. It wouldn't touch The Pipe up there though, it's too high up.'

'I don't think they're worried about that, they just want to kill everyone below that.'

'Nice people.'

'Very.'

'Then we need to go back a bit, take one of the side-tunnels.'

'Oh, and if you see a ginger cat, he's on our side.'

'A cat?'

'Yeah, he's a mean bastard; went after this Clarence. Ain't seen him since.'

Gigali led again with Frankie now bent double to avoid smacking his head on the rocks above, now that they were out of the main tunnel. Frankie struggled as his knees kept coming precariously close to his chin and the faster they went the more likely he would knock himself out. They came out of the side-tunnel and entered another main one. Gigali turned a right and they hurried on.

'Just up here is where I'd put a blockage.'

The "Whumpth" and a flash of searing light came hurtling down towards them at the same time as a force ten gale assailed them; both were plucked off their feet and thrown backwards as the force blew past and went on its merry way to peter out far into the depths beyond.

Frankie sat there bemused as dust settled around him. Gigali lay flat on his back just staring straight up at the roof. Both had trouble with their ears, insomuch as, a band of percussionists were playing a symphony.

When the floor finally stopped moving and shaking, Frankie turned onto his knees and crawled over to the dwarf; the lantern miraculously still alight.

'You alive?' asked Frankie, nudging him with his hand.

Gigali saw the lips move but couldn't hear the words. He shook his head, banged his ears with the palms of his hands and then looked at Frankie again.

'I said, are you...? Oh, never mind.'

'Wha...?' asked Gigali.

'Er?' replied Frankie. 'Can't hear you,' he said, waggling his fingers in the general direction of his ears.

Gigali caught on and indicated the same. They stayed where they were for a few moments and then slowly climbed to their feet. Someone had now turned the volume down on the percussionists and other noises were starting to intrude, like the sound of rocks coming to a rest.

'You hear now?' enquired Frankie.

Gigali nodded. 'Yeah.'

'In that case, what happened?'

'Gonepowder, I reckon. You know about that stuff?'

Frankie sighed. 'I do, one match and it's gone. Yeah, I know it.'

'Well, that's what happened.'

They walked tentatively forward to the junction and looked around the corner. The roof had collapsed, filling the tunnel with rocks and mud. There were little squeaks and squeals and one or two squelches as the rocks and mud oozed to a stop with tapping noises as the rocks cooled from the initial blast.

As things began to settle, Frankie scratched his head. 'So, you would have put the blockage about here, then?'

'Gigali nodded. 'Yup; the good news is it won't take long to clear.'

'The bad?'

'We ain't gonna do it in time.'

'Oh, shit!'

Footstep noises came from behind and then a halo of light bobbed up and down along the walls and roof, and then the light emerged from around a corner in the tunnel. It stopped and then held steady, a small light, as if from a pocket oil lamp, then suddenly it vanished.

'Oi!' shouted Frankie as the footsteps turned into a frantic running away.

Then another noise came, this time, from further away, presumably another blast of gonepowder and a further collapsing of the tunnel.

'Hear that?' asked Frankie, concerned.

'Yeah, it seems someone don't like us much, do they?'

'It appears not. Let's hope that's the last one.'

They ran after the disappearing footsteps and the person making them, ignoring the origins of the latest explosion.

'Where's this lead to?' asked Frankie, ducking his head to miss a low bit.

'The river,' answered Gigali. 'The tunnel under the river.'

After a few more minutes, there was still no sign of the owner of the footsteps and Frankie couldn't understand why. They weren't far behind him when they set off and should have caught up by now. They came to a junction and slowed to a stop.

'Which way?' asked Frankie urgently.

'This way,' said a voice in the dark. 'Youse gets yer arses down 'ere.'

'That you Fluffy?'

"O do youse fink it is, then?'

Yet another explosion came and this time it sounded close, coming from the tunnel directly in front of them, the one that

Fluffy wasn't in.

'Down 'ere quick,' said Fluffy. 'There's two of the buggers now and one o' 'em's that bastard Phimp.'

CHAPTER 42

The Warden lay flat on his back, a couple of promotion seeking juniors tending to him.

Brooksturner and his associates stepped back into the avenue of torches and one of them struck a match, then leaning forward, bent down, shoving the lit end into a crevice in the wall.

He wasn't lighting a cigar.

'Interesting,' said the Bagman turning to the earl. 'I wonder if—'

An explosion came from one of the tunnels leading off the main chamber, interrupting him. A collective gasp came from all the people as eyes switched from the drama with the Warden, to the tunnel from which the noise erupted.

The torches around the chamber flickered as the walls shook.

Someone screamed and pandemonium broke out as the dignitaries began to panic again.

Then came a further explosion but this time louder and definitely closer, if fact, it came from the chamber itself. Above the steps which had recently seen a tumbling Warden, the wall and the mouth of the tunnel erupted in a shower of rock and dust. Everyone dived to the ground, hands covering their ears as the shockwave rebounded inside the chamber.

The Bagman and the earl were the only two humans standing as they observed the destruction of the way out.

'As I was saying,' said the Bagman. 'I wondered if they were going to do something like that.'

A smattering of little rocky shards landed at their feet, bouncing and rolling and making a ticking noise, which sounded remarkably like heavy rain.

The earl leant down to Maud, who had taken evasive action and helped her to her feet. She turned, sniffed, and then brushed herself down.

'I slipped,' she announced, daring anyone to contradict her.

A smile briefly flashed on the Bagman's lips as he angled his head to look around the earl.

Maud stared resolutely ahead as the pitter-patter of the little stones ground to a halt.

'I can see we might have a little problem now,' observed the earl as people began to become aware of their predicament.

'Ah, yes. Then let's hope your son can stop the Sterkle from coming to join us,' said the Bagman, concern remarkably absent from his tone of voice.

Cornwallis scrabbled in the dirt for a bit and then moved around on his hands and knees until he felt a leg. The light had gone out.

'Rose?' he asked, the concern evident in his voice.

'That you, Jack?' replied Rose, a little further away.

'Yes, so this must be...'

'Er...' said Bracic

'What are you doing, Jack?' asked Rose.

'Er... nothing, I just thought Bracic was you.'

'Then why is he swearing?'

'Don't ask.'

As they scrambled to their feet, it became apparent that it wasn't now as pitch-black as they thought. Just the slightest indication of a glimmer radiated from the tunnel in front of them, so low as to be almost imperceptible, but in these circumstances, it was like a beacon of hope.

Cornwallis, Rose and Bracic stood up, picked off bits of the debris that now adorned them and moved forward, Bracic taking the lead.

They moved towards the glow, walking steadily, aware that there could be danger just around the next corner. The further forward they went, the greater the glow became, until a sharp turn came up and the glow flickered menacingly, sending long shadows onto the wall. They tentatively turned the corner to find that the sun had somehow made its way underground.

'Who's there?' demanded Cornwallis as his eyes adjusted to the light.

'Who's asking?' came the reply.

'I am,' answered Cornwallis, stepping forward.

'That don't give me much of a clue.'

Cornwallis hesitated. 'Is that you, Frankie?'

'Jack?'

Cornwallis stepped closer and now he could see Frankie standing next to the lantern held up by Gigali.

'You haven't caught him yet, then?'

'No,' replied Frankie. 'What you doing down here?'

'Phimp.'

'Oh, right. Well, you've come to the right place. He's down here somewhere with that Clarence.'

'Is he now; you saw him?'

'No, Fluffy did.'

'Fluffy? You found him?'

'Well, actually, he found us, but it amounts to the same. Phimp and Clarence are heading for the tunnel under the river.'

'That's where Trugral went, isn't it?' asked Rose.

'Yes, along with a few other dwarfs, so I don't think those

two are going to get away, not with Trugral, anyway.'

'We're not wet yet, and I suspect, not likely to be, not with them two still down here,' said Frankie. 'They ain't volunteered to get drowned, have they?'

'Not by their choice,' said Cornwallis. 'But perhaps Brooksturner has decided otherwise. Come on, let's get down there and find out what's going on.'

'You mean up,' said Bracic. 'We're down and we need to go up to get to the tunnel under the river.'

'Pedant,' said Cornwallis.

'Just saying as it is,' replied Bracic.

Bracic was right: the tunnel sloped up which meant that the water, should it come, would flow down. Cornwallis wondered if MacGillicudy had succeeded, maybe the lack of water indicated he had stopped the crew on the ship from doing whatever it was that they were doing. He just hoped that he had, or they were all still deep in the shit, metaphorically, and if the Sterkle came down, then literally as well.

Two ghostly eyes appeared in the tunnel and rapidly approached. 'Is youse lot coming or what?' asked Fluffy, padding to a stop just in front of them.

'We're coming,' answered Cornwallis quickly.

'Good, 'cause pretty soon there ain't gonna be a place to go to.'

'What's happening?' asked Rose, hurrying forward.

'It's the wet, is what it is, an' it looks like it's gonna get wetter.'

They rushed forward, hearts pumping in anticipation, or dread, at what they might find. The reality of their predicament hitting home as each of them, both dwarf and human alike, as well as the cat, realised that getting out alive might prove to be a lot harder than getting in.

Fluffy was right, puddles were forming on the floor of the tunnel and little rivulets trickled along the crevices.

The tunnel opened up into a big cave with several little caves branching off and up ahead a another tunnel, which, over the proceeding days, had been enlarged to cope with the track and train; now it was ablaze with light, burning brands of torches lined all the way through.

'That's the bit that goes under the river,' explained Gigali, not stopping but increasing his pace.

Bracic hurried too, but Cornwallis, Rose, Frankie and Fluffy all took a moment to look at each other, aware, that perhaps, this would be the last time they could.

Cornwallis grabbed Rose's hand and squeezed it tight. She reciprocated and a message passed between their eyes. They didn't hesitate; they had a job to do.

The dwarfs in the tunnel under the Sterkle were remarkably calm. They ran about with ladders and lumps of wood and various bits of metal sheet, but it wasn't chaotic, there was an order to it, just simple calm detachment as if their own mortality didn't really matter. The light from the torches illuminated the work they were doing: trying to shore up the roof.

'What's happening?' asked Frankie as they tried to take in the situation.

'Some bastard is drilling in from above. Every time we plug one hole, they drill another,' explained the nearest dwarf.

Along the tunnel were four metal plates stuck to the roof with wooden beams propping them up. Just as Cornwallis managed to register the situation, a shout went up and then a whirly pointy thing came spinning into the tunnel. Water came with it, dribbling along the flanges to land beneath it in rapidly increasing amounts. The drill stopped, then reversed and the water started to pour in.

Trugral rushed towards the hole as another dwarf arrived with a ladder; he grabbed a metal sheet then rushed up the rungs and slammed it up as another dwarf rammed a wooden prop beneath it. Immediately the flow of water lessened and then slowly trickled to a stop.

'Jethro hasn't got to them,' said Cornwallis dejectedly, looking at the damage already done.

'Yet,' added Rose. 'He will, he promised he would.'

Cornwallis nodded, his friend had promised; time hadn't run out, they were all still alive, and as the old saying went: where there's life, there's hope. 'How do they know where to drill?' he asked, looking incredulously at the roof. 'They hit the mark every time.'

'We'll have to find that out later,' said Rose, her eyes wide. 'At the moment we need to find Phimp.'

'Yes, and Clarence,' said Frankie. 'They should both be here.'

'Yes, but where? And where has that bloody cat gone to now?'

'He were here a second ago,' said Frankie, looking around.

'Trugral,' yelled Cornwallis. 'You seen a man who looks like a dwarf without a beard and with him a man who looks like a stream of piss?'

Trugral climbed down the ladder, looked at the sheet he'd just rammed up and nodded to himself, then bolted over. 'No, but we've been a bit busy down here.'

'You reckon you'll be able to keep the river out?'

Trugral nodded. 'As long as they only do one hole at a time. The trouble is all these holes are weakening it all, so who knows what's going to happen.'

'That's reassuring,' remarked Frankie.

Trugral shrugged just as a loud screeching noise like a

banshee on an acid trip came hurtling towards their ears from behind; then came a wail, which rose in volume and tone until it seemed certain their ears would bleed. And then came the running: footsteps pounded and splashed and then Phimp and Clarence came tearing towards them, an angry maniacal expression on both their faces.

Clarence had hold of an iron bar which he wielded about his head in a manner contrary to health and safety.

'There's the little bastards,' said Frankie, turning and balling up his fists.

'And there's Fluffy behind them,' observed Rose. 'He's flushed them out.'

The cat's screeching only stopped when he leapt at the fleeing Phimp. Claws out, he jumped, just as the secretary reached the first prop, which Clarence attacked with the iron bar. Fluffy's claws dug into his shoulders, the talons penetrating the cloth of his jacket, and Phimp threw his head back in shock at the unexpected assault and the pain as the flesh began to rip. Just as he threw his head back, Fluffy opened his mouth and sank his teeth into his ear, shaking his head and ripping a great big chunk out of the earlobe. Phimp yelled and spun around, trying to remove the demonic feline from around his neck.

Clarence battered at the prop, trying to move it by sheer brute force; and it appeared that he might well succeed.

'Stop him,' yelled Trugral. 'He'll have the bloody roof down.'

'I think that's the idea,' said Cornwallis, rushing forward along with Frankie and Rose.

With one final heave of the bar, Clarence succeeded in shifting the prop and water began to pour in as the metal sheet clanged to the floor.

Phimp managed to dislodge the cat from his shoulder and

then turned and lashed out with his boot connecting hard with Fluffy's vulnerable midriff, the weight of the kick launching the cat into the air and sending him rolling backwards.

Rose screamed in anger and then ran at Phimp like an avenging angel with toothache.

Clarence moved towards the second prop as Cornwallis and Frankie stepped to block his progress. Trugral and two more dwarfs sidestepped the swinging iron bar and went to repair the damage before it got too wet from the Sterkle pouring in.

Eyeing up the dwarfs, Clarence suddenly changed the direction of his attack, the hatred of dwarfs evident from his look of distaste and the continuous snarling that leached through his gritted teeth. He yelped with glee as the bar connected with the head of his target and the dwarf dropped like a sack of spuds, unconscious before he hit the ground.

Phimp held his hand up to his damaged ear and then yelled defiance as he saw the blood dripping from his fingers. He turned and then rushed forward, only half-regretting that Rose positioned herself to stop him: she blocked his path and crouched low, ready to spring as he sprinted towards her.

Clarence swung again, connecting to the stomach of another dwarf who stumbled into Rose just as she was about to launch her attack on Phimp.

Phimp lashed out and his elbow dug fiercely into Rose's ribs, she grunted and bent double and Phimp registered an opportunity to get through the melee to the other side so he could sprint to freedom down the river tunnel and get out on the other side.

Cornwallis saw Rose's predicament and changed direction, leaving Frankie and Trugral to deal with Clarence. He dived at Phimp as he pushed Rose aside and managed to grab hold of his ankle. Phimp stumbled and fell to his knees; he turned quickly and kicked out with his unencumbered foot, catching Cornwallis on his head. Cornwallis relaxed his grip and Phimp managed to tear his foot away and then scrambled back to his feet.

Confronted by Frankie and Trugral, Clarence eyed them both up menacingly just as three more dwarfs came rushing to help. Frankie leapt at the iron bar in Clarence's hand at the same time as Trugral charged at the diminutive man. Clarence roared as Frankie caught hold and he tried to swing the bar with Frankie still attached. Trugral shouldered into him, and it felt like hitting a bag of concrete. Clarence took a step back and Frankie managed to use the impetus to spin him around and hook his leg behind his knee. The three of them tumbled to the ground. Clarence managed to raise his head up but Frankie could feel the power in the madman's arm and decided the best course of action was to use one of the city's time-honoured traditions: Frankie snapped his head forward and connected fiercely with Clarence's in a Gornstock kiss, just as the three other dwarfs arrived, punches raining, as they dived onto the now semi-conscious man.

Cornwallis made a grab for Phimp's ankle again but missed, giving the man a chance. He rose, but then he slipped in his haste to get away, he scrabbled again then finally managed to get some purchase with his feet, just as Rose and Cornwallis managed to gain theirs. He ran, with Rose and Cornwallis setting off in pursuit just as a ginger blur came tearing from behind.

Just ahead of them, the rest of the dwarfs were shoring up the roof the best way they could. Phimp drew level with them, but his progression halted as the ginger blur morphed into Fluffy the cat, then feline claws and teeth sunk deep into Phimp's undefended rear end.

Phimp squawked, Phimp screamed, Phimp ranted and then he spun around but the cat was like a limpet once he caught hold

316

and the more Phimp struggled the more Fluffy's bite and claws sank deeper into the flaccid flesh.

As the dwarfs finished subduing Clarence, Frankie got up and chased after Cornwallis and Rose. He saw a line of rope and picked it up as he ran, but as he looked up, the drill began to enter the tunnel again.

Phimp rolled on the ground trying desperately to squash the cat just as Rose and Cornwallis jumped on top of him.

Fluffy grunted as the weight began to tell but he still clung on.

The spinning drill sunk deeper and deeper into the tunnel and water began to trickle in around it.

'Stop it!' yelled Cornwallis, more in hope than expectation and Frankie, seeing that Phimp no longer posed a problem, ran to the drill.

He flung the rope around the shaft and tied a slip-knot up as high as he could and pulled tight, hoping to stop the thing from spinning. Two dwarfs rushed to help and all three pulled on the rope as hard as they could, trying to break the thing free from its mooring up in the ship.

Phimp groaned and finally Fluffy relinquished his grip.

'You've had it now, you bastard,' sneered Cornwallis triumphantly.

'Can't hold it, Jack,' yelled Frankie. 'It won't break off and the friction's making it burn.'

The drill spun and then began to retract, the trickling water hitting the smouldering bit of rope making it smoke and steam.

Cornwallis and Rose took their attention away from Phimp for just long enough for Phimp to realise that he had one last chance.

He took it.

Phimp kicked out and then jumped up ready to sprint away

once more, just as the drill reversed into the roof, but he didn't see the trailing rope on the ground and he stepped into the little loop. The rope went up and pulled the loop tight around Phimp's ankles.

'Nooo!' Phimp screamed as he saw the drill disappear back from whence it came with the rope still attached, yanking the secretary off his legs and pulling him up towards the roof.

'Whhooooaaaah!' screamed Phimp as he began to spin like a top, going faster and faster as his body tried to catch up with the speed of the drill. Spinning and whirling he rose quickly, his face pulled in all sorts of directions as the centrifugal force distorted his features. He gave another wail as his feet and legs disappeared into the hole with the water now coming in like a torrent, cascading around his torso and pouring onto the floor. Realising what his immediate future held for him and it wasn't going to be a long one, he cried out in despair. 'Heeeellllppppp!' he screamed as his waist went in, quickly followed by his torso. 'Pleeeeaaasseeee—' and then his head, the final yell of anguish abruptly cut off, leaving just his arms whirling until they too disappeared from sight.

Rose winced.

Dwarfs quickly rushed up with sheets of metal and a few props, desperate to stem the flow of water rushing in. They had just seconds before the whole of the roof collapsed under the pressure; the body of Phimp had enlarged the hole and it now seemed as if the whole of the Sterkle wanted to drop in. Water poured in as Trugral and the dwarfs placed the ladders and pushed the sheets against the roof, trying to slide them into position, desperate to stop the flow before it came too much; but they were fighting a losing battle. The floor of the tunnel had now turned into a second river and Rose and Cornwallis watched helplessly as the torrent grabbed Fluffy and pulled him away,

318

tossing and rolling him in the current.

Rose spluttered and reached out a hand to Cornwallis who grabbed it and held on tight. They managed a look and turned to see Frankie amidst the dwarfs, helping to slam the sheets to the roof. Water washed around them and they fought the flow as they tried to scramble to their feet, desperate to help Frankie and the dwarfs as hope trickled away.

CHAPTER 43

'I'd swear that ship's moved a couple of times,' said Felicity as she stood in the little wheel-house of the sight-seeing boat.

'I think you're right,' agreed Tiffany, gripping the wheel as the boat began to move. 'It's going across the river in a line. I think it's to do with the anchors: it's got one at the front and another at the back. Fore and aft, they call it. I think they're pulling through a capstan, which is a big wheel thing in the ship which they use to raise and lower the anchors.'

Felicity looked at her friend in awe. 'How do you know this?'

'An unconventional upbringing: Daddy likes his ships so he took us on a few when I was young and I remember watching the sailors as they worked. It's amazing what you can pick up when you're young. Look, there's a boat at each of the anchor points and they're raising the anchors then pulling them into the boats, then they row forward a bit, dropping them further away. Then they turn the capstan which pulls the ship along in a set line. Kedging, I think they call it.'

'Kedging? What's that?' asked MacGillicudy, appearing on the steps behind.

Tiffany went into the explanation again as all three studied the ship they were heading for.

'Why are they doing that?' asked the commander.

Tiffany shook her head. 'I don't know but there's definitely a reason; it's a lot of hard work.'

'Whatever it's for, it seems that they're doing it, so I reckon we've got to stop them doing it.'

Tiffany and Felicity nodded solemnly.

'I wonder what's happening in the dwarf tunnels?' mused Tiffany.

'I think we all want to know that, but let's do what Jack asked of us and we'll worry about that after; one thing at a time, eh?'

Below, Dewdrop had found that encouraging the bears had been fairly easy, but he just hoped that Mr Cornwallis wouldn't mind too much when he had to fork out triple pay, he was nearly sure he would understand the urgency of the situation.

With no passengers, the one remaining crewman was at a loss as to what to do, so just stood there, watching the river as they paddled slowly to their destination. Dewdrop climbed out of the hatch which covered the steps to below and came over to stand with him.

'Do you know anything about that ship?' asked Dewdrop.

The crewman raised an eyebrow. 'What do you mean by anything?'

'Anything at all, really.'

The crewman sighed. 'Well, it's been 'ere a couple of weeks or so. Bit of a pain in the arse really, as it sits bang in the middle of where we normally go. Nosher tried to argue with the Ship Masters Guild and the harbour master but they're like that.' He held up two crossed fingers. 'Told Nosher where to go, they did.'

'We've got to stop them doing what they're doing. Do you want to help?'

'What they doing, then?'

Dewdrop turned his head towards him. 'Er... we don't really know for sure, but we think they're drilling; we've got to stop them so there might be a bit of a ruck.'

'Really?' replied the crewman, his interest piqued.

'Yeah, might be a bit of cash in it too, if you help, that is.' Dewdrop thought that Cornwallis, being rich enough, wouldn't miss another few dollars.

'Might do, at that. I'll give it a think.'

'You'd better think quick, we're nearly there as it is.'

'I've thunk. I could do wiv a bit extra.'

Dewdrop smiled, they could always welcome another pair of hands in a scrap.

'How do you slow the thing?' asked MacGillicudy, shouting down, as they neared the ship.

The crewman looked up. 'Ring the bell, the red handle on the left, then yell down that tube thing.'

MacGillicudy's head bobbed back into the wheelhouse and then the sound of a tinkling bell came up from below.

'Slow down,' yelled Tiffany into the speaking tube.

The ship, looming large, blotted out the view. The two crews on the rowboats at the two anchors looked on in confusion as the sight-seeing boat came alongside. It bumped and Tiffany pulled the bell then yelled down the tube to get it to stop.

The top of the wheelhouse came level with the rail at the waist of the ship and MacGillicudy yelled down for a rope to tie the two together. The crewman sprinted forward, grabbed a rope end and passed it up to the commander.

'Keep it there, Tiffany,' shouted MacGillicudy as he leapt onto the ship.

He quickly tied the rope and then the girls, Dewdrop and the crewman piled over.

The deck was empty of crew.

'C'mon,' encouraged MacGillicudy, waving an arm. 'We need to find them and stop them.'

'Where do we go?' asked Felicity urgently, looking around.

'Down there,' shouted Tiffany, pointing to the companionway.

A lot of noise came up through the hatch, and it sounded very much like machinery. MacGillicudy went down first and surprised the man at the bottom of the ladder by immediately giving him a right-hander, not even bothering to ask a question first. The others tumbled down after him and spread out.

'Over here,' said Dewdrop as he ran over to an open door in the side of the ship.

'That goes to that strange bit on the sides of the ship. There's another one opposite,' said Tiffany.

'You look at that one, I'll look at this one,' said MacGillicudy running over.

Inside were two men dragging buckets up through a hole and pouring the contents into a contraption that spun around making a grinding whirly sound, a bit like a wood-saw grinding against metal, they were oblivious at first to the presence of the interlopers.

The two men then noticed they had company and looked at MacGillicudy in surprise, their brains trying to work out whether he should be there or not.

The commander didn't wait for them to form an opinion. 'Hello buoys,' he said with a wink.

MacGillicudy grinned as he grabbed their heads and smacked them together, their previous confusion now academic as they now had a serious concussion to worry about.

'Tie them up,' ordered the commander, throwing the two men out of the bit on the side, shaking his head in disappointment as the men missed his joke.

'With what?' asked Dewdrop.

'We're on a bloody ship, man!'

'Aye aye, sir,' replied Felicity, quickly casting a look at Dewdrop that might indicate a cutting off of supply for a day or two as she bent down and passed him the length of rope which lay practically beneath his feet. 'That one's empty,' she added as she pointed over her shoulder to the other side of the ship.

Without the supply of water, the contraption immediately began to smoke and the grinding noise turned into a clanking sound.

'The power source must be down there,' surmised Tiffany, pointing as she watched Dewdrop and the crewman collect the two men and the one the commander tapped, then tie them up to a pole that came up through the deck.

'Mast,' supplied the crewman when MacGillicudy voiced the question.

'Oh,' said the commander. 'Right, downstairs now,' he added, grinning at the prospect of dealing out a bit more instant justice.

'Below,' said the exasperated crewman. 'We go below, not downstairs.'

'Then that is what we shall do, go below downstairs.'

They did.

The din increased enormously with the individual sounds merging into a cacophony of noise all wrapped up in one. Seven men stood around, supervising bears and a gorilla as they pushed, pulled, spun, twisted and tweaked all different types of pulleys, wheels and levers, all connecting to other pulleys and wheels in what looked like one massive mill-like machine connecting through a gap to the bit on the side.

'Police,' yelled MacGillicudy at the top of his voice. He held up his hand. 'Stop what you're doing, now!'

'What's this?' a grizzled looking man spun around, noticing them for the first time. He took a step forward holding what looked like a cosh which he smacked against the palm of his other hand in threat.

MacGillicudy grinned as he pulled his truncheon out of the pocket of his trousers. 'I did ask nicely,' he said as he brought it down hard on the man's shoulder, disarming him in short order, following up with a severe prod into the stomach and then by a knee into the nose.

The machine continued grinding as the rest of the men stood shocked for a nanosecond and then all hell broke loose.

One advanced on Tiffany who stood her ground and waited as the man charged towards her, swinging a lever in his hand, she side-stepped and swung her locked hands hard onto his back, increasing his momentum, his head charging into a solid capstan bar. He stood up shaking his head and turned, only to have the toe-end of a boot connect to the soft area between his legs; he folded, vomited, and then clutched hold of the rapidly swelling articles, moaning softly.

Felicity faced an unarmed man, but she jabbed a straight arm into the nose then followed up with an elbow into the ribs then stuck two fingers up his nose and wrenched him back before smashing his head against the mast.

The crewman was enjoying himself enormously; he had his opponent in a head-lock, and with the free hand, punched the face to pulp.

Dewdrop lashed out with a lump of wood, which he would later learn was called a belaying pin, with his back to his commander who did likewise with his truncheon, both of them smacking, jabbing and sending crunching blows to any part of their opponents' bodies which presented.

The six animals looked on, straining against the chains that tethered them to their work stations, eager to get at their captors as the fight progressed, their faces a rictus of anger, their voices bellowing encouragement to those who looked to be saving them.

Puffing and panting, the feelers and the crewman stood on the deck of the ship with seven men lying groaning on the floor. They looked around, waiting for more of the crew to arrive but it soon became apparent that there were no more to come.

Slowly, the animals began to settle and the rattling of the chains diminished quickly as the commander acknowledged the victory with a nod.

'Tie them to that thing,' ordered MacGillicudy, pointing with his truncheon.

'Capstan,' sighed the crewman.

The commander ignored the crewman and walked over to a relieved and expectant bear. 'How do you stop this thing?' he asked, trying to sound authoritative despite his wheezing.

The bear looked over at a gorilla who then pushed a lever then pulled a handle and then spun a cog. All the animals waited, looking keenly at the commander to see what was going to happen next.

'What now?' asked the commander as the din subsided.

'What do you want?' replied the bear, grinning.

'Pull the drill up.'

The bear started spinning a wheel and the contraption grumbled as the top end of a large metal spike began to emerge, another bear spun a fly-wheel which corresponded with the revolutions on the drill, which then started to slow down. The gorilla unclipped a bit of the drill and stored it behind him and then pulled on a lever as the bear spun the fly-wheel again, raising the drill up a bit more, then another slowing down and another unclipping.

'It's in sections,' said Tiffany. 'You add bits as it goes deeper, but it's getting very noisy now.'

The bear nodded. 'No lubrication: they pour water onto it from up there to keep it cool and help with the friction.'

Felicity looked at the chains securing the bears and gorilla with a frown of concern. 'How do we release you,' she asked stepping forward and testing the links.

'That one there has the key,' said the bear, a metallic rattle emphasising the pointed finger.

'But you're bigger and stronger than them, those chains wouldn't hold for long. You could have broken them and taken over.'

The bear shook his head. 'This is only half of us. The rest are in the hold. They only work half of us at a time; we kick off up here and those down there are history.'

'But that's terrible,' said Tiffany, a look of angst on her face.

MacGillicudy nodded, he'd heard it all before: a remnant of how the old Morris worked; divide and rule. 'You mean there are more men down there?'

'Just one,' replied the bear, 'With a crossbow; the rest are in the rowing boats out there.'

'Toopins,' ordered MacGillicudy. 'Would you inform the gentleman down there that he had better put down the weapon and get up here.'

'We can do that,' said the bear. 'We would *really* like to do that.'

The commander retrieved the key and unlocked the chains.

'Very kind,' said the bear, rubbing his arms and legs as the gorilla and another bear quickly and with some eagerness, disappeared below.

'What about those rowboats?' asked Felicity.

'Don't worry about them,' said the bear. 'I have a feeling we are going to enjoy pulling them in.'

'What about the drill?' asked Tiffany.

The bear sniffed. 'It's clear now, not drilling into anything at all, see, it's stopped.'

'What's that bit of rope do on that bit of the drill,' asked Dewdrop, peering in.

The bear shrugged. 'No idea: must have got caught on something.'

*

'So, we just wait?' asked the earl, after the initial panic over the explosion had dissipated with the knowledge that everyone was still alive.

'Yes,' replied the Bagman.

'But what about the threat of water?'

'Hopefully, your son has stopped that, which I suspect he has, otherwise we might be a bit damp by now and we wouldn't be having this conversation.'

'I'm still worried about young Mr Cornwallis,' said Maud, a frown of concern on her face. 'And Rose, and Frankie, and all those others who went to help.'

The earl patted her hand and smiled grimly. 'Yes, me too, Maud, but they know what they're doing, and, as Mr Hawk here says, it would probably have already happened. Let's try and be positive.'

'But we're all trapped in here.'

'Not for long,' replied the Bagman. 'Ah, I do believe I can hear something now.'

They all looked up to where the rubble blocked the entrance to the tunnel where a tick-tick noise, indicative of a dwarf using a pick, came through the rocks.

'That'll be Goodhalgan, I should imagine.'

The earl looked askance at the Bagman.

'You did wonder where he went; surely? I had a little conversation with him so he absented himself.'

'You warned him?'

'Of course, strangely, he believed me. I thought it might be better to have some dwarfs outside digging in. Those working The Pipe might not realise that something had happened.'

'What about Brooksturner and his friends?'

'Oh, I wouldn't worry about them. I suspect they're already considering the folly of their ways. I had some gentlemen of mine there too, ready for, er... any eventuality.'

'Why didn't you say?'

'I just did.'

The earl opened his mouth to berate the Bagman and then closed it again when he realised he was talking to the Bagman.

A little later, a hole appeared in the rubble and a dwarf's head poked through like a hairy lump of rock. He looked about then eased himself out then stood at the top of the steps and regarded everyone below. Satisfied with what he saw, he shoved his head back in the hole and crawled back through. Shortly, another head appeared and this one belonged to Goodhalgan, King of the Dwarfs.

Goodhalgan stood at the top of the steps and held up his hands as everyone started talking at once.

'Please, please, ladies and gentlemen. You may have noticed that we've had a minor inconvenience, but I'm pleased to say that we have dealt with it now. Up there, The Pipe is already carrying passengers and from now on, it will only cost you half a dollar to take a trip; but for now, please finish your food and drinks. Oh, you have. Never mind, we'll get this lot cleared in a few minutes and you can go up and take another trip on The Pipe. I hope you've all enjoyed your time here with us, and don't forget to tell your friends. The Pipe is the future, ladies and gentlemen.'

'And that, I believe,' said the Bagman. 'Is where it stops.'

'Apart from Brooksturner, Phimp and everyone else,' said the earl.

'No, it will definitely be *it* for them as well. They wanted a return to the bad old days of summary executions and oppression. Well, we can certainly provide the former for Mr Brooksturner,' replied the Bagman with a wink.

Cornwallis, Rose and Frankie emerged from the tunnel with Fluffy, Trugral and the rest of the dwarfs; Clarence Fogg accompanied them dejectedly, his arms tied and a rope around his torso acting as a lead. All of them were wet, bedraggled and covered in muck.

It had taken all their resources to stop the leak and all their expertise. It took several sheets of metal to stop the flow and several wooden beams to prop it all up. It had been a close-run thing but eventually, they succeeded.

The earl and Maud's faces broke out into a relieved smile as they saw them emerge and immediately they rushed over.

'You're safe,' exclaimed the earl in delight, ignoring Cornwallis and wrapping his arms around the soggy Rose.

CHAPTER 44

'You should really take that smug look off your face,' said Rose, staring at Cornwallis, not unkindly.

'I'm not smug,' replied Cornwallis, smugly.

'Yes you bloody are,' countered Frankie, making a grab for his pint.

'All right, I admit I'm feeling pleased,' said Cornwallis, holding his hands up in defeat. 'But you all saw those queues and it's only day one.'

'Well, it's shut for the night now,' said MacGillicudy. 'I would have thought you'd be down there with Goodhalgan, counting out all that money.'

'Ah, yes, all that lovely money. Did you see the size of that chest? Of course you did, how silly of me.'

'Jack,' warned Rose. 'You're in danger of having that pint tipped over your head if you don't shut up about it.'

'Yes, yes, all right,' he conceded, to keep the peace. 'Bloody heathens,' he added as an afterthought.

Despite everything that had happened deep underground, The Pipe continued to run. The excited passengers drowning out the noise of the explosions as they queued for their turn for a ride on the brand new, new fangled, transportation system.

The first day of The Pipe proved an unparalleled success and Cornwallis felt that he had an entitlement to feel just a little bit pleased with himself.

Fortunately, Eddie had reserved some tables for them in

The Stoat, in the corner where they could have a little privacy, away from the hurly-burly and the rucks. Unfortunately, the earl answered a summons to the House of Assembly to try to sort out some of the mess that Brooksturner and a couple of other ministers left behind. Maud felt that she would rather have a small sherry at home and take things easy; but everyone else was there, including a few dwarfs and the bears that MacGillicudy had rescued from the ship, who were making up for lost time with the pints and the skittles.

The Pipe seemed to be the major topic of conversation amongst the patrons in the pub, most of it positive, which pleased Cornwallis no end. After all the work, the hassle, the danger to those that mattered most to him, he wouldn't have been able to bear it if everybody thought it a total waste of time and effort.

He felt pleased, gratified and he wanted to bathe in the rosy glow of success — but Rose and his friends wouldn't let him.

Rose nudged him, forcing him out of his reverie — again.

'Felicity just asked you a question, Jack. Aren't you listening?'

'Yes, of course I am,' he blustered, his mind still with The Pipe. 'I'm just mulling over my answer.'

'What's to mull over?'

'Er…?'

'It's all right,' said Felicity with a grin. 'Cecil just glazes over sometimes when I talk to him. I think it's a man thing.'

'Well, this man and his thing better get his act together or he'll find his thing will get very lonely pretty bloody quickly,' said Rose, a whimsical tone to her threat.

'Okay, okay, what was the question again?' he said contritely. 'I drifted a bit there.'

'A bit? You were miles away.'

'I was actually just thinking about what could have happened to everyone if it had all gone wrong.'

'Oh.'

'But it didn't, so I think it's time to go over it all, to get it straight in our minds.'

'Good idea,' said MacGillicudy. 'Which was really what Felicity asked you to do.'

Cornwallis smiled. 'See, I did hear the question.'

'Bollocks, you did,' countered Frankie.

'Yeah, Jack. Loads of bollocks,' came the voice from beneath the table.

Cornwallis hardly missed a beat. 'Eddie,' he yelled, as he aimed a kick at the ginger fur-ball. 'Another round here, please.'

'That'll do,' said Rose, leaning down and patting Fluffy. 'He's had a traumatic experience.'

'Yeah, I 'ave,' agreed Fluffy. 'Traumatic it was; used up one o' me lives down there, I did.'

'You're not the only one,' answered Cornwallis. 'And anyway, you cause trouble and I'll be speaking to the Bagman.'

'Wot?'

Cornwallis bent down. 'Talking of bollocks; you like Tiddles, don't you?'

Fluffy looked aghast. 'Youse wouldn't, would youse?' he replied, his eyes widening.

'What do you think?'

'How do youse know I went back there?'

'I didn't, but I do now. Risky business, that; considering what you've got to lose.'

'Bastard!' hissed Fluffy, forming himself into a ball.

'Right then,' said Cornwallis, sitting up and slapping his hand down on top of the table, right into a puddle of beer. 'Erm... just as soon as I dry my hand, that is,' he said, wiping his appendage on the sleeve of Frankie's jacket.

Frankie turned and looked down his nose at Cornwallis in disdain.

'It was your beer,' argued Cornwallis.

Frankie shrugged. 'Yeah, but it was your bloody hand that hit it.'

'A mere detail, Francis.'

'Oi, don't you pair start again,' said MacGillicudy laughing.

The barmaid came over with a tray, collected the empties and wiped the table just as Eddie came over with the refills. Fluffy uncurled from his ball and attacked the cream with relish. Cornwallis waited until everybody had a fresh drink in front of them.

'I'll start at the beginning,' he said smiling at them all, settling himself down. 'Brooksturner had for sometime been accruing like-minded individuals, those hard-liners who wished for the old Morris to make a re-emergence. Over time, he drew in several members of the Assembly and a good few from the guilds. They started planning, what would amount to, a coup d'état. Then we announced that we were going to provide an underground transport system.

'Brooksturner hates dwarfs and anything breathing that isn't human; as it happens, he's not so keen on humans either. However, the thought that the dwarfs were going to build something that was good for the city got under his skin. Being minister responsible put him in a quandary, a position which, as you know, he was appointed to in order to get rid of him, the Warden hoping he would resign. He began to lobby against The Pipe, quietly, using his associates to do the dirty business.

'While all that was going on, Goodhalgan had ordered ore to make the tracks and wood and other materials through his own contacts up north. The dwarfs used their own ships to transport everything down here and that got up the nose of the Ship Masters Guild. The dwarfs couldn't smelt all the ore themselves so they used the iron foundry who were only too pleased to get the massive order.

'Lots of guilds could see money slipping through their fingers: the Guild of Sign-writers, because of all the posters they weren't putting up; the Guild of Lamplighters, because of the candles and oil used to light the trains and the stations; the Guild of Labourers, because the dwarfs were doing all the work; the Guild of Coal Merchants because of the coal supplied by Goodhalgan to the foundry to heat the furnaces. There are others that Brooksturner recruited, but they are the main ones and these began to work in earnest to get the guilds on their side.

'Brooksturner, in his position of Dwarf Minister, had been underground to meet Goodhalgan so he knew that a tunnel ran under the river. That got him thinking on how to ruin The Pipe and overthrow the government at the same time so he changed tack a bit and didn't lobby quite so hard so that the Warden would allow The Pipe to go ahead.

'Wentlebury provided the drilling ship and also knew of a man who hated dwarfs even more than Brooksturner: Clarence Fogg, a dangerous lunatic. Fogg could be relied upon to get into the tunnels and blow them up.'

Tiffany asked a question. 'What about those lads we caught using the ironworkers' houses?'

'Ah, yes. Phimp came across them when they were up to no good, chucking stones at windows, so he paid them to cause disturbances and to scrag Sigi the dwarf at the beginning, they attacked and stripped him on Phimp's orders to supply clothes for Clarence Fogg for when he arrived in the city.'

'Hang on, this is getting confusing,' said MacGillicudy, holding up a hand.

'Bear with me,' said Cornwallis. 'I'll jump around a bit. These were the clothes you found on the ship when you searched it together with that false beard. Clarence Fogg disguised himself as a dwarf, and this is where it gets interesting because Fogg *is* a dwarf. He got banished from his community up north for being a homicidal maniac, killing several dwarfs and injuring a few others, needless to say, he was eager to add to his tally. He shaved and cut his hair and pretended to be a very short human. As a dwarf, he had a natural affinity with dwarf tunnels, so as our dwarfs were busy building The Pipe, he got in and mapped the tunnels; no one would notice an extra dwarf.'

'He wanted to kill his own kind?' asked MacGillicudy, a bit shocked by the revelation.

'A bit like humans, really: don't we like killing each other?'

'You have a point.'

'Now, Wentlebury nicked the keys for the ironworkers' houses from the guild in order to implicate them should it all go wrong, and Phimp gave the keys to the lads that we caught. Is that all clear so far?'

'Er, sort of,' said Dewdrop hesitantly.

'Good, now the ship needed somewhere to drill in order to flood the underground, so Clarence Fogg marked the tunnel under the river. He managed to shove a steel rod through the clay at either end of the tunnel then one of the crew went and put some flags on them during the night so that the ship could line itself up against those rods. Easy when you think about it; they could be pretty certain they could drill in the right place.

'The various guilds supplied the gonepowder for Fogg to take into the tunnels and put it where it would cause the damage to block the necessary tunnels.

'They planned the big day for when The Pipe opened as Brooksturner knew that the Assembly and the guilds would be invited for the event. Once they were all down in the chamber they could set off the gonepowder and block those tunnels needed to flood it all.

'Clarence Fogg had drawn a map for Phimp, showing him where he had put the gonepowder and also the way to the river tunnel and to the exit on the other side once he had set it off; Fogg would blow one tunnel, Phimp, the other. However, Phimp panicked and Brooksturner had to force him to do it, hence we saw him shove Phimp down the steps. Phimp had become surplice to requirements by this time, so it was hoped that he would get killed in the flood; if not, Clarence Fogg was going to do the business anyway.'

'And we stopped it all,' said Tiffany. 'Just us.'

Cornwallis grinned and nodded. We did, all of us. You four when you boarded the ship and us lot down there. The Warden and the Bagman are very grateful.'

Frankie snorted. 'My arse, they are. How grateful?'

'That remains to be seen, Frankie.'

'What about Brooksturner and those others who were on the other side of the collapsed tunnel?' asked Tiffany.

'Oh, yes, I'd forgotten about that bit. The Bagman suspected, or knew, that something was going to happen, so he suggested to Goodhalgan that he, and a few others, might be more useful away from the reception and up near The Pipe where there were a few of the Bagman's men waiting.

'As soon as the blast happened, Brooksturner and the others were nabbed and then the dwarfs cleared the blockage so that we could all escape.'

Cornwallis leant back in his chair and took a pull on his pint to wet his throat. 'The good bit is that apart from Phimp, nobody died.'

'Yet,' added Rose. 'You said the Bagman and the Warden

indicated that there were going to be repercussions?'

'I did,' replied Cornwallis. 'All of them are due to swing for it; the only discussion being, whether it should be a long drop, or the short one. They wanted a return to the old ways, so in some sense, they've got what they wanted.'

'And deserved,' observed MacGillicudy wryly.

EPILOGUE

Isabella came downstairs with Tulip in her arms. She had come to say goodnight to her daddy before bedtime.

'When are you going back home,' asked Rose of Frankie, as Isabella dodged the tables on her way over.

'Tomorrow,' he replied. 'I think it's about time. Can't outstay our welcome or Eddie might get annoyed.'

Rose smiled. 'He won't, but you'll be glad to get back, I should think.'

Frankie raised his eyebrows. 'You mean glad to give up living over a pub? Beer on tap? Food whenever you wanted it?'

'Yes, all right. Maybe not for you, but definitely for those two.'

Frankie chuckled. 'Yeah, I suppose you're right.'

'Here's your daddy,' said Isabella, planting Tulip in Frankie's lap. 'And here's his pint,' she added, swopping one for the other.

'Hey!' cried Frankie in alarm.

'It's okay, I'll get you another,' placated Cornwallis.

'Ahem,' said a voice from below.

'Yes, and you too.'

Frankie was in his element as he bobbed his daughter on his knee, enjoying the soft fresh baby smell, instead of the powerful acrid whiff that generally came from the other end.

Fluffy jumped up onto the table and sat down, licking his paw and eyeing the big detective.

'What?' asked Frankie, as he noticed the cat.

'Nuffink. I were jest wondering how many kittens I got out there.'

'Well, just hope you're not going to get some more in the near future.'

Fluffy grinned. 'Yeah, that's a thought. Imagine, a litter of kittens jest like me, eh?'

'Oh gods,' said Cornwallis. 'That doesn't bear thinking of; I don't think I could stand any more like you.'

Fluffy grinned again and jumped back down, threading his way to the front door and waiting for a punter to let him out.

'Wonder where he's going?' asked Cornwallis.

'Can't you guess?' said Rose.

'Saves getting the cream in,' said Cornwallis. 'Though I reckon he's taking a risk.'

'All's fair in love and war,' said Rose, wistfully. 'Maybe he thinks she's worth it.'

Tulip enjoyed the attention as she was ritually passed to Rose and then to Cornwallis and then over to MacGillicudy, but now there were three others and she stuck her arms out hopefully at Dewdrop.

Dewdrop received her with a degree of unease and trepidation which Felicity found both cute and endearing. Quickly he passed her on just as she began to gurgle.

Once Felicity and Tiffany had had their go, she was once again back in Isabella's arms.

'I'll pop down later, once she's asleep. One of the girls said she'd look after her for a time, so…'

Frankie leapt up, kissed his girl again and then gave the stupid dad wave that every daddy gives and Tulip smiled and giggled then dribbled a nice dollop of saliva.

'So, you make sure there's a drink for me,' Isabella finished.

'Of course, sweetheart,' replied Frankie, meekly.

The door opened and in walked Big George, ready for his shift. Straight away, he saw Tulip and hurried over, sweeping her out of her mother's arms and into his big hairy ones. He grinned stupidly as he always did when he had hold of this little girl.

George acknowledged Eddie with a wave and accompanied Isabella over to the door that led upstairs.

'Shame about George,' said Rose to Cornwallis. 'We never found him a missus George.'

'Not so far, but I'm sure you haven't given up just yet.'

George handed Tulip back and then closed the door gently behind Isabella as she went up. He sighed and then noticed the bears from the ship that MacGillicudy had brought with him to the pub. They were playing skittles and evidently enjoying their new-found freedom. George just stood and stared, his arms hanging loosely by his sides.

One of the bears looked up and saw George staring, and froze, mid-throw.

George's eyes widened and then the other bear dropped the ball in shock.

As far as the two bears were concerned, there were no others in the pub and they staggered towards each other, scattering table, chairs, and punters, alike.

'What's happening?' asked Rose aghast, standing up and staring.

'No idea,' replied Cornwallis, equally stunned.

'It looks like George means business,' observed Frankie. 'He's going for that other one.'

Dewdrop, the girls and MacGillicudy turned in their seats to watch.

'No,' said Rose. 'He's not going *for* them, he's going *to* them.'

Big George and the other bear finally reached each other and with paws out wide embraced in what would seem as the biggest bear hug ever.

The pub lapsed into silence; everyone looked on, knowing that something was happening, but not quite sure what.

'They're hugging,' observed Rose. 'Look, George is crying.'

'So is the other one,' added Felicity. 'They're both crying.'

The reason for the behaviour became clear a little later, once they had broken apart and stared into each other's eyes. They held paws and spoke quietly to each other and then they turned and still holding paws came over towards Cornwallis' table.

'This is Elsie,' announce George. 'You saved her, Commander MacGillicudy, as did you Miss, and you Miss, and you Sir,' he said looking at Tiffany, Felicity and Dewdrop in turn.

Rose still stood at the table, her mouth hanging open.

'You know each other?' asked Cornwallis.

George nodded and smiled. 'Elsie and me were an item, but then she were nabbed and taken away to work on the ship. That were four years ago now. We ain't seen each other since.'

'Oh gods, that's awful!' exclaimed Rose, her hand rushing towards her mouth, tears forming in her eyes.

George shook his head. 'No, it *was* awful, but it ain't now.'

The tears now rolled down Rose's cheeks as she looked at George and Elsie, but no one was immune to the force generated by the two bears in their reunion as they held paws and looked deep into each other's eyes; together once more.

'I don't know what to say,' said MacGillicudy, wiping a bit of moisture off his cheek.

'No need to say anything, Commander,' replied George. 'You've already said it when you saved my Elsie.'

It took a while for things to settle back down into its normal rhythm. Eddie gave George the rest of the night off and he continued his re-acquaintance with Elsie in one of the back rooms.

The atmosphere turned to one of celebration which got to Cornwallis in a big way because he decided to put his hand in his pocket and bought everyone in the pub a drink, sending George and Elsie a crate of champagne to help cement the reunion.

'I think that puts everything into perspective,' said Rose. 'The Pipe is important, but George and Elsie eclipse even that.'

'They do,' agreed Cornwallis. 'I couldn't be happier for him.'

'Me neither,' said Frankie. 'It's just a shame Isabella wasn't down, she would have loved that.'

'She would,' agreed Rose. 'But she'll know soon.'

Frankie nodded. 'Can't be in two places at once.'

'No, but she can arrive soon after. Here she is.'

Isabella sat down and cuddled up to Frankie. 'What was all the fuss about?'

Frankie grinned and then told her all that had happened whilst she was getting Tulip to sleep.

'Ah, bless him. He deserves to be happy.'

'He does,' agreed Frankie. 'Who's looking after our precious?'

'Marie's just going up now.' She waved at one of the barmaids as she headed upstairs. 'Oh, I forgot, have you seen this?' she asked, handing over the evening paper.

Cornwallis grabbed hold and smoothed out the creases. He read the headline and the article below and smiled.

'What does it say?' asked Rose.

'Coggs: his bus service has been approved by the Assembly. Father must have forgotten to tell me.'

'Oh,' said Rose.

'No, it's good,' said Cornwallis. 'It means we've got competition, and I like a bit of that. It'll keep us on our toes.'

'Well, I for one won't be using it,' said Rose, slumping back and crossing her arms.

'Well, I will, if it's handy.'

'Times are changing,' said MacGillicudy. 'The Pipe, and now a bus service. This city is moving forwards.'

'So it would appear,' said Cornwallis. 'Let's hope it doesn't make your job harder.'

'It never gets easier. I'm just glad I've got officers like these three here.'

Dewdrop's face broke into a smile as he heard the praise coming from his commander's lips. He turned and looked at Felicity who smiled back and grabbed his hand and squeezed.

Felicity then turned to Tiffany and smiled at her and then her mouth formed a big "O" as she noticed Tiffany's hand beneath the table, nestling in the commander's. She closed her mouth and then leant towards Tiffany's ear.

'Since when?' she asked quietly, suppressing the excitement in her voice.

'Yesterday,' answered Tiffany quietly, smiling back. 'When we were looking for the Ship Master. We agreed not to do or say anything until this job had finished.'

'But it has now.'

'Oh, yes,' replied Tiffany excitedly. 'And guess what we'll be doing later tonight!'

end

ABOUT THE AUTHOR

Clive Mullis spent a number of years as a paramedic, until deciding that there must be another way of making a living. He lives in Bedfordshire in the UK with his wife, son, and dogs.

Please visit me at www.clivemullis.com where you come and join the **Black Stoat VIP Club** and download a FREE short story about the founding of Gornstock. As a member of the best pub in Gornstock, you will also receive updates about what's new in the bar as well as anything new coming from me.

Look forward to seeing you there!

Also by the same author:

Banker's Draft
Scooters Yard

Printed in Great Britain
by Amazon

52357150R00210